PRAISE FOR MARTINA BOONE

"*Skillfully blends rich magic and folklore with adventure, sweeping romance, and hidden treasure… Impressive.*" — *Publisher's Weekly*

"*So swoon-worthy that it's ridiculous.*"
— *RT Book Reviews. RT Editors' Best Books of the Year*

"*Even the villains and not-likable characters were just so engrossing. I have to say I've already put the sequel on my TBR shelf.*" — *USA Today*

"*Charming and steamy on the surface, with cold-blooded secrets buried down deep.*" — *#1 NYT bestselling author Kendare Blake*

"*Darkly romantic and steeped in Southern Gothic charm.*"
— *#1 NYT bestselling author Jennifer L. Armentrout*

"*Haunting, atmospheric, and absorbing.*"
— *Claudia Gray, NYT bestselling author*

"*Beautifully written, with vivid characters… and romance that leaps off the page. Not to be missed.*"
— *Megan Shepherd, NYT bestselling author*

"*Delightful, charming, and heartwarming!*"
— *Wendy Higgins, NYT bestselling author*

"*Heartwarming, lyrical, soulful, and with just the right amount of humor.*"
— *Jodi Meadows, NYT bestselling author*

"*Perfect for fans of Nora Roberts and Susanna Kearsley…*"
— *Erin Cashman, award-winning author*

HEART OF LEGEND

Also By Martina Boone

Adult Fiction:

Lake of Destiny: A Celtic Legends Novel

Bell of Eternity: A Celtic Legends Novel

Magic of Winter: A Celtic Legends Novel

Echo of Glory: A Celtic Legends Novel

Young Adult Fiction:

Compulsion

Persuasion

Illusion

Love For Two Lifetimes

Legend and Non-Fiction:

Welcome Home

HEART OF LEGEND

—A CELTIC LEGENDS NOVEL—

MARTINA BOONE

MAYFAIR
PUBLISHING

Heart of Legend is a work of fiction, and the characters, events, and places depicted in it are products of the author's imagination. Where actual events, places, organizations, or persons, living or dead, are included, they are used fictitiously and not intended to be taken otherwise.

MAYFAIR
PUBLISHING

712 H Street NE, Suite 1014
Washington, DC 20002
First Mayfair Publishing edition June 2022
Copyright © 2022 by Martina Boone

Jacket design by Kalen O'Donnell
Interior Design by Rachel & Joel Greene
Published in the United States of America
ISBN 978-1-946773-12-8 (Paperback)

HEART OF LEGEND

15 YEARS AGO

Cincinnati, Ohio

T HEY HELD HANDS AS THEY took their bows. Henry's fingers curled around Kath's, warm and slick with sweat. He gave her hand a squeeze so small she wasn't positive she'd felt it, and when she glanced over at him, he sent her a private smile.

They'd done it. Applause swelled through the auditorium, punctuated with whistles and shouts of "Bravo!" Even Kath's mother was on her feet in the front row, with Anna on one side, Meg on the other, and their father on the end like an afterthought. Anna, of course, clapped more for Henry than for Kath, but that didn't diminish the tingling champagne-running-through-her-veins feeling that made Kath feel like she could float away.

Henry pulled Kath back, and the curtain dropped. The clapping grew louder.

They came out for another bow, and another, then Henry picked Kath up in a bear hug and swung her around and around and around, making her feel small even though she stood 5'10" in her bare feet.

"Man, that was great," Henry said, laughing as he set her down. "You were great."

"We were great," Kath said.

They grinned at each, neither of them stepping back. The white shirt he'd worn as Orlando was open almost to his navel, and beads of moisture clung to his bare, hard chest.

He was gorgeous. So gorgeous.

Kath couldn't bear for it all to end: this feeling, the play, the summer, the way Henry talked to her like a real person, as if he knew her, the deep-down her that was more than Anna's sister, or Meg's sister, or Ailsa Cameron's daughter, or Miss Ohio Teen USA—all the labels that crushed Kath tighter than the stupid pantyhose her mother had made her wear to hide the extra pounds she'd gained.

But no matter how much Kath wished otherwise, it *was* ending.

In a matter of weeks, Henry was marrying Anna.

That was a huge mistake. Epic.

Henry was a dreamer, an optimist, a people person. With all her focus and sharpened edges, Anna would grind him down until all that remained was a Henry ghost, trudging through life the way Kath's father had been trudging for years, doing his duty without a scrap of joy.

Henry cleared his throat and let Kath go.

She caught his arm as he turned away. "Are you going to the cast party at Elli's?" she asked. "It should be fun."

"I told Elli we'd stop by," Henry said, "but that's not Anna's sort of crowd."

Kath knew she should leave it there. She couldn't.

The words spilled out of her. "You're allowed to have fun without Anna, you know. Or at least you should be. You shouldn't have to fit your life into whatever neat little box she wants to squeeze you into."

"Box?" Henry's brows knitted together in that adorable way of his. "Anna is the last person who would ever hold anyone back. Are you sure you're okay, Kath? You're looking kind of flushed."

"I'm fine. Great." Kath wasn't drunk at all, only a little warm from the lingering effect of a few airline-sized bottles of Scotch she'd snuck out of her parents' stash. The cast had been warned there would be an important critic in the audience for this last night of the play, and she had needed a boost of extra courage. "You should go to the party," she said. "You owe it to everyone to go."

"Okay. Yes," Henry said.

Kath smiled. "In that case, would you mind if I catch a ride?"

One simple question and a huge mistake.

That was how everything changed

DEVIL WIND

"When one burns one's bridges, what a very nice fire it makes."

DYLAN THOMAS

Present Day
North Hollywood, California

THE DEVIL WINDS OF THE Santa Ana were hot and parched. Unusual in July, they swept down the inland slopes and made LA drivers lean on their horns and cling to each other's bumpers. Kath Cameron inched past a crash that had turned the canyon route into a parking lot. She'd allowed time for extra traffic, but not enough. Now she was late for a breakfast meeting with her talent agent.

More than the right amount of late.

In Hollywood, timing was everything. If she arrived too early, she would seem too eager. Desperate even. Which she was, but she couldn't give off so much as a whiff of that. On the other hand, the longer she kept Joel waiting, the more she risked pissing him off.

She was already a nervous wreck by the time she arrived in front of the restaurant, and then there wasn't a parking space in sight. With no choice other than valet parking, she stopped twenty feet back from the drop-off point and held up a finger to show she needed an extra moment.

Keeping one eye on the waiting valet, she scooped up all the personal items from her center console and dumped them into her purse. Receipts, notes, a yellow highlighter, extra lipstick, dress tape, blonde bobby pins, hair scrunchies, travel-sized gel and hair spray—all the private things a stranger or tabloid reporter could rummage through. She took it all.

That left only the apocalypse-sized first aid kit she kept in a duffel bag behind the seat like a security blanket. And she didn't know what to do with that.

She glared at the emergency kit. If she threw it in the trunk now, the action might invite more attention, and according to her ex-husband, the kit was proof positive she was in urgent need of therapy. Of course, the real reason she couldn't bear to have it out of reach was the one thing she could never discuss with a therapist. Or anyone.

But she could imagine the ridiculous speculation if the valet found it and sold her out:

Ex-wife of HT Lewis is Rabid Doomsday Prepper
—Yet Another Reason the Actor Had to Get Away—

The tabloids had been relentless since the divorce. HT had

cheated on *her*, but he wasn't the one they blamed. Oh, no. It was Kath who was supposedly too difficult to live with—and work with. Too jealous or demanding or crazy.

She'd been so relieved when the attention had finally died down. Then almost immediately, the trade journals had announced the casting for HT's latest film.

That had unleashed a whole new round of tabloid fodder.

The stories were everywhere. First came glowing fairy tales about how Nia Evans had fallen hard for Hollywood heartthrob Henry Thomas—better known as HT, the Hottie—Lewis. Then there were saccharin articles about HT finding true love with his beautiful young co-star. Photos of Kath featured prominently in all of them: paparazzi snaps taken from the worst possible angles, and photos of beautiful "young" Nia side by side with horrible pics of "older" Kath to highlight the resemblance between them like bad before-and-afters.

Considering what Nia was going through now, Kath couldn't even be mad at her.

Exhausted from worrying about everything, Kath flung a couple of Trader Joe's grocery bags over the first aid kit and hoped the valet wouldn't investigate. Then she pulled up the remaining few feet to the valet station and handed off the key.

The valet who took it was one of those slick, mid-twenties guys with a full complement of gym-toned muscles. Everything about him screamed actor-waiting-for-a-break, and he flashed his teeth at her as he drove off in her twelve-year-old BMW.

Kath smoothed the crisp white shirt she had paired with

casual jeans and strappy heels. Pasting on a smile, she straightened her back, opened the patio gate, and walked toward the hostess stand.

The restaurant was a favorite celebrity haunt known for its outdoor seating. Heirloom roses and English ivy climbed the brick walls and spilled over the white picket fence around the patio. Floral patterns on chintz cushions and plump throw pillows softened the white wicker chairs and sofas. The garden theme made the perfect backdrop to "see and be seen," which was why Joel loved the place.

He was already at the table, his nose buried in a trade journal. He didn't look up until the hostess stopped at his elbow. Then seeing Kath, he flipped the paper over to hide a photo of HT and Nia together.

He got up to kiss Kath on the cheek. "Thanks for coming."

Kath took her seat and gave both him and the hostess a brilliant smile. The hostess handed her a thick menu in a leather holder, and Kath waited until the young woman had gone before answering. "Thanks for inviting me, Joel. It's nice to catch up. And you didn't need to hide that article on my account. I read it online, and I feel awful for Nia. I can't even imagine having to cope with a mastectomy at twenty-three."

"It's horrible," Joel agreed, then he ducked his head and busied himself staring at the menu as if he didn't order the same thing every time he came.

He looked older than Kath remembered. That in itself was a reminder of how long it had been since she'd seen him in person. His graying hair had thinned on top, and he'd put on a few pounds, something agents could afford to do that actors couldn't.

The sounds of the restaurant grew louder in the silence. Kath eased back in the wicker chair, doing her best to ignore the other customers staring over at their table.

She wasn't the only one of interest. Joel was one of the top agents in Hollywood these days, thanks to the fact that he'd signed HT not long after Kath had introduced them. The first small breaks, the early Hollywood successes, those had all been Kath's. Then HT's career had taken off, and hers hadn't.

But that was about to change. Kath could feel it.

She leaned forward, eager for Joel's answer. "So, did you talk to him?"

"Talk to whom?" Joel lowered the menu and studied her.

Kath's heart gave an uncertain thud. "HT, of course. Isn't that why you asked me to come? I assumed you wanted to give me tips for the audition."

"Oh, Kath." Joel set the menu down. "I told you on the phone you aren't what Dai Rhys needs."

"But I asked you to try! How can I not be what they're looking for? Nia and I are the same type—as the tabloids keep pointing out. Same size, same hair color. I can fit into the costumes as long as I wear flats. With good editing, at least some of Nia's scenes might be salvageable, and they wouldn't have to pay me nearly as much as they paid her. It all makes good business sense."

"On paper, sure. But Nia is—"

"Nine years younger?" Kath swallowed a bitter taste in her

mouth. "She was too young for the part anyway. Every known fact points to Margaret Glyndwr being at least thirty at the start of the rebellion in 1400. She might have been even older. Owain Glyndwr was fifty by then."

Joel's eyebrows rose, and his lips twitched into a half-smile. "You've certainly done your homework."

"I have," Kath said, ignoring the condescension, "and I've spent the last three days breaking down the script."

"How did you get a copy?"

Kath looked away, her hands pressed together in her lap. "It's a big film. The point is, the screenplay is fantastic, and you know I've always wanted to do a historical drama. Obviously, I feel bad for Nia. But since we do look alike, why shouldn't I take advantage of it? It's the perfect opportunity—"

"Kath, stop. I can't." Joel's brows furrowed, and his voice was sharp.

Kath's heart revved up like a treadmill starting its warmup cycle, a few slow thumps, then a kick up to an all-out run. "Are you telling me you won't ask HT?"

Joel shook his head. "Dai Rhys wants most of the cast to be Welsh since Glyndwr's their national hero. Nia is a major star, and she was born in Wales. HT's grandfather was Welsh. You don't qualify on either count." He paused, and this time, the pity in his expression was unmistakable. "Listen, we're friends, aren't we? And how long have we worked together? Ten or eleven years?"

"Thirteen, and I've made you a lot of money along the way."

"Yes, but you've barely worked since HT left."

"Thanks to the tabloids."

"It's more than that." Joel's looked off somewhere beyond Kath's shoulder. "I hate having this conversation with you, but you aren't getting callbacks. Apart from a few reality shows and the one commercial, I've had no luck sending you anywhere, even for your usual roles."

"I don't want my usual roles. That's why this is perfect. Playing Margaret would open possibilities."

"Playing Margaret requires range. She's complex and subtle, and the accent alone is—"

"I have a good ear. You know I do, and I can get a dialect coach."

Joel paused as the waiter arrived to fill their coffee cups and take their orders. He ordered his usual cholesterol bomb: Belgian waffles with chocolate and bananas, scrambled eggs, bacon, sausage, and a side of hash browns. Kath requested grapefruit juice and an egg-white omelet with spinach and tomatoes. The waiter collected their menus and moved out of earshot.

"It's more than the accent," Joel resumed. "Nia had months to prepare, and she's done character roles. Listen, no one has ever disputed how much the camera loves you. And every once in a while, there are genuine flashes of brilliance in your performances. Casting directors comment on that. But you've never been consistent. You don't dig deep enough. Every role since your soap opera days has been a variation of Diane Weaver, which—let's be honest—was more or less you playing yourself. You could get by with that in your twenties. In your thirties, you need more."

Kath took a sip of coffee, hoping it would warm her up.

Smile. Never show your weakness.

Joel's expression softened. "What I'm trying to say is that it's a good time to stop and consider your next steps. Other career options."

The words hit Kath like a lightning bolt, a quick strike and then a searing pain.

Maybe she should have expected this conversation. In some distant recess of her mind, maybe she *had* expected it.

Of course, Joel would choose HT over her. HT was Joel's biggest moneymaker, an A-list celebrity. That had already gotten him custody of most of their friends in the divorce. Why wouldn't it get him Joel as well?

The knot of fear and loneliness Kath had been fighting these past three years expanded and rose in her throat like a scream pushing to get out. Not that she could scream or make a scene in public. That was probably why Joel had asked her out to breakfast. He hated confrontation. It was easier for him if she had to sit here nodding and pretending everything was fine.

"Are you dumping me as a client?" she asked. "Is that what this is?"

Joel's chair creaked as he shifted awkwardly. "I didn't want to do it on the phone, but it's hard when you put me in between HT and yourself. That's not my job."

"I didn't do that."

"Yes, you did."

In the street behind Joel, traffic streamed along. The sun reflected on gleaming imported cars and bounced off shop windows. A sudden gust from the Santa Anas whipped the fronds of the tall palm trees that lined the road.

The Devil Wind, boding no good to anyone.

Kath should have known not to risk even a little optimism while the Santa Anas blew. And they'd been blowing since her thirty-second birthday earlier in the week.

She started laughing. She couldn't help it. "Old Cow Syndrome. That's what this is. First HT, now you."

"What?" Joel blinked at her as if she'd lost her mind. Maybe she had.

"Oh, come on, you remember. Ashley Judd in *Someone Like You*, 2001? Ashley's character gets dumped by her boyfriend. She takes a study about how bulls won't mate with the same cow twice and adapts it to explain how men are genetically programmed to hunt out fresh meat. I'm the old cow, and you and HT are moving on to someone new."

Joel didn't see the humor. He had never been good at that. "This is business, Kath. I can't keep sending you out for roles that you won't get."

"Send me for this one audition. HT would talk to Dai Rhys if you asked him to."

"Then ask HT yourself. I'm sorry, but I won't."

Kath's eyes felt hot, and she dug in her purse for her oversized sunglasses and slipped them on. Forced a smile and kept her voice even. Professional. "A part like Margaret would turn everything around for me. Give me a chance, and I can nail the audition. I'm an actor, Joel. That's all I've ever wanted to be."

He reached across the table and caught her hand, even though he wasn't a hand-holder. "Sweetheart—and I'm saying this as a friend—it's time to be honest with yourself. Did you ever want to be an actor? Or did you want to be a star? Because they're not the same."

Kath's smile froze.

Around them, the hum of restaurant noise and conversation and traffic continued, people going on with their lives. Going somewhere.

"I know it seems impossible now, but you'll get past this," Joel continued. "You have money, and you're stronger than you think. Look how well you've come through the divorce. You'll be fine."

Kath threw everything she had left at keeping her composure. "Can we at least say it was a mutual decision? I'll need to find another agent."

"Agents won't care—"

"*I* care."

Joel pulled his hand away. "That's your problem, Kath. You waste too much energy worrying about what people think. Isn't it time to find something you love doing? Go out and start enjoying life."

THE LAST PRINCE

*"Time held me green and dying
Though I sang in my chains like the sea."*

DYLAN THOMAS, "FERN HILL" — *COLLECTED POEMS*

DAI RHYS HATED MEETINGS. HE had no patience for them at the best of times, but the discussion on recasting Margaret Glyndwr felt more like a war over creative control between himself and Alan Stickley. A war fought, like most these days, in a sterile conference room against a backdrop of accountants wringing their hands and executives unable to make decisions.

Lizzie Morgan, the casting director, was playing another audition tape on the projection screen. It was one Dai had already watched a dozen times, and he had to force himself to focus.

He already knew what Alan, the executive producer, was going to say.

The irony of being there in Alan's London conference room did not escape him. Dai had joined the British army precisely to avoid the sorts of jobs that involved sitting around and talking instead of doing something useful. But his military career had ended with a mortar round in Afghanistan and two months of indecision by generals and politicians half a world away.

After sending less than a hundred men to hold a compound in Helmand Province and leaving them stranded, the brass in London had sat around debating whether Musa Qala was worth the trouble of fighting the Taliban for it. By the time the talking heads concluded it wasn't, lads they had sent had already run out of ammunition and bled and died there.

Musa Qala and its aftermath had led Dai to this conference room, this moment. But it had also lowered his tolerance for crap. It chafed at him to think he was there now, in London, talking in circles while his cast and crew had to fend for themselves, filming background and battle scenes in Wales without him.

He leaned back in his chair and rubbed his neck to ease the tension. The walls of the conference room were closing in on him, and he needed air. Even the clutter of coffee cups, half-eaten sandwiches, résumés, budgets, and production schedules on the gleaming conference table added to a sense of chaos that churned inside him.

The audition tape ended, and the projection screen turned a solid blue. Lizzie pushed her graying dark braids behind her shoulders, gathered her collection of dry-erase markers, and moved to stand beside the headshot of Nerys Price taped to the whiteboard.

She glanced around the room. "So, what did we think?"

"I'm not excited." Alan sat back with his fingers steepled. At sixty-something, he was still a big bear of a man with a full beard and a tan that came from spending time outdoors. He spoke quietly because he'd earned the right to have people listen to him.

Lizzie turned to Dai. "What about you?"

"I thought she had potential the first time we saw her. Her approach to the character is a bit bland, I'll admit that. Still, I'd like to see how she and HT connect."

"We need a bigger name now. Even bigger than Nia," Alan said.

Dai disagreed. "Nerys has a hit show on BBC, and she's likely to get a second BAFTA nod this year."

"Which won't sell tickets in the States. There simply aren't any other Welsh actors in Nia's age bracket who can deliver the box office draw we need to recoup the losses. The cast insurance won't cover everything."

"We still have HT," Dai said.

"We're looking at a potential twenty-million-dollar budget overrun—more if the delay means extra CGI. We can't rely on HT alone. It's time to be realistic about what a Welsh co-star can bring to the table."

"We agreed on this going in. A story about the fight for Welsh independence deserves to be told by Welsh actors." Dai emphasized every word he spoke, his hands clenched in frustration. "There could be protests or even a boycott if we cast an American actor as Margaret."

"So assume the worst-case scenario. Say there is a boycott in Wales. How many fewer tickets would sell there? Five percent? Ten? Even if it was fifty percent, the population of Wales is less than one percent of the US population. A big American star makes for better math regardless, and most people in Wales will be happy we didn't cast an English actor." He smiled to show he meant the last part of the sentence to be a joke.

And that was the problem. Alan couldn't grasp why it wasn't funny.

In many ways, Alan was fantastic for the project. He'd produced and directed dozens of blockbusters and a string of Best Picture winners, and he had a reputation as the best eye in the business. Dai had jumped at the chance to work with him—to learn from him. But as the director, Dai was meant to have creative control with Alan staying hands-off on the day-to-day. That had been fundamental to all the contract negotiations, because for all that Alan liked to pitch *The Last Prince* as the *Braveheart* for Wales, being English he didn't fully understand.

The English had stolen Welsh blood, land, laws, and even the right to speak Welsh and keep weapons to defend themselves. They had robbed Wales of all dignity and hope. For fifteen years, Glyndwr's rebellion had given all that back.

Glyndwr had been more than a rebel. He had governed and

forged a nation. His vision for Wales was a symbol of justice and power to rival the loss of King Arthur's Camelot, the loss of an ideal. While Margaret and most of their children and grandchildren had died in the Tower of London as captives of the English crown, Glyndwr himself eluded capture. No one in Wales gave up his hiding place, not for gold or their own safety. And without a gravesite where the Welsh could mourn him, legend claimed that, like King Arthur, Glyndwr only lay in an enchanted sleep somewhere, waiting for the moment that Wales would rise again.

Dai had explained all that when he'd suggested the project. But there was a difference between knowing something in your head and feeling it in your bones.

The door to the conference room creaked open, and the other casting assistant came back in from the corridor.

Lizzie raised an eyebrow at her. "Any good news, Jen?"

Jen slipped into the empty chair next to Lizzie's. "Unfortunately not. Catrin Morgan's agent confirmed they're behind schedule on her current project. Photography won't wrap for at least two months, and her next project starts filming in February."

Lizzie made a note on the board under Catrin's headshot. "What about Sian Pryce?"

"We haven't heard from her agent yet."

With almost palpable satisfaction, Alan scratched a double line through Catrin's name on his notepad. "Let's circle back to Sophie Tanner. It would be worth pushing back the release date if we could get her on board."

Dai forced himself to relax the death grip on his pen before he answered. "I'm not ready to give up on casting a Welsh actor yet. And even if I was, Sophie's window of availability is shorter than Catrin's. Not to mention that we would need to pay her at least four times Nia's salary, and she's done nothing but fantasy. We don't want her fanbase coming in with that expectation."

"Maybe adding a bit more fantasy wouldn't be a bad idea. We could focus more on the idea of the prophecies and Glyndwr as a magician," Alan said. "It was good enough for Shakespeare."

"It would make it a different film," Dai said, fighting to control his temper.

Keeping *The Last Prince* from turning into another formulaic Hollywood blockbuster was an uphill battle. With only three minor directing credits and a decade as an actor behind him, letting Dai direct and co-produce had been a hard sell for the investors in the first place. Replacing Nia threatened to push the budget over two hundred million, and that had the investors in a panic. It didn't matter that Nia had gone through all the usual health screenings as part of her contract, or that Dai couldn't have foreseen a particularly aggressive form of cancer. The investors focused on Dai's inexperience and the millions they stood to lose.

For Dai, there was more than money at stake. He'd spent twelve years working on the screenplay. The idea had been born on a rooftop in Musa Qala, where a scared Welsh lad named Robbie Hanmer had told Dai stories about Owain

Glyndwr while the two of them stared down their sniper scopes night after endless night, searching for any movement that could warn them of the next attack. The days had bled together. Against all odds and often outnumbered five to one, the eighty-eight Brits had survived one Taliban assault after another, and the stories of Glyndwr's victories and incredible escapes provided inspiration. Robbie had joked that Glyndwr's ghost had to be watching over them.

Robbie Hanmer had died on the forty-eighth day in Musa Qala. The same mortar round that killed him shredded Dai's back and legs, but the medics kept Dai alive until the final evacuation. Drifting in and out of consciousness, he had heard Robbie's voice telling him stories of Glyndwr's impossible escapes and demanding that he not give up.

Dai couldn't let *The Last Prince* lose sight of its inspiration. He owed that and more to Robbie. Before he let Alan or anyone else change the script in a way that made no sense, he would have to walk away.

Leaning on his forearms, he looked at Alan down the table. His voice was firm and quiet as he said, "Glyndwr wasn't a magician, Alan. He was a man clever enough to use his cultural heritage of bards and prophecy to inspire the Welsh and intimidate the English. That's the project you signed off on, and it's not negotiable. Putting his victories down to magic would diminish what he accomplished."

Alan swiveled his chair around to study him. Moments passed without a sound. Dai didn't look away until Alan broke eye contact first.

"Very well," Alan said. "You're the director. No magic. I'll concede the point, but—as a favor—will you agree to a chemistry reading between Sophie and HT? Just see what she has to offer."

BARGAIN

"When you've lost everything, you've got nothing to lose."

KEN FOLLETT, WORLD WITHOUT END

K ATH COULDN'T REMEMBER DRIVING HOME. She
managed to keep from breaking down until she reached
her driveway. Then the thought of walking into the empty
house she had shared with HT tipped her past the edge. Tears
spilled in hot rivers down her cheeks, making the garage door
blur as it opened soundlessly. Inside the garage, she stopped
the car and cried with her forehead resting against the steering
wheel, her hands and shoulders shaking while the conversation
with Joel replayed itself over inside her head.

She hated herself for begging Joel. For being that weak.

Especially since he had fed her a pack of lies.

All right, yes, her first major role in Hollywood had been
on a soap, playing the social-climbing, much younger wife of a
millionaire businessman. She'd played Diane Weaver for seven

years, and she'd been typecast as the ice-cold femme fatale ever since. A manipulative politician's wife, a demanding girlfriend, a scheming heiress, a cunning murderer, a predatory vamp—she had done them all, but that didn't mean she couldn't do other roles.

She had gotten rave reviews playing Rosalind in *As You Like It* with Henry playing Orlando. And she—not Henry—had been the one who had worked her way up to a leading role. Henry had only done the play by accident, because John Irvine had broken his leg in a motorcycle accident on I-75 and the director was friends with Henry's mother.

Playing Rosalind had taken range. Rosalind was one of Shakespeare's most complex female characters. She had to dominate the stage both as the woman she was and the man she pretended to be. Just look at the actors who had played Rosalind in the course of their careers: Helen Mirren, Vanessa Redgrave, Maggie Smith, Helena Bonham Carter, Bryce Dallas Howard.

Okay, yes, there was a big difference between an amateur production in a Cincinnati suburb and a Kenneth Branagh film, but still. The more Kath thought about it, the more she realized most of what Joel had told her was an excuse. Self-protection on his part while he rid himself of an uncomfortable situation.

Henry "HT" Lewis was the problem.

HT was still, and always, the problem.

So he owed her.

Kath sat up and wiped her eyes. She unbuckled her seat belt and climbed out of the car.

Her footsteps echoed in the cavernous garage, where five of the six bays sat empty since HT had gone. She let herself into the kitchen and threw her keys on the marble counter. They landed with a clank, and somewhere in the distance, claws scrabbled unsteadily on the hardwood flooring.

"Muppet, I'm in the kitchen," Kath called, setting her purse down beside her keys.

Like the garage, the house was cavernous, and the stark white walls and furnishings made it look bigger. Buying the place had been HT's idea, a hyperventilatingly enormous leap of faith they'd made when his career took off and Kath was still working on the soap.

HT had fallen in love with the garage and the way the house and pool sat perched on the edge of the canyon. Kath had loved the garden and the view through the enormous wall-sized windows in the back, but she had spent months terrified an earthquake would send it all tumbling down the hillside. She'd been equally sure they could never afford the mortgage payments.

As it had turned out, they had paid the mortgage off even before the divorce. And after pouring love and countless hours into redoing the garden, letting go of the house would have been just one more loss Kath couldn't bear.

Another symbol of her failure.

Apart from Muppet, the house was just about the only thing she had left.

HT hadn't wanted Kath, Muppet, or the house, and now even Joel was throwing Kath away.

How had she gotten here?

It had been three years since HT walked out. And what had she done since then? The empty shell of a house was just one example. She had meant to change the furniture and paint the walls, add more joy and color. She had intended to reconnect with old friends and make new ones.

She had done none of that. Not to the house. Not to her life. Instead, she had let the days blur together, one after another, time passing while she sleepwalked through the hours, waiting for someone or something to give her purpose.

Well, she had that now.

An undersized geriatric West Highland White Terrier sniffed his way to the kitchen and bumped his head against her shin.

Kath bent to pick him up. "Hello, monster. I hope your day is going better than mine. Are you hungry? It's almost time for lunch."

Muppet bared his teeth at her, but then he licked her face when Kath snuggled him close. He'd come a long way since she had saved him from going to a shelter after biting his previous owner. A visit to the vet had confirmed that the dog was blind instead of cranky. Or at least blind as well as cranky. HT had barely tolerated him, which had only seemed to make Muppet love him more. It had broken his doggy heart when HT refused to take him when he'd moved out.

Feeling the warmth of Muppet's body heat made Kath want to cry all over again. Instead, she opened a single-serving plastic tub of gourmet dog food and scooped the contents into one of Muppet's bowls. He attacked it as soon as she set him down, and she stood and watched him for a while. A delaying tactic. Chickening out.

She couldn't have tears in her voice when she called HT. What she needed was anger. Assurance. Adrenaline.

HT didn't have the power to hurt her anymore.

She snatched her phone out of her purse and crossed to the sliding door that opened to the patio. Her heels clicked on the terra-cotta deck wrapped around three sides of the infinity pool at the canyon's rim. A line of ten-foot Italian cypress trees stood at the edge of the deck, and beyond that was the tennis court with the ball machine that had become Kath's survival mechanism.

She needed to imagine slamming Henry's face a few times before she called him.

The storage bench near the court gate held equipment and a wire basket filled with green, fuzzy tennis balls. Kath armed herself with her favorite racquet and emptied the basket's contents into the hopper of the ball machine. After turning the machine on, she kicked off her shoes, hopping up and down as the heat of the synthetic grass reached her skin.

Taking a position on the far side of the net, she bounced on her toes, waiting for the machine to spit a ball at her. She ran up and slammed the ball over the net, relishing the jolt through her arm and the sound as the racquet connected. The wind blew, and the machine spat fastballs to Kath's forehand or backhand in random order. She smashed them, harder and harder, picturing HT's face, remembering the distorted viewpoint Joel had tried to feed her.

For eight years, she was the one who kept them afloat. Even after the showrunners had killed her character on the soap, she'd had steady work. Not huge parts, but big enough. HT had gotten increasingly larger roles with long stretches of nothing in between. He'd filled those with modeling and tending bar. Then three years ago, he had become a household name almost overnight.

That was when the rumors began. The women.

Kath smacked another ball hard across the net.

Even in the first months of their marriage, he'd had other women. He had told her it would stop, and she had told herself she loved him so often that she believed it.

She should have walked away. They should never have gotten married in the first place, but they had that night between them, and the secrets they couldn't tell another soul.

Another ball flew at Kath, and she nailed it with the sweet spot of her racquet so hard she felt the jolt all the way up her shoulder. The ball sailed over the net and landed in center court.

She had found out her marriage was over by reading the headlines at the grocery store checkout counter. It wasn't until she'd asked HT about it that he'd admitted he wanted a divorce.

How much longer would they have punished each other by staying together if the paparazzi hadn't changed the pattern? By that point, HT was a fixture on the A-list and the producers of his current film had too much to lose. As soon as the first few photos of him with other women had shown up in the tabloids, the PR machine had rolled out to make sure no one would blame HT.

Painting Kath in the same light as the characters she portrayed was easy. The way the tabloids told the story, she was the bitter, scheming witch who had made HT's life so miserable he had no choice except to find comfort where he could.

Kath backhanded another tennis ball, and the world narrowed into that steady rhythm: the *phfft* of the machine serve, the *twang* of the ball against her racket, the *thump* as it hit on the far side of the net.

Green balls littered the tennis court by the time the machine was empty. Kath's shirt clung to her skin, sweat ran down from the backs of her knees, and her heart pounded. But she felt both calm and wide awake.

Before the endorphins had time to wear off, she dug her phone out of the pocket of her jeans and dialed.

The phone rang and rang.

Kath checked the Rolex on her wrist as she strode toward the other end of the tennis court. Wales, located west of England in the UK, was eight hours ahead. With the long days required on location, HT might not have finished for the day yet. But unless he was on set, he usually picked up. Unless he wasn't picking up for Kath.

Then suddenly, he answered. "What?"

No preamble. No pretense.

"Nice," Kath said. "We haven't talked in a while. Maybe try a 'How are you, Kath? Everything good?'"

"You wouldn't be calling if everything was good." HT's voice held more resignation than edge, though.

"Okay, I need a favor."

"We're not married anymore, and I don't owe you any favors."

"See, now I think that depends on your perspective." Kath reached the ball machine and picked up the basket she had left beside it. She positioned the basket above the nearest tennis ball and jammed it down until the ball popped through the wide wire grate at the bottom.

"We've both wasted ten years paying penance." HT released a sigh. "I don't want to fight anymore. I'm past it."

"How nice for you, but Joel just fired me. Don't tell me you had nothing to do with that." Anger swept through her and she felt light-headed. She had spent months fighting this same deep black anger every time it threatened to consume her.

HT let the silence drag on before he spoke. "I didn't know about it, but I'm sorry."

"I'm not looking for apologies. But those so-called wasted years you don't want to think about? They're what got you where you are, sitting on top of the world. You wouldn't be there without me."

"My career has nothing to do with you."

"You wouldn't have come to Hollywood."

"That's not something you want to remind me about." HT's voice was dangerously quiet. "Not when it cost me Anna and my family and everything I had ever planned for my life."

"And you think you're the only one who paid a price?" Kath

positioned the ball basket over another ball and rammed the basket down. "Neither one of us can change what happened, HT. But maybe think about the fact that you were twenty-two, and I was seventeen. With Nia being so much younger now, that might not be a good look for you if the truth came out."

"Is that a threat?" HT's voice was low, cold, and lethal as a knife.

"Your publicist is brilliant. She managed to kill the career I'd been building for a decade with a few well-placed articles, but even she would have a hard time explaining away your part in what happened."

"You know the articles weren't my idea. I never asked her to tell the tabloids you were cold or hard to work with."

"Did you ask her to stop? No, because you were too busy worrying about your own image and career. What do you think would happen to all that if I go to the tabloids and give them the truth?"

"You wouldn't do that. I know you."

"Do you? Your parents are gone. Mine are divorcing. Anna is happily married." Kath had kept the anger in check until that moment, but now she let it uncoil enough to come through, raw and throbbing, in her voice. "I have nothing left to lose, HT. The only thing I can do is try to claw my way into a decent role. Something different from what I've been playing."

"Go back to community theatre and start over. Get a new agent."

"As easily as that?" Kath laughed. "I guess that's what

happens after you film six big blockbusters. You forget how hard it is for the little people."

"For Christ's sake, Kath. Enough. Just tell me what you want." There was a sound like liquid pouring on the other end of the line, then a thud like a glass hitting wood too hard.

HT wasn't much of a drinker, not after that night. But he had a ritual to help him separate himself from whatever character he was playing. He would come home, head straight up to shower, then pour himself a glass of Scotch. Kath could picture him the way she had seen him a thousand times with a towel wrapped low around his hips, his chest still damp and not an ounce of extra fat to soften the hard contours of his muscles.

Had he just poured himself that one glass of Scotch? Or was he allowing himself a second?

A part of Kath hated what she was doing. "I need you to ask Dai Rhys to give me an audition. For Margaret."

"No. Hell, no." HT's voice was like a whip. "I couldn't even if I wanted to, and I wouldn't be doing you any favors."

"Why?"

"Margaret is nothing like what you've done before. And Nia and I spent months preparing. I've put in six months just learning to ride and wield a sword, never mind the accent."

"I've ridden all my life, and I've studied the script. I'm ready. And you know what Margaret and I have in common? Rage. The prospect of losing everything over and over again. So get me an audition, HT, or I swear I'll take the story to the tabloids and deal with any fallout that comes my way."

Silence was a weapon, and HT had always known how to use it. Kath was learning. She didn't rush to fill the void. Instead, she kept busy plucking tennis balls off the artificial turf while sweat beaded on her forehead and trickled between her breasts. A break in the wind had made the temperature even hotter, and the still air bore the smoky-sweet pine scent of the cypress trees.

"Fine, I'll talk to Dai," HT said, giving in. "But I can't promise they'll agree to see you."

"Make them. You're an actor. Make Dai believe I'm perfect for the part."

"That's my reputation on the line—"

"You had no problem trashing my reputation."

"Christ, when did you get so cold? Fine, I'll do it on one condition. My lawyer will draw up a non-disclosure agreement that covers everything from the day you and I first met, and you're going to sign it. One word from you about the accident or our relationship to anyone, and I mean anyone—about anything at all, even if it's as small as what kind of cold cuts I like on my sandwiches—and I'll make sure you know what losing everything really means."

Kath had been wrong. Even now, HT had the power to hurt her.

She pictured his hard, handsome face, the blue eyes that could go from warm to frostbite cold in a fraction of a second. There had been a time when she couldn't imagine breathing without him.

Still, she had to count this as a victory. HT had believed

that she would actually go to the tabloids. That confirmed she was a better actor than either he or Joel believed.

Signing a non-disclosure agreement she would never violate? No problem at all.

"If you want me to sign," she said, "I have a couple of conditions of my own. First, you agree not to speak badly of me. Ever. And that includes keeping any reservations you have about me playing Margaret to yourself. As far as anyone—especially Dai Rhys—is concerned, you think I'll be perfect. That applies before and after the audition. And second, if I get the part, you agree to treat me the same as you would any other co-star—minus the seducing-me-into-bed part."

"Is that all? For a moment, you had me worried. But there's zero chance you'll get the part."

Kath's face burned as if he'd slapped her. She forced herself to go on calmly. "One more thing, HT."

"What?" he snapped.

"If anyone asks, you're the one who gave me the script because you wanted me to audition."

PERENNIALS

"Two stars keep not, their motion in one sphere."

WILLIAM SHAKESPEARE, *HENRY IV, PART ONE*

D AI CLOSED THE DOOR OF the conference room behind him, happy for the excuse to step out of the meeting. The overhead light in the corridor formed a pale puddle on the dark blue carpet, and his face reflected back at him in the glass of the framed posters of Alan Stickley's blockbusters that lined the walls. Seeing himself like that made him wonder at the twists of Fate. If not for Musa Qala, Robbie Hanmer, and that mortar round, Dai might still have been in the army, and he and Laura might still have been together, living near the base in Colchester.

Laura was another part of what troubled him.

She had fought so hard to save him when he'd come back broken from Afghanistan. Laura was the one who had taken him to all of his appointments and supported him as he relearned how to walk. When the therapist recommended Trauma Drama to help him regulate his emotions and learn to cope, Laura had driven him and waited hours for him every day. She'd encouraged him to stick with acting and start writing the screenplay to get Robbie's stories out of his head.

Glyndwr must have needed his own Laura to succeed, so *The Last Prince* was about Margaret as much as it was about Robbie's Glyndwr. Like Laura, Margaret must have needed patience, courage, and fierce intelligence to temper Glyndwr when he returned. Most of all, she'd needed subtlety.

Even if she had been Welsh, Dai wasn't sure Sophie Tanner had the range to show all the qualities Margaret's struggle would have taken. But the chemistry test would prove that much.

He dialed HT's number and leaned back against the wall.

"Hey, thanks for calling me back," HT said. He sounded overly enthusiastic, even for an American.

"What can I do for you? We're still in meetings, but I wanted to make sure the shoot is going well."

"Want the truth or the optimistic assessment?"

"Always the truth."

"Everything we shot today was garbage. I know you're busy, and it's not that Caradoc didn't do a good job directing, but morale is flagging. You can feel it. Everyone is wondering what's going to happen."

Dai closed his eyes. "Alan and I are trying to get things on track as quickly as possible."

"But no decisions yet?" There was an odd, nervous note in HT's voice.

"We're making progress," Dai responded cautiously. "Working through the original auditions and considering some new options. How is Nia doing? Have you heard from her?"

"They're doing a double mastectomy the day after tomorrow. There are some lymph nodes involved, so that means additional treatment. They'll know more after the surgery."

"I wish there was more we could do." Dai pushed away from the wall and walked down the corridor. Nia was still at the age when death wasn't even a blip on the horizon. Sometimes that resulted in more optimism and fight, but he'd seen wounded lads who packed it in for no better reason than not having had the time to dig in and mentally prepare for battle. He hated the thought of Nia facing that.

"Let me know if there's anything she needs," he said. "And if you want time off, that's not ideal, but we can make it work."

"Her family is there for her, and it was early days for us, so she doesn't want me there. I'll do what I can from here."

Dai reached the end of the corridor and turned to walk back. "Give her my best when you speak with her. Where is she having the surgery? I'd like to send her flowers, at least."

"Cedars, but send her a plant instead. She calls cut flowers death in cellophane."

Dai smiled, because Laura felt the same. She'd dug up half the front lawn of their house in Colchester and replaced it with a perennial garden while he was in Musa Qala. Once he was home, that garden became her refuge while he paced the house like a caged tiger. But she never cut the flowers before they faded out of bloom. She couldn't bear the thought of anything dying before its time.

The fact that she'd given up on their marriage without a fight had surprised him. Once he'd come through the physical recuperation and the hardest part of the mental struggle, he had been ready to do the work to get their relationship back. She had claimed it was too late already. What had existed between them had changed and faded, and she felt that the kindest thing they could do for each other was to let go and cut their losses.

Even now, she was the one person who never expected anything from him. Never put any pressure on him. The person he could call anytime, and she would listen.

"Don't worry about the past," she'd said. "Appreciate what you have. Take all you can from today and look forward to tomorrow."

Dai had done his best to take that advice. He'd faced death at twenty-two, and having clawed his way back from that, he took nothing for granted anymore. Seeing what Nia was going through was a fresh reminder to seize every moment.

He realized HT had fallen silent. "You still there, HT?"

HT cleared his throat. "Yeah. Sorry. Hey, so I was wondering… Is there any chance you're flying out to Los Angeles?"

"We're meeting with all the investors on Thursday, and I have some auditions lined up. Why?"

"I've been thinking about Margaret. Actually, I was hoping you might consider giving my ex-wife an audition."

Dai turned again and headed back down the corridor. He vaguely remembered some tabloid gossip and a divorce. Not much more than that. For the life of him, he couldn't remember the woman's name. Which in itself meant she wasn't a possibility.

"I'm sorry, HT. I don't know her work, and it's not a good idea in general. She's not even Welsh, is she?"

"Her mother was born in Scotland, and yes, I realize that's not the same. Also, most of her work has been for television, and she's older than Nia. I know that's not what you had in mind, but if you're going to be in LA anyway, could you give her a reading? You don't even have to send her sides. Do a cold reading. A few minutes in and out, and if she doesn't work, no sweat."

HT wasn't someone who asked for favors. Dai didn't particularly like the man, but he was good at his job and didn't throw his weight around. "You feel like she'd be right for this?"

"She might surprise you."

Dai was getting a little tired of hearing that from people. "There's a lot riding on this. We don't need surprises."

"I get that." HT let the statement hang there.

Dai shook his head, confused. "You get it, but you're asking anyway?"

"Kath's not big, and she's not Welsh, but she's done a lot of roles as the woman pulling strings behind the scenes, and that's definitely part of Margaret's character. As far as audience goes, she got a lot of tabloid coverage during the divorce, and more when I started dating Nia. Sometimes, that kind of drama is enough to get people into the theatre. Anyway, I'd consider it a big favor if you'd see her. The whole Nia thing has thrown me, and Kath could… I mean, you get it, right? Please. A five-minute reading, that's all. And no sweat if you're not impressed."

"You wouldn't have any trouble working together?"

HT laughed, and there was an odd note in it. "There's no chance of that."

Dai found the entire conversation unsettling, but he was already going to waste time auditioning other actors. As soon as he'd agreed to a chemistry read for Sophie Tanner, Alan had argued that they should see Scarlet Johnson, too. Then Lizzie had produced a list of other American stars they hadn't considered earlier. It was almost faster to let them audition than it was to argue, and the same applied to HT's ex-wife. He had no intention of casting any of them.

With any luck, Nerys or Catrin would light up the screen with HT when they came in for the chemistry test. At least they understood the film's importance, and sometimes that sort of fire made all the difference.

"Have Kath send her headshot and résumé to Lizzie," he told HT. "I'll see what she can do, but no promises after that."

CUTTING DEEP

"Your comments are valuable, but I'm gonna ignore your advice."

ROALD DAHL, FANTASTIC MR. FOX

THREE DAYS WAS AN ETERNITY and no time at all. After getting the call from the casting assistant, Kath made a battle plan and set to work. The first thing she needed was a dialect coach.

She'd only had to use an accent twice before, and the coach she had worked with was unavailable. He gave her numbers for other coaches, and after a few calls Kath found one who was available and knew the coach Nia had used to prepare for playing Margaret. Fiona O'Connor, an Irishwoman from Dublin who had worked in Hollywood for over forty years, even promised to phone her friend for insight into the distinct accent Kath would need.

On the phone, Fiona's own speaking voice was deep and

scratchy, with a still discernible Irish accent. When she showed up at Kath's the next morning, she wore a flowing purple skirt and matching tank top that revealed upper arms flapping off her bones like chicken wings. Her flame-red hair had hints of gray along the scalp, and smoking had etched deep lines around her mouth. She smelled sour and ocherous, and Muppet, who had arrived with a flurry of ferocious West Highland barking, skidded to a stop, then backed away.

Kath picked him up and said, "Fiona, it's nice to meet you. Thank you again for working me in."

Fiona looked Kath up and down, narrowed her eyes at Muppet, and retrieved a thin gold cigarette case from her suitcase-sized Gucci purse. "You don't mind if I smoke, do you?"

"Not at all." Still holding the dog tucked beneath her arm, Kath led the way through the house and out onto the pool deck.

Fiona snapped the cigarette case open, lit one, and inhaled as if the time since her last cigarette had been too long. Kath ushered her to one of the conversation areas, where a table and blue-cushioned chairs stood beneath an arbor woven through with wide-leafed grape vines dotted with clusters that hadn't yet begun to ripen.

"I got hold of my friend who worked with Nia." Fiona settled herself in a chair and took another drag on the cigarette. "We talked through a few different strategies for the accent."

"That's wonderful." Kath set Muppet down and took a seat.

"Welsh accents are pretty regional, both in English and in

Welsh. Someone from the North will sound different than someone from Cardiff in the South. Then there's the Valley's accent and the West country. Nia tried to be as authentic as possible, geographically and historically. We don't have that kind of time."

"Two days and counting," Kath said, pretending not to panic.

"What I'm thinking, at least for the audition, is that you stick with what an audience would expect royalty to sound like. Posh British, yeah?" Fiona blew out a cloud of smoke. "Then we can add some Welshness by changing how you pronounce the L's. Like this: All small fellows will follow fall fields bailing balls of bellows." She said the nonsense sentence in an accent that made her sound like Princess Kate, and then repeated it, softening and lengthening the L sounds, which gave it an instant lilt. "Did you hear that?" she asked. "The main thing is that Margaret was educated in a society where being English was rewarded, and that's what Dai Rhys told Nia he wanted to emphasize."

"Great," Kath said, hoping she didn't look as overwhelmed as she felt.

They spent the day running through exercises for basic sound patterns and sentence cadence. By the end, Kath was more or less comfortable Welshifying the sentences Fiona asked her to repeat. She practiced even more intensely after Fiona had left for the day, because she needed to be ready to practice her audition scenes.

She photocopied the pages and had them waiting on the

table beneath the arbor along with an enormous, empty ashtray and a pitcher of iced tea before Fiona rang the doorbell in the morning. The two of them settled themselves, and Muppet found a shady spot upwind, his head resting on his paws. Fiona lit another cigarette and glanced through the sides Kath had given her, then squinted at the notes Kath had scribbled in the margins. They had come through faintly in the copy.

"Don't worry about those." Kath pushed the ashtray toward her.

Fiona let out a long plume of smoke. "Didn't you say the audition was a cold reading?"

"It is, but since I have the script, I want to ask if I can do these two scenes instead."

"Isn't that a little dangerous?" Fiona pushed her chair back from the table and tucked her legs underneath herself.

"What do you mean?"

"Some directors might see that as a bit… well, entitled. Don't you think?"

Was it? Kath had meant it to show she was prepared to do the work. And also, she couldn't do cold readings.

Still, she didn't want to come across as entitled. That was the last thing she needed.

She reached for her phone to call Joel and ask for his advice. Other than HT, Joel was the only person who knew how much cold readings terrified her. Then she remembered she couldn't call him.

She couldn't call Lizzie Morgan, the casting director, either. And she didn't know if Dai Rhys or Alan Stickley were going to be there, or if it would only be the first-line casting team. Alan Stickley had a reputation for being hands-on with casting—as well as every other aspect of a film. Kath had also read that he could be deceptively friendly and generally terrifying. Going to an audition felt like jumping out of a plane without a parachute at the best of times. Now everything she'd ever worked for was riding on this, and she couldn't afford to upset anyone.

Picking up her dog-eared copy of the script from the table, she kept her expression blank. She waved Fiona's concern away as if it didn't matter. "I'm sure it can't hurt if I have the scenes prepared and ask if I can do them. If they want me to read something different, I'll have to figure it."

Fiona stared at her. She had a way of almost pursing her lips that Kath found disturbing. "Are you always this tense, honey?" Fiona said. "Your shoulders are just about hugging your ears."

"I'm fine," Kath said.

"Then try to breathe. Oxygen is good for the brain."

Kath forced another smile. "So, in this first scene, Margaret's husband has come home after fighting for the English king, and he has discovered that their neighbor— Reginald Grey de Ruthyn, an English lord—is trying to claim a piece of land that belongs to Glyndwr. Here. Could you read Glyndwr's part for me?"

She showed Fiona where the scene started, then found the place on her own copy and began.

"Is this how it will be, now that you have come back?" she

snapped. "You will ignore me? Ignore my advice? These years while you were away at war, I have kept peace with de Ruthyn despite every slight and indignity he committed. You have undone it all with a single letter." She glanced up, waiting for Fiona to read Glyndwr's lines.

Fiona's eyes were focused farther down the page, as if she was reading ahead instead of listening.

"That was your cue," Kath prompted. "Or did I do the accent wrong?"

Fiona ground out her cigarette in the ashtray. "The accent wasn't bad. But are you sure you want to play the character with that much anger?"

"Margaret is angry."

"Anger is boring. And it's obvious." Fiona uncrossed her legs and tapped the butt of a fresh cigarette against the table before lighting up. "Let's try something different. Tell me about what happens before this scene. Apart from anger, what else does Margaret feel?"

Kath's stomach tightened. She could feel herself blushing, and she hated that. Hated all of this.

Plus, Fiona was wrong. Angry was exactly how Margaret felt—angry and humiliated and afraid. Only she wouldn't show the fear or the humiliation. That was one of the things Kath liked most about her.

Needing time and air, Kath scraped her heavy blonde hair back and looped it into a knot at her nape before she answered. "Margaret is strong. She's brave. But you'd have to read the whole script to understand, and we don't have time for that."

"You're missing opportunities by being defensive." Fiona blew out a cloud of smoke.

"Sorry, but the audition is the day after tomorrow. I'm out of time."

"I understand, but the way you spat out those lines, all I heard was a woman ready to explode. That seems like a disconnect from how the dialogue reads. The script doesn't show me a wife shouting at her husband. When Margaret talks about the slights and indignities she has suffered, I feel like she's saying something without wanting to say it. Even those few sentences suggest self-control and a world of hurt."

"I wasn't shouting," Kath said quietly.

"You might as well have been. But you see? You latched on to that one word and ignored everything I said after that."

Kath focused on details, the curl of smoke, the deep red color of Fiona's nails against her yellowed fingers as she held the cigarette filter. Details kept her from reacting.

"I appreciate the feedback," she said. "I do. But maybe we should just focus on the accent."

"That's not how I work. I'm a dialogue coach, not an accent coach. I assumed when you told me you got my name from Jonathan that he'd recommended me because you needed what I can give you. Maybe we've gotten our wires crossed somewhere, but I do think I can help you. I took a peek at some of your work after you called, and I can see potential for improvement."

Great. First Joel, then HT, and now Fiona.

Kath had been trying so hard to brush it off, but what if

Joel had been right? Maybe she was kidding herself. How was she supposed to know?

She'd been a working actor for the best part of a decade. She'd studied every acting class she could find on DVD or the internet, from Helen Mirren's *MasterClass* to Uta Hagen to Michael Caine. Method acting had never been her style—she couldn't imagine herself living on set without electricity or running water like Daniel Day-Lewis or working twelve-hour shifts as a cab driver like Robert De Niro. But she'd read book after book, sifting through rivers of information like a prospector hoping for a rare gold nugget. That wasn't even counting her childhood, where her mother had critiqued each step and every smile while parading Kath and her sisters in front of pageant judges.

Kath had spent her whole life learning how to smile no matter what.

She forced herself to smile, and eventually she managed it.

Fiona didn't look convinced. "Listen, I've been doing this a long time now, and I'm not bragging when I say I've got one of the best eyes for talent in the business. I think you have a lot more talent than maybe you've gotten credit for, but you're holding yourself back. Wasting opportunities."

"What do you mean?" Kath asked.

"Nailing an accent is great, but no one is going to cast you because of that. Words—entire scenes—can mean different things depending on the emotion you put behind them. The one thing I haven't seen in any of the work I saw is any sign of vulnerability. You do angry and manipulative. You can do every variation of sexy that was ever invented. But where is the fear? The pain? Try starting this scene again and read it in a way that shows who Margaret *is*."

"That's why I picked these two scenes. Because they do show Margaret."

"Honey, Dai Rhys is one of the most emotionally honest actors in a generation. He wouldn't write a one-dimensional character, and from what I've read so far, he didn't. That scene has all sorts of nuance. But that opening you gave me felt like you had read Margaret's first line of dialogue, decided she was angry, and that's as far as you got. Don't be afraid to push the boundaries. You have to give Dai and the casting team a light bulb moment where they see what you're doing and say, 'Yes! That's exactly what we want.'"

Kath's cheeks flushed hot. "I'm not afraid."

Fiona raised her eyebrows. "I'm going to call BS on that one. You're locked up tighter than a bank vault."

Kath wanted to take the glass of tea off the table and throw it at Fiona's face. Put out the stupid cigarette.

She already had more self-doubt than she could handle. She didn't need any more.

And how was she supposed to know what anyone wanted? She'd read and reread everything *Variety* and the *Hollywood Reporter* had written about Dai Rhys and the film. Not to mention scouring every article and interview in pages and pages of internet search results. She'd watched every movie he had made as an actor and director. She'd even called her friend Olivia, who was the key makeup artist for the film, asking for hints about how Nia had played the part.

"I'd say she was soft-spoken," Olivia had said, "but also smart and patient. Nia didn't give her a lot of fire, if you want the truth. Think Princess Kate instead of Meghan Markle."

Kath had started with anger because of that. She had wanted to give Margaret fire.

Fiona ground her cigarette out in the ashtray and lit another. She watched Kath through a haze of smoke. "I'm not judging you, if that's what you're afraid of. I just think you can do a lot better. If this isn't going to work for you, though, no sweat. There's no point wasting my time or yours, and I won't charge you for today. What do you want to do?"

Kath wanted to jump at the chance to get out of the situation. Fiona had barely given her a minute before deciding that she was wrong, and Kath was so tired of having people beat her up.

On the other hand, if Fiona left, then even the accent would be horrible.

The script pages blurred in Kath's hand.

She blinked away the tears of weakness and shook her head. "Please stay," she said. "I'll try it your way."

"This isn't about me or my way. It's about getting you to open up." Fiona shook her head. "Okay, look, give me some background first. Tell me about the story and why you connect with Margaret. You mentioned her strength and bravery. Well, strength isn't interesting unless the character knows she isn't invincible. And if you want to show her courage, you also have to show that she's afraid. One without the other is only half the job."

A hummingbird zipped over the swimming pool, a fragile flash of iridescence against the gleaming water. It hovered above a fuchsia bush at the edge of the deck. Kath watched it and drew a breath.

What Fiona was saying went against everything she had ever learned. But then, she'd never played a weak character or one who was afraid. She had spent her whole life hiding fear. Showing it went contrary to everything Kath had ever been told.

Then again, everything she had done up to this point in her career hadn't been enough. Something had to change.

She wanted this part. She needed it. She'd burned every bridge between Cincinnati and Los Angeles to come out here, and failing as an actor was not an option.

If she failed, then all the mistakes and pain—her own pain and Anna's and HT's, their parents'—all of that would have been for nothing.

She put everything she had left into keeping herself from crying.

"What do you know about the film so far?" she asked, looking back up at Fiona.

Fiona eased back in her chair. "Mostly what I read after you called. The story is roughly *Braveheart* meets *Rob Roy* meets *Gladiator*, right? About Owain Glyndwr's fifteenth-century Welsh rebellion against the English."

"Exactly," Kath said. "But Dai Rhys made Margaret a driving force all the way through the film. That's what I love most about her."

"Why?" Fiona watched her intently. "And don't give me any BS about anger. Dig deep and give me the honest answer."

Kath had to think about that for a minute. "All right. Things don't just happen to her; she makes them happen. She's the one who's had to deal with the conniving English neighbor while Glyndwr was away fighting wars on behalf of the English king. And she's managed to keep de Ruthyn somewhat contained because of Glyndwr's position, but now that there's political upheaval, de Ruthyn thinks Bolingbroke—who's about to become Henry IV—will side with him instead of Glyndwr. Instead of letting her anger and helplessness make things even worse, Margaret connects that to how the Welsh in general feel about what the English settlers are doing to them. She makes Glyndwr understand that, and she helps him channel that understanding to fuel a wider rebellion."

"So, she's the power behind the throne?" Fiona asked.

"No, that's what Dai Rhys has done differently. Margaret is the power beside the throne."

"Then wouldn't anger be the last thing she would reveal? If that's all that was driving her in this scene, wouldn't she cheer Glyndwr on for doing something to piss de Ruthyn off? Instead, she urges him to be cautious and asks him to let her handle it. That suggests she is more restrained—and politically aware—than he is."

"I think it's more than that. She's lying to Glyndwr when she says de Ruthyn didn't touch her, and she's trying to hide that from her husband. She knows that if de Ruthyn and

Glyndwr meet, de Ruthyn might say something that gives it away. That's why she wants to step in between them."

Fiona studied her. "Is that all in the script?"

"No, but it's the only way the script makes sense."

"Good. Great. Then show me that. All of it. If you can, that's your chance to make yourself stand out from the other actors."

"Okay," Kath said, with no clue where to even start.

"Also, don't forget the audition begins when you enter the room, long before you say anything. Go back into the house now and come out again. Walk over here with all the confidence in the world, as if you're taking your mark in front of the camera. Then give your name like you would for the audition slate, and show me how relaxed and likable you can be. Make it look like you're fun to work with."

"Sure. No problem," Kath said.

Fiona sighed. "Honey, relax. Relax, relax, relax. If you're tense and petrified, Margaret will be tense and petrified. Whatever you are feeling, that's how she will come across."

Kath's glass was empty, but she sat a moment, pushing the straw up and down through the melting ice, gathering up enough energy to get out of her chair.

Looking up, she found Fiona studying her, and she quickly broke eye contact.

Fiona sighed and briefly squeezed Kath's hand. "Never mind. Let's not worry about these scenes or Margaret for a moment. You have to be able to make your body a blank canvas before you can channel emotion into it, so let's try some basic tension exercises."

"Okay."

"Let's start with your shoulders. Make them as tight as you can and hold that while you count to five. Then let all the tension out as you count to ten."

Tightening her shoulders was easy. Making them relax was harder.

Fiona had her repeat the process over and over until Kath could release the tension quickly. Only then did she let Kath do the same for her back, feet, hands, jaw, brows—every place Kath carried tension.

"Good," Fiona finally said. "Your mind is still obviously going a million miles per hour, but at least your body is ready to absorb different emotions. Let's move on to that. Think back to a specific moment when you felt something powerful. Don't tell me the emotion, keep it to yourself for the moment. Have you got something?"

"What kind of emotion?" Kath asked.

"Anything. Maybe something you've felt recently. And don't say anger."

Loneliness, that was what Kath had felt.

She thought back to that moment when she'd driven into her garage after Joel had fired her. How cavernous it had felt with only her car there and the five spaces empty where HT's cars had been. How empty the house had felt when she walked into the kitchen.

How empty her life had been.

"Close your eyes and put yourself in that moment. Think about what you were doing, what you were wearing. What was the weather like? Who were you with? What did you eat or drink? What were you doing with your hands, your legs? Transport yourself back in time and feel the emotion. When you're there, get up and walk across the room for me feeling it. Show it to me."

Kath felt exposed, like a live wire stripped of all its protective shielding. But she did it. She let the weight of that loneliness weigh her down as she walked across the terrace and the pool deck.

When she reached the glass door, her face reflected back at her. She could see the loneliness, the sadness. The empty ache.

Turning to face Fiona and walking back toward her, letting Fiona see what she had seen in the glass, that was one of the hardest things Kath had ever done.

"Aw, come here." Fiona stood up and opened her arms wide as Kath reached her.

Kath let herself be drawn into Fiona's hug. Fiona smelled like ash and smoke, like a funeral pyre.

Like the ashes of Kath's career and self-respect.

Kath sobbed against Fiona's shoulder as if a well of tears had opened up inside her. But eventually, she was all cried out.

Fiona eased herself away. "Ready to try a different emotion?"

"Sure," Kath said, grateful to her for not asking, for not making her talk about it.

Sadness, anger, terror, disappointment, guilt, disgust, shame—a long list of negative emotions were all easy to remember. Kath had years of memories to draw from. But finding happiness, genuine happiness? Kath couldn't remember much of that. Not since she'd left Cincinnati.

She and Fiona worked through dinner, calling in a delivery order of kung pao chicken and moo shu vegetables so they didn't have to stop.

"I think you've made some progress," Fiona said shortly after eleven o'clock. "I'll bet you an even hundred that you're going to feel like a whole new person when we try your scenes tomorrow. But read them through again before you go to bed. Sometimes it helps to sleep on things and let your brain work on them without interference."

Kath nodded and thanked her, and after she'd shut the door behind her, she barely had energy left to take Muppet out and plod upstairs to bed. She fell asleep on top of the covers without changing her clothes, and morning came too quickly. She'd barely showered and dressed before Fiona rang the bell, looking much too cheerful in a bright orange gauzy shirt and pink jeans.

"Ready to do this?" Fiona asked, peering at Kath and Muppet with equal apprehension.

"Absolutely," Kath said, leading the way back out to the table on the terrace.

Kath made it through the first scene without looking at the script, but she focused on a spot to Fiona's left to keep from having to watch for her reaction. When she finished, though, she couldn't resist. "What did you think?"

"Better. Much better. Now go again."

"Why? What did I do wrong?"

"Nothing. Acting isn't about right or wrong. Take it from the top."

Kath repeated the scene, then did it again three more times, and Fiona still said nothing.

"Am I getting better?" Kath asked. "Worse? Come on, Fi, give me some feedback."

"A retake isn't always about you. I've been feeding you Glyndwr's lines a little differently each time."

Kath tried to think back and find the differences. "I didn't notice."

"Actually, you did. You responded a little differently each time, which was exactly what you needed to do. You went in with an approach, but you left room to react to the connection between the characters."

"Sometimes," Kath said, "I want to slap you really hard."

Fiona laughed and went into a fit of phlegmy coughing that ended in a grin. "Finally. That might be the most honest thing you've said to me. I like it."

"You're a strange woman."

"You, too. Now try the next scene and stop wasting time."

They went over the second scene, and after a couple of rounds, Fiona abruptly stood up and scooped her lighter and pack of cigarettes into her oversized purse.

"Where are you going? It's still early," Kath said. "Shouldn't we keep working?"

"You can keep working. But I have a hair appointment and a dinner date, and I've done my best to give you the tools to handle whatever they throw at you tomorrow. Just remember to be open and don't be afraid to show Margaret's imperfections. It's the flaws and contradictions that make people interesting. Trust yourself."

Kath picked up Muppet and followed Fiona out to her black Mercedes. "Thank you," she said as Fiona opened the driver's door. "For everything."

"My pleasure." Fiona gave Kath a hug that felt a little more fierce than her casual attitude suggested. "Knock them dead tomorrow, honey. You're better than you think you are. And let me know what happens, okay? You know, the important details, like whether Dai Rhys looks as good in person as he does on screen."

"Now there's a question I don't need in my head," Kath said.

Muppet gave a series of ferocious "Good riddance" barks while Fiona drove away. Kath carried him back into the house.

Without Fiona, the space seemed too empty again. Too lonely. Days' worth of dishes, script pages, and various articles Kath had printed from the internet lay scattered downstairs as if a hurricane had come roaring through. She felt wrecked herself.

"What do you think, pup?" she asked. "Am I ready?"

Muppet licked her face as she set him down. Kath decided to take that as encouragement.

AUDITION

"Even ashes are a part of your freedom."

SARAH WATERS, *FINGERSMITH*

D AI HAD STOPPED TRYING TO understand why HT had asked for the audition. HT didn't strike him as the type who would stay friends with his exes. Apart from Laura, that wasn't the norm in Dai's experience. And Laura didn't count because she was superhuman. What's more, there was nothing in Katharine Cameron's résumé that suggested she was ready for a part like Margaret. Lizzie had been more than a little furious, and if Dai had seen the résumé before telling HT he would see her, he would have refused point blank.

The preceding audition finished a few minutes early, and Lizzie took advantage of the time to send her assistant John out for coffee. Meanwhile, she and Dai jotted down their notes and impressions, and by the time Dai looked up again, Kath was walking into the room.

On the plus side, her headshot hadn't been airbrushed beyond recognition. Dai looked closer; she had the sort of face that went beyond beauty and commanded a second look. She had also chosen her audition clothing well. The long-sleeved black top with a scoop neck and a full, mid-length black skirt were current but hinted at what she would look like in period dress, and the stark color set off her pale blonde hair, which she had braided and pinned up like a crown. She moved well, reminding him about the teenage pageant titles at the bottom of her résumé. He had wondered why, after all that time, she even bothered to include those anymore.

She crossed in front of the green backdrop, stopped with her feet on the mark taped to the floor, and offered them a tremulous smile. "Thank you for seeing me. I'm Katharine Cameron. I go by Kath."

"Welcome, Kath. Thanks for coming." Dai leaned forward, all of his attention focused. He picked up the stack of sides John had left on the reader's table, then noticed she was already holding pages. "Did you bring something you wanted to read for us?"

"I hope you don't mind. I started breaking down the script and prepared two scenes. But of course, I'm happy to read anything you need."

"HT hadn't mentioned he'd given the script to you." Dai glanced at Lizzie, who sat beside him.

She raised one shoulder in a shrug. "Which scenes are they, Kath?"

If Kath answered, Dai missed it as the door to the corridor slammed and John returned with the coffees. John made an annoying production of tiptoeing to the table, passing the coffee around, and picking up the stack of script pages.

"You won't need those yet," Dai told him. "Kath has something prepared." He glanced back over at her. "Which scene?"

"Page twelve, Margaret and Glyndwr are arguing about the letter he sent de Ruthyn."

Dai thumbed through his own copy of the script, then handed it over to John opened to the right location. John went to stand behind the camera as Dai turned back to Kath. "John will read Glyndwr's lines for you, but since the other actors didn't have a chance to prepare anything, let's limit you to this one scene. Do you have any questions?"

She flashed that smile again, wider and less hesitant. "No, I'm fine," she said. "And thank you."

"Start with the slate whenever you're ready." Dai nodded to the camera operator to start the tape.

Kath nodded, and her smile blossomed into something that kicked him in the chest. This was a Julia Roberts smile, an Audrey Hepburn smile. The kind that came once in a generation, if that. How had Kath not made it as an actor already with that smile?

She looked into the camera and gave her full name, but not her age or agency representation. Then she moved back from her mark several steps, angled her body away from the camera, and bowed her head. The curve of her spine coiled like a spring. She held that for two long beats, then raised her head, the motion slow and carefully contained.

"Is this how it will be, now that you have come back?" she asked. "You will ignore me? Ignore my advice?" Then she turned to face John behind the camera. "These years while you were away at war, I have kept peace with de Ruthyn despite every slight and indignity he committed. You have undone it all with a single letter."

She spoke the words with deceptive softness, like a sharp knife wrapped in cloth. She had taken on an accent that had Welsh elements but was also English and well-bred.

"What slights?" John asked.

Kath paused, and there was a stark flicker of vulnerability. "No more than the English give all over Wales whenever they please."

"Has he touched you?"

Kath stared at the camera, frozen in a shock of fear and pain and fury, each emotion distinct in a near-miracle of the actor's art.

But then she raised an eyebrow with a half-smile of something like amusement. "Would I suffer de Ruthyn to touch me?" She shook her head. "You'd do better to worry that he is every bit as educated in English law as you. That law allows no Welshman to own land within ten kilometers of a township, and de Ruthyn has measured the distance by crow's flight and not by road."

"The land has always been ours."

"All of Wales once belonged to the Welsh, but this is English law, and de Ruthyn has English friends to tip the scales." Kath paused, visibly leashing herself. "You do not know him," she continued more softly. "Reginald Grey de Ruthyn is not a man like his father. The old Lord gave you the respect due to a prince of Powys and a ward of the English king. His son has no respect for any Welsh man or woman."

"I still have Richard's favor."

"Bolingbroke wants the throne himself, and Richard has many enemies."

"Bolingbroke knows me as well or better than does King Richard. Let de Ruthyn bray as he likes. And if all else fails and English law becomes a weapon used against us, then Welsh steel will serve me."

"You would test your sword against an English gallows?" Kath asked, setting up Glyndwr's next line perfectly.

John didn't react, of course, except to deliver the line. "Richard is not yet off the throne."

Dai itched to snatch the pages from him and read the lines himself.

Kath took a step closer to the camera. "Then have a care you do not help him lose it. Bolingbroke is looking for excuses. And remember that the English may accuse where they please. The Welsh may not accuse at all."

She averted her face and held the pause an extra beat before turning back to the camera with all her fear for Glyndwr in her eyes.

"I worry that you do not see how the winds blow," she said. "You have been gone too long, my love. Even your own people do not know you. Let that be your remedy before ever you move against de Ruthyn. Throw open the locks and unbolt the doors of Sycharth so all in Wales may see you are the equal of any English lord. If we feed our own, give them back their pride, we can send them out to be your voice and eyes and ears. Not only here but throughout Powys, Gwynedd, and Deheubarth. Through all the lands once held by Hywel Dda, Llewellyn the Great, and Llewellyn the Last. But until you earn Welsh loyalty, you'll have no protection. Until then, guard your tongue and leave me to reason with de Ruthyn."

She ended the reading with her back stiff and a breath of resignation, as if Margaret knew there was no reasoning with de Ruthyn and dreaded what seeing him would cost her.

Dai found he'd been holding his breath. The room was silent. Then he cleared his throat and Lizzie looked over and raised her brows. He nodded briefly.

Lizzie turned back to Kath. "Thank you. Do you have a few more minutes to read one of the scenes we're having the other actors do for us? We'd like to have that cold reading for comparison."

Dai signaled to the casting assistant. "John, can you give Kath the pages? Then please step out and let Jen know we're running a little late for the next audition."

RISK

"Better by far to live in the truth..."

OWEN SHEERS, *RESISTANCE*

F AILURE HAD BEEN INEVITABLE SINCE the moment Lizzie Morgan said the words "cold reading." Kath tried to push away the familiar wave of sharp, dark panic as she accepted the pages from the casting assistant.

Was the request for the cold reading a good sign? There had been no reaction from Lizzie or Dai Rhys when she finished her scene, not so much as a hint of what they were thinking. And any potential positive impression she might have made was about to be flushed down the toilet.

She needed to concentrate on the scene she was supposed to be reading, but she snuck in another look at the casting table. Lizzie Morgan looked like a dark-skinned Diane Keaton with an extra thirty pounds and a more reasonable clothing budget.

She held her pen in her left hand while she wrote, and she had removed her glasses and held them by one temple tip in her right hand so that they swung rhythmically back and forth.

Dai Rhys was also writing, the pen dwarfed in his hand. He dwarfed everything, but unlike a lot of tall men, he was knitted together so beautifully that there was nothing awkward about him, only a sense of coiled energy as if all that bone and muscle was ready to explode into action and he was keeping it in check by sheer force of will. Kath couldn't tell if that was impatience with her performance or if that was just this nature.

And why had he switched to directing? With that jaw and those eyes, those cheekbones, he should have stayed in front of the camera. She had seen all his films, so she'd known he had that electricity that most actors only dreamed of. It was even more powerful in person.

Focus, she told herself. She had to focus.

The two pages in her hand were mainly monologue, and the section didn't seem to have a turning point or sense of character discovery. From working with the script, she knew Margaret had significant moments immediately before and after these pages, but trying to find an approach in this in-between section was like trying to hold on to smoke.

Maybe that was the reason the casting team had picked it.

As soon as she had that thought, Kath could almost hear Fiona's cigarette rasp of a voice inside her head, "Make your choices bolder. Be original, Kath. Take a risk."

Which risk?

Lizzie Morgan leaned forward. "Are you ready?"

Kath's brain seized up. She hadn't so much as memorized the first sentence or the last.

"It's fine if you aren't," the casting director continued. "It's just that you're standing there, so I wasn't sure."

Nodding like an idiot, Kath moved back to the mark. "Do you need me to slate again?"

"Please."

Kath forced air out of her lungs and then smiled as if she had just received the best gift of her life. "Kath Cameron," she said, gazing warmly into the camera. But after that, she blanked. She hadn't chosen a mood, and she didn't remember the line. Her eyes had to leave the camera to read, and going back and forth made her skip an entire line of dialogue. She backtracked, but then she stumbled over words.

When she finished, her cheeks burned, and her palms were damp. That was it. The last gasp of her career flamed out in spectacular humiliation.

Lizzie Morgan and Dai Rhys scribbled more notes, their expressions even blanker than before. John, the assistant who had read with her, was typing something on his phone. Even the camera guy wouldn't make eye contact.

A desperate apology formed on Kath's tongue. She wanted to ask to start over. Beg. All of that was at the top of the what-not-to-do-in-an-audition checklist, so she clamped her mouth shut and waited.

Dai Rhys put down his pen. "Would you try that again from the top for us?" he asked, his voice low with that Welsh accent that made it musical and smooth as butter. "And this time, try for a bigger hook at the start. More anger. Light it up, then falter as you get toward the end. I'd like to see the scene beat you down emotionally."

"As if Margaret isn't getting the response she hoped for?"

"That's right. Try it that way."

That was the problem with making choices. Too often Kath got them wrong.

Turning her back to hide her embarrassment, Kath gave herself a few more seconds. It felt unfair, almost tyrannical, not having more time to prepare. But if she asked, she'd only look unprofessional, as if she couldn't handle it.

Reaction, she reminded herself. The first lines were always a reaction to what had come before. And she knew what that was. The king had asked de Ruthyn to tell Glyndwr to muster his men at the Scottish border, but de Ruthyn never passed the order on. Instead, he called Glyndwr a coward and a traitor for not arriving. Glyndwr wanted to take the matter back to the English court, where they had already laughed at him once. And where so far Margaret had urged restraint, now she urged Glyndwr to take a gamble and save himself.

Channeling the anger Kath needed to begin the scene wasn't hard. The trick was avoiding the hot, screaming kind that Fiona had labeled boring. Kath needed to transform that into something more controlled, the kind of cold fury that quietly spat each word into the room. She thought of her mother, who rarely raised her voice but could make every word vibrate with venom. But venom wasn't what she wanted either.

She could understand exactly what Margaret felt, the guilt

of not having been able to resolve the situation. The sense that she had made a mistake that started the snowball rolling and rolling until everything in its path became a disaster waiting to happen. Fury at everything and everyone, but mostly at herself for not being able to stop it all from hurting the people she loved.

The night she and Henry had left Cincinnati, Kath had felt like that. That was the night she did her best not to think about. The night that was never far from her mind.

They'd left in the early hours, and they had almost reached St. Louis before Anna had found the letter Henry had left for her. Henry had put the call on speaker when she called, forcing Kath to listen while her sister begged him to come back. While Anna told him they could work through any problems together, whatever they were. While she asked him to think of his parents, their parents, and all the plans everyone had made.

Henry kept himself together while he told Anna it was too late, that there was no future for them anymore. Then he hung up, pulled over on the side of the road, and pounded the steering wheel. The horn honked and honked and honked with every punch, until Kath pressed her hands to her ears and shrank back against the passenger door, afraid of him. Afraid for him.

Henry stormed out of the car and crouched on the grassy shoulder with his arms crossed over the back of his head.

Kath had watched, helpless to help him.

Then her phone had rung, and Anna's name had appeared on the screen.

Kath had been scared to pick up, afraid she would say the things she had been told not to say. Afraid she would drag Anna and her father down with her.

But it had been impossible to keep from answering.

"I'm so sorry, Anna. I—"

"God, you're selfish," Anna said. "You've always been selfish, hogging every scrap of attention, but I didn't think even you could stoop this low. I hope someday someone hurts you half this much. I hope you and HT both live through hell."

"I didn't mean for this to happen."

"Do you think I care what you meant? You better hope you make it in Hollywood, because I'll make sure people spit in your face if you ever come back to Cincinnati. Either of you."

Anna's every word had been soft and rhythmic, like a gloved fist hitting a punching bag.

Kath had felt each blow, and she'd deserved to feel them.

That was how she delivered the lines now, with the quiet desperation that came from being out of options. It was how Anna had felt then, and it was how Kath felt at the moment.

She concentrated so hard on building up to that emotion that she forgot about looking up at the camera. All she thought about was getting the feeling right and not losing her place until she reached the end.

When it was over, she tried to gauge how the scene had gone. But Dai Rhys and Lizzie Morgan were busy writing. They might as well have been playing in a poker tournament for all the emotion on their faces.

Had she given Dai what he wanted? Was that any better than before? But he wouldn't have had to give her any acting notes if she had done the scene right the first time.

Lizzie Morgan straightened the paper on which she'd been writing and took her glasses off again. "Tell us about yourself, Kath. What are your interests?"

Kath blinked and stood there a moment, lost. The dreaded "tell us" question didn't come very often. Most actors hated it as much as Kath hated cold reads. But the years of pageants in Kath's childhood and teens kicked in. She could almost hear the signature double clap her mother used to get attention while she sat on the couch in the living room, firing off questions like bullets while Kath stood in front of her, light-headed and wishing she was anywhere else in the entire world but there.

She could almost hear her mother's voice: Be clear but humble. Make them like you. And for heaven's sake, Katharine, shoulders back. Stand up straight.

Squaring her shoulders, Kath smiled for Olympic gold. "I guess I would say that I'm a glass-half-full person, but I also believe success in anything takes listening, learning, and giving it your all. As an actor, I'm committed to transitioning to more complex roles at this point in my career, and I'm looking forward to putting in the work to achieve that goal. I've been taking more acting classes, and I like to read. Mostly nonfiction about actors, acting, and history, but I also love reading screenplays and fiction with a psychological component. My special interests include horseback riding, which I've done all my life. I also like running and playing tennis. Gardening is another passion, and I have a cranky, blind West Highland Terrier who allows me to live with him." She paused, then added: "Thank you for the opportunity to audition. There aren't many roles like Margaret. She's strong, rich, and challenging, and I would be honored and one hundred percent committed to bringing her to life the way you envision. I'm available to start right away."

She clasped her hands in front of her and stood quietly once she finished. The answer hadn't felt too bad. At least she'd gotten through the whole thing without tripping over her tongue, and she'd kept good eye contact with both Lizzie Morgan and Dai Rhys all the way through.

Lizzie Morgan signaled for the camera operator to cut.

Kath's heart did a double thump as she saw the tally light on the camera blinking, signaling it had been recording. Crap, they'd been taping the whole time, all the way through her answer, and she hadn't once looked in that direction.

Of course they'd been taping it. Why wouldn't they tape her answer if they were taping everything else? They would go through all these tapes and compare them to each other, and all of her mistakes would be there for everyone to see.

Lizzie Morgan leaned over to Dai Rhys and they whispered back and forth.

Feeling light-headed and shaky, Kath forced herself to wait.

"Okay, thanks," Lizzie Morgan said.

Dai Rhys nodded. "Thank you for coming in."

Kath was dismissed. It was over.

She walked out, remembering to project confidence, digging back into her childhood training. She imagined a big, warm yellow ball of light in her chest, felt it expanding and floating up and up and up, out through the top of her head. Her eyes focused on a spot above the door.

She made it across the room without falling on her face. Then she reached the hallway and passed the reception desk.

On her right, there was a seating area with comfortable armchairs and a low coffee table. Two women sat there chatting. Both were actors, both blonde and the same physical type and size as Kath and Nia. Both were Nia's age. Kath had never met them, but she'd seen them in films ranging from period dramas to Marvel movies. They stopped talking and eyed Kath with curiosity, and she flashed a smile at them and said, "Good luck."

CIRCLE OF TRUST

"I'm going up to my room now, where I may die."

DIANA WYNNE JONES, HOWL'S MOVING CASTLE

KATH WALKED OUT TO THE parking lot, across the asphalt, and into her car. Then she drove... and drove. She didn't think. Didn't dwell. At home, she took Muppet out for a potty break and fed him his favorite filet mignon-flavored gourmet dog food.

"At least one of us should get something good. Isn't that right?" She held Muppet close against her chest before setting him down to eat. He didn't move to the bowl. Instead, he moved back to Kath and pressed his body against her legs. She dropped down and sat cross-legged on the floor, and he stepped into her lap. They sat there like that for a while. Kath lost track of time. Later, he curled up with her on the bed while she binged *Gilmore Girls* for comfort.

She let the phone go to voice mail when Fiona called. But

Fiona called again fifteen minutes later and again fifteen minutes after that. Kath gave up and answered.

"How did it go?" Fiona asked.

"Picture the *Titanic* sinking. That's the level of failure." Kath scooted back on the bed and propped her back against the pillows with her knees drawn up.

"That can't be right. You were ready."

Kath tried to find words to explain. "It was like being at a comedy show when the audience isn't connecting, and the comic gets more and more desperate and starts heckling the audience."

"Ouch. Even on the scene that we broke down?"

"That one wasn't so bad, but they didn't react even then. Zero. And after it, they gave me a cold reading, and I didn't even have time to learn the opening."

"Did you ask for time?"

"They offered," Kath said, "but I thought it would look bad."

"How are they supposed to know how much time you need unless you tell them?"

"Well, too late now. They could sell the recording as a how-not-to instruction video for would-be actors."

Fiona sighed. "Maybe it wasn't as bad as you think. You're pretty hard on yourself. Who all was there?"

"Only Dai Rhys and Lizzie Morgan, plus an assistant."

"Only Dai Rhys, she says." Fiona laughed. "What was he like?"

Kath could see him the moment she closed her eyes. "I didn't notice."

"Of course you didn't."

"I was busy failing my audition."

"Okay." Fiona paused. "So, what are you doing to cope? Wine? Ben and Jerry's?"

"*Gilmore Girls* and a stomachache."

"Bad combo, honey."

"On the bright side, at least I don't have to waste time wondering if I'll get a callback. And in a week or two, maybe I'll have recovered enough to figure out what I want to be when I grow up." At the moment, Kath couldn't imagine doing anything other than acting. And at least while she was in Hollywood working, all the bad choices she and HT had made had a purpose. Made some sort of crazy sense.

"I hate hearing you talk like this," Fiona said. "I'm surprising myself by saying this, but don't quit. You were too in your head and up your ass when we started working together, I'll admit that. But you have talent."

"Talent doesn't get you anywhere without an agent."

"Why do people always think that? You didn't have an agent when you first started in the business. So start fresh. Take some acting classes. Get over yourself. People change agents all the time. Want to meet me for a drink and talk about it?"

"I think I need a couple more days to wallow first."

"Oh, good. Glad you have a schedule. I'll check in with you again on Monday. And in the meantime, wallow but don't despair."

"Is there a difference?" Kath asked.

They said goodbye, and Kath watched TV until a little after

two a.m. Two hours later, Muppet woke her up by standing on her chest, asking to go outside. Waiting out in the moonlight for him, Kath felt everything well up inside her again, all the rage and heartbreak. She knew it would be useless to go back to bed, so she put Muppet in the house, stripped off her pajamas, and jumped into the pool, needing to exhaust herself.

Moonlight bathed the water in gold, and she knifed through the silken stillness. Something about being naked felt elemental, like the last step in a process of stripping her bare of all her protective layers. She alternated from breaststroke to sidestroke, and every few laps, she rolled onto her back, her face tilted toward the moon and stars while she swam.

The thought of taking acting classes after ten years as a working actor terrified her. Sitting face to face with people who were just starting in the business, having them judge her work, her failures. She couldn't bear it. But doing the various exercises and breaking down the two scenes with Fiona had helped far more than all the roles she'd had, the DVDs she'd watched, and the reading she had ever done.

Working with Fiona by the end, she hadn't felt like herself. She had connected to Margaret in ways that left her raw. That's what had made the audition such a letdown. Even in the cold reading, she had put herself on the line, reaching into the ugliest moments of her life. There were reasons she'd kept those memories locked away all these years. But maybe she had shown too much of herself, and that was part of the reason she had failed.

She swam until her arms and legs ached and it hurt to pull

herself back out of the pool. Not bothering to dress, she gathered up her discarded pajamas and dragged herself inside. Muppet had waited by the door for her, and she took him upstairs and crawled into her bed. It was almost five o'clock, but that didn't matter. She had nowhere she had to be. No plans. No reason not to sleep in as long as she liked.

The irony of that thought came back to her with a sense of resentment when her phone rang two hours later. And of course, it was her mother, who—like Fiona—would only keep calling until Kath answered. It was ten o'clock in Cincinnati, so of course Ailsa Cameron couldn't imagine anyone in LA could still be sleeping.

Why was it that all the people Kath knew were as pushy as hell?

She injected her voice with sugary brightness. "Good morning, Mom."

"Baby, you sound tired. Are you sick?" Ailsa asked. Her voice still held a Scottish accent after more than three decades in Ohio. "I hope you're not wearing yourself out with parties every night. And drinking. You know that will ruin your skin."

Kath tried harder to wipe away the traces of sleep from her voice. "I'm fine. What's up? Did something happen?"

Predictably, that one question was enough to get Ailsa off and running. She launched into the usual monologue: everything was great, Kath's sisters were blissfully happy with their husbands and their children and their successful careers. Ailsa, of course, was overworked on the boards of two different charities and the fundraising committee at the country club. She barely had time to breathe, and everyone always told her she was doing too much, but they needed her, so how could she step down from any of it? One had to do one's share for the community and the less fortunate. That was a given.

"Absolutely," Kath said when she could get a word in. "You're wonderful, and I'm sure they all appreciate what you do for them. Have you talked to Dad? Are things between you any better?"

"Oh, you know. We have a last few details to finalize." Ailsa's voice grew tight, and the pitch climbed higher. "We're both so busy. He's either in court or preparing for court or going back to his apartment with a stack of reading or pleadings or whatever it is he works on. I keep telling him he needs more exercise. At least I've managed to get him to play more golf. He got a hole-in-one last weekend playing with Ansel Barton. Do you remember Ansel? His daughter Trisha was in that play with you and Henry that summer that... Anyway, she's working as a dental hygienist and hasn't married yet. Her sister Alice, meanwhile, has divorced twice already. So, of course, Ansel and Becca don't have a single grandchild."

"Shame," Kath said, gritting her teeth and bracing herself.

"Speaking of which... Are you seeing anyone yet?"

"Not since you asked last week. And yes, I am making a bigger effort."

"You always say that. And what about a new show? Any news?"

"Still waiting for the right thing. But I'm considering offers. Nothing definite."

"Don't wait too long. You're not getting younger. And come home if you're not working. Come visit. I know you're busy, but I'm sure you could find some time."

Kath pictured herself in Cincinnati, facing her mother in person. She'd slip up; she wouldn't be able to help it. Her mother could smell failure at a hundred paces. One whiff of it, and Ailsa would pounce and move in for the kill. Honestly, if the family ever needed money, they could rent Ailsa out to the CIA.

"I can't get away right now," Kath said. "I still have meetings."

It was exhausting pretending to be fine.

If Fiona had shown her anything, it was the amount of effort that she'd put into pretending all these years.

She hung up and eventually drifted back to sleep. It was almost noon by the time she finished her usual morning run, and the few chores she accomplished in the afternoon felt like intervals of sleepwalking in the midst of hibernation.

Later that night, while the moonlit swimming pool reflected flickers of light across the ceiling above her bed, she decided Fiona had been at least partially correct. Assuming she couldn't find another agent was a form of quitting. Rejection was terrifying, but quitting was worse. Quitting left no room for hope.

Lying awake, she made a mental list of things to do the next day. And having a plan made her finally relax well enough to sleep.

Once again, the telephone woke her. Eyes still closed, she groped on her nightstand and picked it up.

"So listen, Kath." Joel's voice came through the speaker. "This is awkward."

Kath sat up, wide awake. "What is?"

"Lizzie Morgan called me last night. She didn't realize I wasn't working with you anymore. Anyway, they want you to do a chemistry test with HT in Wales. If that goes well, you'd stay and start immediately."

Kath wondered if she'd actually woken up. "What did you just say, Joel?"

He repeated it, then added: "I said I would talk to you. Do you want to go?"

"Aren't they doing callbacks first?"

"They have the tape. But expect everyone to be there this time."

Relief made Kath feel like she was breaking through to the surface of the water after she'd been drowning. But too many thoughts ran through her head at once. All the things she had to do… all the things she didn't know how to do.

Joel cleared his throat and hesitated. "Do you want me to arrange it for you?"

She wanted so badly to tell him to go to hell. But if he wasn't there, who would handle it? The production company might not even be willing to deal with her unless she had an agent.

"Kath?"

"Sure," she said. "If you wouldn't mind."

"It makes sense. And I can handle anything that might come from it. Same terms as before?"

Kath closed her eyes again. "That's fine."

"I sent you a letter the day before yesterday. Tear it up when it gets there, if you haven't received it yet. I'll call when I have more information. But so you know, I wouldn't pack for a long location shoot just yet. If it works out, you can buy whatever you might need. They're bringing in other actors, though. Some big names, so don't get your hopes up."

"Okay." Kath sat hugging her knees after she'd hung up, rocking back and forth. Then she kicked off the covers and kicked her legs in a small shimmy of happiness until Muppet gave a soft whine as if she was making him nervous.

"Sorry, buddy." She swung herself off the bed and set him on the floor. Standing there, she replayed the conversation in her mind.

Muppet still had his head cocked, listening hard, unsure what she was doing or why.

"I'm going to Wales, Mups. I didn't blow it," she said. "I didn't blow it."

Then she jumped up and down like a maniac for a minute. A minute, that was all. No point in tempting fate.

This was only one more step. She wasn't at the finish line yet, but it was a miracle, and she was a firm believer in never looking miracles in the mouth.

Now she really needed to get to work.

Muppet gave a soft bark and hobbled toward the door. Kath picked him up and was halfway down the staircase that floated above the open plan living and dining areas and the kitchen before it hit her: What was she going to do with

Muppet while she was gone? She hadn't worked on location since HT had left. She'd never had to think about leaving Mups with a stranger. He couldn't go to the kennel, and people he didn't know well left him terrified.

Racking her brain, she tried to think of someone—anyone—she could trust to take him. It dawned on her that her circle of trust was shockingly small.

There was no one. No one at all. She was alone.

How had she let it come to that?

HOME

"For only he who has lived in darkness, truly knows and values the light."

STEPHEN R. LAWHEAD, *TALIESIN*

T HE HOUR BEFORE SUNRISE BATHED the valley in shades of blue. Mist clung to the steep-sided hollows tucked between low mountain ridges, and clouds shrouded the higher mountains. Dai's footfalls, the murmur of the nearby stream, and the dawn chorus of birds were his only company.

Wherever Dai was, the blue stillness before dawn was his favorite time to run. That stillness grounded him and prepared him for the day. But here in Wales, the blue hour was magical. Clad in its ancient green fields and time-worn mountains, the countryside was a reminder that the land would remain, regardless of human hubris and attempts to tame it.

Dai had given the land, the place, little thought growing up, but in Afghanistan he'd missed it fiercely. The Welsh word *hiraeth*, that deep longing for home or someone or something you loved, had no equivalent word in English. Homesickness was close, but not enough. *The Last Prince* contained all his longing for a country that never was, but it was also about this ancient stillness.

Steering off onto a narrow track along his left, Dai ran faster as he climbed the hillside, hoping to beat the sunrise to the top. The pastures alongside the track grew steeper, strewn with rounded boulders. Drystone walls topped with rocks like jagged teeth replaced the hedgerows of the valley floor.

Sweat ran in rivulets down his skin, and his lungs burned with welcome pain. Focused on the drum of his footsteps against the earth, his mind stilled. No thoughts of work. No decisions. Nothing except the purity of motion and the smell of earth and grass.

At the top of the hill, he stopped. Hands on his knees, he fought for breath while he waited for the sun.

The low clouds on the horizon bloomed in gold and pink. Then the sun broke through. The sky caught fire and lit the patchwork quilt of fields in the valley below, gleamed on the streams and river, and refracted on the tarmac that formed the web of narrow roads. In Ty Newydd, where Dai and the rest of the main cast and crew were staying, lights had come on as people got up to prepare for work. From here, it all seemed far away.

But he needed to get back. He took another deep breath, then plunged downhill. Two and a half miles later, he was back, approaching the hotel on the outskirts of Ty Newydd, with its large, gold-lettered sign.

He slowed to a walk, head down and hands on hips. Beyond

the hotel was the pub, then the farm shop, a crafts and gift shop, and the only two homes occupied year-round. Until Lord Linley had rebuilt it for holiday homes, the entire village had been a ruin abandoned in 1942 when the nearby granite quarry closed. Brightly painted doors and blooming window boxes marked the five different "cottages" in each of the first two row houses that faced the stream across the road. Then farther down, the stream veered off to the left, leaving room for another rowhouse on both sides of the road, with another two dozen larger cottages bordering a road along the wooded hillside up above.

The production team had booked all the rental units in the village, along with a few farmhouses elsewhere on the Obaith Estate. That saved the extra commute to hotels in Conwy or Caernarfon every day, and apart from some of the Welsh actors and crew members who had their personal cars with them, most of the team commuted to and from the various locations via shuttles.

It was one of the few things that had gone right so far, leaving Dai this extra bit of quiet time. But now that his run was over, he had to face what promised to be the first of many fires that needed to be put out.

As he passed the cottage where HT was staying, he stopped and knocked.

HT took so long coming to the door that Dai thought he wouldn't answer. When he did, his hair was damp from the shower, and he carried a cup of coffee that smelled like heaven.

"The message you left last night said it was important," Dai said. "Sorry I didn't get back to you last night."

"Not that important. I didn't mean to give you that impression." HT stepped back from the entrance to let Dai in.

The door header was low, part of the original structure, and Dai ducked to step inside. The interior was comfortable and modern, with pale wood and light streaming through large windows. HT had the sides of the script for the upcoming chemistry reads laid out on the low table in front of a pair of leather love seats. Two dirty glasses and a bottle of Scotch sat precariously on the edge of the table.

Catching Dai looking at them, HT walked over, scooped them up, and headed for the kitchen. "Can I get you some coffee?"

Dai glanced down at himself and grimaced. Then he pulled the damp T-shirt off and used one of the few dry areas to wipe his face. "Thanks, but my need for a shower outweighs the need for caffeine. So what did you need?"

"I wanted to check in about the schedule." HT topped up his own coffee, then leaned one hip against the counter in a pose that was a study in nonchalance. "All these separate chemistry readings seem like a lot in one day. Is that normal?"

Dai slung the T-shirt across one shoulder. "None of this is normal, but you know the sort of pressure we're under. Alan and the executive team all had a narrow window of availability, and since it's Sunday, we were lucky to get the actors to make themselves available. Are you worried you won't be able to manage?"

"No, it's only that seeing Kath's name there with Sophie and Scarlett and... It's awkward." HT's neck and ears turned red.

And there it was. Dai suppressed a sigh of resignation. "You know I can't give her any special treatment, HT. I told you that."

"But what's the point of bringing her all this way if that's her competition?"

"I'm not sure what you expect me to say to that. We've made no decisions yet. Kath earned the opportunity to continue the audition process, but it's just that: a process. Alan and I have different priorities, and I can't predict how things will fall out by the time today is over. All I can do is give Kath a fair shot, the same as anyone. Now, was there anything else you needed?"

"No. No, sorry." HT looked away and took a long sip of coffee.

Dai's trouble meter pinged a red alert. Something with HT was off, but Dai didn't have time to coddle him. He'd long since pegged HT as a weak man trying to prove himself, and this—whatever it was—only confirmed that assessment.

"If there's something I should know, mate, come straight out with it. I'm still jet-lagged, and I'll be flat out all day, so I don't have the luxury to be polite. I can't fix something if you don't tell me what needs fixing."

HT looked even more miserable and shook his head.

Dai studied him a little longer, but HT's expression went back to being blank and neutral. Dai gave up. "In that case," he said, "I'll see you in Caernarfon later, yeah?"

Back outside, the air felt pleasantly cool against his skin. He hurried the short distance to his own cottage, which was situated up the hill on the wooded side road. After stopping in the kitchen just long enough to start a pot of coffee, he headed up to take a shower.

The overnight bag he'd had with him in California sat unzipped on the chair where he'd removed his shaving kit and toothbrush from it earlier. He snatched up clean clothes and moved into the bathroom. The water coming through the wide, flat showerhead was hot, and the pressure was fierce. He stood beneath it, wishing it could wash away a vague sense of anxiety left over from his conversation with HT.

They'd all moved heaven and earth to get everyone together today: the actors, the casting team, Alan and the other executive producers and studio people, plus the above-the-line crew and principal cast members the decision would impact the most. Getting everyone together in one day was only possible because it was Alan Stickley issuing the invitations. Dai had no illusions about that. But hopefully, these arrangements would allow for a quick decision.

For that to happen, HT needed to be on form. Chemistry—connection—was a two-way street. Dai didn't need HT sabotaging any of the other actors to give Kath a better audition.

Why was it that whenever Dai thought of the chemistry reads, it wasn't Nerys or Catrin, or even Sophie or Scarlet who came to mind? It was Kath Cameron's face and the promise in her first audition that haunted him.

Her audition had been spotty, but she had taken his notes better than he'd expected. And there had been that undefinable something in her performance that had caught them all off guard. Even Alan had commented that the way she'd interpreted the scenes revealed facets of Margaret that made perfect sense. That were, very simply, Margaret.

Dai had found himself replaying her audition over the past few days, trying to figure out what had captured him. The camera had caught more than he'd seen in person. It had captured the fear in her eyes and a vulnerability that lurked below the surface. That's what had made parts of the performance so stunning, but it also made Dai cautious.

That smile of hers could light up the back row of a theatre. Combined with that hint of vulnerability, the smile was a killer. But women like that tended to bring out Dai's protective streak, and he needed to be careful to keep the character separate from the actor.

ROAD TO DISASTER

"To the past's audience upon a stage, of earth and stone"

R.S. THOMAS, "A WELSH TESTAMENT"
COLLECTED POEMS 1945–1990

THE PRODUCTION COMPANY HAD PURCHASED Kath's airline ticket, and she had bought a second seat for Muppet. She could have saved herself the money. Muppet spent the entire flight to Manchester on Kath's lap, snuggled in so tight against her chest that she could feel his heartbeat.

Her driver was there holding a sign with her name on it as she emerged into the airport, and he led her to a cream-colored Mercedes. Even that was terrifying. Having her own car and driver was a stark reminder that Margaret was in a different solar system from the type of characters Kath had received a callback for so far.

The driver, a young man named Davy who wore a suit that was at least a size too big for him, held the door of the Mercedes open for her, and she climbed inside. Muppet whined in his carrier as soon as the engine started, so she took him out and held him on her lap. He curled up with his head on her hand, licking her so softly she barely felt it, as if he was checking to make certain she was there.

She rubbed his ears and bent to whisper. "Don't get used to this, Mups. We're being spoiled."

Davy glanced back at her in the rearview mirror. "Alright, miss?"

"Yes, thanks. And it's Kath, please." She smiled at him.

They crossed the border into Wales, and Davy tuned the radio to a Welsh language station. Kath could make out English words here and there, but mostly everything was indecipherable. She pulled out the pages of the script Lizzie Morgan had sent for the chemistry reading, intending to keep memorizing her lines. There were also the two guidebooks she had bought. She wanted to flip through them as they passed landmarks mentioned in the script.

"You don't get carsick, do you?" Davy asked a short while later.

"Not usually. Why?"

"Traffic report says there's an accident on the coast road like. It'll be faster going inland. Now, me, I like that road better anyway, don't I? But it's a fair bit of up and down and curving along toward the end."

"Does that mean we'll be late?" Kath asked.

"They asked me to have you there by one o'clock. It shouldn't be a problem." He smiled at her in the mirror, and he kept up a running commentary as he drove about the places they were going through.

Used to LA's wall-to-wall suburbs, Kath found Wales almost shockingly green and glorious. Between towns, it was mostly farmland with patchwork fields, stone walls, and charming houses against a backdrop of distant hazy hills.

They passed a turnoff for the town of Ruthin, and Kath leaned forward. "Is that the Ruthyn where Owain Glyndwr snuck into the castle?"

"I'm not much on history, but there's only one Ruthin as far as I know. And Glyndwr was all over Gwynedd and Powys. Sycharth, where he lived, isn't far from Shrewsbury. You Americans have George Washington, and we have Glyndwr."

Kath laughed, thinking of the jokes about B&Bs back east advertising "George Washington Slept Here." Then she sobered, awed by the fact that she was there in Wales, auditioning for Dai Rhys for the kind of film that Alan Stickley made—no, an actual Alan Stickley film—about someone people put in the same sentence as George Washington.

This was Glyndwr's landscape. Margaret's landscape. There was an ancient quality to the air and stone and wind-twisted trees, and the Welsh place names on the road signs looked as though they'd been written in an arcane language of magic spells: Graianrhyd, Llandegla, Pentre-bwlch, Ty-Mawr, and Bryneglwys.

The distant hills and craggy peaks grew closer. Then the road climbed into Snowdonia, which in Welsh was called *Eryri*. Centuries peeled away as though the car was traveling back through time.

Clouds hung low, clinging to rounded hillsides so close that

Kath could almost put her arm out the window and catch a handful. Bald rocks and boulders lay where long ago glaciers had abandoned them, sprouting amid the pastures. She tried to picture herself living there in the Middle Ages, growing up, marrying, building a home, having children and grandchildren, helping them create their own futures. Then watching a foreign army marching in.

Seeing the terrain, she could understand the script much better. Northern Wales would have been a hard place to conquer. The English armies had been bigger and better equipped, but every boulder here could have served as a hiding place for Glyndwr's men. Even the low clouds and mist would conspire to hide defending forces.

Kath grew more anxious mile by mile as they approached Caernarfon. Concentrating on her lines became impossible, and she spent more time staring idly at the land as it rolled by.

Until now, she'd managed to push away thoughts of the actual chemistry test and everything it implied. She'd focused on all the individual tasks: packing, getting Muppet's passport and medical records, preparing the house and yard. A hundred other details, like turning on her international calling plan, would occur to her at two in the morning, and she'd added to the list. In between, she had memorized the lines Lizzie Morgan had sent over and worked with Fiona to break down the scenes.

She'd shied away from thinking about having to perform the scenes with HT. About having the quality of his performance matter at least as much as hers in the casting decision. Not to mention that their chemistry together would be compared back-to-back against his performances with Sophie Tanner and Scarlet Johnson, who were both household names, and with Catrin Morgan, who Kath loved in the police drama filmed in Cardiff. She didn't know the other Welsh actor Joel had told her about, but her film credits were impressive.

HT must have had a heart attack when he saw Kath's name on the schedule. How would he react when she was there in person? The chemistry test depended on how well the two of them worked together.

They didn't work. They hadn't worked for years. Maybe never.

Plus, HT was probably still livid about having to get her the audition in the first place.

Note to future self: be careful who you blackmail.

Muppet whined softly on Kath's lap. They'd already stopped twice, and he'd eaten and had water and gone potty. She was probably stressing him out. She pulled him closer and rubbed his ears again.

"Sorry, buddy. I know you hate it when I'm uptight. Want to go to sleep in your carrier?"

She swung him over, and he growled and bared his teeth at her.

"Oh, no you don't," Kath told him. "You need to be a very good boy today, and that will include staying in your carrier. Especially during my audition. That means no growling, barking, or whining, and absolutely no howling. You have to pretend you're not even there."

Muppet tilted his head, listening. Then he growled again. *No promises.*

Kath tried to reassure herself that he wasn't going to be a problem. But she could picture him howling during the audition, and everyone taking one look and assuming Kath was *that* kind of actor. The kind who showed up on set with a purse pooch and a suitcase full of fido fashion, demanding six bottles of Louis Roederer Cristal Champagne with crystal flutes, three Jo Malone candles, homemade guacamole, and a dressing room temperature set to precisely 78 degrees.

Thanks to HT, she already had a reputation for being difficult.

Not that she'd had a choice. How could she leave Muppet in a kennel? Abandon him in some cramped cage in the blind darkness, with nothing and no one familiar, and unknown sounds and smells pummeling him when he couldn't tell what was a threat and what wasn't.

He wouldn't understand what was happening. And he'd think she was abandoning him forever. Two owners had already thrown him away. Plus, what if he bit someone? He had form, as they said on British murder shows.

Muppet whined and tapped his paw on her hand.

"It's okay, pup. I'll stop. I'm fine—see? We're both fine. And you are going to be good, aren't you? Of course you are."

She absolutely could not afford to screw this up. And she wasn't going to.

Margaret Glyndwr had stared down the English army and the English king. All Kath had to do was face her own ex-husband, make it seem like they didn't hate each other, and convince a room full of way-out-of-her-league industry pros that she wasn't ridiculously underqualified to be there.

What could possibly go wrong?

BITE

"The bad blood rose in me, just like wine."

SARAH WATTERS, *FINGERSMITH*

THE WAREHOUSE-SIZED STUDIO COMPLEX was painted in stark black and red. Davy stopped the car in front of a double door with an awning, and Kath zipped Muppet into his carrier and prepared to exit. Then her door was jerked open, and a dark-haired woman with freckles and enormous brown eyes ducked her head inside the car. "About time you got here, woman."

"Olivia!" Kath was so relieved to see her friend, she felt herself grinning from ear to ear. "What are you doing here?"

A low growl came from Muppet's carrier, and Olivia scowled down at him. "Hello, monster. How are you even still alive?"

"Be nice. He's not a monster, merely misunderstood. And personally, I can relate to cranky." Kath slid out of the car and pulled the carrier after her.

Olivia caught her elbows and bounced up and down. "I'm glad you're he-ere." She sang the words. "And you got the aud-i-tion. You are going to rock it."

Kath laughed, and it felt wonderful to release even a little tension. "From your lips to the acting gods. I can't believe I've gotten this far," she admitted. "Thanks again for sending the script."

"What was I going to do when you reached out? Say no? Although I'm shocked you got it. No offense. Happy but shocked. Now all we have to do is get you through this next part. Starting with that face. Red-eye flights are never a good look, are they?"

Kath stepped back to get her suitcases. "Joel didn't say anything about doing the test in costume."

"No costumes, but that doesn't mean you have to look like you slept on a plane." Palm held out, Olivia traced a circle in the air in front of Kath's face. "There's no filming today, so I packed up my makeup and came down to help you. And yes, you will thank me later." She snatched the suitcase out of Kath's hand and extended the handles on both that and the carry-on case Davy had taken out of the trunk.

Kath dug in her purse and handed Davy a large tip. "Thank you for driving me. And I appreciate you taking that inland route. It helped put things in perspective for me."

"Pleasure, Kath. Good luck. I hope you're here until fall."

Olivia rolled both the suitcases toward the building, but Kath snatched the carry-on to take herself, juggling that with Muppet's carrier and her purse. They walked toward the door beneath the awning. "What is this place?" she asked. "By the time I saw the sign, we were driving past it, and I've been so mesmerized by the Welsh parts of the signs that I forgot to read the English translations."

"It's studios for rent. Film and TV are booming in Wales. And I'll give you a crash course in Welsh essentials later. If you're still here."

"Nice," Kath said.

"Oh, you know what I mean. Don't take that wrong." Olivia pulled open the double doors and then went into a small lobby with a narrow reception desk and an enormous black and red map of the studio complex printed on canvas behind it. Based on the map, there were three empty studios with dressing areas and green room lounges, plus smaller studios with names like "Office Set" and "Police Interrogation Set."

"We're in Studio 3," Olivia said, heading left past reception and turning down a hallway. Once they were out of sight, she stopped and studied Kath. "Are you all right?"

Kath hadn't told Olivia about Joel—she hadn't told anyone except Fiona. The thought of bringing all that up now was too exhausting and humiliating, and the audition was likely to be humiliating enough. "Of course," she said brightly. "I'm just tired from the flight and a little nervous. Thanks for being here. It helps."

"I wish I could see your audition tape. It must have been something."

"No one's said anything to me about it other than to bring me here."

"Doesn't that say enough? Learn to take the win sometimes."

Kath stopped and stared at her. "You know, I've really missed you. Thank you for being here for me."

"Of course. You're the one who disappeared on me. When you stopped returning calls, I figured you were dealing with all the tabloid drama and you would emerge when you were ready. Only you never did."

Even a few days ago, Kath would have said she'd just been busy, or pretended that the tabloids hadn't bothered her. But where had pretending ever gotten her?

"The divorce and the tabloids were hard, and I didn't want to let anyone see me going through that. Then the longer it had gone on, the harder it was to pick up the phone and call. I'm sorry."

"Water under the bridge, babe." Olivia caught her hand and squeezed it. "You're here now, and that's what counts." She opened the door to an empty green room that smelled deliciously of coffee and something spiced with cinnamon.

Kath's stomach growled, and she eyed the craft services table, loaded with drinks and pastries, that stood along the back wall between two conversational groupings of sofas, chairs, and tables on either end of the room. Large televisions suspended from the ceiling in two corners of the room showed a cavernously empty studio with a vacant director's chair behind a three-camera setup. Various men and women sat in a couple of rows of chairs further back, typing on their phones or chatting. A couple more stood nearby, talking to Lizzie Morgan, and off to the side of the cameras, Dai Rhys was listening to an older man with a beard who gestured emphatically with his hands. Kath recognized the legendary Alan Stickley from photos, interviews, and awards ceremonies, and her nerves ratcheted up about a hundred notches. Feeling suddenly queasy, she decided food wasn't a good idea.

HT was nowhere to be seen. Kath wasn't sure whether to be worried or relieved by his absence.

Olivia maneuvered Kath's suitcase next to a sofa. Her makeup kit—an enormous toolbox—sat on a low table nearby. "It shouldn't be long before they're ready for you. We'd better get started."

"I should take Muppet out for a quick potty break first. Is that okay?"

"There's an area of lawn around the back." Olivia gestured the opposite way from which they'd come. "And the restroom's two doors down that way, if you need it. I'll get set up here. You want a coffee?"

"So much. Black, please." Kath didn't think she could keep milk down. She pulled Muppet out of the carrier and snapped on his leash before carrying him down the hall toward a door marked with a lighted EXIT sign.

Tobacco smoke drifted in a cloud past the door as she opened it. She curled her nose as she stepped into it, but it was only as the door clanged shut behind her that she could see back to where the smoker stood leaning against the building. Simultaneously, Muppet growled again, deep in his chest. Kath stiffened and tightened her grip instead of setting him down.

HT stood watching her. He lifted the cigarette back to his lips and took a deep, slow drag. What was it with industry people and cigarettes all of a sudden?

"Since when did you take up smoking?" Kath asked.

"I bummed it from one of the camera guys. Needed an excuse to get outside."

Kath thought about walking away, but it was too good an opportunity to make peace. On the other hand, she might blow the whole audition by setting him off into one of his fits of temper. She could never be sure how HT would react.

"How are the chemistry reads going? Is this leftover energy or nerves?"

"Neither. Both." His voice was strained as he held the smoke in his lungs, then he turned his head to exhale away from her. "I don't know. I just needed air." He reached out to pat Muppet on the head. "Hey, Mups. Remember me?"

Muppet snarled, lunged, and bit down hard on HT's hand.

HT yelped and tried to pull back, but Muppet didn't let go. "Sonofabitch. Get him off!"

"Hold still. Muppet, no. Bad dog." Kath tried to rebalance Muppet since he was halfway out of her arms. Stepping closer to HT, she inserted her fingers into the dog's mouth to pry his jaws open and free the flesh between HT's thumb and index finger. "Come on, buddy. Let go now."

Muppet finally released, but he bared his small bloody teeth in HT's direction and growled again.

HT stared down at his hand, which was dripping red onto the concrete. "What the hell? It's me, you idiot dog."

Kath shook her head. "I'm pretty sure he knows that. It's why he bit you."

HT stared at her as if that was somehow astonishing to him. "What did I do?"

"You left him, and he loved you."

"I didn't leave him—I left you. Has he had his rabies shot?"

"Of course. Also, I'm pretty sure he's a *dog*, so he doesn't understand the finer points of which one of us you left behind. Now, show me your hand."

HT backed away. "Don't come near me with him."

"Don't be such a baby." Kath caught his hand and tried to examine it while keeping it out of Muppet's reach. "This doesn't look too bad. I don't think you need stitches. Go wash it while I let Mups go pee, and I'll put a Band-Aid on it if you meet me in the green room. I've got some in my purse."

"Fine," HT said, glaring at her.

"Fine," Kath said, turning her back on him. Which was all a fantastic start so far.

TRUCE

"What is forgiveness worth without trust?"

SHARON KAY PENMAN, *THE RECKONING*

KATH PUT HAND SANITIZER, ANTIBACTERIAL rub, and several bandages in place on HT's hand. Simultaneously, Olivia worked around that to dab Kath's skin with concealer, foundation, powder, contour, and highlighter. That was one of the perks of working on a soap together when Kath had first been starting out: they knew how to stay out of each other's way. Funny that Kath and HT had never learned that lesson while they were married.

"There you go." Kath smoothed the last bandage in place. "Good as new."

"Easy for you to say." But HT grinned at her, which was probably the most relaxed smile he'd given her in years.

She swallowed hard and looked up at him, and despite all the hurt and anger and fear they had hurled at each other through the years, for that moment, she didn't have the energy to be angry anymore. Also, there was something about him that didn't look right. And the cigarette, that didn't feel right. It wasn't him.

"Hey," she said. "How are you doing? Are you upset about me being here? Worried about Nia?"

He glanced from her to Olivia, then straightened to his full height. "I'm okay."

"You sure?"

"Leave me alone, Kath. Don't pick at it."

"You don't seem yourself. And I need to apologize about… you know."

Olivia stroked a last dab of highlighter along Kath's cheekbone. "You know what, I forgot something," she said. "I'll be right back."

Kath waited as Olivia walked away, relieved when HT made no move to follow her out. Instead, he eased himself down to perch on the sofa's armrest. Kath had been sitting on the very edge of the cushion to make it easier for Olivia to work, so she scooted back and shifted around to see HT better. "I'm sorry about pressuring you about the audition."

"Blackmailing me."

"Yes, that," Kath said. "But I appreciate what you did."

"I don't want you here."

His eyes always surprised Kath, how blue they were. Those eyes were part of what had made her fall in love with him so many years ago. At least, she had thought she loved him. Looking back, it was hard to be sure what she had felt. There had been too much pain that came immediately after.

"Remember the play?" she asked. "Talking about that night has been off-limits for so long, but we had fun before everything went to hell. Didn't we? I know it was only an amateur production and the first thing you'd done, but you were good. Seriously good."

"So were you." He pushed himself off the sofa and walked toward the craft services table.

"We were even better together. Until now, that may have been the last time I was able to become someone else without being afraid too much of the real me was showing through. I was nervous because of the critic in the audience, but when we took our bows, I felt like we were sitting on top of the world. You've probably had that in all these films you've been doing lately. For me, I think that was the last time I felt that kind of pure exhilaration."

HT turned back as if she had surprised him. He smiled at her, and he hadn't done that in a long while, either.

"I think we killed the delight in acting that night," he said. "Don't get me wrong, I know how lucky I am. But when I'm done on set every day, I don't think, wow, that was fun. It's work. I want to do it well—I want to keep getting better. But that sense of freedom and joy that came with playing Orlando? That's gone. Maybe it feels like I don't deserve the success. Or maybe it was because that was theatre instead of film. I've thought about trying the stage for a while. Moving to New York."

"We haven't done any projects together since that night. What if we could get that feeling back? This script is deep and well-written. I love Margaret. I really love her. This role has become more than the desperation for a second chance. That was it in the beginning, I admit. And I was operating out of panic when I called you. But now, I want the opportunity to see if I can bring Margaret to life in the way I see her, in a way that feels true."

HT turned away to pour himself a cup of coffee, and he didn't say anything.

"HT, listen. Can you let me try to do that?" Kath asked. "Can we call a truce for today?"

She reached for the coffee Olivia had brought for her earlier and let the sweet bitterness wash down her throat. It seemed like HT wasn't going to answer her at all, and she didn't know what else to say to him.

He shifted to look at her. "Taking a role like Margaret isn't about seeing if you can do it. You realize that, don't you? You have to know you can, or you're putting the whole production at risk."

"I understand Margaret. I've studied the script, and I know it's an important part of Welsh history. Your history. But it's not just about the past. I see so many parallels in the world right now. In our own lives. Please, HT. I blackmailed you into getting the audition, but now I'm straight-up begging you to help me. Or at least to not stand in my way. Haven't we hurt each other enough? All I want is a chance to do this right."

She could see the tension in HT's shoulders and in his jaw. He'd lost weight lately, and Kath wondered if he'd done that on purpose to play Glyndwr, or if it was a symptom of something else. Worry about Nia, maybe. She tried to assess how she felt about the idea that Nia might be, finally, someone HT loved as much as he'd loved Anna. He'd never said so, but Kath thought it had been the news of her sister's wedding that had driven the final nail in the coffin of their marriage, a reminder of what he'd lost.

The door opened, and Olivia poked her head inside. "They're setting up for you. Can I just do a little with your eyes, Kath? Super quick."

Disappointed in HT and herself, Kath nodded. She shifted forward on the cushion again to make it easier for Olivia to reach her face.

HT crumpled the paper coffee cup in his uninjured hand and tossed it in the trash. "All right," he said. "Look, I've never heard you really say you need help, and maybe I'm not being fair. If you want a truce, I'll try."

He left the room without looking at her again, and Olivia crossed to the sofa and reopened her makeup kit. "You holding up, kiddo? That seemed intense."

"I think it was a good intense," Kath said. "But the jury's still out."

She closed her eyes while Olivia brushed various shadows along her lids. The familiar pattern took her back to the magic of the makeup room on the ABC lot, where she'd sat in a rotating chair in front of a lighted mirror. For seven years, Olivia had transformed everyday Kath into her character, and her career had still been new and full of possibility. They'd been such good friends, and it seemed ridiculous that they'd lost touch apart from being Facebook friends. But that was the problem with people who knew her too well. It was hard to hide that she was miserable, so it was easier not to see them at all.

Olivia applied mascara last, then screwed the lid back on the tube and said, "There. Much better."

The whole exercise had only taken a minute, but Kath felt like she was in a different headspace with better armor. She stood up and hugged Olivia. "Thank you. It means a lot that you're here."

Olivia laughed, caught her by the elbows, and bounced up and down. "You got the au-di-tion," she sang. "You are go-ing to rock it." Then she sobered suddenly and caught Kath's chin in her hand. "You are going to do great, you hear me? Seriously. You've got this."

TOWERS FALLING

"The best thing to do was to brazen it out."

SARAH WATERS, THE NIGHT WATCH

K ATH FROZE ON HER MARK when Dai Rhys called, "Action." Every word of her opening line evaporated out of her brain, her hands tingled, and she was going to throw up. Where was the nearest trash can?

"Action," Dai Rhys said again. There was an edge to his voice this time.

Kath shook her head and took a deep breath. She opened her mouth, hoping the words would come. But nope. Nothing. Blank.

The walls and floor of the studio were lit by the set lights and rows of recessed lighting on the ceiling. Standing there, the space was enormous and felt like an alien abduction scene with the spaceship hidden behind blinding lights. The aliens had obviously kidnapped every ounce of Kath's intelligence and willpower.

"Cut." Dai Rhys stood between two cameras, and he took a couple of steps toward Kath. "Do you need your lines?"

She shook her head. Then she nodded. "Maybe just the first one to get me started. I'm so sorry."

"It's not a problem." He walked toward her holding a script, emerging from behind the cameras all long legs and wide shoulders, and Kath begged silently for him to stop. Alternatively, she wanted the studio floor to open like a trap set and let her drop down onto a net far out of everyone's view.

But he didn't stop. He came in closer, close enough for her to realize how close he was, and close enough to block her view of everyone else who was there to watch her fail.

"Hey, Kath, look at me. You did this before, and you were fantastic. Not perfect, and you're here anyway because we don't need you to be perfect. If you don't remember a line exactly, ad-lib it. You know the action and the overall thrust of the scene. The rest of us here in the studio?" He waved a hand back toward the row of chairs. "We've all been nervous. We're all human, so don't feel intimidated, and don't think about us. Go back into Margaret's skin, and do the same thing you did in that first scene you read for us. Think about being Margaret."

Nerves were a weakness, and there was no excuse. Plus, she knew her lines. Being on a soap had trained her memory. What was wrong with her?

"I'm sorry, Mr. Rhys. I don't want to waste anyone's time."

"First, the name is Dai, and you're alright. This is your time. We're in no hurry. Now, what can I do to make you more comfortable? Are you happy with where you are with the sides? It might help if you tell me what Margaret's feeling."

Seen up close, his eyes were gray, with a darker ring around the outside of the iris. They were kind, but also alive with that same contained energy she had noticed about him earlier. Energy, not impatience.

She stared at him, impressed and mortified at how quickly he had grasped what was going on with her. Maybe that understanding came from the therapy he'd done for his PTSD. She'd read about that. He was open about suffering from it after an injury in Afghanistan and how he had started acting as part of his therapy. Then a student filmmaker had seen him in an amateur play and gotten him involved in a documentary about soldiers with PTSD. The documentary had won an Oscar for Best Documentary Short Subject, and Dai had received four offers from talent agents within a week.

Thinking of that made Kath feel even more useless. Dai had been shot at—actually shot. And she was wasting his time with stage fright.

"Kath? Talk to me," Dai said. "Trust me, talking will help. What's Margaret's mood when she starts this piece?"

"She's exhausted." Kath studied the floor to avoid having to look at him. "She's been going to funerals, tending the wounded, and trying to feed, clothe, and house the tenants de Ruthyn forced off the land he's trying to steal from Glyndwr. She's also furious that Glyndwr botched a retaliatory raid on de Ruthyn and killed one of de Ruthyn's men at arms. That makes her scared for Glyndwr, scared about what de Ruthyn will do to him. It frustrates her that Glyndwr is letting his pride get in the way of what she sees as logic."

"Very good, and what's the first line?"

"I have blood to my elbows, and my eyes are raw from crying at the sight of children and old men laid to rest in earth far from the land they farmed." The line came automatically, from out of nowhere.

"See? I was sure you knew it." Dai smiled, showing faint dimples in his cheeks that made that hard jaw less intimidating. "Do you think you can do the scene off book, or would you feel more comfortable with a script?"

Kath took a breath all the way to the bottom of her lungs. "Can I have just one more minute?"

"Of course." Dai was still watching her closely. "You know, I used to do twenty push-ups before every scene to get my breath moving. Do whatever works for you."

He turned back, and Kath glanced at HT, who was standing nearby looking increasingly pissed and stubborn. But that was okay, because he needed that emotion in the scene. "Sorry," she said again. "Nerves got the better of me."

She walked off a few feet, shook out her arms, rolled her neck, and did a few old exercises to loosen up. She inhaled deep and hummed while exhaling, which she alternated with saying "Ha," while exhaling fast. After doing that five times, she ran through a few tongue twisters with her modified Welsh accent: "I need a box of biscuits, a box of mixed biscuits, and a biscuit mixer," and "The jolly collie swallowed a lollipop," and "Betty bought butter but the butter was bitter, so Betty bought better butter to make the bitter butter better," and finally the old standby, "Peter Piper picked a peck of pickled peppers, a peck of pickled peppers Peter Piper picked. If Peter Piper picked a peck of pickled peppers, where's the peck of pickled peppers Peter Piper picked?"

More grounded, but still embarrassed and terrified, she squared her shoulders and walked back to her mark. Something about that felt off, and on impulse, she lowered herself to her knees and bowed her head, as if the script called for her to still be tending the wounded when Glyndwr walked in.

"And action," Dai called.

Kath brought her head up and turned as if she'd heard footsteps coming. Seeing it was HT, she let the full weight of everything Margaret felt for Glyndwr, love and fear and fury, show on her face. Her breath quickened. Then she stood and pretended to use the corner of an apron tied around her waist to wipe her forearms as she walked to where HT was waiting.

"I have blood to my elbows, and my eyes are raw from crying at the sight of children and old men laid to rest in earth far from the land they farmed," she said. "And here you enter with your sword at your side. What folly do you plan to commit next?"

HT put his hands on her shoulders and bent to steal a kiss. Kath pulled away, but then abruptly she leaned in, put her hands on his cheeks, and kissed him back. She knew the rhythm of his kisses and the taste of him, so it was easy to catch him off his guard. Whether on purpose or out of habit, he pulled her closer and let the kiss go for another moment, until again she was the one who broke away.

He raised his head but didn't step back. "You would wear a sword yourself if you could. Admit it."

"Aye, and run de Ruthyn through happily were he here. Instead, he is where you should be, in London, whispering in the king's ear. The moment he hears you killed his man, he'll tell the king that, too. And what then, when he asks for all you own as forfeit? Or worse, demands to see you hang? What will the king say when you aren't there to plead your side?"

"Bolingbroke will act with reason."

"You men! You rate yourselves as high as the moon!" Kath shook her head and turned to gesture behind her as if there were pallets there filled with men, women, and children recovering from their wounds. "These broken souls are what such pride begets. Children with flesh split to the bone, tended by women whose own wounds are harder to see and take far longer to heal. But what does that matter to you? You and de Ruthyn and the king are *men*. Your friendships, your loyalties, your property—those are the things that drive you." She took a step closer and tilted her chin to look up at HT. "Those are only things, Owain. It's people who matter, but you intend to send them, our own people, back to their farms undefended. What is left for them there? Only the terror of waiting for the fire and sword that will come when de Ruthyn's men return."

"I will see de Ruthyn and his men in hell before I let them attack again," HT snapped.

"And you'll do so how?" Kath turned her back on him, rage roiling inside her as she thought of all the times people had made choices for her for their own benefit and left her to live with the fallout. "Will you kill every man who serves de Ruthyn? Will you march to Ruthyn itself and seize the castle with all its bristling towers?"

"Aye, perhaps I will." HT's voice was quiet.

Kath whipped back around and studied his face, which HT had set into such familiar, stubborn planes. But underneath that was pain. And that, too, was familiar. She thought of their earlier conversation, of all the old hurts—hers and his. Then she did what she had wanted to do a thousand times, reach up to cup his cheek with her palm and beg his forgiveness.

"You would try, wouldn't you? Because you are brave and foolish beyond measure. But if there comes a time to storm Ruthyn Castle, it will require intelligence more than any futile display of strength. I beg you—for the love you bear for all of us, for me—go now to the king. Tell him your side. Court his favor."

HT caught her hand and moved it from his cheek to his lips. Instead of kissing the back of it, he turned it over and kissed her palm. "De Ruthyn will force the king to act long before I can ride to London," he said. "You would have me gallop the length of England and risk delivering myself to the gallows."

He still held Kath's hand near his lips, looking into her eyes. She turned her wrist and interlaced her fingers with his, then brought their arms down to their sides so that she could rest her cheek against his chest, her face turned toward the cameras. She felt his heart beating, steady and a little fast, as if she wasn't the only one who was nervous. Softly, she felt his lips on her hair. With her eyes closed, she could almost imagine the studio had dropped away. Margaret already suspected that Glyndwr's fate was sealed, much as Kath's marriage to HT had been doomed from the start.

They'd had good moments, though. A few. Had Kath valued those enough? If she'd known there was no hope, would she have tried harder or given up sooner? She wasn't sure.

"And cut! Well done, everyone," Dai Rhys called out. "Let's reset, and I'd like to try that again with a few adjustments."

HT and Kath stepped back, neither of them looking at each other. She braced herself for the notes Dai would give her, but she wasn't sure how she and HT could do that scene again and make it seem as natural. Of course, that was the job. They would have to do it as many times as it took until the director believed not only they, but everyone in the crew, had gotten it right.

She wished relationships—life—came with retakes. How much simpler would it be if she could do over every moment of thoughtlessness and selfishness? Unwind every fight, mistake, and misunderstanding? She would give anything not to have all the old hurts stacked up, one on top of another. Since the moment she and HT had left Cincinnati, their lives together had been like an insane competition, both of them racing to see who could build the tallest tower of grievances, until finally one of them collapsed under the weight of it all, and the marriage toppled.

TRUST

"Nobody gets praised for the right reasons."

DIANA WYNNE JONES, *CASTLE IN THE AIR*

T HE CHEMISTRY WAS UNDENIABLE BETWEEN HT and
Kath. It also made Dai uncomfortable.

He tried to fault the two scenes Kath and HT performed
together. He called for retakes, adjusted the shots and camera
angles, and asked for minor changes to see how collaborative
Kath could be and how she would react when he pushed her.
If he was honest with himself, that was more than he needed
to ask from her. But nothing in her history said she should be
this good, and he had to be sure. The result was that the scenes
got even better.

Quite simply, Kath and HT felt genuine, both as Margaret
and Glyndwr and as a married couple under pressure.

By the time he finally called it, Kath looked exhausted,
and Dai felt like a sod. "Excellent work, both of you," he said.

"Kath, thank you, and we'll do our best to phone the hotel in the morning and let you know whether we'll need you to stay on. HT, take a break. I imagine you must be feeling spent."

"Thank you, everyone, for the opportunity," Kath said, taking the time to include the camera and boom operators and the production and creative teams in her smile of appreciation.

There was a moment after that when she and HT looked at each other. Then HT caught her hand, and they crossed to the door together. Dai wondered what their relationship was really like. If he'd learned one thing working in film, it was that nothing in Hollywood was as it seemed.

To compensate for how good Kath had been, he gave extra care to directing the remaining actors. Catrin had already been and gone before Kath, but he found himself asking more of Scarlet, Sophie, and Nerys Price, trying to pull out the same level of performance from them that Kath had delivered. The auditions only cemented what he'd already felt.

The other actors were perfectly fine as Margaret. Better than fine. If he hadn't seen Kath, he could have cast Nerys, simply because she was Welsh and available, and that would have been the best strategic decision overall.

But he had seen Kath.

Watching the others, it reminded him that the longing of *hiraeth* didn't always apply to a place. It could as easily apply to an idea or a person. Directing Sophie, Scarlet, and Nerys, he felt *hiraeth* for Kath.

It was past eight o'clock by the time Nerys had finished.

Dai would have loved to get out for a run to clear his head and game out an approach. As director, he had creative control.

In theory.

In practice, Alan had enough clout to make a handful of calls and get Sophie Tanner and Scarlet Johnson, not to mention everyone else, here on a Sunday with little notice. Alan didn't take no as an answer, and what he couldn't get by asking, he got through manipulation. Take the conversation about introducing a fantasy element in Glyndwr's magic. Had that been genuine? It might as easily have been Alan providing a red herring to maneuver Dai into agreeing to give Sophie a reading.

Before Dai went toe to toe with Alan about casting Kath, Dai had to be sure she was worth the risk. What was he prepared to do if Alan refused and insisted Sophie was still the better choice?

On paper, all four of the other actors made more sense. That was as true now as it had been after Kath's first audition.

Kath was older than Alan wanted. She had no fan base to speak of. No name familiarity, no track record with a role this large. And she had a reputation for being temperamental. Dai had seen for himself how she'd melted down with stage fright.

Then there was HT. For all the drama of the two of them walking off the set hand in hand, a divorced couple working together could spell disaster.

Finally, she wasn't even Welsh. To argue in favor of casting her, Dai would need to abandon his own objections on that score. That meant he couldn't very well argue against casting Sophie or Scarlet, either, on the basis that they had no links to Wales.

Making a case on Kath's behalf was risky. Even so, Dai wanted her.

Having seen her scenes, especially having seen her with HT, he wanted her.

HT's performance with the other actors had been consistent, but consistency wasn't connection. The spark between Kath and HT came from their interaction and something more. It was *hwyl*, in the old sense of the word, the intangible passion and belonging. HT could only respond to what the other actors gave him. That meant Kath wasn't just a better Margaret, she made HT a better Glyndwr.

Still undecided, Dai walked into the green room where Jemma, the production assistant, had brought in dinner and arranged the seats in a circle for the casting meeting. A tall, thin woman in her mid-forties with her dark hair scraped back into a bun, she came and met him at the door.

"How are we looking on the edits?" he asked.

"Almost ready. I've queued up Catrin's audition for you to show on the monitors, and the editors will have the roughs on the last two by the time you need them. Each DVD has the assembly cut with the camera shots and angles you asked for first, then the raw footage for each camera combined with the audio track."

"You're brilliant, Jemma. Thanks. And would you let them know how much I appreciate the help? If they stop in when they're finished, I'd like a chance to say thanks in person."

The room hummed with dozens of conversations as everyone drifted in. It felt increasingly warm and overcrowded.

Dai lowered the temperature on the thermostat, then waited his turn in line at the craft services table. He was spooning chicken and leek pie onto his plate when Alan sidled up beside him. Alan's own plate was already overflowing, and he carried a glass of Jameson's whiskey in the other hand.

"Hell of a long day," Alan said. "So what are you thinking, Dai? Is your mind made up?"

Dai poured himself a coffee instead of the Scotch he would have preferred. "I'd like to see the edited footage before I venture an opinion."

"You know which way you're leaning, surely?" Alan led the way to a pair of empty armchairs.

"Not entirely."

Alan dropped into the armchair with a sigh. "It's been a long day already, and I'm concerned we'll all run out of steam before we finish the screenings, much less the discussions. What if we take a quick, anonymous vote before we start? Whittle down the contenders and save ourselves some time."

"There's plenty of coffee," Dai said, and if his voice had an edge, he didn't mind.

He hated feeling "managed," and that was precisely how this felt. He had no intention of giving Alan an opportunity to throw any auditions out of consideration.

But he was cautious with his answer. "I assume you aren't suggesting that everyone here has an equal vote?"

Alan stiffened slightly. "I only meant it might be useful to hear what everyone's thinking. It can't hurt to get initial reactions in case you or I are still working from a preconceived idea."

"And by that you mean that you think I'll insist on a Welsh actor in the role?"

"I'm hoping we've both kept an open mind, that's all." Alan raised both eyebrows pointedly, and with the collar of his black polo shirt turned upright, he made Dai think of a movie magician orchestrating events to suit himself. The Wizard of Oz, perhaps. The man behind the curtain.

Dai refused to fall for more manipulation. He didn't need Alan pushing him into saying something before he had fully thought it through.

But if nothing else, getting initial input would let him know whether anyone else had seen what he had seen in Kath. If he was the only one, then he'd need to think that much harder about whether she was worth the argument.

"A straw poll is a good idea," he said, "as long as we make it clear from the beginning that we're not casting by majority vote. And regardless of the outcome, I reserve the right to screen and discuss any or all of the auditions."

Alan's eyes narrowed, but then he nodded. "Will you give me the same courtesy?"

Dai agreed, set his plate down, and went to discuss the logistics with Jemma. She left the room, and by the time she had returned with notecards, pencils, and a hat to collect the responses, everyone else had sat down to eat.

Alan assumed the role of moderator. "Before we begin the screenings, Dai and I would like you to try an experiment. Based on what you saw in the studio today, we'd like you to give us the name of the actor you'd most like to see as

Margaret. Write the name on the notecards Jemma is passing around. And if you can't narrow it down to one actor, write in as many as you like. There's no right answer. We're simply looking for your raw impressions to help inform us when it comes time to make our own casting recommendations in a little while."

Faced with the blank notecard, Dai meant to write Nerys's name as well as Kath's. The pencil hovered, but the paper remained stubbornly empty. In the end, he wrote "Katharine Cameron," folded the note, and waited for Jemma to come by and get it.

Alan went back for a second round of food, and Lizzie took advantage of his absence to drop into his vacant chair. She leaned in close to whisper, "Is it me, Dai, or is this the most insane way to cast a film you've ever heard of?"

"Is this how Alan usually does things?"

"No, but then I've never worked with him on recasting a starring role."

Dai drained the last of the coffee in his cup and shook his head. "Do you want to tell me which way you're leaning?"

Lizzie shrugged. "The same direction you are, probably. But I have no idea how we can get Alan to consider her when he's stuck on Sophie."

Jemma came by, and Dai and Lizzie gave her their folded notecards. Dai picked up Lizzie's empty plate along with his own and threw them both in the bin by the craft services table. He'd have loved to follow Alan's example and pour himself a glass of Scotch, but he needed a clear head for what was coming. He compromised on a glass of wine instead and then crossed the room to see if Jemma needed help.

"Can I give you a hand with the tabulations?" he asked.

"Thanks, but the counting is surprisingly easy. I'm nearly finished." She continued flipping through the notecards but made no effort to write anything on the empty notepad beside her. "Do you or Alan want to read the results, or shall I do it?"

"I'll leave it to you. Whenever you're ready." Dai returned to his seat beside Alan.

Within minutes, Jemma knocked on the nearest table to get everyone's attention. Conversation faded.

"I feel like I'm at an awards show and I should ask for the envelope." She smiled around at everyone a little self-consciously. "Are you ready? And the unanimous choice for the best Margaret goes to… Katharine Cameron."

Everyone reacted at once, clapping, commenting to their neighbors. Dai felt like Alan had left him a step behind again.

He turned to him. "Did you vote?" he asked.

Alan nodded. "I did. Did you?"

"So we both liked Kath best, then."

"She surprised me, but I was sure you hadn't let the Welsh thing go yet."

Dai felt a release of the tension that had weighed on him since the moment Nia had told him she couldn't continue filming. "I was dreading having to convince you about Kath over Sophie."

"The chemistry wasn't there, though, was it? I'll admit, I thought you and Lizzie were crazy for considering her with no background to speak of. That said, you're the one who will have to make sure she delivers this same level of performance. And we can't afford to take months immersing her in the character. Can you find time to work with her considering how far behind we are already?"

"Do you still have reservations?" Dai asked. The question came out a bit too sharp.

Alan rocked back on his heels and studied him. "I'm not the enemy, Dai. Whatever you may think. If there's anything I've learned today, it's that both of us need to do a better job of trusting one another. This film is special, and you have an enormous level of talent. That said, you have a tendency to charge into battle even when the situation calls for a more diplomatic approach."

"I prefer to think of it as being direct," Dai said, grinning. "But you might be right."

"The investors who are here today won't need to be convinced. As for the rest of them, a unanimous straw poll and the fact that Kath stood toe to toe with the likes of Scarlet and Sophie will go a long way."

Dai raised his brows. "Are you saying you planned this?"

"Not to you," Alan said, smiling. "But if it helps me make a case to other people, will I fudge a little for the sake of diplomacy? You bet. What I'm saying is that this business isn't about talent alone. You can't always charge ahead will all guns blazing."

Dai had to respect the man, even if he didn't necessarily like the methods. "Point taken."

"Good. Now with that said, we both know that casting Kath is risky. The investors, the studio, even the media will need convincing. You leave that to me, but make sure you do whatever it takes to get her ready to deliver. Can you do that?"

Nerys would have been the practical choice. Sophie would have been the commercial choice. Dai went with his gut instead.

"I think she's worth it."

Looking pleased with himself, Alan clapped him on the back. "I agree. But keep me in the loop if it looks like she's in trouble. We can't afford any more delays."

REPRIEVE

"There are narrow windows for certain beginnings."

OWAIN SHEERS, *I SAW A MAN*

T HE FORTRESS TOWERS OF CAERNARFON Castle loomed dark and forbidding in contrast to the sunrise. Kath had barely slept, so she was outside with Muppet when the quiet pre-dawn blue turned orange and red. The city began to stir. She waited for Muppet to do his business, then tied off the bag, picked Muppet up, and went in search of a trash can. After that, she kept walking with no particular destination in mind.

Seen without the bustle and hum of traffic, the cobbled street was an invitation to explore. She strolled past restaurants and shuttered shops in the direction of the castle, which looked to be only a couple of blocks away.

It had been built to intimidate and subdue, to make anyone who lived in its shadow feel insignificant. Following the castle walls down to the Menai Strait, she tried to imagine how it must have felt to be Welsh in the 13th century and have to watch it rising stone by stone.

At the water's edge, she paused to take in the view. The wind whipped her hair, carrying salt spray into her face and making her feel alive and wide awake. But Muppet was growing heavy and restless, and she hurried back. In the time that she'd been gone, one of the restaurants near the hotel had opened. She settled into a chair at one of the outdoor tables and set Muppet down beside her feet. He lay down tight against her legs, his pink tongue lolling, just as he did at home.

A waiter came out almost immediately with a dog bowl full of water and a menu, and Kath opted for coffee, yogurt, and a croissant with jam. She had kibble for Muppet back in her room, but she ordered him a scrambled egg anyway as a special treat. Then, when the waiter had gone, she sat back, tipped her face toward the sun, and practiced breathing and patience and trying to quiet her mind.

The aroma of coffee alerted her when the waiter returned, and she was just setting the egg down for Muppet when her phone rang. She pulled it out of her pocket and stared at the name on the screen: Dai Rhys.

Her heart kicked into a jackhammer rhythm, but she told herself he could be calling for any number of reasons. To soften the rejection, for example.

Except he wasn't.

"I'm happy to say that we'd all love to have you join the cast," he said. "Everyone loved what you did yesterday."

A rush of sound in Kath's ears blocked out anything else.

Or maybe it was just her brain that was incapable of processing additional information. "Excuse me, could you repeat that?"

Dai gave a low, deep chuckle. "Congratulations, Kath. And welcome to the cast."

Kath closed her eyes, drew a breath, and let it out. "Thank you. That's fantastic news."

"I assume your agent told you we were hoping you could start right away. Will that work, or do you need to go home and make arrangements?"

"I'll need to pick up a few extra things here, but other than that, I'm set. How long will we be filming?"

"The plan was to finish up here in mid-November. We'll all have to work longer hours to make that now, but it would be better if we didn't have to extend the shooting schedule."

"I understand."

"Good. In that case, I'd like to have you on set by Thursday for fittings and so forth. If you and I can get up to speed by then, we could plan to shoot your first scene next week. Unfortunately, I'll be going flat out playing catch-up. Would you mind doing a working dinner tonight to kick things off? I should be able to get free around seven to pick you up."

"Here in Caernarfon?" Kath asked, envisioning disaster. How was she supposed to concentrate in a restaurant?

"Sorry, no. I've done this entirely backward. I'll have Jemma email you with all the details, but in a nutshell, we're all staying in a village on the Obaith Estate. It's not too far, and there's easy proximity to most of the location shoots. Jemma will include a number to call whenever you need a car and driver and information about picking up your keys. You'll be in Nia's old cottage, and I can pop round there to get you tonight."

He said all that so casually, as if Kath had dinner with a gorgeous director every day of the week and called around for a car and driver as a matter of routine.

"Now…" His voice became more businesslike. "We haven't covered money and contract details yet. I assume Joel will handle all that for you?"

"Yes, please." As much as it made Kath furious to think of Joel getting ten percent of her earnings after everything he had said, she didn't have much choice.

"In that, I hate to cut this short, but we're arriving on set and I'd better go. Do you have a million questions?"

"Only a thousand. And nothing that can't wait."

"Brilliant." She heard the smile in his voice. "And I'll look forward to speaking more tonight."

He hung up, and Kath sat at the table with the phone half-forgotten in her hand. Eventually, she forced herself to eat her breakfast. Her coffee was almost cold. Then she carried Muppet up the street to the hotel.

It all felt like a dream.

Checking her watch, she decided to call Olivia. After everything she had done to help, Kath wanted her to be the first to hear the news.

"No way. Seriously?" Olivia yelled loud enough that Kath might not have needed the phone to hear her.

"Does that mean you're happy?" Kath asked, laughing.

"Are you kidding? And I'm going to take all the credit. I deserve points for saving the whole production. You have no idea how worried everyone has been. It sucked not knowing when we were going to finish shooting here—whether we were going to have to shut down and pick up later. Not to mention all the doom-and-gloomers who were sure Alan Stickley would end up scrapping the entire project."

"Why? They had some amazing actors auditioning."

"Actors who are booked years out. Oh, you know how production sets are. Rumors and fur flying everywhere. Word is Dai and Alan have been at each other's throats—in the politest possible way—over how to recast Margaret. And no offense, because your audition was great, but I don't know how you pulled that off. Good for you, though. I assume the champagne's on you at the pub tonight?"

"Actually, I have a dinner meeting with Dai to go over the script and schedule."

"Poor Dai. He's working all hours. But hey, if I wasn't jealous before, I am now. He's yummy, right? I can't help wondering how HT's going to react to you and the director hanging out. There was some definite leftover sizzle between the two of you last night."

"That was audition sizzle, not actual sizzle. HT couldn't care less. Plus it's a working dinner."

"That's the most threatening part for him. Think about it. HT has Glyndwr all mapped out, and now you're stepping in. That's going to change the whole dynamic. You actors are all neurotic and paranoid anyway."

"Thanks very much. I'll call you if I get done early tonight. Or we'll figure out another time. Oh, and what are the cottages like?"

"Nice. Loud inside, quiet out. I'm up the hill in the village where the larger cottages are, but five of us are sharing. And unless we can get a ride from some of the locals who have cars, the pub is the only option for food and entertainment until Sunday, when there are shuttles back and forth to Conwy."

"So it's a six-day shooting schedule?"

"Usually. And the hours have been reasonable so far. Oh, hey, I'm supposed to be on set. See you later!"

It was too early to call anyone in LA, so Kath sent Joel an email and typed a text to Fiona. Then she checked online for clothing stores nearby. The options all seemed like small boutiques, which she would have loved if she'd had time. But she decided that leaving Muppet alone in a hotel room wasn't fair.

The production assistant had sent the details Dai had told her to expect, and after Olivia's description of the cottages, Kath called down for a late checkout so she could take advantage of the quiet and go over the script again. At noon, she arranged for the car company to send a driver and picked up a sandwich to go while she took Muppet out for air. Packing took only a few minutes, and since the production company was paying the hotel bill, checkout was quick and easy. She was outside waiting fifteen minutes before a white Mercedes arrived, and an older man in a black shirt got out. He looked around, then came toward her.

"You Miss Cameron?"

"Yes, I'm Kath."

He grunted, which Kath wasn't sure how to take, and his phone rang as he steered the car up the street. He answered and spoke in Welsh, then as soon as he hung up, he immediately made another call. Kath snuggled Muppet on her lap.

The route out of town followed the Menai Straight, then curved along the coast of the steel-gray Irish Sea. Near the medieval town of Conwy, the site of another of Edward I's castles of doom and intimidation, the driver turned the car inland into a green valley bounded by bald, green hills. For twenty miles, a broad river flirted with the road, curving away and back again, growing narrower the farther they drove inland. On the hillsides, streams and rivulets flashed in bright silver ribbons, and the white walls of farms and village houses gleamed whenever the sun came out from behind racing clouds.

After half an hour, they passed a sign that said "Entering the Obaith Estate," and a few miles later a house the size of a city block became visible in the distance. A long drive branched off toward it, but the driver continued straight and eventually turned onto a narrower road that approached the village of Ty Newydd.

The village was straight out of a screenplay:

EXT. VALLEY — DAY

A cloud-shrouded ridge plunges into a valley, and a
brook tumbles over rocks. Sunlight refracts on

windows softened with boxes of flowers in a
charming village of white and stone homes climbing
up the hillside. Apart from a dusty delivery van
parked in front of a shop and a handful of cars, the
main road lies deserted. A girl of fifteen or sixteen
slips out of a cheerful green door, looks both ways,
and walks off with her head down and her face
hidden. Minding its own business, a ginger cat trots
away in the opposite direction.

There was something almost painfully ordinary about the girl that made her stand out. Without her and the handful of cars, the rest of the village could have been plucked straight from the 19th century. Kath felt out of place as well, an imposter who would be caught any moment and told she didn't belong.

CLIFF'S EDGE

"Life is not hurrying on to a receding future…"

R.S. THOMAS, THE BRIGHT FIELD

FOLLOWING DAI'S INSTRUCTIONS, KATH ASKED John to stop at the first of the two detached houses past the village hotel, pub, and shops. With Muppet safely back in his carrier, she climbed out of the car and knocked on the bright blue door. The door creaked open, and two eyes peered around the edge.

Kath smiled and said, "Hello, I'm looking for Glenys Jenkins. We spoke earlier about getting a key?"

The door opened wider, revealing another teenage girl, perhaps a little younger than the first. She was thin and small, with blonde hair a bit darker than Kath's and a sharply pointed chin. Her arm was in a cast, and mascara and tears stained the skin beneath her eyes and her cheeks.

"Are you Katharine Cameron?"

"Yes." Then she couldn't help asking, "Are you all right? Is there anything I can do?"

The girl's face closed like a book slamming shut. Kath assumed she didn't realize the tears had left their marks. "I'm fine," she said. "Nain had to run out to the estate. She left the key for you. I'll get it."

She disappeared, leaving the door open about four inches. Despite the musical cadence of her Welsh accent, her tone had said she was anything but fine, and her expression said she would rather die than let anyone know that.

That was a feeling Kath understood. Some things needed to be worked through alone. But she hated that any child should have to feel like that.

The girl returned with a key attached to a wooden fob carved in the shape of a spoon with two hearts intertwined to form the handle. Kath was careful not to let her sympathy show. She trotted out her first word of Welsh, which according to the guidebook meant thanks. "*Diolch.*"

"You're in cottage three. You can count the doors starting there." The girl pointed toward the nearest of the rowhouses. "We had it cleaned this morning, and there's a number in the kitchen to phone if you need anything."

She had wiped off the tear smudges, but there was still something so heartbroken about her that Kath couldn't bring herself to leave. "I guess we'll be neighbors for a while," she said. "What's your name?"

"Ceridwen. Anderson, not Jenkins, isn't it? I'm called Wenny, mainly."

"You said Glenys Jenkins was your *nain*. Is that Welsh for 'grandmother'? I'm still trying to figure things out."

Apparently, a virtual eye roll that didn't involve any actual rolling was a skill mastered by Welsh teens as well as American ones. Wenny got the point across. Even then, Kath didn't feel right about leaving her alone. There was just something... *off*. She thought about asking whether Wenny's arm was hurting or if she needed help. But no. It wasn't Kath's business, and the girl wouldn't tell her anyway. She had her grandmother and her parents.

Kath was still searching for something else to say when Wenny's expression became even more defiant. She was staring at something to Kath's left, and Kath turned and saw the same teenager she'd seen earlier approaching. The girl glared at Wenny and walked up to the house next door. Wenny stepped back and slammed her own door in Kath's face.

Kath turned to examine the girl more carefully. She was a stunner, with high cheekbones, wide lips, dark eyeliner around eyes that even across the distance were very blue. Her shoulder-length hair could have used a good brushing but fell in gorgeous curls around her shoulders. Instead of being uncomfortable that Kath was staring at her, she raised her chin and eyebrows and paused aggressively before opening the door, as if daring Kath to say something. After holding Kath's gaze for several beats, she disappeared into the house.

Kath felt like she'd walked into the middle of a high school drama, and the whole incident left her unsettled. She shrugged the feeling off as she unlocked the green door that was the third one down the rowhouse. As if he couldn't get out of the village fast enough, the driver took Kath's bags out of the trunk, left them in the street, and hopped back in the car so fast she didn't even have time to tip him.

"We're not off to a great start so far, are we, Muppet?" she asked as she took the dog carrier inside to set it down.

But inside, the "cottage" was modern and designed for comfort, and despite having been a little concerned by what Olivia had told her about sharing, it looked like she was going to have it all to herself. Windows framed in warm, natural wood looked out across the road at the rocky stream. A two-story wall of windows looked out back into woods that climbed the hillside on the other side. In between, the downstairs area was open plan, with a cathedral ceiling along the back and stairs leading to a loft with what Kath presumed was at least one bedroom. Beyond the small entryway, the living area contained a sleeper sofa and matching love seat, a low table, and a wood-burning fireplace. The kitchen had a wide counter with barstools, and to the right of that was a separate dining nook with a round table and four upholstered chairs.

Kath set Muppet's carrier beside the sofa. "Hang on a minute here for me. Let me get my bags, and I'll take you out and find some kibble for you. Sound like a plan?"

Muppet whined in answer, and Kath retrieved both the suitcase and her carry-on bag from the street and maneuvered them upstairs. The large bedroom looked out over a half wall to the kitchen and dining nook, and the queen-sized bed looked out across the wall of windows. There was also a walk-in closet and a bathroom with a frameless shower door and a Jacuzzi tub.

She rummaged for Muppet's kibble in her suitcase and had just removed it when the phone rang. Fiona's name flashed across the screen.

Kath didn't bother with a greeting. "Isn't it amazing, Fi?"

"Honey, I am thrilled for you," Fiona responded in her throaty-cigarette voice. "I've had my fingers and toes crossed for you. I even said a few prayers to my personal deities, Meryl Streep and Jameson's Irish Whiskey."

"Well, it couldn't have happened without your help," Kath said, grinning. "I do know that."

"True. And I'll expect you to leave me a gushing five-star Yelp review. Oh, and tickets to the premiere. Preferably in the seat beside Dai Rhys. I'll look forward to telling him and anyone who'll listen about how terrible you were before I turned you into a star."

"I really hope you're kidding."

Fiona laughed. "Relax, honey. Of course I am. You'll be great, but remember I'm here for you if you need to work through any more scenes. Did you—"

Kath's phone beeped with another call, and she saw it was Joel. "Oops, that's my agent calling. I'd better take it."

"After what that pig did to you, make him cut his commission before you sign the contract. It's a damn shame you have to take him back."

"It is, but don't worry. He'll probably fire me again as soon as this project wraps. Bye, Fi. Thanks again for everything."

She braced herself before switching the call and kept her voice professional. "Thanks for calling me back. You got my email?"

"Yes, that's great news, and I've already reached out to them. They're eager to get you on contract, so that means they'll be less likely to nickel and dime us about the terms. The bad news is that they want you working as fast as possible. You won't have much time for preparation, so don't expect the scenes to go as smoothly as the auditions. Manage your expectations."

"I expect the schedule will be brutal since they need to make up time, but I can handle that. And HT and I worked well together."

"That's not what I mean. You did four scenes for the auditions and you had days to prepare those. Now you're going to have to deliver every scene Margaret is in as well as you performed those four. Maybe even better. There will be times when you won't be able to give Dai what he wants, or scenes when the two of you disagree about approach. If you handle that badly, it could affect the entire cast and crew as well as your own career. Keep the budget and the number of people counting on you in the back of your mind."

Kath's feet landed firmly back on earth while Joel was talking. In fact, she felt like she'd crashed through the surface and ended up buried chest-deep in the dirt, squeezed in so tight there wasn't room to breathe.

"Good pep talk, Joel. Thanks for that," she said.

"I'll give you all the pep talks you want after you sign the contract. Right now, I need to hear that you're positive you want to sign. That you're ready to sign. You can't do this on a whim. If you aren't sure you can handle this role, tell me now, not in two days, two weeks, or two months."

Kath closed her eyes. "Of course I want to sign. I worked damn hard for this."

"Fine," he said, but she heard him sigh, letting her know he wasn't convinced. "Did Dai talk money with you? I'm sure Nia had deal points. You're not her, obviously, so I may not be able to get that for you, but I'll do my best."

"Please remember that I want this role more than I want the money. Don't push too hard."

"They won't walk away before you get on set. Recasting again would be disastrous. What about other details? Did Dai tell you anything else?"

"I'll forward you what the production assistant sent me."

"Good. And what about a publicist? You'll need one, and if the production won't pay for it, you'll have to foot the bill. Don't be surprised to see some ugly rumors in the tabloids once the news goes out. And stay off social media completely. We'll have the publicist take over your accounts."

Kath inhaled sharply. "Why?"

"There are always trolls, and Nia's fans may be angry if they think you took the part away from her. They may recycle all the old tabloid fodder and speculate about how you got the part. And be prepared in case the paparazzi show up there. Don't give them any opportunities."

"You're so encouraging lately, Joel. It's a gift, really."

"I don't think you're getting this. The level of pressure. Are you absolutely sure you're ready?"

"Just do your job and send me the contract. I'll sign it, and then I'll go do my job." Furious, Kath didn't bother saying goodbye. She disconnected, wishing there was a way to slam a mobile phone. Her stomach had clenched into a knot that kept pulling tighter and tighter until she felt like throwing up.

She wasn't going to let Joel get to her. Not now when she should be celebrating. How had he managed to turn great news into a torture session?

Snatching up the bag of kibble, she headed downstairs and released Muppet from captivity, trying to sound cheerful. "So, this will be home for the next three and a half months, Muppet pup. What do you think? Do you want to sniff around? Let's figure out where to put your food and water."

She shook the bag of kibble and walked back toward the kitchen. Muppet trailed behind her, snuffling at everything along the way and making occasional detours. By the time he reached her, Kath had found two plastic bowls in the well-stocked cupboards, and she adopted them for Muppet's food and water.

Muppet drank half the water as soon as she set the bowl down, and then he sniffed the kibble. He backed away with an expression that said, "What? This *again*?"

Kath sighed. "All right, yes. It's not great, but we'll see what they have at the shops here. If worse comes to worst, I'll find a pet store in town. In the meantime, you get to see how the other dogs live."

She refilled his water bowl, then investigated the double French doors that opened out onto a narrow flagstone patio occupied by a small table and two chairs. A supply of firewood stood in a neat stack against the wall, and beyond the flagstones, ten feet of mowed area created a transition zone before brush and trees climbed sharply up the hillside.

While Muppet sniffed the patio and ventured off the flagstones for a potty break, Kath looked around. The air smelled like mountains, of rain and trees and blooming, fertile things. Dozens of different birds called out, a reminder that there was more to life than traffic and human chatter.

Her father had told her once that cities were like cages, and only the birds could fly away. She'd been too young to understand. She'd told him that was silly because airplanes flew away, too.

"Airplanes mostly go to other cages," he'd said, and he'd tried to teach her to identify different birds from their calls and by appearance. She'd never learned more than a handful, and Anna was the only one who'd been any good at it. Meg, their middle sister, would tease him by making up outlandish names. "Isn't that the song of the Green-Tongued Warbler, Dad? Or is it a Purple-Crested Pigeon Toe?"

Standing there in the absence of human noise, Kath missed him, missed them all. She wanted to call and share the news, but also just talk, really talk with them. She hadn't done that in years.

Before the divorce, she had flown to Cincinnati a handful of times to see her parents, although never when Anna might be there. Since the divorce, she couldn't face going back. It was too hard to find something positive to say while her life was falling apart.

She finally had good news. But what she'd done to Anna hadn't changed. What if the news brought up all the old hurts again?

As much as Kath and HT had hurt Anna by leaving, Anna might not be happy to hear they were working together. Even happily married now, every photo, clip, and trailer could be a reminder of old pain.

She'd have to call them all before the news got out. But not just yet. Not until the contract was in her hand and she was sure it wouldn't all disappear in a puff of smoke. Thinking of Anna was a reminder of why Kath didn't deserve good luck, no matter how much she wanted it.

She hated Joel for reminding her that she could still spoil everything. Unfortunately, he wasn't wrong.

Every scene they had to shoot was an opportunity for failure. When she'd blackmailed HT to get the audition, she had told him she had nothing left to lose. That wasn't true anymore. Once the announcement went out, any failure would be very public and the crash would be spectacular.

Kath couldn't breathe. Seriously. She needed a paper bag.

She crouched and put her head between her knees, inhaling and exhaling to the count of three, over and over, until her heart slowed and she wasn't in danger of passing out.

Unpacking took less than fifteen minutes, including setting up Muppet's blanket by the fireplace. Then Kath curled up on the sofa with the script again. By the time Dai came to pick her up for dinner, she intended to know Margaret's emotional arc cold. Whatever questions Dai threw at her, she was going to be ready. Failure was not an option.

DEPARTURE

"No one gossips about other people's secret virtues."

BERTRAND RUSSELL, *ON EDUCATION*

D INNER MOVED TO SEVEN THIRTY. Jemma, the production assistant, phoned to say warn Kath that Dai was stuck on a conference call. She sounded rushed off her feet, so Kath didn't bother her with questions about the restaurant or dress code. A meal at a village pub wouldn't be too dressy, but it was still a business dinner. That meant dressy casual as a compromise, and nothing remotely sexy. She had Olivia to thank for putting that thought in her head.

It wasn't that she hadn't noticed that Dai Rhys was incredibly attractive, but she'd thought of him more as a director than a man. Now, thanks to Olivia's comment, dinner didn't seem like a great idea.

She dressed in a pale pink sweater with black piping around

the sleeves and neckline, paired with dark jeans and espadrilles, and made it downstairs with thirty minutes to spare. Leaving Muppet still worried her, so she used the extra time to help him get more familiar with the cottage. She used a handful of the homemade dog cookies she had found at the farm shop earlier to lure Muppet to every corner of the cottage. Whenever he reached her, she gave him a treat and lots of praise and then she moved to a different location and called him again. She had him back on his blanket by the fireplace when someone knocked loudly on the door at seven-fifteen.

"Stay there, Mups," she said, then she opened the door and found Dai Rhys standing there.

"Is it too early? I hope Jemma didn't throw you off on the time," he said.

He was wearing a green V-neck sweater and jeans, and standing just a foot away, he made Kath feel a little tongue-tied.

"Of course it's not too early. Come in. I'll just grab my notes and make sure Muppet's all right."

"Muppet?"

"My dog," Kath said.

He gave her exactly the sort of look she had dreaded. Then he ducked his head to avoid hitting the low doorway and stepped inside the cottage. Muppet growled at him from over on the blanket.

Dai glanced over and smiled. "He's very ferocious."

"Isn't he? I won't pretend he's exactly friendly, but the growl doesn't mean anything. He can't see, so he warns everyone away on principle."

"Not a bad strategy, actually. And that's right; I remember you saying he was blind during your audition. Is that why you brought him with you?"

It was a small thing, Dai remembering and making the connection about why she couldn't leave Muppet behind. But it made Kath like him.

"I'm glad you understand," she said. "I was afraid people wouldn't."

"He's a West Highland Terrier, right? Small, though. We had a Scottie when I was growing up. And by all means, feel free to ask why a self-respecting Welsh family would have a Scottish terrier instead of a Corgi."

"Okay, why is that?"

He grinned at her. "Because we found him on the side of the road and never found anyone who would admit they'd owned him. Believe me, we tried. The first week he stayed with us, we referred to him as The Beast often enough for the name to stick. He chewed up half the house—pillows, furniture, doors, shoes. And he hated everyone outside the family so much that we felt honored by the fact that he tolerated *us*."

"Stockholm syndrome," Kath said. "He held you hostage."

"Basically, yes."

He had a wonderful smile. The kind that felt so genuine Kath couldn't help smiling back.

"Do you mind if I say hello?" he asked.

"Be careful. He did a number on HT's hand yesterday. I'd feel terrible maiming the director before I even set foot on set."

Dai's smile widened again, and he crossed to where

Muppet was still doing his best impersonation of a German Shepherd. "If I lose an arm, I promise to tell everyone it happened in a freak shark incident."

"A great white that got disoriented, mistook itself for a salmon, and swam up the River Conwy?"

"Exactly that." He crouched in front of Muppet but didn't immediately reach for him. "Hello, old man. Yes, you're terribly fierce. I can see that. And brave. Now me, I'd be dead afraid if I were in a strange place in the dark. Good job Kath is here with you so that you have someone to protect."

Muppet sniffed at Dai's jeans, then cocked his head.

"Is that an invitation?" Dai rocked forward and slowly offered his hand. "There you are. Good lad."

Not only did Muppet not bite Dai's hand, he even leaned into it to encourage Dai to pet him.

Fascinated, Kath moved closer. "If you ever need a second job, you could take up dog whispering. Dai Rhys, tamer of frozen actors and savage Westies."

Dai gave Muppet a last pat on the head, then straightened and turned toward Kath. Unfortunately, she had miscalculated the distance when she stopped beside him, so now they stood too close. Not kissing close, but still too close for comfort.

Lord, where had *that* thought come from? There was zero chance of kissing in the forecast.

Smiling brightly, Kath hurried to grab her notes, script, and purse. "Where are we going, by the way? Do I need a coat?"

"The temperature doesn't change much from day to night at this time of year. It might drop to 15—sorry, 60 degrees in

Fahrenheit. But it's only just up the road. I thought I could make dinner at my place if you're comfortable with that. But I could just hop back and bring everything here if that would be easier with Muppet. It's only that I thought it would be better to have more space and quiet than we'd have at the pub."

He was babbling a little, which was adorable since he was the kind of guy who could probably take out half the Hollywood muscle at an Oscars ceremony without breaking a sweat. Kath wondered if he'd suddenly had #MeToo thoughts.

Was going to his cottage out of bounds?

Not that she didn't trust him. He seemed perfectly trustworthy. Only she was feeling stupidly awkward, and the very last thing she needed was for someone to catch her going in or coming out of the director's cottage and sending rumors flying.

Or were they going to fly anyway?

Was that what Joel had meant about people speculating about how she had got the job? That everyone would assume she had to have slept her way into it? Was that what Joel was thinking?

Probably. Because in Joel's mind, Kath didn't have the talent to earn the part.

She wanted to throw something. Preferably at Joel. But that wouldn't solve the immediate problem.

As she saw it, none of the options were great. She could insist on going to the pub, and she and Dai could sit around having stilted conversations for however long it took for him to feel comfortable with her approach to playing Margaret. That would waste his time and give her less insight than she'd hoped to gain. Potentially, it would mean longer rehearsals on set while the cast and crew all stood around and watched. She would be even more nervous, and that would lead to mistakes.

She should tell Dai that going to his place was fine.

Or invite him to stay here, where the chances of people seeing them were possibly even higher.

She had been thinking too long. Spots of color were rising in Dai's cheeks. "Sorry, Kath. I should have thought this through better. The pub is clearly the better choice."

"Anything is fine. It's nice of you to offer to cook after you've been working all day. I'd offer to stay here instead, but the choices come down to yogurt or a cheese and tomato omelet. I didn't pick up much at the shop."

"An omelet sounds great, actually." Dai ran a hand across the back of his neck, a curiously vulnerable gesture. Then he glanced around the cottage, hunting for something. "Did you get the gift basket, by the way? It was supposed to be here when you arrived."

Kath shook her head. "I haven't seen one."

"It was supposed to be here when you checked in so you wouldn't have to worry about going shopping right away. There's also a notebook with all the how-to and where-to instructions Glenys put together for the rest of us. Opening and closing times for local shops and restaurants, the sorts of things you would be better off getting in town—and which town—where to drop dry cleaning, and so on. I'll have to check with her and see what happened."

"Her granddaughter mentioned she had been called away."

"Wenny," Dai said, with a tone Kath couldn't place.

"She'd been crying when I went to pick up the key, so I didn't ask a lot of questions."

"Poor kid. And poor Glenys." His expression had gone blank, and he stepped away. Then he added with a rueful smile, "It's like the village version of *Coronation Street*. There are only two families who live here year-round. Glenys and Wenny, and the Davies in the next house over. They also have a teenage daughter. Apparently, the girls don't get along."

"I saw the other girl. Pretty, but she glares."

"Yes, Lona glares, and Wenny sulks."

"Poor Wenny. I remember that age. Everything feels like the end of the world." Kath made a mental note to be nice to her. "So, are we having omelets?"

"That would be brilliant." Dai looked relieved to change the subject. "I have bread, salad, and a Welsh apple pudding to go with them, if that would help. I can dash back to mine to get them. It's only up the hill. Even quicker if I cut through the woods behind you."

Kath waved him toward the doors that opened to the patio, and she couldn't help wondering if he was really thinking about it being a faster route, or if there was just less chance of being seen. Sneaking around was probably the surest way for them to get in trouble.

He turned back to her as he was about to shut the door behind him. "I don't generally invite myself over and make people cook for me. Are you sure you don't mind?"

"I was worried about leaving Muppet since it's the first

night here, so this is easier all the way around. I'd hate to have him howling for hours, annoying the neighbors."

"I wouldn't worry about that. It's HT beside you on the left, and Harri Rice on the other side is about the most easygoing man you'll ever meet. He's playing the bard, Iolo Goch. Then past him, the next cottage is occupied by Ifor Jones, my co-producer, when he's here. Alan and some of the other executive producers also use the second bedroom there if they're around. Then it's the Davies house after that. And going back in the other direction, there's Emris Morris next to HT. He plays de Ruthyn. Then Thomas Hughes, who plays Bolingbroke, is after that; and Caradoc Thomas, the second unit director; and—" He stopped himself. "Too much?"

"It will probably be easier to keep straight once I meet them," Kath said, smiling.

He smiled back. "Right. See you in a few minutes."

"How many eggs in your omelet?" Kath called after him. "Two, three, or four?"

"Three, if you can manage."

Then he was gone. Kath watched him stride up the hillside between the trees as if, even more than a film set, the woods were his natural element. The trees were thick enough that she lost track of him once he'd gone a dozen yards in or so. Sunset was an hour away yet, but she couldn't help wondering how much light filtered through the tree canopy. It might be easier to explain a shark attack than why he had broken an arm or a leg skulking through the woods.

HUNGER

"Hunger is the best seasoning."

KEN FOLLETT, THE PILLARS OF THE EARTH

DAI KICKED HIMSELF ALL THE way up the hill and down again. How had he not considered that having dinner at his cottage would make Kath uncomfortable? That was precisely the sort of thing that could get a bloke in trouble, and trouble was the last thing he needed.

He knocked on the patio door, and Kath turned and waved him in without leaving the stove where she had an omelet in the pan. The cottage smelled of toasted butter and onions lightly fried, and he realized how long it had been since he'd eaten.

"Alright if I come and fix the salad?" he asked.

"Please. Especially if the lettuce came from the farm shop. The produce there was beautiful. I even bought sheep's cheese and sheep yogurt."

He couldn't help laughing. "And yet you told me you'd only bought the basics."

"Basically, when in Wales?" She smiled, and he found himself smiling back.

"I feel as though I should be offended on behalf of every self-respecting Welshman," he said. "We do have cows, you know."

"Also a lot of sheep."

"And a lot of sheep," he said, grinning broadly.

He put together the salad and sliced some of the crusty bread he'd brought. She lifted the edges of the omelet with the spatula and let the runny eggs ooze underneath. The space in the kitchen was tight and difficult for them to maneuver in at once.

"Are you through with that butter?" he asked. "I can put it on the table."

"All yours," she said.

She flipped the omelet, one of those practiced flips that take talent or practice, neither of which Dai had ever possessed. He watched as Kath scattered chopped tomatoes and basil over the top and added a layer of the sheep's cheese that she had already grated. Then she folded the omelet in half and slid it onto a waiting plate.

Looking up, she met his eyes, and he felt like he needed to explain why he was staring. "I'm admiring your technique," he said, "and I also didn't want to throw you off by reaching for the butter."

She slid the package over to him, then turned the burner

off. Between them, they transferred the food to the table she had set while he was gone. Muppet was already lurking underneath it, and he whined as Dai dropped into a chair. Dai stooped to pat him, then poured the wine, a deep garnet red that smelled like peppercorns and chocolate.

The omelet was delicious, the wine was good, and both paired perfectly with the bread and salad. For the first time all day, Dai felt the tension roll off his shoulders. "This is perfect, Kath. Thank you."

She smiled—that smile. "It's very basic."

"You've no idea. I've seen gastropubs serve something similar and pass it off as a gourmet ploughman's lunch for £15."

Brows furrowed, Kath stopped eating to look at him. "You realize that I'm American, so literally everything in that sentence requires a translation?"

"Britain has pubs," he said, teasing. "You may have heard of those?"

"There are rumors. In fact, you'd be amazed at the number of Americans who are jealous of those. Men who want a place to drink beer with their friends every night, not to mention the wives who'd love to send their husbands away to watch sports somewhere else."

"Yes, but man—and woman—can't live on beer and sports alone. Enter the gastropub, offering craft beer and gourmet versions of Toad in the Hole and Bubble and Squeak at three times the acceptable price."

"Ignoring the toads and squeaks, what is a ploughman's lunch, exactly?"

"A do-it-yourself sandwich. A hunk of bread, a chunk of cheese, maybe a boiled or Scotch egg, and pickles or tomato chutney. If you're lucky, a bit of lettuce."

"Okay, so that explains the connection to a tomato omelet with bread and salad. But doesn't that miss the point? I'm imagining a medieval serving wench run off her feet with customers. Medieval man comes in demanding lunch, so she throws the stuff on a plate and tells him, 'There you go: bread, cheese, pickles—now fix it yourself and don't bother me again.'"

Dai could picture that exactly, and he laughed out loud. "That's it in one."

Their eyes met and then broke contact. They both concentrated on their food.

In a little while, she looked up again. "Do you mind if I ask about the audition? Why me?"

It was there again, that vulnerability he had found appealing. Only now, it was clearly Kath, not Margaret. Which was fine. Those small flashes that came through the cracks, blending the actor and the character, could be wonderful.

"That's a hard question. The obvious answer is that you were Margaret. You kept her contained within the space her class and gender allowed, but you let us see her reaching beyond the box in which society had placed her to steer. We could see her strength and her willingness to fight for what she believed, even if she knew the chances of winning were slim. Her intelligence shone, as well as her love for Glyndwr. And you and HT were great together. That combination of familiarity and tension, even a bit of resentment toward each other—it made her and Glyndwr real."

"Our 'tension' has graced the supermarket checkout counter a few too many times. I'm glad it was finally useful."

Dai watched her lips, waiting for her to smile, finding himself disappointed when she didn't.

He took a bite of his omelet and firmly changed the subject. "Is there anything about her you'd like to discuss? General approach? Any particular character traits?"

"I was going to ask you the same thing. Since there's not much historical information about her, I'm curious about your inspiration. What can you tell me that would help me understand what you're looking for?"

"I can't think of anything I want you to change from the auditions. In any case, Margaret will be your creation at least as much as mine."

"That's not really true, though. Is it?" Kath toyed with a piece of bread, breaking off small crumbs as if she wasn't aware that was what she was doing. "You're not only directing, but you also wrote the screenplay. I imagine it has to be hard having to watch an actor changing things from the way you wrote them. The interpretation at least, if not the dialogue."

"That's where the casting process comes in," Dai said. "It lets us all see the package—both the interpretation and the actor's skill."

Kath had a way of tipping her head down to shade her eyes when she got uncomfortable. That was another thing she'd given to the character.

She was silent a moment, as if searching for words. "This is awkward," she said eventually, "but I can't help asking. Margaret was a soldier's wife, and I know you were a soldier. How much of this script is personal to you and your wife? Am I likely to trample on things that have special meaning for you? I guess it would help if you could tell me what the boundaries are, what makes Margaret special to you."

"Ex-wife," Dai said.

"Excuse me?"

"Laura and I are divorced. Really, there's nothing I'd consider sacred or out of bounds. And if there's ever a point where you feel I'm being resistant or not listening to your ideas, I hope you'll call me on it."

The words were automatic, but even as he said them, he realized it wasn't fair to dismiss her concerns so easily. He sat back in his chair.

"You're right, of course. I based some of Margaret's experiences on Laura, but they're also very different people. Glyndwr was away a long time, off and on. Margaret had to manage the estates all that time, and when he came back, he expected—was expected—to take back the reins. That was obviously true in the fifteenth century, but even now, that's often the way it is for military families."

"But it felt like that was a big issue for Margaret, and Glyndwr never acknowledged it. Is it okay to let her show some resentment for that in the tension between them?"

"In the scenes before the one you did for the chemistry read, do you mean?"

Kath nodded. "Every scene that involves decisions about de Ruthyn, you have her opposing Glyndwr. But she doesn't push back on anything more ordinary—the finances, the children's education, decisions about running the estate. Was she picking her battles, or did you mean for that to be a signal about the importance of her relationship with de Ruthyn?"

"Relationship?"

She looked less certain as she answered. "Either an affair, or something she didn't want to happen. You hint at it when you ask if de Ruthyn touched her, but she denies it. It seems like keeping that secret is huge. Glyndwr never brings it up again, but obviously he has to suspect."

Dai had to stop and think. He'd helped dozens of actors through character breakdowns over the years, but she was right. Thinking about characters he'd written was different. Neither Nia nor HT had picked up on these sorts of questions. They hadn't recognized Dai's own life within the characters. Or if they had, they hadn't dared to mention it.

He hadn't intended to write in the difficult transition from military life to civilian life as clearly as Kath was reading it, but now that he looked for it, it was there.

"I was probably too much like Glyndwr," he admitted. "I started the first draft of the screenplay while I was still healing. There have been a lot of drafts since, but maybe things still bleed through. Coming home as a soldier between deployments, I always felt like I needed to do as much as possible to make up for the extra work Laura had to do while I was gone. But I didn't ask her whether that was making her life easier or harder."

Kath watched him with those eyes that seemed to see too much. "You figured it out at some point, though."

Dai set his fork down, and his hands felt useless. "When I was wounded in Afghanistan, I came home from the hospital barely able to walk. Laura had to nurse me through the physical and mental wounds and navigate the military bureaucracies to get me the care I needed. I didn't make it easy for her—I kept trying to do things myself, run things. She went out of her way to find things I could do, to give me back some dignity. Honestly, if she hadn't let me feel like I was pulling my weight, I don't think I would have made it. Maybe Margaret is giving Glyndwr what she thinks he can handle."

Kath's eyes shone with tears when he looked up at her, and he realized he'd probably revealed too much. Even now, it was hard to think how close he had come to putting a bullet in his brain. Outside of therapy, he'd never admitted that to anyone, or discussed the role Laura'd had in bringing him back from the brink.

"I'm not sure Margaret was as kind as Laura," Kath said gently.

"I think she was. In fact, I always imagined their relationship starting with Margaret's kindness."

She studied him, but then she accepted the change of subject. "Her father was a judge, wasn't he? And Glyndwr apprenticed with him."

"I had a sort of Dickensian impression of their origin story while I was writing. Glyndwr hunched over his law books in a dark corner, and Margaret bringing him lunch—"

Kath smiled at him. "A ploughman's, obviously."

"Obviously." Dai smiled back at her. "And I imagined her seeing that Glyndwr was lonely and stopping to discuss points of law with him. English versus Welsh law, maybe, with Margaret pointing out how the Welsh laws had been more humane and fair. Especially when it came to women."

"And Margaret would have been clever enough to know that men hate to be beaten. She'd have made her point and let Glyndwr think it through on his own." She shifted forward to pick up her wineglass, and the light above the table pooled on her hair, her cheeks.

Her skin reminded Dai of the texture of the orchids he'd given Laura when the divorce had been finalized. The memory surprised him, and he rummaged inside, searching for a reason why it had surfaced. Why that specific orchid?

"Can I ask you something else?"

"Of course," he said.

"I can't see Margaret having an affair with de Ruthyn. She loves Glyndwr too much, and Glyndwr isn't the kind of man who would blame her for anything that wasn't her fault. So does she keep it secret to protect him or to protect herself?"

"Protect herself in what sense?"

"I can't see her wanting anyone—especially Glyndwr—see her as weak or afraid."

"She has to know Glyndwr wouldn't think less of her."

"But she would think less of herself, wouldn't she? Until that moment, she never suffered the way most of the Welsh have under English occupation. Her birth and position protected her, and she grew up believing that she has a measure of control in her life. De Ruthyn strips that away and shows her that security and control are illusions. Everyone and everything she loves is vulnerable. Including Glyndwr, and she's afraid that if she tells him what de Ruthyn has done, Glyndwr will do something rash and get himself killed."

"Men aren't always rational," Dai said.

Their eyes met as she looked up, and he found himself unable to look away. She didn't either, and he felt his pulse quicken dangerously.

A faint wash of pink stained Kath's cheeks. She played with the stem of her wineglass, rubbing it between her thumb and forefinger, watching the liquid moving. He could almost see her thinking, the wheels turning. Her lips tightened, and it occurred to him she didn't smile enough, that there was something essentially sad about her.

With a smile like hers, she should have smiled all the time. He wanted to make her smile.

Dai leaned back in his chair and shook his head to clear it. "I like where you're going with this. And you're right. Margaret sees how what de Ruthyn is doing to her family—what Bolingbroke allows him to do—has been happening all over Wales."

"She helps Glyndwr connect to that."

"War is always personal. It doesn't matter what the politicians say," Dai said, unable to keep the bitterness from his voice. The first time the army had sent him to Afghanistan, he had been naïve and idealistic enough to believe the public reason for being there. But in the trenches and on the rooftops, it came down to fighting for the people beside him.

"Ready for dessert?" Rising abruptly, Dai gathered up the plates and cutlery.

He'd forgotten that Muppet was under the table until the dog growled in protest. The tags on Muppet's collar jingled as he emerged and shook himself, and he positioned himself uncertainly between Dai and Kath.

She reached down to reassure him. "It's fine, Mups. You're good. Do you want a cookie?"

Muppet answered with a commanding bark, and Kath crossed to the kitchen, retrieved a dog treat from a bag on the counter, and tossed it to him. Dai carried the dishes to the sink and removed the beeswax wrapper from the pudding he had left out on the counter. Kath retrieved two parfait glasses from the cabinets and spooned out individual servings.

"Would you like some coffee?" she asked. "Or maybe tea?"

"Nothing for me, thanks."

Dai took the glasses to the table, and they both sat down again and concentrated on eating. The table seemed smaller than it had before. Kath held the stem of the parfait glass, and her hand was close enough that Dai could have reached out and touched it.

She had been right about *The Last Prince* being personal. Every part of it was tangled up in things that mattered deeply to him. And watching Kath climb inside Margaret's skin was dangerously seductive.

He pushed back from the table and stood up to put more

space between them. He needed to stay professional. "I'm sorry," he said. "Thinking about coffee has made me realize how tired I am, and I have to start early again tomorrow. This might be a good place for us to stop."

Kath came around to walk him to the door, looking confused. "Do you want to pick this up again tomorrow night?"

"It's up to you. Do you need more time before you get on set?"

Her shoulders and spine had stiffened, but the glow from the light showed that vulnerability in her eyes again. "It's hectic during read-throughs and rehearsals when everyone is there, and I still have questions. I'm sorry. I know you're busy."

Dai felt like a sod for being abrupt with her. They'd thrown her into the role too fast, and most actors would have demanded more time. Turning to apologize, he found Muppet under his feet again, and he quick-stepped to avoid him. Kath moved in the same direction. They collided, and Dai reached out to steady her.

Her eyes were like stained glass, dark until the light shone through them. Seen this close, there were shards of green and gold and violet amid the brown. He wanted to trace her cheekbones and learn the planes and angles of her face, to feel them like the camera saw them. He wanted to push her hair back and find out if it felt like spun silk, the way it looked.

They both stepped back.

She stooped to pick up Muppet and stood with him as a barrier between them. She didn't look at Dai. "Thank you for taking the time to let me talk through this."

"I'll phone you about another session," he said. "And Kath, you can have as much time as you need. I promise."

LIGHTS

"A little magic can take you a long way."

ROALD DAHL, JAMES AND THE GIANT PEACH

F OR THE SECOND NIGHT IN a row, Kath barely slept. She lay in bed awake, listening to Muppet snoring beside her and thinking about not sleeping. Thinking about Margaret and the conversation with Dai and wishing she wasn't thinking about Dai at all. She couldn't afford to think about him.

Talking to him about Margaret had made her feel, at least momentarily, better than she'd felt after Joel's phone call. He'd made her feel more confident about Margaret, about belonging in the role. But now that she was alone again, her brain replayed Joel's warnings on repeat, and reminded her of all the ways she could fail.

The clock read 2:42 a.m. when she pulled the chain to switch the bedside lamp back on. Sitting propped up against the pillows, she thumbed through the script and counted up the number of scenes in which Margaret appeared. Eighty-seven.

Eighty-seven scenes.

And if she screwed up, it wasn't only her career on the line. The director usually took the blame for box office failures. She could torpedo Dai's career and waste all the years he had put into the project. Then there were the producers and investors taking a risk on her, and the actors and above-the-line crew who counted on box office percentages. Not to mention the rest of the cast and crew, effects people, supporting staff... They all needed the film to be successful.

Nope, no pressure there at all.

And leave it to her to develop a crush on Dai. Not that she could blame herself. He was kind, smart, creative, emotionally aware, and dangerously, undeniably yummy—as Olivia had pointed out. Kath hadn't met a decent guy in... she couldn't even remember how long. And what was that thing again? Oh, yeah. Sex. She would probably need an instruction manual and a crash helmet if she ever had an opportunity for sex again. So yes, there was a perfectly rational reason she had made an idiot of herself in that awkward moment before Dai left. Perfectly rational and absolutely out of the question.

She had to work with him. Work *for* him.

In full view of the cast, the crew, and anyone else, including any idiot with a camera and a social media account.

For months.

A crush? *Such* a bad idea.

She set the script back on the night table and was about to

close her eyes when she noticed lights moving on the hillside behind the cottage. They weren't flashlights, more like glowing orbs of golden-green gliding in graceful, mesmerizing unison along a clockwise circle a few feet above the ground. There were nine of them, the spacing between them never changing, with no hint of a bob or wobble that suggested human motion. That graceful and effortless glide pulled Kath out of her bed and toward the window. She stopped when her toe stubbed against the half wall before she realized it was there.

She swore, and the lights winked out. All of them without so much as a fraction of a second in delay. They were there, then not. And an instant after that, they winked on again, but farther to the left behind HT's cottage.

Kath raced down the steps to let herself out the back door. Small twigs and pebbles on the flagstones dug into her feet, and her satin pajamas soaked in the nighttime chill.

She moved toward the lights, shivering. Fascinated. A puddle splashed cold water across her toes, and she stopped again. But the lights changed course and descended toward her, floating diagonally through the woods, slowly at first, then faster but with the same eerie glide above the earth.

Her heart thundered, and her chest tightened. She told herself it had to be a teenage prank. Candles in jars strung up on wires, a video and projector. Maybe Wenny, or the Davies girl out with her friends and having a little fun.

The lights increased their speed. And still she was walking toward them. It stopped feeling like a prank, and goosebumps climbed up the back of her neck.

She stopped. Then whipping around, her hair fanning out around her, she darted back inside and slammed the door behind her.

Safely behind the glass, she looked for the lights again, but they were gone. The woods were dark.

Feeling ridiculous and more than a little ashamed, she slid the door back open and stepped out to the edge of the flagstones. Nothing happened. She waited five or six minutes, listening, searching the darkness. Then she retreated back inside, shivering and more than a little shaken. Desperate to get warm again, she slipped a pair of socks on her dirty feet to protect the sheets and climbed back into bed beside Muppet, who was still blissfully sound asleep and snoring. Kath threw him an envious look, then switched the light off and rolled to her side to watch the window in case the lights came back. Eventually, she must have drifted off.

The phone ringing on the nightstand jerked her from a restless dream. Lifting her head off the pillow, she checked the bedside clock, which read 4:27 a.m. She made a mental bet with herself and won when she saw the Caller ID.

She answered, "Hi, Mom."

"I wanted to tell you before you heard it from your father." Ailsa's voice sounded clipped and vibrated with outrage. "He's going to Scotland."

Kath sat up and practically knocked the lamp over as she reached to turn it on. "Did you say Scotland?"

"Yes, that's what I said. He booked a ticket, packed a suitcase, and he's going."

"Well, why shouldn't he go see Anna and Connal? You made one flying visit for their wedding, and you were there for two days when the baby was born. It makes sense he wants to spend more time."

"You're not listening to me. He's staying with Anna, but it's my sister he wants to see. Apparently, he and Elspeth have been video chatting every day, and he says he's getting too old to take things slowly to spare my feelings. What kind of thing is that to tell your wife?"

"Ex-wife, if you'd be reasonable and sign the papers."

"Why should I make it easier for him?"

"Because it's the right thing to do?"

"This is not what I need right now. I thought you, at least, would understand. After all, you did the same thing to Anna, and I've supported you all these years."

"The same thing?" Kath repeated, stunned.

Tears burned her eyes, and she felt gut-punched. Her lungs squeezed, and her throat tightened at the unfairness of it. Elspeth had never married, but she had tried to get past what Ailsa had done. Despite being happily married, Anna still hated Kath—and it hadn't all been Kath's fault. Some of it, a lot of it, was. But if it hadn't been for the accident, it might have all blown over.

It wasn't the same thing at all.

And even though, ridiculously, talking back to her mother still terrified her, she couldn't let it go. "I think you need to remember what really happened that night," she said. "Because you're the one who made a snap decision and told us we had to leave. You're the one who said we couldn't tell anyone."

"I was protecting the family from scandal. Just as I've always done."

"You got pregnant on purpose and made Dad marry you."

"So now even you are taking Elspeth's side? She only met John because I brought him home. You girls all think she's so wonderful and charming with her fairy tales about one true love and destiny. She has everyone saying, oh, poor Elspeth, how awful for her. Not one of you has any sympathy for me."

"Since when do you want sympathy? You've always said it's just pity wrapped in pretty paper."

"There's a difference," Ailsa said in an icy tone, "between feeling sorry for someone with genuine problems and pitying someone who's looking for an excuse to fail. What has gotten into you, Katharine? This is not attractive."

Kath let her head fall back to the pillow and closed her eyes. "I'm tired, and it's 4:30 in the morning. Look, Dad asked you for a divorce ages ago. He's moved out. It's not your business who he wants to be with anymore. He and Elspeth fell in love, and they gave each other up for the baby. Even after you miscarried, Dad stayed with you, trying to do the right thing. He may not be in love with you, but he's proven that he cares for you—loves you—year after year after year. Now he's finally trying to move forward, and you need to let him go."

"He's leaving me without a shred of dignity—"

"Mom, seriously? What happened to 'No one can take your dignity unless you give it away'?"

"Why are you regurgitating greeting cards?"

"That was another vintage Ailsa Cameron quote. You're the one who taught all three of us that no one likes a display of weakness."

"So now you're minimizing how I feel?"

"I'm not minimizing." Kath rubbed her temple, trying to get rid of the throbbing ache. "I hate that you and Dad are going through this, but in the long run, won't it be better if he is happy? And you can find a new beginning, too."

"Tell me about all the wonderful men you've met since your divorce. It's not that easy."

Kath's mind jumped straight to Dai. Which was ridiculous. She had no business thinking of him like that. "I have to hang up now," she said. "It's early, and I'm jet-lagged, and I have to get some sleep."

"What do you mean, you're jet-lagged? Where are you?"

Kath sighed, but there wasn't any point trying to keep it secret. "I'm in Wales until November, working on a project. It's a last-minute thing, and I had to leave right away. I didn't have a chance to tell you."

"Did you say Wales? In Britain?" Ailsa asked. "You're not talking about *The Last Prince,* are you? With HT?"

"Yes, Nia Evans dropped out and—"

"Please. I don't live under a rock. So you're replacing Nia in the film? Well, finally, that's some good news. You know how devastated we all were when Meg quit her job at the network. I'm glad at least one of you girls is still making use of your talent."

For a brief second on hearing the words 'good news,' a Pavlovian rush of pleasure rippled through Kath, only to disappear as her mother mentioned Margaret. And how pathetic was it that a small part of Kath was still hoping for her mother's approval? But she didn't want it at her sister's expense.

"Meg and Anna are both doing something they love," she said evenly, "and they are happy. It sounds like Dad is moving toward happiness, too. Maybe it's time we all let go of our grievances. I'll try to call you later in the week, okay? I really have to go."

"Of course. Just remember that it's heartbreaking when no one in your own family has time for you. I hope you never have to experience that," Ailsa said, and she hung up.

Kath didn't even try sleeping after that. Sleep would have been impossible.

SUNRISE

*"There's a sunrise and a sunset every single day,
and they're absolutely free. Don't miss so many of them."*

JO WALTON

K ATH DRESSED IN LEGGINGS AND running shoes, set a
playlist of Bear McCreary songs on her phone, and
popped her earbuds in. The tar dark sky was bleaching into
blue, but the moon shone on the road, providing light to run
by. She walked west in the direction she had come from the
day before until her pulse picked up. Then she eased into a
run.

She needed to turn her brain off. These kinds of
conversations with her mother weren't really anything new.
What was different was the way she had reacted. The accusation
that what she had done to Anna was the same as what Ailsa had
done to Elspeth was too unfair to go unanswered. Or maybe she
had finally been tired enough to let the truth slip out. Either way,

the conversation had opened a cesspool of thoughts she'd always kept safely contained.

It didn't matter that the circumstances of what she and her mother had done were different, or even that Anna and HT wouldn't—couldn't—have been happy together. To Anna, the betrayal must have felt the same. Hurting her sister had always been one of the many regrets Kath had about that night. She was glad that Anna had finally found happiness with Connal, but that didn't change the truth. She had been selfish and immature, and she had caused Anna years of pain.

She didn't know how to atone for it. All these years later, she and Anna still hadn't managed to discuss it like grown women instead of brokenhearted girls. That conversation grew more impossible with every year that passed. Kath wondered if that was how it had been for Elspeth and her mother.

The road was smooth and level as she ran, curving between the river and the low, green foothills. Moonlight's last hurrah turned the river the color of mercury, and the sky blanched from indigo to dark navy and then to lapis. She drank in the stillness, letting her legs stretch into longer strides until she felt her shoulders slough off the tension she'd been holding in.

Then something moved behind her on the right. Startled, she stumbled, and her heart revved up. But then she saw it was Dai, and he passed her and ran backward, facing her. He was smiling, saying something. She couldn't hear over the music, and she tapped an earbud to turn it off.

"I didn't mean to startle you," he said. "I remember you

mentioned you were a runner, but I wasn't expecting to see you out so early."

"It was a spur-of-the-moment decision," she said. "Good morning."

He dropped back beside her. "Would you rather run alone? If not, I usually do a five-mile out with a hill and the sunrise in between. We still have time to catch it."

Kath's heart thudded for a different reason. "Sure."

They ran in silence, and the awkward tension from the night before had eased into a warm awareness. It was more comfortable, but even now Kath was doing too much thinking. About Dai, mostly, and they were thoughts she shouldn't be having.

She should have told him she couldn't run with him. She wasn't interested in the sunrise.

She lengthened her stride again, and he matched her. Part of her wanted to keep increasing her speed, to prove herself or test herself—she wasn't sure which. But if there was a hill, she needed to save her strength.

He tapped her arm and gestured toward a trail that cut to the left, and he let her make the turn first so she could set the pace. The trail climbed steeply past stone-walled paddocks of sheep with their coats clean and short from recent shearing.

Kath's legs and lungs felt good. She loved the concentration it took to keep her footing on the uneven ground. She pushed harder, faster. Her heart pounded, and Dai's footsteps matched hers.

The trail grew narrower, worn deep with repeated use. She

wondered how long human feet had been taking this same route. How many thousands of years had people used these same pastures? How long had it been since someone cleared the rocks from them to make the first stone walls?

She reached the smooth breast atop the hill and stopped to wait for Dai. He was only steps behind her.

Placing his hands on his knees, he took deep breaths. His shoulders were wide, and the damp T-shirt clung to every muscle and the curve of his back. Hands on her hips, Kath walked away in a wide circle, letting her breath slow gradually. Dawn had lightened the sky to a faded cobalt blue, and the hills and valley were watercolor smudges of shadowed greens.

"It's very different from LA, isn't it?" Dai asked. "Do you like it?"

"Wales? It's beautiful. But it's a haunting kind of beauty. A land of mists and shadows." She laughed at her own flight of fancy. "Clearly I've been reading too much, but I think I would have felt the sadness even if I didn't know some of the history."

Dai watched her as if he was trying to read something beneath the surface of her eyes. He didn't say anything, and after a few seconds, he walked toward the eastern edge of the summit and sat down, his legs bent in front of him and his arms wrapped loosely around them.

He looked completely at ease, as if he never questioned himself. Kath thought back to the articles she had read where interviewers asked about his injuries and his struggle with PTSD. In its own way, PTSD was a kind of haunting, wrestling with ghosts and demons from the past. None of that was visible on his face, and if she hadn't known some of his history, she wouldn't have guessed at it. She would have envied his sense of peace.

Sitting down beside him, she stole a glance at his profile. His face was interesting, not the typical handsome that was common in Hollywood. His features had strong, sharp angles that looked like someone had instructed a sculptor to carve a warrior.

As if he felt her watching him, he turned. "You're up early considering the jet lag."

"Not by choice. I tried to sleep, but there were odd lights in the woods in the early morning. It must have been kids playing pranks."

"Or the *Tylwyth Teg*," he said with a smile. "The fair folk. My *nain* used to tell stories about the *Gwyllion*, the female fairies of the mountains who lure unwary travelers away from safety or punish those who aren't virtuous. Then there are the *Ellyllon* who inhabit the groves and hollows. Be careful they don't knock on your door and ask to sit by the fire."

Kath shivered again, remembering the hypnotic, eerie quality of them. "When you hear hoofbeats," she said, "think horses, not zebras. I'd rather believe in teenagers."

"But you were worried?"

"No, sorry. I mean, I didn't lie awake because of that. My mother called at four thirty, which in her defense would only have been eleven thirty in Cincinnati. I hadn't told her I was leaving the country."

"I suppose I should be grateful my mam's sound asleep by nine these days. Then again, she's up at five every day, and she's probably a good decade older than yours."

"Do you have a big family? Brothers? Sisters?" Kath put her cheek on her knee and turned to look at him.

"I'm an only, but my mam was thirty before I came along. They married late. They're still living down the valley in Conwy where I grew up, and she can't understand why I can't spend every evening with them since I'm finally close to home."

Kath smiled at that. "You spend most of your time in LA and London, don't you? Do you miss living here?"

"Yes and no. I love Wales, especially *Eryri*—Snowdonia— and the north. That will always be home in a way no other place can be, but I know how lucky I am to be making films. I had hoped to have more time to spend with my parents while I was here... What with Nia leaving, I've barely seen them."

"It's good they still have each other, though."

"Yours are divorced, then?"

"In the process of." Kath looked down across the valley where the headlights of a car were slowly making their way toward Obaith Hall. "My mother hasn't signed the papers yet. I think she's still hoping my father will change his mind."

"That must be hard. Do you have siblings?"

"Two sisters."

"Does that make it harder for you all to stay connected?"

Kath started to give a polite answer and shrug it off. But she was tired of pretending. Tired of lying and calling that polite. Tired of everything her mother had taught her about minimizing her feelings.

"We haven't been connected in a long time. My family is great at ignoring things. If I'm honest, my father has done nothing more than go through the motions of being married for as long as I can remember, and I've only seen my sisters twice in almost fifteen years. That's awful, isn't it?"

"Do you regret that?"

The question surprised her. "Yes. I didn't realize how much until recently."

"Can you do anything to change it?"

"Not about their marriage. My father's gone to stay with my oldest sister in Scotland, and it's finally sinking in for my mother that he's gone. It's strange how people get stuck, knowing they're unhappy without knowing how to change that. HT and I were that way, too."

"Are you over him?"

Kath considered before answering. "Are you asking if we're going to be able to work together without problems? Definitely. We had some last things to resolve, but we talked before the chemistry test. I've finally realized that I spent years holding on to the idea of loving HT instead of *being* in love with him. Does that make any sense? Can you fall in love in self-defense?"

"The mind is good at protecting us from ourselves. That includes hiding things we're not ready to face." He watched her, his gray eyes alive with intelligence and compassion.

That combination was probably what made him good as a director.

"I'm glad it's not just me," she said.

He smiled and shook his head. "How did you and HT meet?"

Kath watched an ant crawling up the slope of her running shoe. Given its relative size, the shoe must have seemed like a mountain.

"He and I did a community theatre production of *As You Like It* together. It was his first play, and I was Rosalind to his Orlando. But he was engaged to my sister Anna, and I was seventeen and self-absorbed," she admitted. "On closing night, I was also drunk and too stupid to see disaster coming."

Dai's expression showed no trace of judgment. "What happened?"

"We went to a party, and it went horribly wrong." She looked off at the clouds that were becoming visible, gunmetal gray against the lightening sky.

"That still bothers you, obviously," he said.

"Instead of facing the people we hurt, we ran away to Hollywood and hoped that becoming famous would magically make us better people. Clearly, that didn't work. I mean, at least not for me."

"Are you saying that you're not famous—yet—or that you aren't a better person?" Dai asked, smiling at her gently. Teasing her.

As if what she'd told him wasn't horrible. He was an actor, though. He could pull that off.

It should have terrified her that she had said so much. It was more than she'd ever admitted to anyone. And there was the non-disclosure agreement, now.

"Please don't mention any of this to HT," she said, half panicking. "He'd hate it if he found out that I had told you. And he's not a bad guy—I'm sure you know that. But as a couple, we never stood a chance. I keep hoping Nia will be okay, not only for her own sake but also because HT deserves to be happy with someone."

The sun cast its first warmth across the sky, separating clouds from the gray-blue dawn and rimming them soft pink above and tangerine below. Kath and Dai turned simultaneously to watch. Kath's temperature had dropped, and she pulled the sleeves of her running jacket down over her hands.

"Are you cold?" Dai asked.

"Not really. So, do you come here often?"

They both laughed at that, and then he said, "Whenever I can. It still takes effort to quiet my mind. Running helps. And sitting up here, the sunrise reminds me that I can't control everything, that I have to let things go." He paused a little self-consciously, as if aware of how much he, too, had revealed. "What about you? Do you run every morning?"

"I don't know yet."

"That's a diplomatic answer."

They were smiling at each other, and she looked away.

"Diplomacy isn't something I'm accused of very often," she said.

The tangerine clouds grew brighter, and gold layers appeared between them. Kath and Dai watched in silence as the sun broke the horizon and climbed until the pink had faded from the sky and left it a clean, dusky blue.

A fresh slate to begin the day.

It was extraordinary, all of this. Being there in that moment, Kath felt like she had won the lottery, and it made her even more determined not to let it all slip through her fingers.

But she also made herself a promise. As Dai had pointed out, watching the elements and the miracle of the planet revolving around the sun was a reminder that human beings weren't meant to control everything. Compared to the immensity of the universe, there was so little that Kath could control. She needed to let go. To worry less about the past and what came next and focus on whatever the day would bring, do her best to live in every moment.

Dai pushed to his feet and held his hand out for her. His palm was warm and rough against her skin, alive with an energy that opened her veins and made her blood course faster. His touch lingered even after he pulled away.

"Ready to run back?" he asked.

There was no sign he'd felt any of that.

Kath folded her fingers into her palm, trying to keep his warmth a little while longer. "I'll race you," she said, and she bolted toward the track that led downhill before he answered. Keeping her footing required all her concentration, so she couldn't think about what it felt like when he touched her, or wonder whether she'd made a horrible mistake saying the things she'd said. There was only the sensation of being slightly out of control, hurtling full speed toward something new and slightly dangerous that lay beyond the horizon.

GENERATIONS

"Sometimes the shortest journeys take longest, don't they?"

SARAH WATERS, THE PAYING GUESTS

K ATH FELT CAFFEINE-OVERDOSE AWAKE as she let herself back into her cottage. Muppet greeted her with a grumbling admonition for having left him, but at least he hadn't torn apart his blanket or the sofa. Kath considered that a win. She sat on the floor and rubbed behind his ears, telling him he was a good boy until he'd had enough. He sniffed his way to the patio door and gave a commanding, "Woof."

She put coffee on to brew before she took him out, and she studied the wooded hillside while waiting for him on the patio. Determined to prove to herself there had been a perfectly logical explanation for the lights, she let Muppet back into the cottage and went to explore the woods. Dog-roses bloomed an ethereal pink at the edge of the trees, along with elder brush and something with yellow blooms clinging among spiky leaves. The dark scent of soil and decaying leaves mingled with the sweeter flowers and the tang of the pines that grew among the oaks and beech. Deeper in, the undergrowth grew sparser.

Apart from animal tracks, she found only what she presumed were Dai's footprints coming and going. There was no sign of wires in the branches of the trees, no disturbance of the bark or leaves, and a complete absence of beer bottles, vape pens, and other teenage paraphernalia. For a prank, if it had been a prank, it had been well executed and someone had gone to a lot of trouble.

The hillside grew steeper, and then about a hundred yards up the hill, she emerged from the trees onto a narrow road. A row of small, neat houses lined up on the opposite side. She studied them, then dismissed the idea that the lights might have come from inside one of those. Maybe there had been a vehicle on the road that accounted for the way the lights had moved. But that made no sense, either.

No wiser, and even more curious, she walked about twenty feet down the road, then descended through the woods behind HT's cottage. Nothing had been disturbed there, either. An owl watched her with large round eyes from high up in a pine tree, and something gray and white and ferret-like weaseled away into the brush.

Reluctant to pop up behind HT's cottage and have him spot her through the window, she cut back through the woods until she was behind her own door again. Then she scrabbled through the last few feet of brush and trees, and went home to shower and eat a quick breakfast of coffee and the surprisingly delicious sheep's milk yogurt before going back to the sofa to check her email, where she found a message from Joel with the contract ready for her review and signature.

Twenty minutes later, as she was about to send the contract back, someone knocked on the cottage door. She had a moment of panic at the thought of Dai seeing her when she hadn't even bothered to put on a bra under her thin sweater and her hair was still damp from the shower. But Dai had already seen her without makeup and her hair damp from sweat. Anyway, it shouldn't have mattered what she looked like. He was the director—nothing more.

She pulled the door open, and it wasn't Dai standing there. Instead, an older woman stood on the stoop holding an enormous gift basket that barely fit into her arms. She was slight, no more than five feet tall, and her dark hair had a thick gray streak at the front, which she wore pulled tightly back.

"Good morning," she said, sounding a bit out of breath. "Dai asked me particularly to make sure this basket was here waiting for you when you arrived. I've only just found that it wasn't, and I'm terribly sorry."

She looked so worried that Kath smiled broadly to reassure her. "You must be Glenys. It's nice to meet you, and your granddaughter mentioned you'd been called away. Would you like to come in? And here, let me take that for you."

Glenys surged past her instead of letting her take the basket. "It's a bit awkward. Probably easier if I just set it in the kitchen for you." She stepped farther into the room, then noticed Muppet making his way toward the door. "Oh, he's lovely. Is he a Westie or something else? Jemma called to ask if we had rules against dogs a few days back. That must have been for you. I'll have to let the cleaners know to expect him."

Kath hadn't realized there was a service, although she supposed she should have thought of it when she saw the Davies girl coming out of one of the cottages.

"He'll usually be on the set with me when I'm working," she said, "but can you ask the cleaners not to come in if he's here by himself? It's not that he's unfriendly, but he's blind, so it's better not to upset him. I won't need cleaning very often anyway."

"Of course. Poor little man." Glenys smiled at Muppet, and wrinkles fanned out around her eyes.

She set the gift basket on the counter above the barstools, where it took up most of the space. It seemed to have most of the staples Kath could possibly have wanted—most of which she had already bought. But there were a few luxuries as well: homemade pasta, fresh herbs, apples, plums, vegetables, and more. There were also two bottles of wine, assorted pastries, a small cake, bath potions, several candles, and the notebook Dai had mentioned.

"This is so kind of you," Kath said. "Thank you for taking so much trouble with it."

"It's Dai's idea. He wanted you to feel welcome, and it gave me a chance to pick out and share my favorite things from the shops. No need to worry if anything's gone off, either. We restocked it all fresh this morning." She let out a sigh. "I am sorry about the delay. I can't make sense of teenagers these days. Too busy brooding to remember anything useful."

"I wondered if Wenny's arm was hurting when I picked up the key," Kath said gently. "She seemed upset."

"Oh, I'd never have asked her to bring it in herself. She was supposed to take the key to the shop when it opened so that they could leave it here for you, but she claims you arrived sooner than she'd expected and she assumed you would let them in. Never once thought to ask herself how they would know you'd arrived if she hadn't told them. But that's teenagers for you, isn't it?" Glenys put her hands on her cheeks, and she shook her head, clearly overwhelmed. "Sorry. Here I am going on about this when it's the last thing you need to be hearing about."

"It's only natural you'd be worried about her," Kath said, searching for a way to broach the subject of the lights diplomatically and ask whether the Davies girl and her friends might have been playing pranks. "I saw another girl about Wenny's age yesterday. It must be hard when it's only the two of them. Teenage friendships can be like kegs of gunpowder."

"You'd think it would be good for them to have each other. And they did used to be friends when they were younger. They're chalk and cheese now, and it's a shame because Lona Davies is a lovely girl. Not that my Wenny isn't," Glenys added hastily. "But I suspect there's a reason grandparents aren't meant to raise their grandchildren, isn't there? Too much difference in age, and it makes it impossible for us to understand each other."

"Can I get you a cup of coffee or tea?" Kath asked. "Or are you in a hurry?"

Glenys checked her watch, a Rolex even more expensive than the one HT had given Kath for Christmas a few years back. "I have a few minutes before I need to head down to the hall if it's no trouble."

She didn't wear a wedding ring, and she didn't seem like the type of woman who would spend money on herself. Kath wondered if the Rolex had been a gift and who it had been from. Maybe when you worked for an aristocrat with a title, that was the customary Christmas or anniversary gift. Then she felt terrible about making assumptions.

Kath poured coffee into another cup and handed it to Glenys, then took the milk out of the refrigerator and set it on the counter beside her. "I hope you don't mind my asking, but I was wondering about teenagers last night, actually. I saw some odd lights in the woods."

"What time was this?"

"Almost three in the morning."

"It can't have been Lona or her friends at that time of night. Fireflies or fairies more likely, or someone up on the road above you," Glenys said, smiling as she added a splash of milk to her cup.

As easily as Glenys had dismissed it, Kath didn't want to press the point. "Dai mentioned you're the hospitality manager here?" she asked to change the subject. "Is that for the rentals in the village here?"

"For the entire estate, which includes about fifty square

miles. There's a map and a bit of local history in the notebook there, if you're interested." She gestured toward the basket. "Lord Linton restored forty-two units here in Ty Newydd when he inherited, and another thirty or so cottages and converted farmhouses elsewhere. My team also runs the garden tours, weddings, and events for Obaith Hall, as well as the shops here, and the gift shop and restaurants around Obaith Hall."

"That sounds like a lot to do with a teenager in the house. I know I was a handful at Wenny's age." Kath also remembered how lonely it could be, and she thought of how fiercely Wenny had said she was fine even though she clearly wasn't. "Actually, I wonder if Wenny might be willing to help me. I need to pick up some extra clothes, and since it means leaving Muppet alone, I don't have time to hunt through the small boutiques in Caernarfon. I'd love to have someone local show me where to go."

"Wenny's only fifteen, so she can't drive for two more years, but if you have a driver, I'm sure she'd properly love that. Even if she pretends it's nothing out of the ordinary. I'll ask her and have her ring you, but I'll warn you, she can be a right little madam. You might regret it."

Kath gave Glenys the number, but an hour and a half later, she remembered the older woman's warning as Wenny stared sullenly out the window on the drive to the shopping center.

Since Wenny was quiet, Kath chatted with Mari, the driver, for a while, hoping it would give Wenny time to get more comfortable so they could have a conversation. "How did you break your arm?" she asked a while later. "Was it only recently?"

Wenny managed to look even more sullen and long-suffering. "I fell, didn't I?"

"I don't know," Kath said gently. "That's why I was hoping you would tell me."

Wenny did the invisible eye roll thing again, conveying her contempt.

"It's an expression," Mari said, flashing Kath a sympathetic look in the rearview mirror. "In Welsh, we often put questions at the end. That's a habit that carries over into how we speak English."

She dropped Kath and Wenny outside the shopping center and then pulled into a nearby parking space to wait. Inside, Wenny lagged behind and gave monosyllabic answers to anything Kath said while they went from store to store. Kath tried not to regret bringing her, and she remembered how tempting it was to appear "too cool" whenever she felt uncomfortable.

She wasn't picky about the clothes she needed, so it didn't take long to buy a handful of extra sweaters, two pairs of jeans, dressier slacks, riding boots with flat heels, and black ankle boots with a two-inch heel that was wide enough to be stable regardless of the terrain. She also picked up extra leggings and some T-shirts.

"So what do you think?" she asked Wenny as they walked through the shopping center on their way back to the car. "Have we earned a snack after all of that?"

Wenny nodded, staring at a short skirt in the window of a

shop. She had looked at the same skirt on the way to the department store as well. "Is that something you would wear?" Kath asked, stopping in front of it. "Because I'd like to give you something as a thank-you for coming out here with me."

Wenny's face lit up, but shuttered almost immediately. "I don't need it."

"Why not?" Kath asked. "If you like it, I'd be happy to buy it for you."

Wenny spun around to face her. "Why are you trying to be nice?"

Kath hesitated, then remembered that being lied to was the thing she'd hated most when she was Wenny's age. Teenagers could sense that at a hundred paces.

"I guess it's because I remember what it was like when people were always telling me not to sit around moping, but then criticized anything I wanted to go out and do. Being sixteen felt like I was constantly running toward a wall and slamming into it."

For the first time, Wenny actually looked at her. "Nain means well. She's only busy, and there's no one around where we live except Lona, who's horrible."

"What kind of horrible?" Kath asked.

Wenny shrugged. "It doesn't matter."

"Aren't there any other kids in the villages nearby?"

Wenny's cheeks flushed. "No one who isn't boring."

Kath hoped she was wrong, but that sounded like code for 'no one who wants to hang out with me.' "What about school?" she asked. "Anyone there worth the time? Especially with the cast and crew staying in the village, it must be fun to see HT and Dai Rhys and some of the other actors, right? I bet people like coming to Ty Newydd hoping to catch sight of them."

Wenny turned back to the shop window, her face averted, and her shoulders hitched with a silent sob.

"Oh hey, I'm sorry." Kath felt awful. "I didn't mean to upset you. Do you want to talk about it? Sometimes it's easier talking to a stranger."

"I'm fine." Wenny sniffed and started walking toward the car again.

"What about the skirt?" Kath asked.

"Nowhere to wear it, anyway. So what's the point?" Wenny rushed back to the car with her shoulders hunched and her head staring at the pavement, looking even more miserable than before.

Kath had to admit to being out of her depth. When had she gotten too old to communicate with a teenager? Half the time, she still felt like one herself, faking her way through life. She ran to catch up and pushed her hip against the door to buy herself some extra seconds. "Wenny, I meant what I said. If you ever need someone to talk to, I promise to listen and try to help if I can. I remember how hard everything was at your age. You feel like an adult, but adults treat you like a kid, and you don't always get a say in your own life. Or am I way off base? Is this something you're going through yourself, or is it a problem between you and Lona?"

Wenny raised her chin and glared. "Who says I have a

problem at all? So thanks for offering, but no thanks. All I want is to be left alone."

NOTES

"For there are ghosts in the air and ghostly echoes on paper,
And the thunder of calls and notes."

DYLAN THOMAS, "I HAVE LONGED TO MOVE AWAY"

KATH MET DAI AT THE pub at seven fifteen that night. Rain had stormed in late that afternoon, and wind swept down the hillsides hard enough to bend the trees. Kath was thankful for her waterproof Burberry coat that went to mid-thigh and came with a sturdy hood. Between that and the new riding boots, she was dry and warm walking the short distance to the pub, and since there weren't any cars out front, she assumed the place would be empty.

Before she'd even walked into the bar, laughter and conversation and the clink of glasses let her know that assumption was wrong. Inside, light walls and white-painted beams on the dark green ceiling made a change from the stereotypical pub décor, and the room seemed larger than she'd expected. People crowded two deep along the wooden counter, watching sports on the televisions, and still more people sat at leather couches and armchairs by a fireplace and at several round tables along the walls. Behind the long bar, wide wine racks that reached to the ceiling flanked the expected array of bottles on either side.

With the entire village occupied by the cast and crew and no cars in sight, it stood to reason that everyone in the room was with the production in one way or another. A familiar pang of awkwardness made Kath want to wait for Dai outside, even though she knew she had to meet everyone sometime. She searched the faces, hoping Dai was already there somewhere, or that Olivia or HT were there. The longer she stood there, the more people turned to stare at her. She wrapped confidence around herself like a cloak, smiled at everyone, and walked toward the bar to order a drink. She was only halfway to the counter when the exterior door opened behind her.

"Kath," Dai called.

Relieved, she turned and found him hurrying over, his eyes locked on her. "I was behind you," he said, "but you must not have heard me shouting in all that wind."

He'd thrown a battered waxed jacket over a navy button-down shirt and jeans, and raindrops glistened on his hair and cheeks. He was gorgeous and everyone was looking at him, at them, and she felt a tingling sense of anticipation until he reached her. Then he tipped his head and whispered, "Follow my lead."

He turned back to the room, but the touch of his breath

seemed to linger against her ear. Too aware of him, she wanted to step away. But she couldn't.

Dai raised his voice. "Alright, you lot? This is Kath Cameron, who's come to be Margaret for us. Wave to her from a distance, because I'm tired, and we have work to do."

There was general laughter and a shout of "Alright, Kath?"

She smiled and answered, "Alright, all? I'm glad to be here."

There was another round of laughter at that, and the ice broke enough for people to look away. Dai led Kath off to the restaurant in a side room. Black-and-white photos of varying sizes hung above sea-green wainscoting on the walls, and the pale stain on the tables and chairs kept the room light and cheerful. Dai settled into a booth at the far corner, and Kath was grateful to be tucked out of the way.

"I thought I'd save you the usual crush of introductions. They'd have been overwhelming all at once. I hope that's okay?" he asked.

"Are you kidding? I could kiss you—" She stopped, mortified.

His eyes had dropped to her lips, and he looked away abruptly.

"Sorry," Kath said. "What I meant was, thank you. How was filming today?"

He flashed a wry smile and shook his head. "They'll be doing some of the fill-in shots until the light is gone. I was hoping to finish the last of the shots for the battle of Mynydd Hyddgen this week, but it has a lot of moving parts."

"I'd love to see that."

"It's bloody tedious most of the time. Parts of the battle scenes—and most of the castle interiors and building reconstructions—will be done with CGI, but getting close to HT and the major cast requires live-action in the background. And I may be a dinosaur, but I still believe that brings an element of realism and tension that CGI can't quite achieve. Come watch tomorrow, if you like, though. That will give you an extra day to observe and meet people before starting fittings and makeup design, and we may get some work done here and there."

"As long as I'm not in the way."

He grinned at that. "Don't be daft. Your trailer won't be there until we move locations for Monday, but you're welcome to use mine anytime."

A shout came from the bar, followed by laughter and more shouting. Kath had trouble hearing the rest of what Dai was saying. He fell quiet, smiling at her in a way that he probably smiled at everyone but that felt like it was for her alone, as though they had a secret shared between them. Smiling back, she realized he looked tired. She wondered if she should offer to cut the night short, but she didn't want to. Selfishly, she didn't want to, but she told herself it was only because she needed all the help that she could get.

"Do you need a mental break while you eat?" she asked. "Or do you want to dive right in to work? I have a few things to go over." She pulled her script out of her purse and set it on the table. She'd tabbed the pages with sticky notes where she had questions or suggestions.

"Just a few things, then?" Dai raised his eyebrows with a teasing smile.

At least Kath hoped he was teasing. Maybe she had gone overboard. He'd been so open the night before, but it was his screenplay. And he and Alan Stickley knew what they were doing. What was she even thinking, bringing any of these things up?

Someone stopped at her elbow, surprising her. She looked up and found Lona Davies with a pencil poised over an order pad. "Alright, folks? What can I get for you?" Kath must have stared a little too long. The girl's smile faded, and her blue eyes narrowed. "Do you need more time?"

Kath hadn't so much as picked up either of the menus that were stacked against the wall of the booth. Dai leaned in closer. "There's no ploughman's of any sort on the menu, but you can't go wrong with the mushroom and garlic risotto, and the spiced lamb is good. My favorite is the marinated sea bass."

"In that case," Kath said. "I'll have the fish."

Dai nodded. "Same for me."

"And to drink?" Lona Davies asked, watching Kath with slightly more focus than was strictly comfortable.

"How about a bottle of the pinot grigio?" Dai asked Kath.

She nodded and watched the girl walk away, hips swinging as she moved in heels so high they would turn to torture devices long before her shift was over. A man coming through into the dining room stopped to ask her a question. There was another roar from the bar, and he bent closer so she could hear him. Lona turned her head so their lips were close enough that the man could probably feel her breath.

Something about the way she stood made Kath feel sad for her. That had been the start for Kath, testing her sexuality and trying too hard. Desperate for someone to care.

That same neediness was there in the way this girl was dressed, a black skirt too short over black tights that made it barely acceptable, a sweater cut low enough to show the effects of a push-up bra.

And what was she? Fifteen? Sixteen?

"I feel bad for her," Kath said.

"Poor kid," Dai agreed. "If she were mine, I'd have grounded her for life by now."

"She seems to be making life a misery for Wenny. The sad thing is that she probably won't feel really guilty about that for years yet. If ever."

The man who'd stopped to speak to Lona moved away and walked toward their table. "Hiya, Dai. *Sut dach chi?*"

"*Tsiampion, diolch.*" He gestured to Kath. "Kath Cameron, Caradoc Thomas. Caradoc directs our second unit team."

"I was there for your chemistry read, Kath. It was phenomenal, and I can't wait to see what you bring to the role," Caradoc said, smiling at her with the kind of smile that was probably very successful after a few too many drinks. He was dark-haired and light-eyed, well but leanly built, and dressed fashionably in jeans and a sweater that showed his muscles. His teeth gleamed white against a short beard, and he angled his head down just enough to make his hooded eyes suggestive.

Kath found it all a bit too deliberate compared to Dai's lack of pretense. "Thank you," she said, smiling wider to compensate for her reaction. "I'm looking forward to starting work."

He eyed the script with all her sticky notes. "It looks as though you have done that already."

"Kath has some intriguing ideas for Margaret," Dai said.

Caradoc's attention switched back to him. "Anything I need to know?"

Dai's expression shuttered. "Not just yet. Weren't you meant to be heading toward Cardiff for the next few days?"

Caradoc shifted his balance, rocking back onto his heels. "I'm working out some changes. I'd like to take some of the additional shots we need for Bolingbroke's march from Shrewsbury before heading farther south. That way, I'm around in case you need me."

"You'll have to work that out with Bowen and the location manager, but you've done a lot of juggling already."

"I've had no choice the past few weeks while I had to cover for you."

"Bowen accounted for that in the schedule, didn't he? Which is why we had hours to make up this week, and that included the added time for travel."

"I've got that sorted. The crew will make up the time."

"It isn't only about the time. I've had some… questions, let's put it that way, from your unit. Check in with Bowen first, then maybe take some time for team building, yeah? Get everyone back on side. I know we're all under added pressure, but that's important. Also, I'd like to have everyone together on Sunday afternoon to finalize the schedule revisions now that Kath is on board."

"Sunday was my first day off in weeks, and I was heading home."

"I know, and I'm sorry." Dai rested his forearms on the table. "If you have to, you can call in. But all of us going through the schedule together is the best way to make sure we don't lose more time."

Caradoc nodded reluctantly. "What did you mean by questions, by the way?" he asked. "Questions from whom?"

"We can talk about that later."

"I'm not the one going over budget, Dai."

The muscles in Dai's neck and shoulders tightened, but his expression didn't change. "*Diolch yn fawr* for your concern," he said pleasantly, "and for letting me know about your plans. Enjoy your evening."

Caradoc stood a few seconds, clearly debating whether to say anything more. Then he thought better of it and walked away. At the opening to the bar, he bumped into two women who were standing there talking to HT, and he stopped to apologize, all smiles again. HT called something after him, and Caradoc raised a hand in acknowledgment, then walked out of sight.

"Sorry about that," Dai said to Kath.

"I got the impression you don't like him much."

"I shouldn't have let that show. He's a bit full of himself, but he's an excellent director." Dai sighed. "Having to recast

Margaret has been a lot of added work and stress. Caradoc and Ifor Jones are the main reasons we've been able to continue filming at all instead of having to hold production." Another burst of laughter and shouting erupted from the bar, and he glanced in that direction before giving Kath a smile. "Now, let's get back to these notes of yours."

Kath waited for the noise to die down again, then started working through her notes in order. The first few were simple clarifications she needed about logistics, action, or motivation. Then Lona Davies came back with their wine and meals.

The noise in the bar grew increasingly louder, and Kath grew more nervous as she reached the Ruthyn Castle scenes. She licked her lips and took a sip of wine to fortify her courage. Not wanting to overstep with either Dai or Alan Stickley, she considered skipping her suggestions altogether, and she searched through the sticky notes to skip ahead.

"I don't charge extra for questions," Dai said.

Looking up, she found him watching her, and for a moment she lost her concentration. "Maybe you should. Your working hours would be shorter."

"Don't worry about that, and if you're worried whether I'll like an idea or interpretation, don't be. This really is a team effort from start to finish, and I want you to feel comfortable."

She flipped the pages back. "I've been thinking about what we discussed last night. How Margaret wants revenge even though she's urging Glyndwr to be cautious. She's also seen the damage from de Ruthyn's raid on the disputed land." She raised her voice to be heard above another outburst in the bar.

"After helping to treat the wounded and bury the dead, she's seen firsthand what can happen to bystanders during an attack. She knows Glyndwr and his men are angry, and she knows that's usually when soldiers lose control and bystanders suffer."

"Are you saying you want to add dialogue like that before Glyndwr leaves?" Dai asked, raising his voice.

"I think Margaret would want to go with Glyndwr and his men when they sneak into Ruthyn Castle. Being Margaret, she'd demand it."

"What?" Dai asked, leaning closer over the table.

Kath repeated herself, practically shouting this time, and watched for his reaction. He shook his head and looked down at her half-eaten plate. "This isn't working. Are you finished with your dinner?" His plate was no emptier than hers, but she nodded, and he said, "Do you want to go back to yours?"

They walked out through the bar together, and Kath was too aware of him beside her. And of people watching them. She said a brief hello to HT and wondered if she should have talked to him about her suggestions before speaking to Dai about them. It was possible he would assume she was overstepping, but it was too late now. And any kind of serious conversation in the pub seemed to be impossible.

More of the cast and crew had come in, and there were still more upstairs by the sound of the laughter and conversation coming from that direction. She wondered if she would ever be as comfortable among them all as they seemed to be with each other. She'd never been the one with that magical ability to connect with groups. It had always been Anna who could walk into a room full of strangers and have everyone's phone number five minutes later. Meg was like that, too, to a lesser degree. Kath had missed out on that gene completely.

She waited as Dai stopped to answer a few questions on his way out the door. He introduced her each time, and she smiled and said a few words, and repeated the names several times in her head to make sure she kept them straight.

The wind had blown the rain farther south, and the sunset was setting fire to the clouds on the western horizon. A small mixed group of men and women was walking down the street toward the pub, avoiding cars parked up too close to the rowhouses. They called out to Dai, and he waved to them while Kath unlocked the door of her cottage. Then he followed her inside.

Muppet stood and shook himself before climbing out of his bed. That took a while since Kath had emptied the gift basket earlier and folded his blanket up inside it. She had wondered if it would be too hard for him to get in and out, but he had climbed in immediately, turned in a circle twice, then settled in with a sigh and a soft, contented whine.

Kath and Dai hung their coats on the hooks beside the door, and he sat down on the end of the sofa.

"I wish I'd thought to suggest bringing the rest of that bottle of wine with us," Kath said. "Glenys brought over a couple of bottles this morning, though. I could open one?"

"Not for me, but don't hold back on my account. So, what were you saying about the attack on Ruthyn Castle?"

The tension Kath had felt earlier all came flooding back. She bent to scratch Muppet's ears as he reached her and butted his head into her shin. "We talked about Margaret wanting revenge on de Ruthyn. Wouldn't she want to be there herself when Glyndwr and his men infiltrated the castle? It was her idea, and she knows Glyndwr and his men are angry. She would want to be there to make sure things don't get out of control."

Dai's expression grew wary.

"What I'm thinking is that, being Margaret, she would demand to go. I can see her arguing that Glyndwr's men might go unnoticed moving in one or two at a time on market day, but Glyndwr himself is too well-known. On the other hand, if she went with him, he'd be in less danger of being caught because the guards might pay less attention to a man and woman coming in together. The whole attack would be more likely to succeed."

"That would make Margaret an active participant in the rebellion, not only in the planning."

"Isn't that what she would have wanted? I don't mean she has to fight, although that could be interesting. At Ruthyn, if she saw someone about to be attacked, I could see her wading in to save them."

Dai opened his own copy of the script and thumbed through to find and read the scene. "We'd have to rewrite this scene, and the departure scene." He considered for a moment. "I don't hate it. We'd be adding tension and giving Margaret a better payoff for her tactical planning."

"Exactly." Kath sat down at the edge of the love seat kitty-corner from him. "Expectations about women in combat have changed since *Rob Roy* and *Braveheart*. In real-life military operations and everything from Marvel movies to Disney series. I'd love to see the story take advantage of that."

Dai propped his forearms against his thighs, leaning toward her. "Are you asking for a more active role overall?"

Kath hadn't even let herself get that far in her own thoughts. "The Ruthyn Castle scenes jumped out at me, because the castle belonged to de Ruthyn. It's a way for Margaret to avenge herself without having to admit that's what she's doing. I can't see her passing that up." Cheeks growing hot, she stared down at her hands folded on top of the script in her lap.

"Kath," Dai said. "Look at me."

She met his eyes, even though she wanted to look away, and it was probably only a tenth of a moment, but it felt much longer. Her heart sped up.

Dai smiled at her gently. "That wasn't a criticism. I don't want you to be embarrassed about bringing any idea to me, however small. It's normal to feel self-conscious when you're walking into the role now after everyone else has already gelled into a team. But Margaret is one of the driving forces through the film. We all want her—you—to succeed. And this is actually a bloody good idea."

Kath nodded, and her face felt even hotter.

"Good." He reached out and touched her hands, squeezing for an instant before he pulled away. "With a change this big, we'll need to talk it through with Alan. That will be easier if we can show him what it would look like on the page. Do you want to help me tackle a rewrite?"

"Now?" Kath asked, relieved, but also exhausted.

"What time is it?" Dy glanced at his watch and shook his head. "Well, never mind. Let's call it a day for now and pick it back up on the drive tomorrow. If you'd still like to come in with me?"

Kath followed him to the patio door, and he turned back toward her. There was an awkward moment when they both stood there, not knowing how to say goodbye. He looked down at her, and Kath's lips tingled, as if there should have been something more than words.

Did he feel that, too? He was the one who paused, his eyes intent on her face, her lips. She wasn't naïve—she could sense interest. Or was that wishful thinking on her part?

Confused, she wrapped her arms tightly around herself and said, "Thanks for listening."

He smiled and reached for the door handle, then ducked back and kissed her lightly on the cheek. "Thanks for trusting me enough to say what you were thinking. But don't be afraid to trust yourself."

CURVES

"At night, dreams became the devil's own accomplices."

SHARON KAY PENMAN, *THE RECKONING*

A NIGHTMARE WOKE DAI EARLY in the morning. Too early. The process of getting back to sleep was routine by now. Instead of lying in bed with his heart thumping and his mind overworked, he threw off the covers and hopped into a warm shower to wash away the film of sweat that soured his skin. Forehead pressed against the wall, he let the water needle into his shoulders and upper back, grounding him in the present and washing away the guilt and dread. Those changed nothing. Accomplished nothing.

The nightmares weren't frequent anymore, but he'd never gotten rid of them. Triggers varied: sights, sounds, smells, images on the news. More often they came of general anxiety, a sense of futility or powerlessness. He'd felt that weight on him for weeks, and the aftertaste of the nightmare made it worse.

He dried himself off and climbed naked into the clean side of the bed, where the sheets were dry. Then he found the guided meditation for restful sleep on his phone and lay back with his eyes closed, listening.

The alarm woke him a few hours later. Briefly, he considered turning it off and sleeping a little longer, but if he didn't get his run in, it would only make him prone to more anxiety.

Then, too, there was Kath. He could see her standing by the patio door, her hair shining in the light and her lips looking like an invitation. Walking away had felt harder than before, which was dangerous for them both. Still, he'd told her he would knock on her door this morning, and he didn't want her getting up and waiting for him.

He rarely drank coffee before a run, but he thought about it now. Instead, he sipped water from the bathroom faucet and took a couple of paracetamol tablets for the ache his head was brewing. After dressing in shorts and a long-sleeved T-shirt, he laced up his running shoes and stopped downstairs in the kitchen for another glass of water. Altogether, it took ten minutes to get up and out, which left him time to follow the curve of the road back down toward the river and the main route that led past the rowhouses, the pub, and the hotel and continued out of town.

There were a few faded stars still visible in the deep blue stillness, but the ground swirled in curls of fog. He stopped where the road curved to stretch, easing the tight muscles of his neck, shoulders, calves, and quads. He shook his arms out, then jogged the rest of the way to Kath's door.

She opened almost immediately when he knocked, light streaming overhead and behind her. He wasn't prepared for that, the glow on clean skin and silver-gold hair, the smile that created light by itself.

He stared a moment, then collected himself and said the obvious, "Good morning."

"Morning." She stepped out and locked the door behind her, then paused to look at him. "Are you okay?"

"I was up late and woke with a nightmare," he admitted. "I still get them. What about you? Any strange lights, or did you get some sleep?"

"If there were lights, I was blissfully unaware of them."

She fell in step beside him, and he was struck all over again by the way the light hit the angles of her face. His mind raced with all the ways the camera could play with that.

"Does it help to talk about the nightmares?" she asked. "Or is it better to ignore them?"

"Thankfully, I forget the details as long as I don't dwell on them. It's mainly the emotion that lingers."

She was quiet for a beat or two, and then she said, "I read an interview where you talked about Musa Qala. I was looking for insight into what you were looking for in *The Last Prince*. You mentioned that the inspiration went back to someone you served with there."

"Robbie Hanmer."

"Hanmer, like Margaret's maiden name?"

"The same. He said he was related to Glyndwr, but it must have been a distant connection. Still, he knew stories I've still never found anywhere. And he was a brilliant storyteller. I didn't appreciate that at the time, since I couldn't give him my full attention while I was looking for Taliban movement."

Dai eased into a run as they left the village, and Kath matched him. The swirl of ground fog added an eerie mood to the landscape, muffling the sound of their footsteps and making him feel as if they were both floating above the earth.

"It must have been hard, constantly waiting for disaster," Kath said.

"After a while, I don't know that any of us expected to survive. But you stop minding about yourself. It's the thought of watching the other lads dying and being powerless to stop it. The Taliban soon figured out there were only eighty-eight of us and we didn't have any way to get food or medicine in, or our wounded out, except by helicopter. They threw a hundred attacks at us in forty days. The mortar team was almost out of ammunition by the end, and the machine gunners were manually recycling rounds the Danish troops we replaced had left behind."

There wasn't anything useful that could be said to that, so it didn't surprise him when Kath didn't respond. He was grateful she didn't roll off the usual platitudes: "I'm sorry," or "That must have been difficult," or "How did you survive?" They'd survived because there wasn't any choice.

He picked up speed. Kath didn't complain, but she was breathing hard, and he eased up on the pace to give them both time to catch a second wind before starting the climb uphill. The fog clung to the track, making the footing treacherous.

He let Kath set the pace, assuming she would slow down. She didn't, and he didn't ask her to.

At the top of the hill, the fog blew away. They both took a few minutes to recover, and when he went to sit in his usual spot, she sat down beside him.

"Might not be much of a sunrise today," he said.

"Or it could be spectacular."

He grinned. "Is that your glass-half-full outlook?"

She bit her lip and looked down briefly before lifting her eyes back to his. "I might have exaggerated about that."

"Should you be confessing?"

"Probably not, but I feel like…"

"Like what?" he prompted.

"Maybe because you're honest, I should be, too."

"But you aren't as a rule?"

"I am about most things."

"Only not about your feelings?"

She drew back, then pulled her knees to her chest and curled around them in a self-protective gesture. "It's not that I don't recognize my feelings. More like I think it's pointless to wear them on my sleeve. How often did you soldiers talk about being afraid during the siege?"

"What's the point of talking about it? Everyone is afraid."

"You see? The very British stiff upper lip."

"You aren't British, or a soldier. And being Welsh, I prefer to remember that the source of that attitude goes back to Marcus Aurelius. He said something about being more upset by our reactions to an event than by the event itself."

"Maybe if we don't admit we're afraid, it makes it easier to face ourselves," Kath said.

"Training and adrenaline kick in when you're in the thick of it. That's as true for an actor as it is for a soldier. It's mainly in the stretches after or leading up to combat or a performance when you flashback to a negative experience. That's when it's paralyzing to think about having to go out and do it again, and you have to rely on discipline and routine. Laura reminded me of that after I came home. Going from having a purpose every day to having nothing to do left me floundering."

"Is that why you run in the morning?"

"The routine is part of it. Running in the quiet helps remind me that the world will keep turning regardless of my problems. It's all perspective." He smiled at her.

She shivered as her body temperature dropped, and the morning was also cooler than it had been the day before. Dai scooted closer and put his arm around her. It was automatic, and she leaned in automatically, too. Then they both tensed as if they'd realized at the same time what they had done.

He didn't move away, and he hoped she wouldn't either. They sat like that, rigid and uncomfortable, and then they both relaxed. Neither of them acknowledged it, as if saying something would break the moment.

"Did you mean to write what you felt in Musa Qala into Margaret? That sense of fighting for the people beside her, even knowing they couldn't succeed, because that was all she could do?"

"I didn't realize I had written that. Not until you brought it out in her. I'm still not sure if it was her or you."

"Why Margaret instead of Glyndwr?"

"Every uprising needs an optimist."

"Or at least a fanatic."

"I don't see that in either of them."

The sun broke over the horizon, waking the landscape and clothing it in vivid color. Kath's cheek dropped to Dai's shoulder, and her warmth felt like summer, inevitable but fleeting as she leaned against him. Her curves fit as if someone had specially carved them to fit within the space beneath his arm and up against his ribs. It would have been easy to turn his head and kiss her hair. He didn't, though, because he shouldn't have been holding her at all.

FLAMES

"Some things are so frightful that a bit of madness is the only response."

SARAH WATERS, THE PAYING GUESTS

K ATH TENSED AS DAI'S ARM curled around her shoulders, and she knew she should have pulled away. It wasn't that he meant it as anything more than a chivalrous gesture. She'd been cold, and if he'd had a coat, she knew he would have given it to her. Instead, he'd given her his body heat, and contact like that could lead to too many misinterpretations. It confused her hormones. It quickened her heart. But she didn't pull away.

She wanted to be there. That was the simple truth. She wanted to feel his arm around her because it made her feel equally safe and unsafe, in the best way of each. He warmed her, calmed her, and made her feel even more awake than the sun climbing above the horizon. And if the sunrise was a reminder that they were both insignificant in the grand scheme, that they couldn't control everything, in that moment, she didn't mind. She could accept that there was something new and unexpected coming.

He helped her to her feet, and she retained enough good sense not to look at him. That would have been too dangerous.

Neither of them spoke as they started the long run back. Kath let herself enjoy the downhill scramble, that sense of flying out of control. It matched her mood. Then once they were back on the paved road, their footfalls and breaths came in sync.

They were almost back to the village when Dai stopped abruptly.

"What's wrong?" Kath asked.

"Shh." He held up a finger, his chin raised and his eyes narrowed as if listening intently.

Kath listened, and then she heard it. Something like a moan and a whimper. Someone crying softly.

They both turned toward a fifteen-foot break in the low stone wall that separated the road from the bank that sloped down toward the stream. All the way down, brush and grass looked crushed, and a patch of light blue stood out among the green at the bottom. It took a moment for Kath's mind to register the shape of a girl with jean-clad legs and a dark blue rain jacket. She lay facedown, mostly, only a small bit of cheek visible beneath blonde hair.

Wenny.

Kath and Dai both scrambled down the slope. Kath slid part of the way on the wet soil, but when she reached the bottom and ran toward Wenny, Dai caught her and held her back.

"Kath, stop," he said. "Don't move her."

Just like that, with Dai's arm holding her back, Kath was at another accident.

Fifteen years fell away.

She was seventeen and sitting in the passenger seat of Henry's car.

He'd barely spoken to her at Eli's party, but they'd both had too much to drink. And both of them were high from joy and praise.

The stupid pantyhose were cutting off Kath's circulation, and she couldn't stand it a moment longer. She wriggled out of them beneath her skirt, and Henry watched her. She could feel him watching her.

Neither of them noticed Henry's car drifting across the dividing line, not until the headlights of another car whipped around the corner. Henry swerved back.

Kath closed her eyes, bracing for the impact. But there was only the screech of brakes and then a crunching sort of thud and thud and thud. Then silence.

Awful silence.

No collision, no pain.

Henry slammed the brakes and threw his door open when the car had barely stopped. He raced across the road. Kath had to get the damn pantyhose off the rest of the way, but then she ran barefoot over the cold asphalt, pebbles and small stones gouging her feet.

The other car lay on its side down the bank, all bent and crumpled. The engine was still running. Kath smelled smoke, but that registered only a second before the explosion. She fell, and Henry flew backward, landing a few feet from her.

Flames engulfed the car. Kath scrambled toward it.

Henry caught her, held her back while her feet slid in the grass. She tried to run forward. "Kath, stop. Stop! There's nothing we can do."

There had to be something. She had to do something.

But there was no movement inside the car. Their phones were both back in Henry's car. Kath wrenched free of Henry's grasp and said she was going back to call for help. He ran back with her, ahead of her. Then as he'd almost reached his car, he stopped and threw up in the bushes alongside the road. He retched again, and she hesitated beside him, then kept running. But as she reached in through the open driver's door to get the first phone she could reach, he ran up behind her.

"Kath, we can't. We can't call anyone."

"We have to." The phone was in Kath's hand.

He wrestled it away. "There's nothing we can do for the driver, and I've been drinking. I need to talk to someone. A lawyer."

"There's my dad," she said. "He'll know what to do and who to call."

She didn't mean that to be the start of the cover-up. But it had been.

All these years later, panic clawed at Kath's chest, as fresh as it had been that night.

The world spun around her, and her heart hammered in her throat. Light-headed, she tried to breathe through it, but she had to put her hands on her knees to keep from collapsing.

Dai had Wenny's wrist in his hand, checking her pulse. Then Wenny moaned again.

Shaking, wishing she had her first aid kit, Kath knelt beside her. Not that any of Wenny's wounds were visible. She pushed Wenny's hair off her forehead.

Wenny's skin was cold. So cold.

Dai dug his phone out to dial for help.

"Wenny, can you hear me?" Kath asked.

Wenny's eyelashes fluttered, but her eyes didn't open.

Still, it was something. Hope.

Dai was talking to someone, so Kath gestured back toward the village and mouthed, "I'm going to get Glenys."

He nodded. Kath scrabbled unsteadily up the slope and stopped at the top when she was out of sight, still trying to get her equilibrium back. Refusing to think about anything except the present.

She couldn't waste time. Pushing herself into a sprint, she raced back to Glenys's house and pounded on the door until Glenys answered.

Glenys had thrown a bathrobe over her pajamas with the sash untied, and she held it closed. "Kath, what's wrong? Are you hurt?"

"Wenny's had an accident. We found her off the road by the river. She isn't conscious, but she's alive, and Dai is calling for an ambulance. I can take you to her."

Glenys's hand flew to her throat, and the color bled from her face. Her fingers tightened on the robe, then she blinked twice, grabbed a pair of boots from beside the door, and pulled them on bare feet. She snatched a jacket off the coat rack by the door and tugged it on over the bathrobe while she left the house.

"A blanket," Kath said. "We need a blanket for Wenny."

Glenys pulled a quilt off the corner of a sofa in the front room and crumpled it against herself as she held it.

"I didn't even know Wenny had gone out," she said. "How badly is she hurt?"

Kath couldn't speculate whether Wenny's skin was so cold from having been out there most of the night or whether she was bleeding internally. She knew nothing, so she only put her arm through Glenys's and supported her as Glenys stumbled.

"How can I not have known she wasn't home?" Glenys asked. Her voice was hollow and ragged.

"She's a teenager. That's what teenagers do. They're reckless, and they sneak around, and you can't blame yourself for that." Kath guided Glenys down the bank to where Wenny lay. "Has she moved? Anything?" she asked Dai, who was crouched beside Wenny.

He shook his head. "She's breathing, but her pulse is thready." He put a hand out to caution Glenys. "Don't move her. She could have a back injury, and we don't want to risk making anything worse. A pediatric Air Ambulance out of Caernarfon is on its way. They should be here soon."

Glenys crouched beside Wenny and stroked her hair,

speaking to her in Welsh. Kath had to walk away to catch her breath. Tears ran hot down her cheeks, and she wiped them with her fists. She didn't deserve to cry. It would only make it worse for Glenys if she broke down.

Dai came over and threaded his fingers through hers. "She'll be alright," he said. "We have to believe that."

"How did she get there?" Kath asked. "She didn't fall—not that far. But there aren't any skid marks on the road."

She looked up toward the road, but her vision blurred. Years melted away, and she was on a different road again, a long dark road where the houses were a hundred yards from the street behind locked gates. Henry turned off the headlights as he drove away.

The flames grew smaller in the rear window, and a dark plume of smoke was barely a smudge against the darkness. Kath shook, tears streaming down her cheeks. Henry drove up a side street, then turned off onto a parallel road before switching his lights back on. Unlike Kath, he was eerily, frighteningly calm.

The same feeling of dread had Kath shaking now.

Had someone hit Wenny and knocked her down the bank, then driven away like Henry? Calmly driven away, with no idea of the price they would pay for keeping that secret locked inside them?

If they had, if they'd hit Wenny and left her, the pain of their conscience wasn't enough.

They deserved to burn in hell.

SHOCK

"When cold as snow he should run the wended vales..."

DYLAN THOMAS, "A WINTER'S TALE"

T HE HELICOPTER CAME, AND THANKFULLY Kath had already made it back. After watching Glenys and looking increasingly panicked, she'd had the common sense to run back for Glenys's phone, purse, and some clothing to change into once they reached the hospital.

Dai watched how Kath supported Glenys while the team of two medics stabilized Wenny, loaded her onto a stretcher, and then onto the H145 Airbus. Glenys stood quietly, probably in shock but able to follow instructions. Kath nudged her forward to ask if she could travel with Wenny, and Dai caught the quick assessment the pilot gave Glenys before he nodded, took Glenys's purse and bag for her, and settled her in the helicopter.

Sirens announced the police arriving, but the radio car hung well back to let the helicopter leave.

Kath stood too close, and he drew her back to a safer distance before the rotors started turning. She shivered and her face was pale. He wrapped his arm around her as the rotors whined and the wind picked up. Her hair whipped into her face and up against his chest.

"Police first," he said, "then we'll get you some coffee and warmer clothes."

They walked forward to meet the police car, but the officers were more interested in securing the scene. Dai gave them a quick sitrep of what had happened and where exactly they'd found Wenny.

It was only then that he noticed the crowd that had gathered behind them, including HT and virtually everyone staying in the cottages along the river. Kath saw them too. She stiffened like a soldier at attention and tried to step out from under the arm he had around her.

He moved with her and bent his head to whisper, "Don't, Kath. No one will think anything about it under the circumstances, unless we draw attention to ourselves." Turning to the police officer, he asked, "Is that everything for now?"

The officer's yellow jacket was bright against the black tarmac of the road, and he nodded. "I've radioed for a supervisor, and someone will be along to speak with you both." He'd been writing everything down in his notebook, and now he asked for their names and phone numbers.

Dai ran a hand along his neck, mentally doing the calculations about the day's workload and what it would take to reshuffle things again. "About how long will you need us?"

"I couldn't say. They'll be sending a detective for this. You're with the film crew, aren't you?"

"Kath and I are, but Glenys Jenkins works for Lord Linley at the Obaith Estate. The girl is her granddaughter."

The officer looked at Kath, who was still shivering but trying to hide it. "You'd better get her inside where it's warm. We'll try to get someone to speak with you as quickly as we can."

Dai thanked him and showed him Kath's cottage, then he waved HT over. "Would you give me a hand? I think Kath could use a familiar face."

"I'm perfectly fine," Kath said, drawing herself up.

HT wore jeans and nothing else except a small towel around his neck. Traces of shaving cream clung to his jaw. He moved to Kath's other side to put his arm around her shoulders.

She rummaged in the pocket of her running jacket for her key and unlocked her door. Once HT had followed her inside, Dai turned back to the others waiting curiously, hoping for information. Nothing moved faster than gossip on a movie set, and he needed to make sure there wasn't any speculation.

Ifor Jones and Caradoc walked up to meet him, with the others close behind.

"Alright? What's occurring?" Caradoc asked. He was fully dressed, a step up from HT, but his hair curled wildly as if he hadn't combed it yet. "Was that Glenys's granddaughter? Is she alright?"

"Kath and I were coming back from a run, and we heard her moaning. They're taking her to Caernarfon."

"But she's alive?" Caradoc looked shaken. "Hell of a thing to happen. She seems like a nice kid, and she means the world to Glenys."

Dai nodded and turned to Ifor, who—thankfully—appeared ready to go to work. "It pains me to say this, especially after all you've already had to pick up for me, but I'll need to wait for the detectives to come in from Colwyn Bay. No telling how long they'll be."

In his late thirties, Ifor could have passed for a teenager. A *Game of Thrones* T-shirt stretched tight over a barrel chest and even larger stomach, and he gave Dai the one-shouldered shrug that was his usual approach to setbacks. "Caradoc and I will handle it. Is HT still coming in?"

"Soon. Kath's tough, but she's had a shock, and she's been standing out in the cold too long. I asked HT to stay a while in case she needs anything before I get back with my laptop. Then she and I will work here until the police are through with us. She has a great idea for the Ruthyn Castle scenes, and I want to get that fleshed out before we run it past everyone."

"It can't be easy to have this added to all the pressure she's under. Did she run your usual route with you?" Ifor asked.

Dai nodded.

"Five-mile run, finding an unconscious teenager, police statement, and still planning to rewrite scenes. On top of stepping into Nia's shoes at a moment's notice. You're not asking much of her, are you?"

"Nothing she can't handle," Dai said. "She's surprising the hell out of me."

CONFESSION

"All the dark things came out of hiding
And had the world all to themselves."

ROALD DAHL, *THE BFG*

A HOT SHOWER THAWED KATH on the outside, flesh and skin. Tears slipped down her cheeks, but inside, she felt frozen in a silent scream. The thought of HT downstairs didn't help. When she emerged from the bathroom, she could hear him moving, banging cabinets, cursing at Muppet cheerfully. She could also hear Muppet growling.

She threw on a sweater and a pair of black jeans, brushed her hair out, and left it to dry naturally in long, loose waves. Socks were her last concession to the cold, and then she padded down the stairs.

The scent of coffee and butter browning greeted her, and her stomach turned over. But it was nice of HT to try.

It hit her that she was falling right back into the habit of making excuses for him. She'd blamed herself all these years, while HT blamed her and her mother. And Kath had let him do that because she felt responsible. She wanted to kick herself for that. Maybe Muppet had the right idea, biting him.

Still wearing only his jeans, HT turned at the stove as she approached the kitchen. "Feeling better?"

"Should I get my phone and post a photo to social media? Breakfast prepared by your favorite shirtless hottie—you could sell it as a charity giveaway."

HT's brows furrowed, and he studied her. "Are we back to dripping sarcasm all over each other? What happened to the truce? You and your demon dog are both growling at me."

"I took an unwanted drive down memory lane after finding Wenny. Muppet, come here, buddy." She found the bag of treats while Muppet trotted toward her, and then lured him back to his bed and sprinkled out a handful of treats for him there. "Good boy," she whispered, and kissed him on the head. "Stay here."

She went back toward the kitchen. "Do you ever have flashbacks of that night, HT?"

"No." He shook his head, but he was lying. She could have won a fortune from him at poker.

"Always? Or only recently?" she asked.

"Off and on since that night, especially right after and again when my father and then my mother died. It's been worse since you brought it up again. Not necessarily just flashbacks. Anxiety. Being moody, not really processing things logically. You?"

"I thought I did okay not thinking about it. But maybe that

was never true." Kath poured herself a cup of coffee and added a dab of milk. Then she moved around to the other side of the counter and sat on a barstool to watch as HT finished what he liked to call his deconstructed omelet. Or as Kath preferred to call it, scrambled eggs with cheese.

HT flicked the burner off and spooned eggs onto a waiting plate. Before he could start on a second plate, she said, "Not for me, thanks. I'm not sure I could keep anything down."

"You need to keep your strength up." He slid the rest of the eggs onto the second plate.

She was tired of him not listening to her. "Someone hit Wenny with a car and didn't stop, HT."

"You don't know that. She could have fallen."

"How? That section of the wall is broken, so it's not like she could have been walking on it and fallen. Did you notice how she crushed the vegetation all the way down, rolling over it? That took more momentum than a trip and fall." She took a breath. "Maybe because I'd already been thinking about it, seeing Wenny like that sent me right back to that night. It was like I was standing there when the car exploded. I remembered every detail, every bit of conversation. How does the mind dredge up something so clearly after all this time?"

"I don't know. Try not to think about it." HT set the plate of eggs down and slid it in front of her.

Kath ignored it. "You turned your headlights off and drove away," she said. "I didn't remember that until tonight. Or at least, I didn't know that I remembered. I told you we could talk to my dad, but you weren't going to him for legal advice. You were running away. I've spent all these years thinking it was my mother who talked us out of turning ourselves in, blaming myself for not telling my dad in spite of her, or going to the police." Tears brimmed in Kath's eyes, blurring her vision, but she shook her head. "We left that man, the way someone left Wenny. We left him burning in the car because we were worried about what was going to happen to us."

"There was no smoke in his lungs. He was dead before the explosion."

"You don't know that. We didn't have to slink away. No one should have to die alone."

"I'm telling you, he was already dead. It wouldn't have made any difference."

"It would have to us, don't you see that? Are you the same person you would have been if we hadn't run away? All this time, I let you make me the bad guy while you painted yourself as the victim. I'm not saying it wasn't mostly my fault. I threw myself at you and drank too much, and I distracted you. But you were driving, and we both made choices. We chose to listen to my mother and run away. All these years, we made one terrible decision after another." She held the cup in both hands, trying to let it warm her from the outside at the same time she took a sip.

HT moved to stand across the counter from her. "We were in shock that night. Which doesn't excuse what we did. I'm not trying to excuse it. And you're right. It was easier to cling to my anger instead of facing my actions. I needed someone to blame, especially after my father died and my mother accused me of having killed him. The thought of not being wanted at his funeral... I'm not sure that I could have gone anyway, but hearing her say that she didn't want me there—her voice was so quiet, so matter-of-fact. It tore me apart. The two of them had all those plans for after I took over at the factory from him. All the vacations they'd put off over the years, the time they had lost together. Looking back, I think I was relieved not to have to follow in his footsteps. I'd never felt like I had a choice about taking the business over. Your mother sending us away gave me an excuse."

He looked down at the floor instead of meeting Kath's eyes. She stared at him as if she hadn't really seen him for a while. Maybe she hadn't. Neither of them had wanted to see what they had done to each other.

HT finally raised his head. "I knew you blamed yourself, Kath. But instead of admitting that almost none of it was your fault, I made you the scapegoat. I blamed you for the accident, for running away, for hurting Anna, for ruining my father's plans. At the same time, I let myself buy into what your mother said and convinced myself it was kinder not to tell Anna or my parents or your father the truth. What it comes down to is that I wasn't brave enough or strong enough to do the right thing. I ran because any of them would have made me turn myself in if they knew about the accident."

"They would have been right," Kath said quietly. "It's what we should have done."

"Yes. I just couldn't bring myself to make the phone calls. By the time Dad had his heart attack, I told myself it was all too late. I'd let four years go by while my parents believed they'd raised a selfish jerk who didn't care about them. It wasn't fair to blame you for any of that, but I needed to punish someone. I couldn't seem to make myself stop. Maybe Catholics have the right idea. Confess your sins in private and be genuinely repentant. Then let it go."

"I'm not sure it's that easy."

"Probably not." He turned away and leaned back against the counter with his fingers gripping the edge behind him. "As long as we're confessing, I know for sure that the man was dead. I hired a private investigator after my mother died. I had him dig up everything he could find about the accident—the autopsy results, what happened to the man's wife, all of it. The wife is sober now, remarried, and they have two kids. I sent them some money anonymously, enough to send both kids to college. That won't make up for what I did, but—"

"You wanted to soothe your conscience. Nice. And you didn't tell me."

HT dropped his chin and looked away. "You're right to be angry."

Kath shivered, cold all over again. "You didn't tell me, and you went out and got caught with other women, then demanded a divorce. That wasn't long after your mother died, either."

"I didn't plan any of that. Not consciously. Looking back, I realize I went off the rails when I found out my mother was sick. I felt so guilty that I didn't care anymore, and I got reckless. The irony is that doing my own stunts, taking bigger risks, putting everything out there—that's what changed my career."

"And destroyed mine in the process," Kath said quietly.

But she was tired of being bitter. Tired of being angry.

HT turned back to face her. "You were right, Kath. When that stuff hit the tabloids, I should have defended you. I'm not trying to make excuses, but I was weeks away from a film release where I was playing a good guy, and the studio couldn't have me looking like an asshole. I told myself they didn't give me a choice."

"You always had a choice."

"I know. I'm sorry." He looked away and stood there. "And for the record, those women… that was never about you. I think I needed someone who wouldn't look at me like you're looking at me now. Someone who didn't see me as a crap person—a crap son, a crap husband. Like I said, when my mother got sicker, I stopped caring. Hell, maybe I wanted to get caught after she died. Blow things up. Maybe subconsciously I was afraid that I would take wanting to punish myself, punish you, too far."

Kath didn't know what to say. And they had already spent too much time trying to hurt each other.

She leaned across the counter and took his hand. "Hey, I'm sorry. I didn't realize how much you were hurting. I wish I could have helped you."

He looked down at her hand on his and then turned it over until their palms touched, neither of them holding the other, only touching. "I wish we'd helped each other more," he said, "and hurt each other less."

Tears filled Kath's eyes, but she blinked them away. "So, what now? Should we turn ourselves in?"

He came around the counter and braced a hip against the other barstool facing her. "I'm not trying to shrug off responsibility, I swear, but you need to think that through. Think about how many people it would hurt. Everyone on the production here, for one thing. And how would it really help? If your mother had let us talk to your father about it, he would have taken us to the police station. He might have waited until we were sober before marching us down there, but even then, the worst that would have happened is that I would have gotten a conviction for driving drunk and maybe a misdemeanor because I left the scene. Me, not you. A half-decent attorney might even have gotten me off. The investigator I hired said the police report had the guy leaving a bar completely hammered, and he was speeding. They could tell that by the way the car traveled and landed.

Kath drew back. "There's a difference between legal and moral responsibility, HT. Even if he was drunk, he might not have crashed if we hadn't been there."

"I know that. And I should have done the right thing then. Instead, I made things worse with every choice from leaving to asking you to marry me and trapping us both in blame and guilt."

"It felt like I was the only one you couldn't forgive." Kath didn't mean for the pain to come through, but it did. She heard it in her voice.

HT winced and reached for her hands, holding them between his. "I'm sorry—for everything. You telling me you would go public, seeing you, talking it through, all of this is making me reexamine it all. Maybe seeing what Nia's going through is finally making me grow up, too. But I see what I've done to you. Every time I cheated on you, I told myself it didn't matter because it wasn't a real marriage, but I knew you thought things were real. Or at least that we were going to try to make it real. I hurt you."

"Why did you even propose?" Kath asked, her own voice sounding distant and small.

"I don't know. We were living together, trying to save money. You were the only person I didn't have to pretend with. And you were so happy about it, for a while I convinced myself it was the right thing to do." He caught her chin and turned her gently so that she had no choice except to look at him. "Can you forgive me, Kath?"

"I'm trying." Her voice came out as a croak. She wasn't sure if that was relief or pain.

"Does that mean you can let it go?"

Kath didn't know what to say to that. There were so many people she had hurt.

"There's a girl here who reminds me of you," HT continued when she didn't answer. "I see how she looks at men, and I want to shake her. But I should never have taken you to that party with me because you were clearly in the mood for trouble. I shouldn't have let you drink, and you shouldn't have been in my car going home. I shouldn't have been driving at all that night."

"I need to think, HT. We've never taken responsibility. I need to fix things. Maybe not with the police, I'm not sure, but at least my dad and Anna."

He let go of her hands and leaned back. "Don't do anything rash. Will you promise me that?"

"Don't pressure me, okay? Please, HT. Just give me a little time."

She could see him making himself relax, making himself smile. "Then eat your eggs," he said. "They're good brain food."

She pulled her plate closer without thinking and took a bite. Then she had to force herself to chew and swallow. One bite was all she could manage. "Good," she said. "Thanks."

HT laughed. "I'm sorry, they're cold, aren't they? I forgot how much you hate cold eggs. Let me stick them in the poptyping. That's Welsh-English for microwave, by the way, according to the cleaner. It's perfect, right?" He picked up Kath's plate, put it in the small microwave that was hidden behind one of the cabinet doors, and quick-started it for a minute.

Thinking of the cleaning and Lona took Kath's mind back to Wenny. To the accident. She looked out the back windows toward the woods. "Hey, have you ever noticed lights in the woods behind your cottage at night?"

HT glanced back at her. "What kind of lights?"

"Eerie ones, floating in a circle. It was probably a teenage prank. Maybe Wenny or Lona and her friends."

"Weird. No, I haven't seen anything like that. But then I'm usually asleep by eleven." He turned to look at her as the microwave pinged. They both smiled faintly. "You think that had something to do with what happened to Wenny?"

"Maybe. I don't know. I'm just trying to connect the dots, I guess."

HT took the eggs out and handed her the plate. She forced herself to take a couple of bites, but instead of cold and rubbery with congealed cheese, the eggs were now hot and rubbery. And she still wasn't the least bit hungry. She could picture Wenny lying facedown by the river too clearly.

"She could have died alone down there, HT."

He came back around and put his hands on her shoulders. "Kath, listen to me. I'm saying this with love and because I'm worried about you: stay out of it, okay? Let the police handle it. Especially if it was a hit-and-run. You don't want to get involved."

FEELING

"Thy spirit within thee hath been so at war,
And thus hath so bestirred thee in they sleep . . ."

WILLIAM SHAKESPEARE, *HENRY IV, PART ONE*

THE POLICE DETECTIVE WAS PROFESSIONAL and not very forthcoming with information. He would only confirm that they were looking for a driver who might have hit Wenny. But passing on details wasn't his job. Kath understood that. Still, as she closed the door behind him when he left, she couldn't help wondering how a police interview would have gone back in Ohio if they'd had the courage to turn themselves in.

The more she thought about it, the more she suspected HT was probably right. Her father wouldn't have let them say anything incriminating, and in the end, they would have gone home. Kath's mother would have seen to it that the whole incident became someone else's—anyone else's—fault.

None of that made Kath feel less responsible.

The human conscience was ingenious and sadistic in equal measure. It didn't come with an instruction manual or a reset button.

She walked slowly back to the living area where Dai had picked up his laptop again. Muppet had settled beside him on the sofa, which meant he had bullied Dai into lifting him up there the moment Kath had turned her back. She paused and watched them both a moment.

Dai turned to look at her. "Are you okay?"

She didn't trust her voice, so she shrugged.

Dai set the laptop aside and gave her his full attention. "It seems like this has hit you hard."

Kath took a breath, ready to make an excuse. But she was through with lies and secrets. "It has. It's not only because of Wenny. I helped cause an accident when I wasn't much older than she is. A man was killed. But I got away with it, and seeing Wenny today, it all came rushing back."

"You were the driver?"

"No, but it's complicated."

He was silent, but there was no sign of condemnation. A moment later he said, "I remember you mentioned being seventeen and drunk and too stupid to see disaster coming. Is this what you were talking about?"

Kath nodded. "But you're leaving out self-absorbed."

"Isn't that mandatory at seventeen?"

She gave him a half-smile and circled around the sofa. "You don't seem shocked."

"It isn't my place to judge, Kath. But I can listen if you want to tell me."

She sat on the other sofa kitty-corner from him and debated grabbing Muppet to snuggle like a ten-pound security blanket. But maybe because Dai understood guilt, she wanted to tell him. She left nothing out.

He leaned forward and held her icy hands in his when the tears started rolling down her cheeks. And when she was done, he held her. Just held her. Between crying in the shower and now, she'd probably cried more in the past hours than in the last fifteen years combined.

He wiped her cheeks with his thumb. "That's a lot to carry on your own."

She shook her head, embarrassed. "Thank you for listening. I didn't mean to dump it all on you."

"It's no wonder Wenny hit you so hard."

"I wonder how she is doing. And how Glenys is holding up."

"Glenys probably has her phone off at the hospital, but I can leave a message for her," he said, accepting the change of subject. "We should ask if there's anything we can do for her."

"Yes, please." Kath nodded, then checked her watch. It was almost noon, which was still early for a crew on location. "And we should go in if the police don't need us anymore. I'd hate to throw your schedule off any more than we have already."

Dai gave her a searching look that encompassed every bit of body language and incongruity in her expression, and she tried not to squirm beneath it. She was already feeling too exposed.

"Are you sure?" he asked. "Costume fitting and hair and makeup can wait another day, and I do want to get these scenes rewritten. Also, you have at least another fifty sticky notes in that script of yours that we haven't covered yet."

She pushed off the couch, picked up Muppet, and went to feed him. "It's Wenny in the hospital, not me. The news is probably all over the set by now, along with speculation about why you and I were out running together."

Dai didn't look convinced, but he gave a nod. "I'll call for the car. It'll take them a while to get out here. Are you hungry?"

"Not really."

"We can grab something from craft services later."

He dialed the car company, and Kath took Muppet to the kitchen to feed him. That finished, she put the pan HT had left on the stove into the sink to soak and cleared away the dishes. Dai finished the call and brought in the coffee cups from the living area. He stopped behind Kath, close enough that she could feel him there.

"You know that if what happened today opened a window into the past for you, that may not be the end of it. If it happens again, whether that's a flashback or anxiety or guilt or anger—whatever it is, don't try and ignore it or minimize it. The harder you try, the more it will bubble up in other ways."

"Bubble up how?" Kath asked, zipping the bag of kibble.

"That's why Laura and I fell apart, I think. I pushed her away, even convinced myself she was seeing someone else because I wanted someone else to be responsible. But it was me. As soldiers, the army trained us to react when the bullets flew, to shoot back, to run toward them. You react during a trauma, and your body floods with adrenaline. The brain doesn't have time to process the emotions or file the experience away as a memory. No one prepares you for living with an event that always feels like it's still right there, still happening, still producing emotions and guilt, but never letting you change anything."

Kath's throat clogged at the raw note in his voice, and she turned toward him. "I hate that it was like that for you."

"It isn't only me, Kath." His expression softened. "It can happen to anyone who goes through something traumatic—a car accident, for instance."

"I don't have PTSD," Kath said.

"It's not binary, full-blown or none at all. Something can trigger symptoms after years, decades even, without warning. That doesn't make it less real. People think this is some recent phenomenon, something we invented after Vietnam or the Gulf War, but it's universal. Shakespeare gave one of the best descriptions of PTSD I've ever read in *Henry IV*. Have you ever heard it?"

"I don't know." She was still reeling from what he'd said. "No, wait. Nothing to do with Glyndwr, right? You mean Lady Percy's speech to Hotspur when he tells her he has to leave."

"That's it," Dai said, holding her eyes as he recited it from memory:

"O my good lord, why are you thus alone?

For what offense have I this fortnight been
A banished woman from my Harry's bed?
Tell me, sweet lord, what is't that takes from thee
Thy stomach, pleasure, and thy golden sleep?
Why dost thou bend thine eyes upon the earth,
And start so often when thou sit'st alone?
Why hast thou lost the fresh blood in thy cheeks
And given my treasures and my rights of thee
To thick-eyed musing and curst melancholy?
In thy faint slumbers I by thee have watched,
And heard thee murmur tales of iron wars,
Speak terms of manage to thy bounding steed,
Cry "Courage! To the field!"
And thou hast talk'd
Of sallies and retires, of trenches, tents,
Of palisadoes, frontiers, parapets,
Of basilisks, of cannon, culverin,
Of prisoners' ransom and of soldiers slain,
And all the currents of a heady fight.
Thy spirit within thee hath been so at war
And thus hath so bestirred thee in thy sleep,
That beads of sweat have stood upon thy brow
Like bubbles in a late-disturbed stream;
And in thy face strange motions have appeared,
Such as we see when men restrain their breath
On some great sudden hest.

O, what portents are these?

Some heavy business hath my lord in hand,

And I must know it, else he loves me not."

Dai's features hardened while he delivered the lines, as if the ghost of the soldier he had been was slipping back inside his skin, giving him steel and strength, but also pain. Hearing him recite Lady Percy's words, it was easy for Kath to imagine what it must have been like for Laura to have to watch him struggling. Watch him suffering.

He was only steps away. Kath closed the distance and placed her hand on his cheek to bring him back to himself. Just a touch, and that was all. He looked down at her, and everything else fell away. There was only the warmth of his skin, the heat of him.

His lips came down to hers. She stood on her toes and met him with all the hunger of someone who'd been starved and locked in darkness. Every part of the kiss felt brand new, the way his lips moved, the size of his hands flattening on her back to draw her close, the mingling of their breaths. Their tongues tangled, a dance, a duel. Neither of them conceded.

Kath needed more. She pulled his shirt out of his jeans so that her hands could explore his back, all velvet skin and solid ropes of muscle.

There were scars. Small and large, her fingers found them by the dozens, and she slid open a button from his shirt and moved to the next, but his hand cupped hers and held her still.

"Are you sure?" His voice was rough. "We shouldn't."

259

"Probably not, but I don't care. Do you?"

His lips descended again, offered himself, asked more from her. Then he drew back, pulled his shirt over his head and threw it toward the table. He paused with a question in his eyes, giving her another out and time to think. She didn't want it. Inhaled the scent of him, cedarwood and rosemary, and something clean and salty like the sea, she needed him. She tore her sweater off, then unclasped her bra.

Her skin throbbed, standing in front of him as naked as the secrets she had bared. He didn't look away. His touch was reverent. He cupped her breasts and bent his head to kiss her nipples.

The ability to think short-circuited. There was only electric feeling, the rough skin of his thumb, his fingers, zippers rasping, denim scraping down their legs. Dai lifted her, carried her to the couch, and she wanted him, ached for him. She pulled him closer even as he raised his head and whispered one more time, "Are you sure?"

Her answer was a growl of frustration, and she drew his hips to hers. "Please."

He laughed softly. Then there was the silk of skin on skin, muscles straining, moving. The primal dance, the sheen of sweat that came with effort and giving, accepting, giving more, and shuddering until they both were spent.

He eased her over on the sofa and lay beside her. She pressed her ear against his chest, listening to the drumbeat of his heart, her fingers restless, wanting to memorize every inch of him. He kissed her hair and traced the curve of her ear, the line of her cheekbone, the angle of her jaw.

"Will you roll over?" she whispered. "Let me see the scars."

There was a moment of refusal. She saw it in the flare of his nostrils, the way his pupils constricted. But he pulled away, and she shifted her hips to let him roll to his stomach, exposing the old wounds on his back and legs. Seeing them, her heart ached. The number of them. The pain.

"You're beautiful," she said, and she bent to kiss them, one by one.

She reached the long scar along his spine, tracing it with her tongue. He gasped and turned, and they began the dance all over again.

Kath watched him move above her, and for all that every part of her was so, so alive and her breath came hard, she felt peace. Every bit of joy and uninhibitedness that she had kept locked away felt released.

His eyes never left hers, and she liked that. It felt as if he saw her, wanted to see her. As if he didn't shy away from any of the dark and twisted and undeserving corners. As if he saw the scars she wore beneath her skin as clearly as the shrapnel wounds that he'd had to work so hard to heal.

"You're more beautiful each time I see you," he said when they both fell back. "From every new angle. But this is going to be messy."

"Complicated," she said, propping herself on one elbow as she eased herself down beside him.

"Complicated," he agreed. "So, how do you want to play it?"

DISCRETION

"I may not always have this, but I have this now…"

JO WALTON, THE JUST CITY

M ARI WAS THE DRIVER WHO came to get them at Kath's cottage and drive them to where the cast and crew were filming. In addition to having driven Dai many times, she was also the driver who had taken Kath and Wenny to the shopping center and back. She waited outside when they were running late.

"Hiya. Trading up on your traveling companions, are you?" She grinned at Kath as she and Dai slipped into the rear seat of the Mercedes. "Where's your Miss Snotty Pants?"

"She's at the hospital, actually. There was an accident."

"Gosh." Mari glanced back in the rearview mirror. "Is that what the police and the reporters are doing up ahead there on the road? Or was that something different? Either way, you must think I'm a right cow for saying that."

Kath reached forward and squeezed Mari's shoulder. "Getting hurt doesn't change the fact that she was a snotty brat. I think she's just very unhappy."

"Will she be alright?"

Kath opened the dog carrier and let Muppet out onto her lap. "I don't know. We're hoping for news from her grandmother when she has time to let us know."

"Her grandmother." Mari switched on the ignition, then she swiveled to look at Kath and Dai in her seat. "You don't mean Glenys Jenkins? I didn't put that together the other day. Neither of those two needs any more tragedy in their lives. They've had more than their share already."

Dai had taken out his tablet to check emails, but he reached out and took Kath's hand and folded it in his. "Glenys has been kind to all of us. I wish there was something we could do."

"She is lovely, isn't she? She's always the first to help anyone. My parents have a farm not far down the main road, near the edge of the estate," Mari said, pushing the dark sedan into gear. "Everyone knows, so it's not like I'm spilling secrets. The girl came to live with Glenys when she was two or three, I think. Her mother died giving birth, and the baby only lived a few months. The husband knocked on Glenys's door one night, dropped a bag on the step, and pushed the poor girl over the threshold. Then he left. Hasn't been back since, has he? Hasn't called once, from what my mother says. Not a card for birthdays or a gift at Christmas. It's no wonder if the girl's a handful. She and Glenys used to live on the estate, but they couldn't keep her out of trouble there."

"What sort of trouble?" Kath asked.

"Wandering into places she shouldn't have gone at Obaith Hall. Going off with people who were there for tours. Nothing horrible. How badly is she hurt?"

The police still had one side of the road blocked near where Wenny had gone down the bank. Mari drove slowly past the parked police car and the officer who waved them around. A news van stood parked a little farther on.

Kath averted her eyes, and Dai squeezed her hand. "She was unconscious when we found her," he said to Mari. "I'm afraid that's all we know."

He and Kath must have repeated those words two dozen times in the minutes after they arrived on set and people came to introduce themselves and satisfy their curiosity. Dai stuck around for a few minutes, then took Kath to his trailer and gave her a brief rundown on where to find hair, makeup, and costuming before he disappeared to where the crew was filming.

Kath told herself she didn't mind. They'd decided to be discreet and professional, at least on set.

The collection of trailers that served as a basecamp stood clustered in a flat area off the narrow road. Kath set Muppet on the floor and let him explore the space, still weighing whether to leave him there in his carrier or to take him to makeup with her. But word traveled fast around a movie set. Olivia showed up within minutes and practically knocked Kath off her feet as soon as she had opened the door.

"Ohmygod. I *still* can't believe you got the part."

"Flattery will get you everywhere."

Olivia backhanded her upper arm and crinkled her freckled nose. "You know what I mean. I was hoping we'd get that champagne last night, but I popped my head into the restaurant and saw you and Dai were working. Then you left and someone saw him go into your cottage with you, so I assumed you would call me when you got free."

Kath tried not to look guilty, and she felt bad that she hadn't called. "He didn't stay long because I basically passed out. Emotional reaction and jet lag and everything, all catching up at once."

"But I hear you were out running together at the butt-crack of dawn."

"And look how that turned out."

"But if you and Dai hadn't been there, who knows how much longer it would have been before poor Wenny was found. Only don't go hogging him all to yourself, will you? Some of the rest of us want a shot, now that HT's mostly taken."

Kath raised her eyebrows. "Mostly? I thought he and Nia were an item."

"He didn't say anything to you? Maybe the rumors are wrong, but I heard she broke up with him. I'm pretty sure he's had late night drinks at his cottage a couple of times since she left."

"That's a shame. Who's he drinking with?"

"Not one who. At least two, from what I heard," Olivia said. "What is it the French say? *Plus ça change, plus c'est la même chose.*"

"The more things change, the more they stay the same," Kath said. "I don't know. I think maybe he has changed. Or he's trying to."

"You shouldn't be nice to him after everything he's done. But at least he's not your problem anymore."

That was true. It wasn't any of Kath's business who HT slept with, if he was sleeping with anyone. After their recent conversations, though, she hoped he found someone to make him happy.

"What about Caradoc?" she asked. "He seems available."

"A bit full-on for my taste, although I may get desperate enough in a few more weeks." Olivia shrugged faintly. "I don't know. He's nice enough, and good fun at the pub when he comes. Also, now that I think about it, I can't say that I've ever seen him taking anyone home from the pub. He's Welsh, though, so maybe he has a girlfriend at home."

Kath decided she and Dai would need to be even more careful about their own comings and goings. People leaving the pub were apparently all too happy taking notes of who slept where.

"Are you okay?" Olivia cocked her head and studied her. "Asking about Caradoc wasn't your way of changing the subject, was it?"

"Not at all. Like I said, HT can date who he likes. I hope he can be happy."

"Good, then let's walk you over to the Painted Palace so we can figure out how to get your medieval on. Are you bringing Muppet? The girls will love him. Except Raymond because he doesn't love anything or anyone. You know that Nia's the reason I got this gig in the first place? I worked on her last film with her and she requested me. Which means you're stuck with me doing your makeup, too."

"So disappointing," Kath said, deadpan.

"I know, right?" Olivia caught Kath's chin and angled her face toward the light. "What have you been doing to your skin? Whatever it is, you need to stop. Are you even drinking water? Sleeping? We'll figure out the makeup first, and then you're going to get the mother of all facials."

They made their way to the trailer, and Olivia called out a long list of introductions to the other makeup artists who were either working on actors, cleaning or organizing their equipment, or chatting with each other. The names were mostly Welsh, and all but one man at the end raised a hand or offered a greeting as Olivia called them out. Olivia had Kath sit in a chair in front of a lighted mirror. But she'd barely pinned Kath's hair up and started cleaning her skin before a thin, wiry little woman in her late fifties swept in, looked around, and marched toward them.

"Bethan," Olivia said a little sourly.

"Olivia." The woman sniffed. She wore measuring tape draped around her neck and a pouch on her hips that bulged with scissors, dress tape, and a flapped pocket that was probably full of pins and thread. After complaining that Kath hadn't come to see her first, and asking Kath to make sure the dog stayed in his carrier, she led Kath to the trailer where Margaret's costumes were kept. A couple of costume assistants worked on costume repairs while carrying on a conversation in Welsh with a few English words scattered in. They smiled as Kath approached.

Kath had tried to learn a few Welsh phrases from her guidebooks, and she tried out the Welsh for 'good afternoon' as she passed the costumers: "*P'nawn da.*"

The men smiled broadly and one responded, "*Su'mae! Croeso i Gymru,* Ms. Cameron."

Kath thought that translated to something like 'Hi, there. Welcome to Wales,' and she thanked them with "*Diolch yn fawr,*" and hurried to catch up with Bethan. The costumer had stopped to wait for her beside a full-length mirror mounted between two more curtained dressing rooms.

"Arms out," Bethan said. "I'll need to double-check your sizing first."

She wrote down every possible measurement, then brought out the first of the costumes to make minor adjustments and sent Kath into the fitting room. Fortunately, the dress covered enough that Kath was able to keep her own bra and underwear underneath.

"We're not staying historically accurate," Bethan said, talking through a mouthful of pins while she turned Kath back and forth and pinched in her bust and waist. "Alan and Dai wanted lower necklines and shorter tippets—those are the long, draping part of the sleeve that hangs from your elbow. You'll want to practice working with that to use as part of your character's movements. Nia made it look quite elegant. Now shoes. There's enough hem on this dress for me to let out, but not on some of the others. We've ordered various heel heights in your size to account for that, but I've only received one pair in so far, and I'm waiting to hear which of the scenes Dai wants to shoot next week. We may need to swap some of the costume choices around based on the shoes we have."

Kath had almost forgotten how tiring standing around could be, and she was even more exhausted by the time Olivia had finished with her and turned her over to Erin, her hair stylist, to highlight and tone her hair to match the clip-in extensions she would have to wear to add length and volume. Thankfully, Margaret's hairstyles wouldn't involve the uncomfortable headpieces women wore in the early fifteenth century, and Kath would wear her hair long instead, with ornaments or braids pinned in various ways.

Before she knew it, it was eight o'clock, and her stomach reminded her she had never made time to eat. She'd barely had a chance to take Muppet out and give him some water and treats to tide him over until dinner. Erin rinsed her hair out, sat her in front of the mirror, and combed through the tangles. She was starting on the blow-dry when the trailer door opened and Dai poked his head around it.

He smiled when he saw Kath, his eyes softening. "Need another few minutes?"

Kath felt a start of guilty pleasure, but she squashed it down. "I can take the crew shuttle with Olivia if you're ready now."

"I'll wait. We need to keep working on those scenes on the drive back. I spoke to Alan, and he thinks the changes could be interesting. He wants a look as soon as we can get the ideas to him."

Kath turned to Erin. "Can we skip the blow-dry? Or were you going to make any more adjustments?"

"Nothing that can't wait," Erin said, smiling at Dai in a way that made Kath want to grit her teeth.

Kath peeled off the hairdressing smock, folded it, and laid it across the back of the chair. Then she thanked Erin and picked up Muppet's carrier.

Outside, the evening chill was even colder with her hair wet, but she didn't care. It was all she could do to keep from taking Dai's hand as they walked together.

They were actors. There was no reason they couldn't pull off a discreet relationship.

Neither of them talked on the way to the car, and maybe that was the problem. Kath had nothing to focus on except how close Dai's hand was to hers, and her awareness of him built with every step. He sent her a half-smile, like a secret shared between them, and she wondered if he felt the same.

It was a good thing, she decided, that they were going to work on the drive back. She wasn't sure how much actual work they would do once they reached her cottage. What she had in mind was more along the lines of improvisation.

STRATEGY

"One should never assume anything."

DICK FRANCIS, *CROSSFIRE*

D AI MENTALLY CURSED THE LENGTH of the drive back to Ty Newydd and the reduced speed on the narrow roads. Kath's thigh pressed against his while they worked and sharing the laptop screen was a slow form of torture. And Muppet lay on Kath's lap, the Westie's chin resting on her arm while he listened carefully in Dai's direction as if he knew precisely what Dai would rather be doing.

They finished the rewrites on the Ruthyn Castle scenes and talked through a few other places where Margaret could take a more physical role. Kath had a way of thinking through what Margaret would do in any given situation that was entirely separate from what Kath herself wanted to do. That was what made the difference between her and the other actors. Sophie and even Scarlet had brought the best parts of their signature selves to the role. Kath was the only one who had given Margaret life.

Dai loved the potential that was bringing to the story. But he also needed, genuinely needed, to take her clothes off and take her to bed.

There were extra cars at the pub and hotel, but no one was out on the street as Kath unlocked her cottage door and the car continued up the road to turn around. Inside, Dai set his laptop and backpack on the dining table and took the phone out of his pocket. He poured them both a glass of wine while Kath went to let Muppet out back and feed him.

By the time she had finished, he ignored the wine and kissed her. Their clothes peeled off, and he pressed her back against the wall for support while he held her wrists above her head so that she couldn't touch him. He needed to take his time, to kiss every inch of her he could reach.

When neither of them could wait any longer, he scooped her up and carried her upstairs, and made love to her the way she deserved, slowly and tenderly at first, then hard and fast, because both of them needed that. They fell asleep on top of the covers, tangled together, arms and limbs and pounding hearts.

He wasn't sure what woke him. Disoriented, it took him a moment to wrap his mind around where he was. Then his stomach growled and reminded him he'd never eaten dinner, which was also a reminder that he needed to get back to his cottage so that no one caught him creeping home in the morning.

Lying there beside Kath, he didn't want to leave. He

watched her in the dim light filtering through the window. They'd done something with her hair, and it was lighter, the same color as the moon outside. She had a tiny crease between her brows as if, even in her sleep, she was worrying about something. He wanted to take his thumb and wipe it away. He wanted to kiss her and clear all the worries from her mind.

He couldn't leave without letting her know he was going. But he couldn't bear to wake her when she needed sleep. He crept downstairs and dressed, poured himself a glass of water, and went to retrieve his things from the table, intending to leave a note for her.

When he turned around, she was standing in a blue silk robe on the last step of the staircase. "Were you going to say goodbye?"

He walked toward her, and she moved to meet him. "I'll be back in a few hours unless you want to sleep instead of running?"

"Can I at least fix you something to eat? You must be starving."

"If it's something quick and simple."

She spooned yogurt into two bowls, added walnuts and honey, and carried them to the table. He brought over the glasses of wine he'd poured hours earlier.

They settled into chairs and ate, and she paused with her spoon in the air. "How are we going to do this? Assuming you want to continue doing it. Filming on location is hard enough between the long hours on set and all the preparation. We're going to need to sleep."

"Sleep is overrated."

"Based on what I heard about HT today, the crew is very good at keeping track of who is sleeping where."

"Does it matter if people know?"

She went still and her eyes dropped away from his. "Tell me something. Did I earn the part? Or did any of this factor into your decision?"

That vulnerability always surprised him. Kicked him in the chest.

It also made him want to shake her.

"Are you asking if I risked my reputation and a $200 million budget to get you into bed?" he asked.

"That's not what I'm saying." Her cheeks reddened, and she concentrated too hard on scooping up a spoonful of yogurt.

"Kath, listen. I expected a long argument with Alan before we agreed about casting anyone. I wanted someone Welsh, and he wanted an established American star. You fit neither of those categories, and despite some good work at your original audition, neither of us thought you had the background for this. Lizzie was the one who pushed hardest for you to read with HT. But after we had finished the chemistry reads, we took a straw poll of everyone who had been in the studio. They all picked you. You blew us all away."

"Really?" Her head lifted, and her eyes brimmed over.

"You've no idea how good you are."

"But Joel said—" She shook her head. "Never mind. Except that what you just said underscores the problem. I don't have the background for this. Maybe that wouldn't matter if there wasn't anything between us. But if it gets out that we're involved, everyone will assume that's why I got the part. The tabloids have already made me out to be difficult to work with. If people assume I slept my way into this part, no one will take me seriously."

"They will as soon as they see you as Margaret. And that's not a bad idea, actually. We can leak the straw poll results and release some clips from next week's filming."

"Would you do that if you weren't sleeping with me?"

"Yes, because it makes sense to prepare audiences to see you instead of Nia. Joel asked us to hold off on the press release until you hired a publicist, but I'm not thrilled about that idea. The news is bound to leak out with a production this size, and Wenny's accident will only draw more attention."

"You want to make the announcement now?"

"We already have it drafted, and I don't see any point in holding it. Trust me, I'm good at my job, Kath. We'll get it out there now, then after next week's shooting, we'll pick out some clips to show the rest of the world what the rest of us have already seen. Not because I'm sleeping with you, but because it will help build excitement for the film. And as far as you and I are concerned, anytime you want to stop, all you have to do is say the word. Or we can put it on hold until we wrap. It's up to you."

He watched her, waiting for her answer, his heart heavier than he would have expected at the thought of seeing her every day without being able to touch her. It was more than physical, though. If they waited, they might never see what might be possible between them. At the end of the film, they would each go in their own directions. Dai already had another project lined up, and if Kath did half as well as he expected as Margaret, it wouldn't be long before she had offers to choose from.

She had bent her head, her hair tumbling forward to hide her expression from him. He braced himself for what was coming.

"I don't know what we're doing," she said. "HT and I were so broken, it didn't give me a lot of confidence to put myself out there. It's all different now with dating apps and people having whole personas that have nothing to do with who they are. But this—you and me—it feels like what it must be like to fall through space, all glittering stars and darkness, and not knowing where I'm going to land. And please don't say you'll catch me, because that would be the cheesiest line of dialogue ever written. Also, you can't promise that. We can't know what will happen."

"Do you want to stop?" he asked, his voice quieter than he'd intended.

"Maybe it's better if you at least go home at ten o'clock from now on when everyone can see you."

"Or if I stay until the pub closes, there will be no one to see."

"You'll be tired and people will notice your lights aren't on."

"They have gadgets for that. Look, I never cheated on Laura, and since my divorce, my relationships have been mutually casual. If you don't want to go public with it, we don't have to. The British army paid good money to make me good at skulking through the woods."

She gave him a reluctant smile. "I think slinking is the word you're looking for."

"*Cariad*, I can't tell you what to do." Dai got up and gently drew her to her feet. If you want to stop, that's all you have to say. One word. Until then, let's see where it takes us." He pressed his lips to her forehead, and then kissed the tip of her nose, avoiding anything below that, because that would just make leaving harder. "Agreed?"

She nodded, her face tipped up to his.

"In that case, go back to sleep, and I'll come knock on your door in the morning if you still want to run with me and drive out to the set together. We have to be ready to discuss your changes with Alan, and if he's on board, there will be more scenes to revise. I still want to finish the new production schedule by Sunday night."

"We should talk to HT about the revisions, too. It'll mean extra work and longer hours for him."

"I already mentioned you had some ideas. It's more Caradoc who concerns me. He's the one with an ego that bruises easily."

Kath took the bowls and glasses to the sink while he slipped his laptop into his backpack and picked up his phone. He'd missed several calls, including one from HT and another from Alan. There was also a text message from Glenys and he read it aloud to Kath:

> Wenny doing okay. Regained consciousness but
> doesn't remember anything. Cracked ribs and pelvis
> and concussion. Could have been much worse. I'll
> be back tomorrow afternoon to catch up with work.
> She'll be a few more days. Thanks for everything.
> You didn't find her phone by any chance?

"That's great news," Kath said. "But poor Wenny."

Dai typed a response to Glenys, then kissed Kath again and crossed to the patio door to let himself out. At the edge of the woods, he turned back to see Kath standing in the doorway, light spilling around her to catch the sheen of the silk in her robe and turn her hair the color of the shining moon. She looked rumpled and breathtaking, and he wished he was taking her back to bed instead of heading up the hill.

Clouds chased each other across the moon, and when it was covered, the darkness in the woods was near complete. He picked his way through knobbed roots and spikes of fallen branches. Small creatures skittered unseen through the underbrush, though now and again he caught the yellow gleam of wary eyes. The back of his neck tingled with the sixth sense from years on patrol, warning him that something more intelligent than the usual fox or marten was watching. He stopped to listen, but nothing moved.

Dai continued up the hill more cautiously, telling himself it was nothing more than his imagination. He wondered if he should ask Kath a bit more about the lights she'd seen. Perhaps he'd accepted her idea that it had been a teenage prank too easily.

He didn't believe much in coincidence. If Lona and her friends were playing around in the woods at night, he could imagine Wenny walking off from them in a huff and a teenage driver not seeing her until it was too late. To be honest, he had more trouble imagining Wenny being part of Lona's group in the first place. But why else would she have been outside that late at night?

FAKING IT

"Tomorrow maybe love; but now it is the rain
Possesses us entirely, the twilight and the rain."

ALUN LEWIS, "ALL DAY IT HAS RAINED"
RAIDERS' DAWN

A N EMAIL FROM JOEL CONFIRMED that he understood the
announcement was going out and suggested a meeting
with the publicist he was recommending. He also passed on a
suggestion that Kath have some photos taken for social media:
her in the cottage with Muppet, in the cottage studying the
script, in the makeup chair, having her hair done, having her
costume fitted, etc. She discussed that with Dai while they
watched the sunrise, and he took her phone and snapped a shot
of her sitting beside him.

"That's gorgeous," he said, showing it to her. "And I'm
emailing it to myself."

"And you know that's not what they mean. The last thing

anyone wants to see is me all sweaty and not wearing any makeup."

"Why do you need makeup?"

"What did I tell you about cheesy lines? But stand up and let me take a selfie of us with the sunrise behind us."

He mock growled at her bossiness and kissed her, hard and fast, as he pulled her to her feet. She ducked away and snapped the photo, then slipped the phone back into her pocket.

The clouds raced, and the wind battered them both. His eyes were the same color as the clouds, changing just as fast. Mount Snowdon lay behind them, *Yr Wyddfa,* in Welsh, the tallest mountain in both Wales and England. But standing beside Dai far below, Kath still felt perched on top of the world.

On the way back, he stopped at the place where the medics had brought Wenny back up to the road.

"What are you doing?" Kath asked.

"I've been thinking about Wenny's phone since Glenys asked about it."

Kath scanned the tall grass, brush, and rocks, and it seemed like a hopeless task. "I'm sure the police have metal detectors. And the phone may not even be missing. Or she left it somewhere completely different."

"You're probably right. I've been thinking about the lights, too. Wondering if there's a connection."

Kath repeated what she'd told him before as they walked the rest of the way to her cottage. There wasn't anything new to add.

Mindful of curious eyes and gossip, Dai didn't come in, and they didn't kiss goodbye. Kath fed Muppet, drank her two cups of coffee, and ate half a pastry and a piece of cheese. She told herself she needed to do a better job with meals and sleep or even Olivia wouldn't be able to salvage the wreckage. Not to mention that she'd find herself unable to fit into her costumes.

She showered and dressed quickly, putting on a little extra makeup and taking the time to blow her hair dry before Dai and the car came for her. He kept the car waiting long enough to duck inside and take advantage of the morning light to take the photos the publicist had suggested of her and Muppet in various poses.

The driver was the one who had driven Kath from Caernarfon. He was on his phone again, speaking in Welsh, and he ignored Dai and Kath as they did a read-through together of the scenes they had rewritten. The first time through, both Kath and Dai stopped to make suggestions. After the second time, it was mostly changing the dialogue or stopping Kath to ask a question. It took eleven readings before they got all the way through to the end.

Kath grew more anxious with every reading, not knowing if that was Dai, the writer, trying to get the lines right, or whether it was her interpretation that bothered him. She wondered if this was what it would be like rehearsing with him. With the crew and HT and other cast members there, that would be excruciating. Or even worse, what if it took a dozen takes before she managed to get it right on film?

"Is something wrong?" Dai asked, looking up from his laptop.

"I hope Alan will like the changes," she said weakly.

"I don't see why he wouldn't. He's more hands on than I'd expect an executive producer to be, but he's the one who's been pushing to make the film more commercial. With luck, he'll be able to text me back soon about what time he'll be available to talk." Dai slid out of the car and held the door open for Kath. "Do you want to take the photos you need before coming to watch the filming? I can see who's available to take them—we'll need someone with an eye. Where are you going to be?"

"Makeup first, if Olivia has time, or hair. Hopefully, the photos will look better if we do them in that order. Then costumes last. I want to wheedle a dress out of Bethan to take home as well. She told me Nia used the movement of the sleeves to help her build Margaret's character."

Dai's brows furrowed almost imperceptibly and then went still while he gave that careful thought. "Your Margaret has more energy and less patience than Nia's. She'd be more likely to be annoyed by the tippets dragging everywhere, wouldn't she?"

Kath could see that, but not all the time. "I think she could be graceful with them when it suited her. When she wanted to fit in. I can see her code-switching between more courtly manners and being impatient with them."

"I like that. It would make the Welsh and English sides of Margaret clearly visible. Or the public and private sides. We should think about other movements that could help convey that."

There was a careful distance between them, but he brushed her hand as they turned in their respective directions. "I'll see you later," he said. "Try not to worry about things."

She made her way to the makeup trailer and found HT in Olivia's chair, a drape over his costume to protect the cloth from makeup and powder stains. Kath set Muppet down a sizable distance away from him as she said hello to them both.

HT half rose to kiss her on the cheek. "It's nice to see you on set."

"I'm not officially here yet. Is it strange for you?" she asked quietly, sliding a look at Olivia, who had—possibly intentionally—given them privacy while she rummaged through a drawer in her makeup station.

"You and I are fine. Muppet not so much." He gave her that sideways smile he used to charm people.

"I was thinking it might be hard for you having me here instead of Nia. By the way, I heard you two broke up. I'm sorry."

His eyebrows rose. "She doesn't want me staying out of a mistaken sense of loyalty—her words, not mine—since we weren't seeing each other long."

"Do you want to keep seeing her?"

"I like her. I know she's young and my track record's not very good at being there when someone needs me, so I'm worried about that. But we're still talking. If nothing else, I want to be there for her as a friend."

Kath sat down in the empty chair beside him. "How is she doing?"

"They've done the mastectomy, and she has another few days to wait before they do the surgery for the reconstruction. Meanwhile, she's starting a charity to raise money for reconstructive surgery for cancer survivors. Since it's not covered by insurance, most people can't afford it. That's giving her something to focus on other than what she's going through."

"She sounds nice." Kath leaned over and touched his arm. "You deserve someone nice in your life. You really do."

"You, too." He settled his hand over hers and squeezed, then turned his attention back to Olivia, who had found the fresh package of contour she had been searching for.

Olivia dabbed it under his cheekbones and jaw and blended it in. "Did you just pop in, Kath? Or did you need something?"

"My publicist is asking me to get some photos in the makeup chair for her."

"Like fake selfies?"

"Pretty fake selfies. So could you work your magic again?"

"My wand and I are at your service." Olivia scanned down the length of the trailer until she found someone who wasn't busy. "Hey, Sara. Can you go see if Erin's available? Tell her Kath needs some publicity photos and see if she has time to do her hair. If not, ask her what's a good time for it. Same for Bethan." She glanced back at Kath. "Assuming you'll need costume, too?"

"I love it when you're the boss."

Olivia laughed. "We've come a long way, baby."

"In theory. In practice, I did a table reading with Dai on the way in this morning, and it took eleven run-throughs before he was happy. Do you remember when every scene was a one and done?"

"Yeah, and you were mostly crappy. Although to be fair, it was the same run-of-the-mill level crappy that everyone produces on a soap opera after one take, day in and day out. We were also shooting the full episode every day."

"On a film like this, we're happy if we get through a single script page," HT said.

"Does Dai usually ask for a lot of rehearsals or retakes?"

"Not usually. It depends on how many moving parts there are."

"So it's just me then?"

HT rolled his eyes but couldn't talk while Olivia finished blending the contour into his skin and started applying powder. Then he eyed Kath out of the corner of his eye, moving his mouth as little as possible. "Which scene were you going over?"

"The run-up to the infiltration of Ruthyn Castle. Dai said he'd already mentioned to you there might be some changes?" Kath wasn't sure if she should dive into this with HT at all, but she also didn't want HT to feel like he was being left out of something secret. "We had an idea about Margaret being more involved in the attack instead of staying on the planning side of it. He and I rewrote a couple of sample scenes to go over with Alan. But it's just an idea for now. I'm sure he'll go over everything with you before it becomes more than that."

"Okay." HT hitched one shoulder, not seeming to mind.

Olivia used a large brush to get rid of any excess powder and took the protective cape from around his shoulders with a flourish. "Now don't go spoiling my handiwork when you put on your silly helmet and chain mail."

"Yes, Mother." HT gave Olivia a mock salute, grinned at Kath, and hurried out.

"Hop on over, milady." Olivia patted the chair he'd vacated, then worked quickly to replicate the look she'd designed for Kath the day before.

In the midst of it, Erin came in. Standing inside the trailer with the door open, she shook out a green umbrella, closed it, and hung it over a rack on the wall beside half a dozen others. She headed down to Olivia's station and started unpacking a tote bag.

"*Su'mae*, Kath, Olivia. I heard you needed some photos, so I figured I'd come pop the hot rollers in for you now, then you can come over whenever and we'll do some shots putting in the extensions." She used a couple of oven mitts to pull a set of hot rollers out of the bag and plugged the unit back into the nearest empty outlet. Next, she removed a set of long, blonde hair extensions that were already wrapped around jumbo pink self-grip rollers.

She held the extensions up beside Kath's own hair to check the color. "We got lucky the first time out on matching these. And I think the lighter color and cooler tone we put on your hair yesterday look good on you. Do you like it?"

"Love it. You did a fantastic job," Kath said, realizing for the first time that she hadn't given the color a second thought since she had gotten up out of Erin's chair the night before. Now that she noticed it, she did like it. It made her eyebrows and eyes stand out more.

Erin had all but the last two rollers in place when a woman in a rain hat and yellow raincoat opened the trailer door and peered inside. On spotting Kath, she headed over, making clomping noises in bright pink rain boots pulled up over her jeans. "Kath? I'm Ranya, the director of photography. Dai was looking for someone to take some photos of you, and I wanted a chance to get out of the rain."

Olivia punched Kath's shoulder. "Look at you! So important these days that you get Ranya Singh coming to take your fake selfies for you. *The* Ranya Singh, mind you, winner of not one but two Best Cinematographer Oscars."

Ranya rolled her eyes at Olivia, then glanced around. "Do you still have that tea station set up in here? I could murder a cup."

"That's the real reason you came, isn't it? You only love us for our tea. Help yourself." Olivia gestured toward the opposite side of the trailer, and Ranya clomped off. Olivia turned back to Kath. "Seriously, the DP taking photos for you? Who even are you?"

Thanks to the hot rollers, Kath couldn't hide the embarrassment that reddened her cheeks. "Dai wants to do the casting announcement today. I think that's why. I have what you might call a deficiency of box office compared to Nia. That means managing the publicity more carefully."

Olivia looked over Kath's head at Erin and gave a shrug. "Okay, that's fair."

Erin took the hot rollers out and fluffed Kath's hair with her fingers. "So what's Dai really like? I hear you're spending loads of time with him."

Kath forced herself to answer casually. "He's been patient, helping me develop Margaret, so I'm ready to start work. And doing his best not to terrify me."

"Why would you be terrified?" Erin asked. "I hear he's a perfectionist, but not unfair."

Ranya returned, blowing on a steaming cup of tea. "Who's a perfectionist? And whose bright idea was it to film in the bloody mountains where it feels like winter when it's barely bloody August?"

"Dai on both counts," Erin said. "I was asking Kath what he's really like to work with."

Ranya laughed, finally looking something other than miserable. "If I wasn't already married… Only kidding, but I like him. He's good at his job, but he doesn't throw his weight around. Unlike some people I could name. Caradoc for one."

A scar dissected one of her eyebrows. Makeup could have hidden that easily, but she hadn't bothered with any. Altogether, she gave off a vibe of being perfectly content with who she was and to heck with anyone else's opinion. Kath envied that.

Ranya took a cautious sip of tea and then set the cup down on the next counter over where it wouldn't be visible in the photos. "Do you mind if I move some things around, Olivia?"

"Knock yourself out." Olivia had finished with Kath, and she watched as Ranya gathered a copy of a Welsh language magazine and set it on the counter before rearranging Olivia's makeup cart to angle various pots and brushes in artistically random ways. Finally, she took off the cape Olivia had put around Kath's shoulders, twisted a strand of Kath's hair, tucked one side behind her ear, and had her cross her legs. "Swivel the chair just about ten degrees to the left. That's it. Perfect."

"How are you faking a mirror selfie when I'm not actually looking in the mirror?" Kath asked.

"I'm not. I'm just shooting the mirror as background. Mirror selfies are overdone anyway. Simple. Now Olivia, stand over there, and take out a lipstick brush to outline her lips. Kath, pucker up just a little. We want that kissable look, yeah? Now hold your phone like you're reading messages."

She took about ten shots on her iPhone, showed them to Kath and then to Olivia and Erin.

"See? This is why Dai sent Ranya." Erin smiled. "Are you ready for me next?"

She packed up her hot rollers and the hair extensions and headed out in Ranya's wake. Kath got up to follow, but Olivia grabbed her arm and tugged at her until Kath bent closer. "Don't think you're fooling me. What's going on between you and Dai?"

Kath debated lying, but what was the point? "Wow, I must really suck as an actor."

"So I was right? There is something?"

"We didn't plan it, Liv. We—"

"Don't stop there, dammit."

"I have to stop, because I don't know what else to say. I like him, and I think he likes me. Beyond that, who knows? And I have to catch up with Erin and Ranya. Thank you for the magic, though."

"I hate you so much right now," Olivia called after her. "So, so much!"

SABOTAGE

WHILE KATH WAITED IN DAI'S trailer for him, she let Muppet out to wander around and stretch his legs. He worked his way to one end of it, then back in the other direction. Kath sat cross-legged on the sofa and pulled the script out. She went over the lines again until Dai opened the door in a burst of wind.

"Sorry, I'm running late," he said. "Wanted to finish up the last of the rehearsals so we can be ready when the sun comes out this afternoon."

"How do you keep continuity when the weather is constantly changing?"

"The good news is we can always count on it to start raining again. Nothing like consistency." He smiled and dropped a kiss on her lips. "Ready to call Alan? I'll explain what we're thinking, and you stand by to chime in or read the scene if he needs convincing. He might have me send the pages to him and leave it at that."

Kath watched him as he placed the call and paced the trailer up and back on repeat. She liked seeing him full of energy and intent on getting what he wanted, and she found it oddly comforting to know that even he felt like he was stretching himself beyond his experience and had something to prove.

"Audiences are already used to seeing women in combat. In the real world and in fantasy and science fiction," he said, and then he frowned as he listened to Alan's response. His pacing stopped. "It does make sense in this film. It makes perfect sense."

He didn't have the phone on speaker, so Kath couldn't hear what Alan was saying, but Dai's body language said enough. Dai's laptop was open on the table, and she slid it over, clicked open the browser window, and typed "Welsh treatment of women versus Norman law" into the search bar and hit return. The second listing from the top was for the article from the Department of Celtic Languages and Literature at Harvard that she had found when doing her research. She found the section in the sample text where the author confirmed that medieval Welsh and Irish sources perceived men and women symmetrically and provided examples. Kath took the laptop to Dai and pointed.

He took it, scanned the article briefly, and asked Alan to hold on a second. Then he read more carefully and set the laptop down before resuming the conversation. "I understand that this might be a more significant rewrite, Alan. But how many times has that happened and resulted in a better film? They hadn't even finished the screenplay for *Gladiator* before photography began."

Kath pointed to the laptop again, and Dai held up a finger, gesturing for her to wait. "Consider how other types of diversity are being treated in film and television now."

He started to pace again, all coiled muscle and sinew like a cat, the fingers on his free hand half-curled into a fist. There was a pale strip of skin at the nape of his neck where he'd recently trimmed his hair, and it made him look a little less impregnable. Kath wanted to go and kiss it. Instead, she sat back down.

Dai paused and stretched his neck to the right and left as he listened, then walked past the table, the cream-colored leather armchairs, and the sofa in front of the wide-screen television. Before reaching the bedroom, he stopped and turned again.

"Alan, these changes *are* in the spirit of history." He crossed back over to the laptop. "I'm looking at an article from Harvard now. There are examples of women in battle from every Celtic country. Here in Wales, Gwenllian led a Welsh army against the English, and they beheaded her on the battlefield in 1136. She inspired rebellion even after her death, and *Ddail Achos Gwenllian!*—Revenge for Gwenllian!—was a

Welsh battle cry for centuries. Glyndwr and his men may well have shouted it as they swept down on the English from the mountains."

He paused at the end of the trailer instead of turning. Kath saw the release of tension in his shoulders even before he answered.

"Yes, I'll send the pages over soon," he continued. "And I know it's short notice, but we have a meeting scheduled for Sunday afternoon to go over the revisions to the production schedule. If you have thoughts on the down-line scenes or overall impact—even if it's as simple as a 'change this,' I'd be grateful."

He disconnected and strode toward Kath. Stooping to cup her face in his hands, he kissed her soundly. "That article was a stroke of genius."

"Where did you get the Revenge for Gwenllian part?" she asked. "That's what sold it."

"I've seen references before. I never chased them up, because I didn't see how it would advance the script. But Margaret would have known about Gwenllian. And she would have used that to support her argument for going on the Ruthyn Castle raid."

"Absolutely." Kath was still sitting, and Dai was leaning over her, hands on either side. He was there, inches away, and she wanted to stand up and turn the tables, because this was new and dangerous, and he made her feel incredibly, vividly alive. But she needed to keep things separate, work and this—whatever this was.

She turned toward the laptop on the table. "So," she said awkwardly. "Alan agreed to look at the changes?"

"Yes, he did, and he did love the battle cry." Dai sat down beside Kath and slid the laptop closer. She watched as he added two lines to the discussion before the departure for Ruthyn, and then the battle cry for Kath to scream as she used a pottery milk jug to knock one of de Ruthyn's men unconscious. "Enough?" he asked.

"I like that Margaret's the first one to shout it in the rebellion. She can't admit she's at Ruthyn to avenge herself, but shouting Gwenllian's name could be her way of striking a blow for every woman in Wales who has suffered under the English occupation. We could also use it in the scene after the Battle of Bryn Glas, where the peasant women castrate the English dead. It would make the motivation easier to understand, bring in how much women suffer in a war."

Dai leaned forward and kissed her. "That," he said, "is bloody brilliant."

They grabbed salads and sandwiches from craft services and ate back in the trailer as they worked through a few more scenes. The changes came more easily now, the ideas sprouting and blooming between them. Dai compiled the changes and sent the document to Alan. He shut the laptop and swung to his feet. "I'd better get back to the shoot. Thanks to the weather, we had to pivot to doing some more of the foundation shots for the CGI models, but if the last of the rain is over, we can get back to HT's scene. Do you want to come and watch?"

"I'd better wait a bit and then come up."

"Afraid to add fuel to the gossip?"

"No," she said. "Exercising common sense."

Dai's expression sobered. "I've been thinking about being more open about our relationship. I'm not saying we shouldn't be discreet. But there's a difference between discretion and misleading people—"

"I don't think you understand how damaging rumors can be to women. And if Alan approves these changes, the gossip could be even more vicious."

"How?"

"People will think I used my influence with you to make the part bigger for myself."

"That's ridiculous."

"Yes, but that doesn't mean it won't be said. That's literally the way the industry has me typecast—as the woman manipulating things for her own benefit behind the scenes. Stepping in for Nia weeks into filming is hard enough, especially since the cast and crew already know each other. I don't want to create more distractions."

"People will say what they like, regardless of the truth, Kath. You know that. Isn't it better to be upfront? We can't control what people think, so why waste the energy worrying about it?"

Kath stared at him. Joel had accused her of the same thing the day he'd fired her. She'd thought Dai was better than that. That she had come farther than that.

Swallowing her disappointment, she picked up Muppet

and carried him to the door. "Can we finish this conversation later? I need to take Mups out, and you need to get back on set."

"Hold on, Kath. I'm sorry. Don't be angry."

"I'm not," Kath lied, and she quietly shut the door behind her.

She hated how easily Dai brushed off her concern. But then he'd spent years chasing bullets for a living. She was a coward, and that cowardice came from experience.

Was she wrong to worry? She didn't want to let fear and old habits sabotage something potentially wonderful before she gave it a chance. She'd finally started being honest with herself and others, and here she was piling on new secrets.

ACCIDENT

*"All the history of human life
has been a struggle between wisdom and stupidity."*

PHILIP PULLMAN, *THE AMBER SPYGLASS*

THE SCENE CALLED FOR FIVE hundred people and more than a hundred horses and hill ponies, which also required enormous tents where the cast could stay dry, and dozens of costumers, handlers, and added crew. An unexpected gust of heavy rain and a runaway horse forced him to stop the shoot and set up all over again, moving the horses back to the top of the hill to wait out the storm. The day already called for many of the actors to change costumes and switch back and forth between the Welsh and English armies.

Dai and the crew plodded back and forth through the mud, resetting, checking continuity, checking equipment. With a thousand and one things to do, he had no time to think of Kath. Still, it seemed as though he'd developed a compass in some back corner of his brain that made him aware of where she stood even when he wasn't looking at her.

He hated that he'd upset her. He wasn't even entirely certain how the argument had escalated so quickly. Had it even been an argument? But one thing he'd learned from Laura was that it didn't matter whether he'd intended to say or do something hurtful. It mattered only that he'd upset Kath, and he hadn't wanted that.

The rain slowed to a light mist, and he and his assistant directors ran through the final checks. The master shot was critical, creating the framework of movement that editing would later combine with closeups and alternate angles. With everything in place, he called for "Action."

The first line of English cavalry appeared at the top of the hill while HT led his army through the valley below. Shouting a command, HT wheeled to face the English, his bowmen scrambling to take cover and knock their arrows. Mounted on more nimble hill ponies, his cavalry charged up the slope, followed by ranks of foot soldiers. But the English kept coming, a wall of heavy horses and armored men, more and more of them sweeping over the ridge and streaming downhill through the mud.

Arrows flew, mingling with rain and wind. The English horses plunged and reared, the movements carefully choreographed to loosen the tight formation. Between the armies, the distance closed. Two hundred yards, a hundred. Then one of the heavy cavalry horses fell to its knees and threw its rider—which wasn't part of the plan. Behind them, riders tried to pull their mounts aside and collided, hooves slipping in the churned-up mud. Another rider went down, and then another. A horse reared and fell backward, its rider crashing to the ground under the hooves of a horse that couldn't stop in time. In desperation, the man behind him tried to jump over the fallen horse and fell as he landed.

"Cut!" Dai ran forward, waving the remaining riders to both sides, clearing a path. There were five riders and a horse still on the ground. Others were struggling to get up. Medics and vets and ambulances raced to get there. Trainers and handlers waded in, everyone trying to calm the remaining animals.

The next hours were chaos. Medics triaged the fallen riders and the vet treated the horses. For good measure, Dai had the handlers look all the remaining horses over. He rushed between checking in on the injured, calming the other actors and crew, and working with the safety team to assess what had happened and ensure they could resume more safely. In the end, the accident was bad enough, but they were lucky it hadn't been worse. One horse had broken a leg, and others had sprains and strains. Two men went to the hospital, although neither of them had critical injuries.

Logically, it wasn't Dai's fault. There were handlers and trainers and safety staff on set precisely to ensure that everyone was safe. But he couldn't absolve himself of responsibility, because in the end, everyone answered to him. And in the back of his mind, he couldn't help hearing Kath's voice mentioning distractions.

He pushed that aside and focused on getting the shoot back on track. In an abundance of caution, he moved the setup to a fresh area of the hillside where the turf was still intact and had the ground inspected for any holes or potential problem areas. By the time the light faded, they had only completed a single take of the master shot, and none of the closeups. He had juggled the camera positions to add additional angles, hoping to avoid a second run-through of the master the next day.

It wasn't until he and the team sat watching the dailies together on the big television in his trailer that he breathed a little easier. More often than not, they each watched the day's footage on their own to see what would need to be adjusted or reshot. Tonight, he had enough doubt that he wanted them all to watch together. And for the sake of morale, he passed out drinks all around.

By the time the screen went blank, the mood had changed from subdued quiet to an undeserved jubilation of relieved laughter and clinking glasses.

"Damned if you didn't pull it off with that extra camera, Dai." Ranya Singh stood up as Dai turned the projector off.

"We were bloody lucky, if we're honest," Ifor said. "There's the one big hole in the English cavalry formation as they start down the hill, but we should be able to edit that with the aborted footage and a bit of AI. I don't think we need to reshoot the whole thing. Do you?"

Dai's head ached, and he rubbed his temple. "I think we can move the closeups to tomorrow and skip the alternate angles. That alright for everyone?"

"I'm good," HT said, and the others nodded.

"I'll send out the call sheets in an hour or so," Dai's assistant director said.

Everyone gathered up their belongings and trooped out, milling around outside the trailer. Ifor stayed behind to talk to him, and over his shoulder, Dai spotted Kath walking toward him.

Ifor glanced back at her and shook his head. "You know there's a limit to how hard you can push yourself, don't you, Dai? I know you're trying to get her up to speed as quickly as possible, but you're burning the proverbial candle. Frankly, you look like hell."

"I hate having anyone get hurt on my watch," Dai said.

"We all do. That doesn't mean there was anything you could do about it."

"I know."

"Should I worry about you?" Ifor asked.

"Not at all." Dai forced a cheerful tone, and Ifor gave a doubtful lift of his brows and headed to his own trailer.

By the time Dai and Kath were in the car for the drive to Ty Newydd, the headache was even worse. He threw back a couple of paracetamol and rubbed his temple.

Kath handed him a bottle of water and a sandwich she had wrapped up for him in a napkin. "Why don't you eat and then close your eyes for a few minutes until the headache wears off."

He shook his head at the sandwich but thanked her for the effort. "Maybe I'll take you up on closing my eyes, though. At least until the meds kick in."

"Today can't have been easy," she said.

He didn't mean to sleep, but the next thing he knew, the car had stopped in front of her cottage, and his head was resting on her shoulder. "Did I sleep all the way here? Hell, I'm sorry. You should have woken me. I wanted to clear the air and apologize about earlier."

"We can talk tomorrow. You're too tired for anything else tonight."

"I'm fine—"

"Go home, Dai. It's not fair to you or anyone else to keep you up all hours." She got out of the car before he could stop her, and she leaned back in through the open door. "I'll see you for our run in the morning."

She closed the door and went to unlock the cottage. Dai asked the driver to wait and hurried to follow her inside.

"Kath, hold on."

She set her purse and the dog carrier down by the sofa and carried Muppet to the patio out back. The sun had set while Dai slept, and he felt disoriented, as though a chunk of the day had disappeared. More than that, he felt like he'd missed out on something critical with Kath, and he didn't quite know what.

"You're still upset about this morning," he said, following her out onto the patio.

She stood watching Muppet sniffing the ground, and her shoulders stiffened. "I'm not. Honestly. This isn't me being a drama queen, or punishing you—nothing like that. You need sleep, that's all. It was a rough day."

"That's all? Are you sure?"

She turned to face him. "You've invested ten years of your life in this film, not to mention the debts you feel you owe to Robbie and Laura. And for me, this is a once-in-a-lifetime chance. I don't want to pile more pressure on either of us when we both need to focus. I definitely don't want to spend time talking about my feelings when you've got so much going on."

Dai knew enough to realize that relationships didn't happen without talking. Whatever Kath professed, he could feel her pulling away. He'd learned that from Laura. When he felt someone pulling back, it was because they were.

He'd also been around enough to know that connecting with someone the way he had with Kath was rare. Time and possibilities could too easily slip away. He already had other projects lined up, and he was rarely in one place for long. After this, her career would change as well. Who knew where she would be?

Still, he didn't want to pressure her. Some people, the harder you held them, the faster they disappeared.

"Are you sure you don't want to work at least a little while?" he asked. "It'll be a long day tomorrow."

She reached for his hands and stepped in closer. "Exactly. Your schedule is hard enough as it is. I want to sort back through all the questions I have marked and figure out which ones I really need to have answered before the read-throughs and rehearsals. It's not fair for me to take up your time unless I have to."

"I enjoy spending time with you," he said softly.

"I'm glad, and that's a choice we can make. Spending time together relaxing is one thing. Going over questions as a crutch because I'm nervous about not being ready for rehearsals is something else."

"Getting us both comfortable with how you interpret Margaret isn't a crutch. That's my job."

"Okay, yes. But you said something today about me worrying too much about what other people think. It made me realize that I've spent most of my life feeling like I'm not good enough, so I've compensated by pretending to be perfect, pretending things come easily for me. I went into a tailspin imagining that if I didn't get things right in one or two rehearsals or takes, the crew would think I shouldn't have gotten the part. Admitting any of this to you is hard. Admitting it to myself is a big step forward."

Her hands were warm in his, but he wanted to pull her closer.

"What does any of this have to do with sending me home tonight?" he asked.

"If I'm going to be the actor I would like to be, I have to learn not to panic about failing. I have to stop giving up, and I have to trust that you—as the director—will be honest with me about how well I'm doing."

"Of course I will." Dai brushed the worried line between her brows with his thumb.

But that wasn't what she needed. She needed him to respect her decision.

Maybe a decent night's sleep would give them both more perspective. She wasn't wrong about that.

She stepped closer and stood on her toes to kiss him. He met her halfway, and she leaned in, her palms flat against his chest so that he felt the heat of her through the fabric of his shirt. The wind blew her hair across his cheek, silk on skin. He wanted more. He wanted *her*, but he swallowed that down and made himself step back.

"If you change your mind, you know where I am," he said. "You can come up anytime."

That got a smile out of her. "I don't know, actually."

"You have my number. And it's the fourth house to the left along the road once you're up the hill." He turned and stepped back through the door.

She followed him, and it wasn't until they'd both taken a couple of steps that he saw the front door standing open. And the car stood in front of it with the engine running where he'd asked the driver to wait.

Kath stopped short beside him, her face bleached of color. He tried to imagine what someone walking by might have seen.

"Kath, I'm sorry," he said. "I must still have been half-asleep when I came in. I wasn't thinking."

"It's fine," she said with her voice tight. "I'm sure it's fine. Get some sleep, and I'll see you in the morning."

FEAR

"We see what a punishing business it is, simply being alive."

SARAH WATERS, *THE LITTLE STRANGER*

KATH FOLLOWED DAI TO THE front door, trying to bury the rising tide of panic. A group of people stood together in front of the pub, but other than that, the street seemed mercifully empty. She waited until Dai slid into the rear seat, then held her hand up in goodbye as he waved to her. The car drove off, and she shut her door.

She didn't blame him. Yes, he should have shut the door after following her inside her cottage. But he was tired, and she should have noticed herself that the door stood open.

The problem wasn't that anyone and everyone could have noticed the car idling in front of her cottage and looked through the front door out of curiosity. The trouble was that she'd been doing things she felt like she needed to conceal. He'd been right about that. And if she couldn't be comfortable with the crew knowing she and Dai were seeing each other, then she and Dai shouldn't be seeing each other. Simple.

All her life, she had hidden anything that might make people think less of her. She couldn't do that any longer. She certainly shouldn't ask Dai to hide things from the team whose trust he needed.

She fed Muppet and sat on the floor beside him with her back propped against the oven door while he ate. The cottage felt empty. She missed Dai, which was ridiculous because she barely knew him. But he knew more about her than anyone except HT, and he hadn't run away screaming yet.

From what she had seen, if Dai had a weakness, it was that he had a blind spot when it came to people. Because he was honorable himself, he didn't see that there were people who could twist even something innocent into something ugly. He saw and expected the best in people.

She'd watched him while he directed the shots and kept track of a hundred different things at once. After the accident, he had walked alongside the wounded actors as the medics moved them to the ambulances and took them away. He had consulted with the horse's handler and the veterinarian and made sure that not only the injured animal but all the other horses involved received checkups. He'd consulted with the safety supervisors and the rest of his team to make conditions even safer, and then he'd spoken to the actors to boost morale.

Dai seemed always to put other people's needs ahead of his own, and that made her realize how self-absorbed she had been most of her life. It was time she made herself accountable for that.

Tired of thinking, she washed out Muppet's empty food bowl, gave him more water, and went to skim through her emails. Joel had sent an invitation to an introductory conference with the publicist, and she accepted and marked it on her calendar. Ranya Singh had sent over the photos that she had taken that morning—most of which were wonderful—and she sent them on to Joel. Alan Stickley's office had sent a copy of the press announcement they'd released, and she already had a few dozen congratulatory emails from friends and acquaintances. She answered a few before finding a rambling, guilt-inducing one from her mother.

> Hope you are enjoying your time in Wales. I've let
> Anna know you and HT are working together again.
> I didn't want that to come as a shock.
>
> She says she hopes you get everything you wanted
> from the role. Try calling her when you can. Maybe
> you can talk to your father at the same time.
> Apparently, he and Elspeth are having a wonderful
> time together. Everyone here says congratulations.
> They would love to see you if you can make time to
> come home.

Kath wondered briefly who her mother meant by "everyone," then decided it didn't matter. She typed out a brief, polite reply, and then struggled to write an email to send to Anna. That consisted of typing a couple of sentences, erasing them, starting over. Then she erased that, too. Finally, she gave up. She contemplated making dinner, but her mind wouldn't stay quiet. She phoned HT to ask if he had eaten yet.

"I'm just getting out of the shower," he said.

"Want to go see if they have anything left at the pub buffet?"

"Not particularly. I'm beat. I don't know how people here live with twenty-two days of rain a month."

"They don't have to ration water, for starters."

"I miss the sun. Do you remember how much I hated LA when we first moved out there? It's grown on me."

"I'm glad," Kath said. "Good night."

In the spirit of being a better version of herself, she decided to brave walking down to the pub on her own. She brushed her hair out, slipped her arms into a warmer sweater, and hid treats for Muppet in various parts of the cottage to give him something to do while she was gone.

The night was dusted with stars and swollen with wind and silence. Now and then, the door to the pub opened and people stumbled out in twos and threes. As she passed the Davies house, a lace curtain twitched in an upstairs window, but it wasn't until she'd reached Glenys's house that she noticed the lights were on. Deciding it was only marginally too late to visit now but would definitely be too late if she waited until after she'd eaten, she stopped and knocked.

Glenys answered wearing the same clothes Kath had thrown in the bag for her two days ago. Fluid had puffed beneath her eyes, which were bloodshot from lack of sleep.

"Oh, hello. Did you need something? I was going to call Dai and give him an update, and I forgot."

"I don't mean to intrude," Kath said, "but I thought I'd see if there was anything you needed."

"I could do with some company, if you have a few minutes? It's too quiet here without Wenny's music and her sulking."

The inside of the house had barely registered with Kath the day before. Dark green walls in the living room contrasted with white built-in floor-to-ceiling bookshelves and linen curtains in a maroon and white floral print. The same pattern carried through in the throw pillows on a pair of small white sofas, and an enormous ottoman with a maroon and gold throw served double duty as a table. It held a tray with a teapot, cup and saucer, sugar bowl and creamer, and half a sandwich on a plate.

"Would you like some tea?" Glenys turned into the room and gestured for Kath to sit. "It's no trouble at all. I'll just bring an extra cup." She bustled out before Kath even answered, returning a short while later looking calmer, and she poured tea into Kath's cup and handed it to her.

Kath declined milk and sugar. "How are you holding up? And how is Wenny? Has she remembered anything yet?"

"She claims she doesn't, and the doctor says that's not unusual. Only she barely talks to me, and I get the impression there's something she's not saying. And she's not arguing about having to stay in the hospital, which isn't like her. It makes me wonder if she's afraid to come home, and looking back over the past few weeks, she's been even moodier than usual. I can't help thinking there has been something else going on."

Kath balanced the teacup and saucer on her knee. "Do the police have any idea what happened yet?"

"They've found a tire track on the shoulder near where Wenny went over. The driver must have known he'd hit her." Glenys poured more tea for herself and added a lump of sugar. "How could anyone do that? Hit her and leave? And her phone is still missing, which is odd. It's not in her room and the police searched the ground and river."

"People get scared in situations like that, weak people," Kath admitted. "Selfish people. Maybe they'll still do the right thing and come forward. They may need time to work up the courage to confess."

"Lord Linton offered a £10,000 reward for information. That may help."

"It's kind of him to do that."

Glenys concentrated too hard on stirring the sugar into her tea. "He has always been kind to us, but it isn't fair to involve him."

"Nothing about this is fair," Kath said. "Offering the reward may make him feel better. It hurts to have to stand by and do nothing when someone you care about needs help."

Glenys started to cry, and Kath set her own tea on the tray and rushed to put her arms around her. "I'm sorry," Glenys said, sniffing against Kath's shoulder. "You're right about doing nothing. For years I've sat by and watched Wenny closing in on herself, and I haven't known what to do. I should have made her talk to me."

"Admitting you have a problem is hard, especially at that age. Wenny may have thought she could work it out, or maybe she didn't want you thinking less of her."

"She used to be such a happy little thing, always talking to people and getting herself in trouble opening doors, poking around in drawers and under furniture. And she and Lona were like shadows of each other when we first moved to the village."

"What happened?" Kath asked. "Do you know?"

"Not really. A few years ago, Wenny began to lock herself in her room and never spoke of Lona. I assumed it was only the sort of fight that girls have at that age, and that they'd get over it. But you can't force friendships, can you? I've tried speaking to her parents many times. They tell me she tries and it's Wenny who won't have anything to do with Lona. They're probably tired of the whole situation. I rang them yesterday to ask if Lona knew anything about who Wenny has been involved with or why she might have snuck out that night. All they'll say is that she has already told the police she doesn't know anything, and they don't want her dragged into Wenny's poor decisions."

Kath winced at the cruelty of that, but she had to be careful about what she said. Glenys would have to continue living next door to them. "Lona might not want to tell her parents everything, either. Maybe she's afraid of getting in trouble."

Glenys looked up sharply. "What for? It was an accident. It had to have been. Someone passing through and not paying attention. That's the only likely explanation, isn't it?"

"Probably," Kath said. "But if that's the case, then why would Wenny be afraid?"

Revisions

"You tread upon my patience."

WILLIAM SHAKESPEARE, *HENRY IV, PART ONE*

D AI'S MIND DARTED FROM THE accident to the production schedule to revisions to Kath and a half dozen other things as he lay in bed. Despite being knackered, he couldn't shut off the torrent of thoughts, and even the words and soothing tone of the guided meditation took far longer than usual to send him drifting off. One of his last conscious thoughts was that the best sleep he'd had in weeks had been those few hours with Kath's warmth beside him.

The alarm woke him at 4:30 as usual, and he made himself a cup of coffee, then opened his laptop and took his phone from the charger. Alan had already sent a text at 4:07 a.m.:

Call when you get up!

Dai drank the coffee and woke himself with a couple dozen

push-ups and some leg stretches. After that, he felt more ready to cope with whatever Alan had to throw at him.

"You're up early," he said when Alan answered the phone.

"I received a rather disturbing email from Caradoc as I was going up to bed last night, so I made time to run through your revisions first thing this morning."

Dai switched the phone to speaker, leaned back against the kitchen counter, and took a beat to breathe before he answered. "I'm not entirely sure which part of that sentence I should query first."

"Let's say Caradoc is not your greatest fan."

"He's a talented director with the potential for greatness. Crap as a human being," Dai said.

"He says the same about you, leaving out the part about you being a talented director."

"And?"

"And the reason I dove into the revisions this morning is because he thought it was his duty to let me know that the pub in Ty Newydd was awash in gossip last night about what you and Kath were up to on her patio."

Dai closed his eyes and rubbed the bridge of his nose. "Well, that was fast. And unfortunate. Did he provide any details?"

"I assume he wanted me to use my imagination. Apparently, he is 'concerned.' He wonders if I know that, in addition to already running substantially over budget, you are letting your attraction to a woman with no serious background as an actor, let alone as a writer or director, cloud your judgment.

Apparently, she is prodding you into making changes that will increase the overrun and add pressure on the crew, which—in his words—you have overworked to the point that fatigue and stress have led to accidents."

Dai took a deep breath and let it out. "By crew, you understand Caradoc is speaking about himself? We had a bit of a run-in earlier this week."

"And the accident he's referring to?"

"A horse went down in the mud yesterday. It left two actors and one animal injured, but that had nothing to do with overwork. We followed all the safety protocols."

"I notice you're not denying a relationship with Kath."

"Why would I deny it?" Dai answered evenly.

Alan was silent for several beats. "You do like making things difficult for yourself, Dai. I presume you've heard of Bryan Singer, James Franco, Kevin Spacey, Les Moonves…. I could continue, but you know where I'm going. You're the director and co-producer. In effect, Kath works for you. If things end up going sideways, that won't reflect well on you or any of the rest of us. Something like that could shadow you for decades."

"Kath isn't like that, and it didn't start until after we had cast her."

"Obviously, but Caradoc was happy to jump straight from one to ten without connecting any dots in between. Other people might reach the same conclusion, and the fact that she's suggesting revisions—"

"What did you think of them, by the way?"

"They're bloody brilliant, and I wish we'd made them

sooner. They'll mean reshooting a few scenes that you've already filmed, which is unfortunate. Not least because Caradoc is right about adding to the overrun. But it won't be an enormous expense, and it will pay off with a better film."

"So we're going with them, then?"

"Of course. I started thinking beyond the scenes the two of you have rewritten so far and penciling in suggestions for similar changes elsewhere. I'll finish that and send it over to you this afternoon. Meanwhile, tell Kath congratulations. For the Gwenllian thing especially."

"And Caradoc?"

"I assume you won't change whatever you and Kath are doing on my account."

"I'd rather take my lead from her, not you, and certainly not from Caradoc."

Alan's sigh was audible. "Fair enough, unless Kath complains. Now, what do you plan to do about him?"

"Tread as carefully as I would with any venomous snake. I'll stick to the letter of his contract, give him all the credit he's due, and take extra care to see to it he doesn't sour the crew enough to damage morale."

"I don't suppose there's much else you can do. It's my wife's birthday on Sunday, so I can't make any promises, but I'll do my best to phone into the meeting and support you. Feel free to remind Caradoc—as publicly as you like—that this is your project and you have my trust. Running to me with schoolgirl tittle-tattle isn't doing him any favors. I don't plan to respond to him directly."

Alan rang off, and Dai's smile was grim. He refilled his coffee, then pulled up the overnight emails on his laptop. But Caradoc hadn't so much as had the courtesy to share his "concerns" with Dai directly. Any small shred of respect Dai might have had left for the weasel vanished.

He hadn't checked email before going to bed last night, and thanks to the casting announcement having gone out, there were far more than the usual twenty-odd emails that needed an urgent response, so he sorted through and typed out replies that couldn't wait. By then, he was late meeting Kath. He picked up his phone to ring her, but thought better of it and decided he was in the mood for a bruising run. Something to burn off a slow coil of fury that was only growing the more he thought about Caradoc's tactics.

And his own stupidity.

If he didn't waste another second, he could still catch Kath up. He needed to catch her, because she deserved a warning before she found out about the gossip. She also deserved an apology.

Most importantly, he needed to make things right.

BOUNDARIES

*"But one discarded dreams and got dressed,
and made what one could of the day."*

DICK FRANCIS, *WHIP HAND*

KATH HADN'T FALLEN ASLEEP EASILY. Her head whirled with random thoughts about Wenny and Dai and HT and Anna. Then she dreamt of being naked during rehearsal for a battle scene, trapped alone in a bubble of space like an enormous snow globe where she delivered the same line, over and over, as an endless army on horseback swept down the surrounding hillside under a barrage of arrows. She woke with her mouth dry and her heart thudding in the early morning, struggling with the realization that whatever she had told herself about facing up to her fears wasn't keeping her from being afraid.

She dressed and took Muppet out, then waited an extra fifteen minutes for Dai before setting off. When he didn't come, she told herself that maybe he had overslept. His absence didn't have to mean anything. If he had changed his mind about running with her, he would at least have sent a text. She knew that, but she worried anyway. The thought of not seeing him made it clear how much she valued their time together.

Clouds hung low in the blue hour, and the air was thick with moisture that clawed its way into her bones. Kath zipped her waterproof jacket all the way up and set a pace fast enough to outrun any wayward thoughts. Missing the echo of Dai's footsteps beside hers, she pushed herself even harder.

By the time she reached the top of the hill, her lungs burned and her legs ached. Everything hurt.

A few shards of sky had appeared between low, tattered clouds, so she waited hopefully to see if there would be a show of color as the sun came up. Standing at the edge of the hill with her face tipped toward the sky, it felt like balancing at the threshold of the world. The wind snapped at the fabric of her jacket, and on impulse, she held her arms out like Kate Winslet in *Titanic*, trying to let go of everything that wound her tight. Almost like a reward for that thought, the sun arrived in slivers of deep red to outline the edges of the clouds.

"I was afraid I was going to miss this," Dai said, coming up behind her. His breath huffed like a locomotive.

Kath wanted to throw herself at him, but she made herself stand still. "So was I."

"Alan sidetracked me for a bit this morning."

"About the rewrites?"

"The rewrites were the good news. He asked me to tell you they were 'bloody fantastic,' by the way, and those were his exact words. He'll be sending us notes later with ideas about how to carry the changes through the remaining scenes."

Kath allowed herself to bask in the warm satisfaction of that for a moment, but then she turned to face him. "And the bad news?"

"Have I told you that your mind is dangerous?" His eyes were dark, his features stiff with caution.

"My mind and I both get nervous when you dodge questions," Kath said.

"Then let me start with an apology. I was wrong not to take your worries more seriously. You gave me your concerns and your reasons, and I should have listened better and taken you seriously. I was careless. I'm truly sorry." He reached out for her hand.

She stepped aside, her back to the hill. "Is that your way of telling me someone saw us last night?"

He nodded, watching her carefully. "Caradoc wrote Alan to say there was gossip at the pub last night about what you and I were doing on your patio." Dai's voice was gentle, almost the tone Kath used when Muppet needed to be soothed when he was nervous. "He felt Alan needed to know that he was 'concerned' I might be too besotted with you to judge your suggestions rationally."

Kath's lungs emptied, and she stepped back when Dai reached for her. Her right foot found empty air instead of earth, and she lost her balance.

He caught her as she fell.

His skin had gone pale beneath his tan. "Christ, you nearly gave me a heart attack."

Her heart banged against her ribs, and she tore out of his grasp and pushed past him, trying to sort through the jumble of thoughts and feelings that all threatened to pour out of her in hot, furious tears. But she refused to cry.

"Say something," Dai said, following her. "Please talk to me, Kath."

"Did Alan have a problem with it?"

"He wasn't thrilled, but no. He and I are fine. What about you?"

"This is exactly what I didn't want to happen," she said.

"And you were right. I didn't take you seriously enough, because gossip isn't important to me. That wasn't fair, and I'm genuinely sorry." He watched from a wary distance, then looked down at his hands as if they didn't belong to him, as if he found them helpless.

Except that he wasn't helpless, was he? No one would assume that he was incompetent or using her. He'd already proven himself to the cast and crew and earned their trust. That had been clear from the way they treated him on set.

"What do you want me to do? What can I do?" he asked.

"Nothing."

"This doesn't change what you bring to the table. Everyone will see your talent."

"You still don't understand."

"Then tell me."

She had told him. More than she'd told anyone. She had opened herself and let him see all the fear and ugliness inside her, and for once, she hadn't protected herself. Now she was going to have days of obsessing about what the cast and crew might say behind her back before she had to face them all on set for the rehearsal. Any notes Dai gave her would make her feel even more like a failure, and that would become a self-fulfilling prophecy.

What if she froze? Or never got her lines out well enough to satisfy Dai?

It was all very well to tell herself she wouldn't let herself fail. Emotions don't follow instructions.

Needing to find some warmth, she walked back toward the edge of the hill, tipping her face to where the sun was slowly emerging. "I was actually on my way to the pub to eat last night. I thought it might help if I went and introduced myself and made an effort to let people get to know me. But Glenys was home, so I stopped in to see her, and we ended up talking until a few minutes before the pub closed."

She shivered, and Dai moved up behind her. And it didn't matter what her brain wanted. Her body needed his warmth and his arms around her. He didn't touch her, and she didn't turn around, but she could sense how close he was. She let herself lean back against him and felt him sigh against her hair. When she didn't move away, he wrapped her in his arms. They stood in an unspoken truce, delaying the rest of what needed to be said.

It was only when the sun had fully climbed above the

horizon and the hot edges of the clouds had faded that she made herself move away. She headed back toward the trail, and Dai fell in step beside her until they reached the top of the trail. He let her go first, and she launched herself down the rocky track, her eyes focused on the rocks and crevices and unevenness beneath her feet. Twice she was on the verge of stumbling, but she needed the adrenaline.

Back on the road, she ran even faster, disappointed in herself.

She had wanted too much. But that was always the problem, wasn't it? She should have known better than to let herself invest so much into anything.

She ran even faster, wanting to outrun Dai and her own thoughts. He kept up too easily, and when they reached the spot where Wenny had fallen, he caught her elbow. "Let's walk the rest of the way. Please."

He let her go almost instantly.

Lights were on in the upstairs windows of about half the rowhouses. Kath thought it was funny that so many people flipped their switches automatically, even when there was enough light to see by. People were hardwired to look for light, around them and inside them.

She had told Dai and Lizzie that she was a glass-half-full kind of person, and she wanted to believe that. The best version of herself was glass-half-full. She wanted to look for the joy and magic in the world. Just once, she wanted to fully let go and not worry about what was coming next.

She wanted to be the kind of person who didn't care how many people might have seen Dai catch her arm just then.

"Glenys told me Wenny claims she doesn't remember what happened, and the police are still looking for Wenny's phone," she said, to change the subject. "Glenys thinks Wenny is afraid of something."

"It's probably normal to be afraid when you've been hit by a car."

Kath shook her head. "She doesn't seem eager to go home. Who wants to stay in the hospital? So, what if the fear is more specific? She could be afraid of whoever was driving the car that hit her."

"The car would have come up behind her on that side of the road, wouldn't it? She wouldn't have seen the driver."

"Unless it crossed from the other lane. And even if it didn't, she would have heard the engine and seen the headlights. What if it's all connected to why she was upset the other day? She didn't just sneak out of the house to walk along the road in the dark all on her own. There has to be a reason. She was going somewhere, coming back from someplace, meeting someone. And if that someone wasn't involved in the accident, wouldn't they have come forward?"

"Maybe they have. The police wouldn't necessarily share that with Glenys."

"And the phone? I've probably watched too many crime shows, but I can't help imagining someone going down to take it out of her pocket after she had tumbled down the slope. What if she wasn't unconscious right away? She could have seen them. It might have been the same person she was meeting."

"You're saying that it could have been someone she knew? Or at least had been in touch with?"

"Maybe they'll still find the phone somewhere. But if they don't, why would someone take it unless there's something on it they don't want anyone to see?"

Hanging in the air, the words sounded worse now that she had said them aloud. But ironically, the village still looked as charming as a movie set. The same ginger tomcat swaggered around the corner of the pub. The same dusty delivery van stood in front of the farm shop.

"The road continues past the village, straight through to the A5 between Bangor and the English border. The car could have been going anywhere. It doesn't have to have anything to do with the village at all."

"No, you're right." They had reached the front of Kath's cottage, and she moved to unlock the door. "Maybe I'm overthinking it because of what HT and I did. The accident."

Dai put his hand on top of hers. "You can't change the past, Kath. None of us can, no matter how much we wish otherwise. But that one incident doesn't define you. If I've learned anything from my own experience, it's that I have to learn what I can from it and then forgive myself. That's hard, far harder than forgiving someone else, but that's the only way to heal."

Kath's eyes burned, and she swallowed a lump the size of a grapefruit that seemed to block any chance of her being able to respond coherently. "Thank you."

Dai nodded, his eyes concerned, and his brows knitted as he studied her. "And the gossip? Are you alright?"

"I will be by the time I need to be on set. Although, I think I'll skip that today. I have an appointment this afternoon with Joel and the new publicist, anyway."

"Are you sure? I hate the thought of you being here alone all day, feeling like this."

She didn't tell him she was fine.

"I'm sure," she said. She pushed the door open and stepped inside. Dai waited a moment longer, then he nodded again and turned to walk up the street, his head down and his dark gray T-shirt damp and clinging to the muscles of his back and shoulders.

Kath didn't want to watch him, but she couldn't help it. And even though the village was small, and the clouds pressed in close to make it even smaller, she felt as if in a matter of days he had stretched the boundaries of the world for her, like ripping the brown paper from a painting starting at the middle and pulling apart the edges until more and more and more emerged.

At the intersection, he glanced back toward her door before heading up the hill. She raised her hand and then closed the door. It felt strangely final.

HONESTY

"You cannot change what you are, only what you do."

PHILIP PULLMAN, *THE GOLDEN COMPASS*

K ATH HAD NEVER BORROWED THE COSTUME she had
wanted from Bethan, but she had dress tape, safety pins,
and a pair of dishcloths. After a quick breakfast and another
run through her emails, she folded the dishcloths lengthwise
and pinned them to her shirt above each elbow to simulate the
floor-length tippets that were part of the fifteenth-century
sleeve style.

The idea of code-switching Margaret's movements
intrigued her more and more. She had grown up in Wales, but
her father had been the Justice of the King's Bench and argued
petitions in the House of Lords. Margaret had spent much of
her time in England, and around the English, so she would
have been familiar with their manners and expectations and
would have been careful not to give them a chance to criticize

her. On the other hand, the Welsh who didn't have Margaret's wealth and good fortune would have been busy worrying about how to pay the exorbitant English taxes and survive the oppressive laws intended to subdue them. Kath doubted they would have cared as much about courtly manners. Seeming too English might even have worked against Margaret and the uprising.

Kath walked around the cottage, wearing her makeshift tippets and imagining her movements hampered by a dress that trailed behind her on the floor. She concentrated on learning how to shift the fabric out of her way while she cleaned the kitchen and the bathroom and removed Muppet fur from the floor and carpets with a sweeper she found in a downstairs closet.

Once she had that down, she blocked out specific movements for various scenes, changing the way she moved her arms, the way she walked with longer strides when she was with the Welsh. In scenes with the English and on court occasions like Glyndwr's coronation and meetings with the Pope or the French and Irish ambassadors, she adopted a more mincing, ladylike step.

Muppet quickly tired of following her from room to room, and he plopped himself beside the sofa with his chin resting on his paws. Shortly after ten o'clock, he lifted his head and gave two sharp barks as Glenys knocked on the door.

She looked more rested than she had the previous night, and she had dressed for work in black slacks and a red silk blouse. Kath stepped aside to invite her in.

"I can't stay. I'm running late back to hospital as it is," Glenys said, remaining in the doorway. "But I wanted to stop in and thank you again for listening to me last night. I must have sounded half-hysterical."

"Not at all, even though most people would have under the circumstances. Have you heard anything more from the police?"

"The detective rang a while ago, asking about Wenny's arm. Exactly how did she break it, and where was she, who was with her? He also asked about her father and anyone who might want to hurt her."

"So they think it was deliberate?" Kath asked.

"They're only trying to be thorough. Apparently, her phone received text messages from an unregistered number that night, but pay-as-you-go phones are available in any shop, so that doesn't tell them much. But again, thank you, Kath. I'm sure you'll be run off your feet with the film, and I'm at the hospital until they kick me out, but if you'd ever like to stop in again, please pop round."

"I'd like that, if I get a chance," Kath said. "Please tell Wenny I hope she's feeling better."

"I will." Glenys turned to walk away.

Kath called after her. "Who do I call to let Lona know I don't need any cleaning today? Is it the main number, or do I let her know directly?"

"Lona?" Glenys turned back with a frown and waited for the noise of a passing car to subside. "The Davies have nothing to do with that side of things. They only handle the hotel, pub, and restaurant."

"I must have gotten the wrong end of the stick, then. I saw Lona coming out of one of the cottages a few days ago."

"She was probably dropping off a meal. The restaurant delivers on request. Oh, and the number for the cleaning service is in the notebook I brought over."

Back in the cottage, Kath found the number for the service. The man who answered was only too happy to skip her cleaning for the day, and he confirmed Glenys had already left instructions not to enter if the dog was home. With only a brief break for lunch around noon, Kath worked diligently on the script until three o'clock, when the phone rang.

"I saw the announcement in *Deadline* just now. Congrats on being official," Fiona said in her smoker's rasp. "I thought I'd check in and see if you needed anything."

"A giant vat of self-confidence, maybe?"

"Is Dai being hard on you?"

Kath found herself smiling at the sound of his name. "No, it isn't Dai. We're not even shooting with Margaret yet."

"Then what?"

Kath thought that over. "Bad habits? My inner voice of doom?"

Fiona laughed, a sound like shredding paper. "Try music, honey. Something by Shania Twain. That'll drown out the doubt every time."

"Really?" Kath asked.

"Hell, no. But it can't hurt. Try 'Don't Be Stupid' and 'Life's About to Get Good' for starters, or 'I Ain't No Quitter'—if you can ignore the double negative. Or maybe try reading the press release, because I think the exact quote was 'She brings an exciting new dimension to the role of Margaret Glyndwr.'"

"You want to come to Wales?" Kath asked. "You're better than *Gilmore Girls*."

"You don't need comfort, Kath. Once you start filming, you'll be great."

Kath downloaded the songs Fiona had recommended, along with some others, and as she dialed up the volume, she found her foot tapping. Fiona was right—she felt better. Stronger.

That lasted until late in the afternoon, when she had the introductory call with Joel and the new publicity team, which consisted of a no-nonsense woman named Jane Kim and her assistant, a young man with a voice that seemed to default to breathless excitement. They asked for her social media passwords, gushed over the photos she had sent, and gave her a laundry list of additional photos they wanted her to get. They also told her they wanted to set up a couple of softball interviews with the trade magazines in the next few days.

"Nothing earth-shattering for now," Jane assured her. "We mainly need to establish your professionalism and let people see that you have a lot to offer for the film. Your credits have been thin lately, but Joel mentioned that you'd read a lot of the history behind Margaret and Glyndwr. That might be where we'll need to focus. How carefully you prepared and why you connected with the character."

"Dai mentioned releasing some clips from next week's

filming, and leaking the results of an unofficial poll they did after the chemistry test."

"Careful with that. They don't want anyone else who auditioned getting upset," Jane said. "And it would be nice to get something out next week in the trades."

"Maybe something from the chemistry test? I could see what they'd think of releasing that, and you could offer it to whichever of the trades would be the most strategic?"

"If the footage can be edited into something fantastic, maybe." Jane's voice pitched slightly higher. "It would be news. Auditions aren't something fans usually get to see, so it might get some buzz. Especially since HT's in there. Can you sound Mr. Rhys out about that? Or is that something you need me to do?"

"I can ask."

"And what's it like to be working with HT now that you're there? Once we get your credentials established, we were thinking it might be good to start some speculation about the two of you rekindling your romance. Are there sparks flying between you?"

"That's not a possibility," Kath said firmly.

"Too bad," Jane said. "But it doesn't have to be real—"

"That's beside the point. Nia would get dragged into that, and I won't do that to her."

"I can talk to Nia's people—"

"No," Kath said.

"I see." Jane sounded disappointed. "In that case, maybe we can focus on the tension. Make people wonder if you and

HT can get through the film without killing each other or getting back together. That might be an even better angle."

Kath needed to be calm and make herself clear. She took a breath and slowly let it out. "I appreciate what you're trying to do, but I want people to know I earned the part. I don't want more tabloid drama."

"Drama is how your name stays in front of readers until the film comes out. If it wasn't for confidentiality, I could rattle off dozens of A-list showmances off the top of my head."

"I want to do my job without making it any harder for anyone else to do theirs."

"Even HT and Nia may not be having the relationship you think they are," Jane said.

"Which has nothing to do with me. Think of something else. Meanwhile, I'll ask Dai about the chemistry clips."

"This isn't coming from Jane, Kath," Joel cut in. "It was part of the original discussions when you got the role—"

"You never mentioned that. And I went over the contract. It says nothing about a showmance, which means I don't have any obligation."

"It was a side conversation. It was mentioned to me that Alan Stickley would find it helpful if we could get people talking."

"No." Kath took another breath to rein herself in. "If that's what you and Alan discussed, then call him back and admit you overstepped. Or I'll do that myself. I fought hard to get this audition, Joel. And I got it without your help. If I want to have a relationship with anyone, it will be on my own terms. My terms, not part of a deliberate media circus."

"Joel, why don't we circle back to this another time?" Jane inserted smoothly. "Kath understands how important the opening weekend box office is going to be. She knows that her performance will stand on its own after the film is out, but that the Monday morning headlines will be about the number of tickets sold. Which in turn will impact ongoing ticket sales, international box office, streaming, and everything else. She's smart enough to see that. In the meantime, she can keep us in the loop about anything we need to take care of for damage control and work on getting the audition clips from Mr. Rhys. Isn't that right, Kath? We really are all on your side here."

"Jane, with respect, I don't need you to 'manage' me or interpret what I know or do not know. I appreciate your expertise and guidance, but that kind of help doesn't work for me. I prefer to be honest. And I'm sorry, but I have to get back to work."

She hung up, tore open the safety pins above her elbows, balled up each of the dish towels and threw them across the room. They were too light to make for a satisfying gesture and fell limply to the floor.

Why had she let Joel recommend the publicity firm? In what universe could that have been a good idea? She was starting to hate Joel, and Jane Kim's condescension was almost just as bad.

If either of them had been listening to her at all, she might have mentioned the gossip about her and Dai, in case it escaped the pub and Alan Stickley's office. But she could imagine the look on Joel's face when he found out and the type of things he would say. He and Jane would either tell her to steer clear or they'd want to exploit that relationship, too.

Thinking of Dai, she sent him a text about the clip:

> Hope you're having an easier day. Spoke to the new publicist. They're arranging some trade interviews, and I was thinking about your idea of leaking clips. Was there anything in the audition or chemistry test that my team could use to build some credibility?

He didn't text back right away, which wasn't surprising, but it was discouraging. Kath checked her email in the meantime and discovered that he had already forwarded her the notes he'd received from Alan earlier about the later scenes. Reading through the comments, she started adding her own thoughts plus a few suggestions for dialogue changes or additions here and there.

Amid all that, she received Dai's reply:

> Clips are not a bad idea. Ranya has two in mind and will speak to editing. Also wants to look through the first audition. How soon do you need them?

Given the gossip, Kath would have loved the clips to be out there for the cast and crew to see before she had to meet anyone else or set foot on set. *Now* would have been ideal.

> They're setting up interviews for me in the next few
> days. They can probably hold off as long as you
> need. Today going well?

A few seconds later, he responded:

> Will need to work on Sunday morning, but should
> be able to change locations for Monday per the
> schedule. Thinking you could start then.

So that was that. Strictly business.

Fine, that's what she had asked for. They both needed to focus on the film.

It was probably a long shot to ask if Olivia wanted to eat together, since she probably needed to stay on set until they wrapped for the day. Kath texted anyway, and Olivia replied that she was walking back to catch the shuttle and expected to be back around seven thirty.

> Are you finally buying that champagne? Not going
> to lie, it's past time. Assume since Dai is still here,
> he will join you later?

Kath texted back:

> So you've heard the gossip?

And Olivia answered:

> Don't know who saw you, but Caradoc made sure
> everyone heard. Figured if you wanted to talk about
> it, you'd let me know. You okay, tho?

Kath had never stopped to consider the difference between answering someone who was asking how someone was for the sake of being polite, versus a friend who was asking because they cared. She had let her friendship with Olivia slip away once already by trying to hide the fact that she was a walking disaster.

And had she really fooled anyone? How many other friends had she pushed away out of pride?

When she had needed someone to stay with Muppet, there had been no one she could call. The people who saw only the mask she wore were there for the polite answers and the fun, and she could count on them for exactly as long as the laughter continued and the champagne was cold.

Joel had accused her of wanting to be a star more than she wanted to be an actor. That wasn't true. What she had wanted was a chance to escape herself, to have enough fame to make people like her even when, deep down, she wasn't sure she deserved to be liked. Out of sheer exhaustion, she had let her guard down, and she felt like she had made more genuine friendships in two weeks than she had in a decade.

Dai had been right about living in the moment. And Dai was her one regret. What if all they had together was a moment, and she had thrown that away?

She typed an honest answer to Olivia's question:

> I'm embarrassed and sad, but I'll get over it. Is there any blowback on Dai for this?

There was a long pause before Olivia answered:

Not that I've heard. I wouldn't call any of it blowback
anyway. More like surprise because Dai doesn't flirt
or respond to flirting. There's some jealousy, I'm not
going to lie. And some of the a-holes are being a-
holes. But that's because they're a-holes.

Kath answered *HaHa* to that, and asked Olivia to stop by
to get her on her way to the pub. She put on jeans, running
shoes, and a thick, comfortable sweater, and did her makeup
carefully to make sure it didn't look too "done up." Then she
took Muppet out for a short walk on the leash while the village
was still quiet. There was a man sitting in a car in front of the
hotel, and sure enough, on seeing Kath, he got out with a
camera in his hand and started hurrying toward her.

Kath walked faster, surprising the ginger cat who had been
sitting beside a flowerpot. The cat trotted away, his tail straight
up in the air. Muppet stopped and sniffed, then suddenly tore
off after him, jerking the leash from Kath's hand and running
headlong into the flowerpot.

He stopped and looked mildly dazed. Kath scooped him
up and crossed the road while the photographer snapped
several photos. "Idiot," Kath said to Muppet. "What's the
point of running at full speed if you can't see where you're
going?"

Muppet licked her face and wriggled in her arms, asking to
be set down again. The photographer called Kath's name, and
she thought it through for a second before she turned and
flashed a smile. With luck, the photo wouldn't be half bad, and

maybe the guy would be content with that. Or maybe not. For all that she had promised to live more in the moment, she had still been fighting for control and closing the door on opportunities. Doing that was too exhausting.

SHOTS

*"Nothing solves insomnia like a warm glass
of regret, depression, and self-loathing."*

D.D. BARANT, *DYING BITES*

EXPECTING OLIVIA TO DISAPPROVE OF her casual look, it surprised her when Olivia looked her up and down with narrowed eyes, then nodded and said, "Yes, that will do nicely."

Kath pulled the door shut behind her. "Does that mean I should expect judgment?"

"Honey, from the second you walk in there, you will get more judgment than a mother with a kid who's throwing a public tantrum. For getting the part, for being HT's ex, for all the old tabloid crap. You did well the other night—or at least you didn't do anything wrong. But hearing you're with Dai now, people are going to wonder what you have that they don't and whether you're all that. Plus whether you're full of yourself."

"Dai and I aren't together." Kath paused as they were walking toward the pub.

"Don't even try that when we get inside." Olivia caught her elbow and started walking again. "Trust me, even if it was true, it wouldn't help. And I'm not hating, by the way. There's something incredibly sexy about a guy who's got that old-fashioned sense of honor and decency. Never mind the guts to take on a project like this. And the fact that's he's Willy Wonka–level eye candy? That's a bonus. But it's the steady and no drama, no temper part that makes him exactly what you need."

"What about what he needs?"

"He wasn't running the other direction, from what I heard. He's one of the most grown-up men I've ever run into. Trust him to know what's good for him."

"We may have put things on pause until after we wrap photography, anyway."

They had reached the pub, and Olivia paused with her hand on the door. "You both decided that?" she asked, studying Kath. "Or you decided it on your own? Out of fear?"

Kath stared at an old, dry piece of chewing gum stuck on the wall beside the door.

"You see what I mean?" Apparently, Olivia didn't need her to say the words aloud. "I swear you are the dumbest smart person I know. Relationships don't come with a pause button. They go from zero to sixty and build from there, or they start with that long, slow burn of trust and friendship that keeps getting hotter and hotter. You can't turn the engine off and expect it to fire right back to where it was when you start it up again. For all you know, you and Dai might be on different continents once this film is over. Have you seen how hard he works? He's not going to be flying back and forth all the time. So if there's something between you, why not see where it can go?"

"The gossip. The disruption. He and I both need to focus on our jobs."

"So don't let it mess with your focus. And screw the gossip. Unless it's only a physical thing, it's worth seeing where it goes. But we've already established that Dai doesn't bed hop, and you don't, either."

"I'll think about it." Kath reached past Olivia and pulled the door open.

The bar wasn't as full as the other night, but conversations and laughter bounced off the low-beamed ceilings and the hardwood floors. The volume dipped as people noticed her and stared while pretending not to stare.

Olivia stepped past her. "Hey, everyone! Kath's buying a round, and I'm making introductions."

Kath forced herself to laugh and wave, and she walked to the counter to get the bartender's attention. "What's easiest for you?" she asked, leaning over the bar. "A round of champagne or getting everybody another of what they're already having?"

The bartender was about twenty-five and blue-eyed, with a thick crop of dark hair that curled into his eyes. Tattoo sleeves covered his arms to the knuckles. "I doubt we have enough champagne, and taking orders would take a while. I can do beer, yeah? Or a good Welsh whiskey."

"Whiskey shots it is," Kath said. "Mind if I pass them around myself?"

"Can you handle a tray, love?"

"As long as you don't load it up too much."

"Come back and load it yourself, if you like. So long as you don't tell anyone I've let you." He gestured for her to come around behind the bar. "Get those shot glasses for me and line them up on the tray so they're touching. That'll get you started, and I'll do the next tray while you're working."

Kath lined the glasses up, and he took down a nearly full bottle of whiskey and moved steadily down the row, never lifting the bottle until it was empty. While he opened a fresh bottle from a cabinet beneath the bar, Kath set the filled glasses on a round serving tray and ventured out to pass them around.

"Good thinking." Olivia leaned in to whisper in her ear, then she snatched two glasses and held one out for Kath while she kept the other for herself. "Down you go. Get your courage up."

"I'm not sure courage is in my vocabulary yet." Kath struggled to balance the heavy tray, but she didn't argue. Olivia held the shot to her lips and Kath threw it back. The whiskey burned down her throat, leaving behind a welcome warmth that slid along her veins.

"Do one more." Olivia held up another glass.

Like HT, Kath hadn't been much of a drinker since that last night in Cincinnati. Control was her security blanket. But it had been a long couple of days.

She downed the second shot when Olivia held it to her lips,

then she moved to the far end of the bar and let people take them off the tray. Olivia went with her, introducing her to everyone along the way. Most were welcoming and friendly as she held the tray out for them, but there were a few who smiled like they didn't mean it. Kath took extra time to be friendly with those, but she tried not to read too much into anyone's reactions.

She hadn't expected people to wait for a toast, but they did so automatically. After the last of the shots had been poured and distributed, Olivia shouted, "To Kath, who is going to be genius as Margaret and save our butts."

People laughed and shouted, "To Kath," and downed their shots.

Kath's throat burned less on the third shot than it had on the first, but that was a hint that three was the magic number. No more. Then she spotted Lona Davies carrying a tray of food from the kitchen to the dining room, and the fire the whiskey had ignited in her veins cooled by a few degrees at the dirty look Lona gave her.

Olivia noticed it, too. "What's with the kid? Did you set fire to her cat or something?"

"Not a clue. Have you noticed her around much?" Kath asked. "What's she like?"

"A bit starstruck. You've met the type."

"Any star in particular?"

"Apart from HT? I don't know. Anyone with a Y-chromosome and on-screen credits. Can't say I've paid much attention beyond thinking that she's way too young for anyone here and that I hope to heaven no one here is remotely that stupid. Not that I give men much credit." She shrugged and tugged at Kath's hand. "Hey, are you feeling those shots? Because I am. It's time to eat before I embarrass myself."

She put her arm around Kath's waist and started up the stairs, then paused as a commotion started up behind them. Kath turned in time to see the same photographer from before moving toward the bar, his camera hanging around his neck. Several crew members were shouting at him to leave and crowding him to get him to walk backward.

Kath didn't wait to see what would happen. She pulled Olivia up the remaining steps.

The room at the top of the steps had rows of large tables and chairs, and three separate buffet stations that overflowed with food. Besides the standard buffet fare that ranged from salads and steamed vegetables to baked fish, chicken, and beef, there was roast lamb and various dishes Kath didn't recognize. Everything had a card written in both Welsh and English. Kath took a green salad and some clementine-glazed salmon, along with some Conwy mussels.

"You'd better take some of those potatoes. They're delicious, and they'll soak up the shots so you can drink more."

"I think I'm done drinking, Liv."

"Party pooper."

They found seats at a table for eight with a mixed group of makeup and crew members from sound and lighting. One woman barely waited until Kath had sat down before pinning her with an avid look. "What's it like working with HT and seeing Dai? Awkward, isn't it?"

Seven pairs of eyes watched Kath carefully, and she struggled to keep her smile. "I'm not sure you can say that Dai and I are exactly seeing each other. We're more interested-but-too-soon-to-tell," she said, mindful of Olivia's warning. "We definitely don't want to make things awkward for anyone. And as far as HT goes specifically? I'll have to come back to answer that next week. The chemistry test was the first time we've ever worked together, but we're good friends. I don't think there's going to be any problem."

Olivia looked around the table. "Show of hands. Who would go out with Dai if they had the chance? Working together or not?"

All the women, including Olivia, and one of the men raised their hands.

"*Et tu*, Brute?" Kath said, sending a mock scowl at Olivia.

"What? I'm telling you, snap that man up while you have the chance."

"Thanks, but I'm not sure I should run my love life based on popular opinion."

Olivia leaned in and whispered in Kath's ear. "Really? Because it kind of feels like that's exactly what you're doing."

Kath stared back at her a moment, then concentrated fiercely on eating her dinner and asking the others about their jobs and families and how things were going on set. By the time they went back downstairs, the pub was packed. Olivia dragged her from group to group for a bit, but since nearly everyone had to be on location first thing in the morning, most people headed out of the pub shortly after ten. Kath seized on the opportunity to go with them.

"Are you coming or staying here?" she asked Olivia.

Olivia downed the last two sips of the red wine she had been refilling since dinner and slid off the stool a little unsteadily. "I'm definitely coming. Might have overdone the alcohol it a bit."

She wasn't much steadier on her way to Kath's door, and she stopped and leaned an arm on the wall while the group said, "Good night, Kath," and Kath said her own "good nights" in return. But as Olivia made no move to follow the group, Kath studied her critically instead of going in.

"You sure you're okay? I can walk back with you," she said. "Or you can sleep here, if you want?"

Olivia shook her head, sending her dark hair flying in every direction. "Nah, I'm good. You're good now. We're all good. Also, you can thank me later. Again. Because I shaved your bacon."

"You did shave it," Kath said, smiling back at her. "So, thank you for being my wingman and taking care of me. And I still owe you champagne."

"I know that, shilly. And don't worry, I'll collect. But not anytime shoon, because I'm giving up alcohol. Also, you should listen to my advice about Dai. It's good advice." Olivia rubbed her temple and then shouted for the group to wait up. Her steps were wobbly as she ran to catch them.

Kath went in and gave Muppet an extra treat and lots of

love for having left him. Then she stood and looked around. Now that she was alone, the evening felt anticlimactic. She'd built the gossip and potential judgment into an enormous obstacle in her mind, the way she'd been letting too many things become obstacles all her life.

Sure, there had been a few people in the pub who weren't friendly, and she was still going to have to deliver on Monday and prove to everyone why she deserved the role. That terrified her just as much now as it had before. And yes, the pressure was going to be worse if everyone thought she and Dai were seeing each other.

On the other hand, now that people already believed she and Dai were seeing each other, what was the point of breaking it off? Apart from a bit of extra sleep.

"I think it's time I finally grow up and put on my big girl pants," she said to Muppet, scooping Muppet up and snuggling him beneath her chin. "What do you think? Want to see if Dai is still awake?"

She started to phone him, but she didn't want to ask permission to come over. She wanted to make the gesture. If he didn't want her there, she would turn around and go home again. At least she would have a chance to let him know that she, at least, had changed her mind.

Muppet waited at the bottom of the steps while Kath ran up, changed into running clothes, and slipped her toothbrush, toothpaste, and hairbrush into her purse. Downstairs again, Kath scooped a bit of Muppet's kibble into a plastic bag, added his blanket and leash, and then switched off every light except the overhead in the kitchen. The only directions she had for Dai began with cutting through the woods, so she went out the patio door even though it meant leaving the cottage unlocked. She wasn't sure she could find his house any other way.

"We are going to be brave, Muppet. We're going to march straight up that hill and not look back. But keep your ears open, okay? Let me know if we're going to trip over any bears or vicious teenagers."

SELF-DEFENSE

*"Unnatural voices, my mind broken
By a sudden acquaintance with man's rage."*

R.S. THOMAS, *TALIESIN 1952*

THE LIGHTS MATERIALIZED AROUND KATH in a circle. There was no warning, not a sound or a stir of wind. But Muppet's hackles rose and a low growl rumbled through him.

Kath's heart became a jackhammer in her chest. She spun around. "Who's there?"

There were nine lights again, unevenly shaped orbs floating clockwise around her in that slow, eerie movement, pulsing, flickering like fire. She could have taken two steps in any direction and touched one, they were so close. Close enough to make it clear nothing human held them up, and no wires or strings suspended them from above.

Muppet growled again, louder and fiercer. The hair rose on Kath's neck, and she felt like she'd plunged into a tub of ice. Her body felt heavy, rooted to the ground.

"What do you want?" she croaked.

The lights stopped, hovered in place. Then they floated closer, chest level a foot away. Kath could almost see a figure inside the one in front of her, a woman with long gold hair. But that was an illusion, because in a blink the impression vanished, leaving only an orb of light so bright it hurt to focus on it.

Kath took a step uphill.

The light ahead of her darted closer. Kath jumped back, but it followed, pressing her, pulsing brighter. Kath expected heat, but her face ached from cold instead, a glacial, searing cold.

Muppet whimpered and buried his nose in her chest.

Kath stepped back more slowly. The lights began to circle again, slow at first, then faster and faster until they blurred together into a solid ring. The raw, searing cold burrowed into her, forcing her backward step by step. Pushing her downhill.

Then the lights winked out.

There was darkness. And a ringing silence. Not so much as a rustle in the underbrush around her.

Kath spun around, searching the woods.

Then below her, a shadow moved. A small figure slipped along the back of the Davies house, and the light above the first cottage patio illuminated Lona's face. She paused at the edge of the building and peered inside through the glass. No lights were on, and a moment later, she darted across the patio to the next wall, peered in, then ran to the corner of Kath's cottage.

Kath had left the kitchen light on, and Lona waited longer before crossing to HT's cottage and from there to the next. After darting across the empty space between the two rowhouses, she peered around the corner of the first unit there, and moved to the second unit, where she stopped and watched. Then she smoothed her hair, adjusted her jacket, and crossed the patio to the door. She pulled the handle, and when it didn't move, she knocked and waited, but not for long. She knocked again, then pounded with her fist.

Kath tried to remember the names Dai had rattled off: the man who played Bolingbroke, and Caradoc Thomas, and Emris Morris, who played de Ruthyn. But she couldn't remember the order and who lived where.

She patted Muppet's nose, trying to keep him from growling. One foot at a time, so slowly she made no noise at all, she moved farther down the hill.

The door finally opened, and Lona started talking. Kath couldn't hear what she was saying, and she couldn't see who was there. Then Caradoc Thomas abruptly stepped past Lona and moved to the edge of the patio to look right and left down the row of buildings.

Kath held her breath and didn't move. Caradoc gave no sign of having seen her. He snarled something at Lona, his expression vicious. Grabbing her by the arm, he shoved her inside and slammed the door closed so hard it bounced back open an inch or two.

Kath charged down through the woods and across the open stretch in front of her own patio. Throwing the door open, she set Muppet inside and dropped the plastic bag with his blanket and food on the floor. Next, she shrugged her purse off her shoulder, pulled out her phone, and dialed Dai's number.

"Pick up, pick up. Please pick up," she whispered.

He did after a couple of rings. "Kath?"

"Please come down through the woods and go to Caradoc's through the back. Lona Davies just knocked on the glass, and he pulled her inside. Roughly. He looked furious, and I'm afraid she's in danger. Calling 9-1-1 might take too long for them to get here."

There was a moment of silence. Then Dai said, "I'm on my way. If something happens before I get there, call 9-9-9 for emergency services. Don't do anything else. Wait for me, alright?"

"Hurry," Kath said.

She dropped her purse beside the bag, then shut the door beside her and tiptoed across HT's patio, and the next one over, then past the break in the buildings and over to the wall before the second patio. The sound of raised voices carried through the stillness. Kath paused and listened, but it was all in Welsh.

Carefully, she peered around the corner of the wall.

Caradoc and Lona stood by the door, his hand still clutching her upper arm. Lona screamed something at him, and Caradoc's face turned red. He put his hand over her mouth.

She tried to wrench out of his grasp, but he held on, and then she bit him. He slapped her hard.

Kath took out her phone to call 9-9-9. Lona's hand had flown to her cheek, then suddenly she shoved Caradoc in the chest. He stepped forward and caught her by the throat. Fighting to breathe, she clawed at him. His other hand came up and his grip tightened. He shook her.

Lona's eyes bulged. Her mouth opened, but no sound came out.

Kath ran to the sliding door and threw it open. "Let her go."

"What the hell—" Caradoc turned. Seeing Kath, he dropped his arms. "This is none of your business. Get out of my house."

"Your hands around a girl's throat is everybody's business. And she's fifteen."

"Sixteen," Lona corrected, but she stepped away from Caradoc and rubbed her throat. Black-stained tears streaked her face.

"Lona, come over here to me," Kath said. "Let's get you home."

Caradoc grabbed Lona's arm again. "Tell Kath we're fine. We were rehearsing a scene for an audition you want to do. Isn't that right? We don't need her butting in."

"I'm fine," Lona said, looking anything but. "We were rehearsing."

For Kath, the pieces were falling in place like dominoes: Lona coming out of a cottage, Wenny's expression when she'd seen Lona coming home that day, Caradoc changing the second unit schedule so he was around more in the afternoons when Lona wasn't at the restaurant.

She tried to step between them. "Tell me," she said, "was it you or Lona who knocked Wenny into the ditch, Caradoc? Was that an accident or did you deliberately hit her? Were you trying to scare her?"

"Shut up." Caradoc moved so fast Kath didn't see it coming until his hands were around her throat, the same way he'd been holding Lona.

Kath stomped on his instep with every bit of force she had. Then she pivoted and brought her other knee up into his groin.

He let go of her and doubled over. She reached for Lona's hand and pulled her toward the door, but Lona resisted, watching Caradoc as if she couldn't decide what to do. Kath didn't let go, towing her along. Then Caradoc grabbed Kath's other arm.

Kath released Lona and jammed the heel of her hand into his nose. Blood spurted, hot against her palm, but he didn't let go of her. She whipped around, dropped to one knee, jerked him forward, and hoped to throw him over her shoulder.

He pulled out of her grasp instead.

Her heart hammered at her chest. She'd exhausted the few tricks she'd mastered in her self-defense course. He grabbed her hair and jerked her to her feet. Screaming, she spun behind him and kicked him behind the knees. He stumbled and released her.

She shoved Lona toward the door. "Run! Go now!"

Lona still hesitated, but Kath pushed her outside, and Dai

was there, sprinting across the patio. He stepped past Lona, his expression calm and cold. "Stop there," he said to Caradoc in a dangerously quiet voice. "Don't move, and I won't have to hurt you."

"Go to hell, both of you." Caradoc lunged at Dai, his arm drawn back.

Dai caught the fist coming at him in his palm and stopped the momentum. Closing his hand around it, he forced Caradoc's arm behind him and pushed his wrist up onto his back. Leaning into the painful hold, he pressed Caradoc's cheek up against the glass. "Don't so much as twitch, or I'll bloody break your arm in pieces."

Caradoc went still. "I'll have you both arrested for assault. You forced your way in without permission."

"That's an excellent idea. Kath, let's make it easier for Caradoc to file his complaint. Would you call emergency services for me?"

Caradoc tried to twist his head around to look at Dai. "Come on, mate, this is all a misunderstanding, innit? The girl came in, spouting all sorts of lies. And your girlfriend here got the wrong end of the stick. I can see how she might get confused, but there's nothing wrong. Lona and I were rehearsing a scene for a screenplay I'm writing. There's no need for police."

Kath searched the floor for her phone, which she had dropped without even realizing it. "Do you have a screenplay with that scene somewhere? I may know nothing about British law, but I'm pretty sure a thirty-something-year-old man forcibly pulling a girl half his age into his cottage and then trying to strangle her in front of a witness is a slam-dunk case even here. You might want to think of a different story."

She dialed 9-9-9, and once the operator picked up, she explained she was calling to report an assault that was possibly connected to an ongoing hit-and-run investigation. "It's Ty Newydd, in the rowhouses along the main road. Cottage number 7."

The operator asked whether everyone was safe and asked Kath to stay on the line.

Kath put the call on speaker and went out to take Lona by the shoulders and gently bring her back inside. As soon as Kath let go again, Lona backed away from all of them until the dining table stopped her.

"Did Wenny try to get you to stop seeing Caradoc, is that what happened?" Kath asked. "Did she threaten to tell someone?"

"She's a cow, and it's none of her business," Lona snapped.

"So you told her to stay out of it?"

"Why shouldn't I?" Lona started to sob, and Kath's heart broke for her. At some point, the girl would understand how many mistakes she had made, and she would carry the guilt of those for the rest of her life. But however much she might have thrown herself at Caradoc, he was the one who was supposed to have the good sense and judgment to protect them both.

"Wenny was trying to help you," Kath said, trying to remain sympathetic. "Was it you or Caradoc who talked her into setting up a late-night meeting?"

"Shut up," Caradoc snapped at Lona. "You don't have to answer her."

Lona stared at him, and something inside her deflated until she looked even younger than her age. "He told me to text her on a phone he gave me," Lona said, "but I didn't know what he was going to do, I swear. I thought we were only meeting her out of the village to talk where it was quiet. Only she wouldn't listen. She called Caradoc a pervert and said she was going to the police. He only grabbed her, trying to explain, didn't he? But she ran away, and he got back in the car and took off after her. I wasn't even in the car then."

Kath's heart broke all over again, for Wenny and Lona both. "And the phone? Was that him or you?"

"He told me to go down and get it while he parked the car. And then he asked me if she was dead, and I lied and said she was, because I didn't want him to do anything more to her. I saved her."

"You knew she was alive, and you left her there?" Dai's voice was glacial, but his face held no expression.

"Lona, for God's sake, shut up!" Caradoc shouted.

Kath's legs felt numb. Her heart felt numb. She stumbled to the table and sank into a chair. The thought of Lona leaving Wenny like that... leaving anyone like that... But they had been good friends at one point. How could she? But Kath had done the same thing.

No, it wasn't the same. The explosion would have been heard in the nearby houses, and the flames were visible. The wreck could be seen from the road—someone would have found it.

Most importantly, the poor man had already been past help. Kath and HT had still been horrible to leave, but it wasn't the same.

What Lona had done was colder and more heartbreaking.

Sobbing now, Lona looked from Dai to Caradoc and back again. "I saved her. I wanted to save her."

Kath set the phone on the table and went to pull Lona into her arms. "You should wait and talk to your parents before you say anything else. Do you want me to call them for you before the police arrive?"

That set off a fresh round of sobs, and Kath wondered if that was from fear or remorse. She held Lona anyway, thinking of all the pain that lay ahead for her.

When Lona's tears finally ended in hiccupping breaths, Dai asked Kath to find something to tie Caradoc's arms together. Kath pulled out a chair for Lona, then went to the kitchen to look for something. The best she could do was a dishcloth and a knife, and Dai helped her rip the cloth lengthwise, tied Caradoc's hands behind him, and made him sit on the couch. Caradoc's face was mutinous and stained with drying blood, which made him look like the soul-sucking predator he was. Lona, meanwhile, looked young and scared and shaken.

The police arrived about fifteen minutes later. Kath asked them to get Lona's parents before speaking to her. Then she and Dai gave their own statements.

"You may both need to come in to the station tomorrow to make more formal statements," one of the officers said. "Someone will be in touch about that, but you did enter the premises."

"That's right. They broke in and assaulted me," Caradoc said.

"Not until you assaulted us first," Dai said calmly. "And Lona."

The police didn't argue with him, and Caradoc glowered then looked away. Dai slipped his arm around Kath's waist, and they walked out through the patio door together.

Muppet charged over to her and bumped into her shin as soon as they slid Kath's door open, and he had attacked the purse Kath had left on the floor while she was gone. Shredded leather and the contents lay scattered all around as if he had shaken the bag to death.

She scooped him up and snuggled him close. "Did you hear us over there, puppy? And you wanted to be in there fighting tooth and claw."

"I can't blame him for that. I'd have liked to get a few good punches in myself," Dai said. "Not that you needed help. Remind me never to make you angry. And I'm sorry, Kath. For everything."

Reaction was settling in. Kath trembled, and her legs and arms felt like wet noodles instead of something that could hold her up. Dai took Muppet out of her arms, set him on the floor, and picked Kath up and carried her to the sofa. "You did the right thing," he said against her hair. "I wish you'd waited for me, but you saved Lona."

"Caradoc scared me. You should have seen him before you got there. I don't even want to think about what he might have done to her if I'd waited."

"But he didn't—you stopped him. You put yourself in harm's way to protect someone else, so never think of yourself as a coward. That isn't who you are."

Broken Pieces

"She was unique; there was something abnormal about her,
and it was that abnormal something that made her magnetic."

Ken Follett, *The Pillars of the Earth*

K ATH SHOOK IN DAI'S ARMS, and he looked around for a
throw or something to put over her to warm her up. In
the end, he tucked his jacket around her shoulders and excused
himself to make her a cup of tea heavily laced with sugar. "I'm
turning into my *nain*," he said, handing the cup over. "She
always passed out tea and honey as a remedy for emotional
shock."

"I saw a study that said glucose could help ward off some
of the effects of PTSD," Kath said, wrapping her hands around
the mug and letting the steam warm her lips.

Dai pulled her toward the sofa and sat down with her
beside him, surprised at how much even having her nearby

seemed to fill the empty spaces inside himself. "You looked up PTSD after your flashback?"

"After I watched your documentary," she said. "Before I auditioned."

He wondered how many of the people he knew well had tried to learn more. Most people looked away from anything uncomfortable. He shifted around on the sofa and pulled Kath back against his chest. Her head nestled beneath his chin as though it had been made to fit there.

"Your grandmother might have been right about the fairies, too," she said. "What did you call them?"

"The Tylwyth Teg?"

"I saw them tonight, the lights. They pushed me back out of the woods to where I saw Lona sneaking off to Caradoc's. Does that sound crazy?"

"The mind plays odd tricks, doesn't it? But then, a lot of people swear the *Tylwyth Teg* are real. What were you doing in the woods in the first place?"

"Coming up to see you. I pushed myself out of my comfort zone and went to the pub tonight to try to fit in. People were nice, mostly. But there was also a photographer here earlier, snapping pictures of me when I took Muppet out. It made me realize that whatever is going to happen will happen and I can't hide from it. The cast and crew will judge me next week based on how I perform, and when the film comes out, there will be more judgment. People will hate me or love me or not give a damn, or they'll claim I slept my way into the part. And the only thing I can do is give my best performance and hope that's good enough."

He wanted to kiss away the worried crease between her brows. "Good enough is always subjective, *cariad*. And what people say has little to do with truth. They'll talk to get attention for themselves, or out of their own jealousy, meanness, or insecurity. What they say reflects more on them than it does on you."

"The tabloid stuff with HT tore me to shreds inside, and I couldn't face even going to the grocery store. I imagined everyone was thinking horrible things. I could hear them inside my head, a parade of the worst things anyone could say. Partly that was my mother's voice in my head and growing up with two sisters who never put a foot wrong, but a lot of it was guilt going back to the accident and how we had to sneak away."

Dai pulled her even closer. "What do you mean, you had to?"

"I was a wreck, and Henry—HT—was so badly shaken.... It got worse as the shock wore off. My father is a lawyer, and I wanted to talk to him, but my mother said we would only bring him down with us. She said we would ruin both our families and everything they had built if we stayed, because we wouldn't be able to hide what we had done. But if we left, we had been convincing enough as Rosalind and Orlando falling in love on stage that people would believe we were running away to Hollywood together. We didn't have time to think it through. She packed a few things for me and gave us money, and HT wrote a letter to Anna breaking off their engagement. And then we left."

Dai's heart broke for her. He imagined her at seventeen,

carrying the burden of all of that. No wonder she was so afraid of failing as an actor. Even if acting had been something she originally loved, it must have become a prison.

"What did you think would happen if you didn't make it as an actor?" he asked.

Kath's brows pulled together, and she studied her hands as if an answer was written on the pale half-moons at the base of the fingertips that rested on her lap. "I don't know. Taken the excuse away and let my family—Anna—down all over again."

He kissed the top of her head. "That's a lot of pressure to carry all these years."

She pulled away and turned to face him. "I'm only telling you so you know what kind of a mess I am. In case you want to turn away, now's your chance."

He found himself smiling at that. "No chance at all. Everyone's broken in their own way, love. But someone has badly let you down. They made you believe what you are isn't enough, and they couldn't have been more wrong. You're intelligent and kind, and you keep saying you're a coward, but the more I know you, the more I see your courage. And this may be my personal form of brokenness, but I find it incredibly sexy that you can beat the shite out of a man when you feel like it."

She smiled that incredible smile of hers, and he traced the outline of it with his thumb. Then he kissed the red bruises that Caradoc's fingers had left on her throat.

Dai wanted to break Caradoc into pieces all over again. He wanted to kiss all her pain away, the way his mam had used to soothe his hurts.

How long had it been since anyone had done something to make her feel better?

When he raised his head, she was looking at him. Her beautiful eyes swam with tears. "I'm not crying," she lied. "But that may be the nicest thing anyone has ever said to me. Not the part about shite, obviously."

"Obviously," he said.

Their faces were so close, Dai felt the warm moistness of her breath. He couldn't have said which of them moved first. There was only that moment when their lips found each other and he was able to say all the things he couldn't put into words: the relief that Caradoc hadn't hurt her worse, gratitude that she had been coming through the woods to him, that she'd chosen to come to him, the anticipation of not knowing where they were headed, and the certainty that wherever that was would involve joy and adrenaline and turbulent highs and lows. He hoped it would be joy more than anything else. He intended to make sure of that.

In the bedroom later, he propped himself on one elbow and watched her while she slept in the moonlight. It fascinated him that, despite all her insecurities, being with her filled him with a sense of peace. He wanted to call and tell Laura about her. After all, Laura had predicted he would find her.

Laura had been weeding the perennial garden when he returned from a slow, painful run. He'd come up from behind and kissed the back of her neck. She had turned to look up at him, her eyes squinting against the midday sun.

"Do you realize that you've stopped kissing me?" she asked.

"I kiss you all the time."

"No. You kiss my cheek, or my forehead, or the back of my neck. Sometimes, you kiss my lips, but you're only recreating the memory of kisses we used to share. Somewhere between here and Afghanistan, you took yourself apart and reassembled yourself in a way that keeps us from fitting the way we used to."

That had come from out of nowhere. He'd been working hard, pulling himself back together. "I'll do better," he said. "There's still a war inside me, but it can't last forever."

"You're already better." Her smile was both wistful and determined. "Everyone is broken in their own way. You and I used to make sense, and I'll always love you. I know that in your own way, you will always love me, too. But there will be someone else whose brokenness makes you stronger, and when you're with her, you won't feel broken at all. You'll give her courage and strength, and you will make each other better. I'm not that person for you anymore, and I'd never forgive myself if I held you back."

"Are you saying you want me to leave?" he asked.

"I'm saying we'll always be friends, but we're at a point where a divorce is best."

"I can't imagine being with anyone else."

She'd put a hand on his cheek, her eyes full of all the sadness he had given her. "Stretch your imagination, Dai. Look for a woman who brings peace to that war you carry inside yourself. Someone who fills you up and makes you look forward to every sunrise. And call me when you find her, will you? Because I'll want to thank her for doing that for you."

Lying beside Kath in the moonlight, Dai stretched out and pulled her into his arms. She sighed in her sleep, and he kissed the top of her head. For the first time, he thought he understood what Laura had meant. It didn't matter where he kissed Kath, he was kissing all of her, the part that made his body quicken, the part that made his brain work to keep up with hers, and the part that made him want to make her smile.

He closed his eyes and slept.

DANCING

"I'll be no longer guilty of this sin."

WILLIAM SHAKESPEARE, *HENRY IV, PART ONE*

KATH WOKE ON MONDAY MORNING with a sense of dread. Checking her phone, she saw Dai had texted he would be a few minutes late for their run. Apparently, he hadn't gotten back until after two in the morning from his meeting in London about the fallout from Caradoc's arrest, but he wanted to shoot her first scene anyway.

She took advantage of the extra time to pack a tote bag with everything she and Muppet might need for the day. By the time Dai knocked on the door, she had nearly finished.

"You look exhausted," she said, laying her hand along his cheek. "Do you want coffee first?"

"Let's just run."

He seemed to need to push himself, so Kath tried to

keep up. Her heart pounded, and he was barely breathing hard.

At the top of the hill, they sat down to watch the sunrise. "You didn't say much in your texts yesterday," she said. "How did it really go with Alan?"

"I meant to ring you while I was driving back, but I had other calls I had to take. By the time I got off, I didn't want to wake you. It's a big day for you." He smiled at her, a smile that wrapped itself around her so she could almost feel his arms holding her close.

"You still haven't said what Alan's thinking."

"It's not the sort of publicity any of us want, but he's grateful it was Caradoc and not anyone English or American. He thinks that would have made the scandal worse."

"It's awful either way."

Dai looked off toward the distant ridge where the first hints of light were rising against a sky streaked with dark clouds and whipping winds. "Maybe he isn't wrong. I'd poured so much into this project, and I know how hard Wales has fought to keep its own identity. Whenever we had a difference of opinion, I put it down to Alan being English and not understanding. But he's good at seeing the bigger picture. We all hate that anyone took advantage of Lona. I hate that in the twenty-first century, we're still wasting time thinking about where a person's from instead of focusing on what they've done, but it all comes down to sound bites. In social media terms, it will play better if it isn't someone from 'outside' coming in and taking advantage of a Welsh girl. The story hasn't broken widely yet, but it will as soon as Caradoc goes before a judge."

"Olivia and I made dinner for Glenys last night, and she says Lona's parents think she'll get some kind of rehabilitation and community service sentence instead of jail time. I can't imagine what it will be like for her and Wenny having to see each other every day. The same village, the same school. I feel sorry for them both."

"Come here." Dai settled her against him. "Did you call your mother yesterday?"

She could feel his heartbeat, strong and reassuringly steady. "Not yet, but HT and I called Anna together. My dad was there, too, and I talked to him afterwards."

"And how'd that go?"

Kath thought back to the phone call, and how hard it had been. She had been glad that Anna's husband had been there with her, and they had put HT and Kath on speaker. They'd all struggled to know where to begin.

"Just spit it out, both of you," Anna finally said. "It's old pain, if that helps. I'm over it."

The words had been a release. "I've never gotten over it," Kath said. "I don't think HT has either, but it didn't happen the way he said in his letter. We didn't run off together. He didn't want to leave you."

"I knew you had a crush on him—"

"I flirted with him like an idiot, but he wouldn't have let it go any farther than that."

"God, no," HT said. "I left because I loved you."

Between them, they'd told the entire story, and Anna and Kath had both been crying by the end. "I'm so furious with you," Anna said. "You could have trusted me. I would have told you Mom was wrong."

"She said you would have been an accessory after the fact if we said anything. It could have ruined your life."

"You think I would have covered for you? If Dad hadn't done it, I would have marched you down to the police station myself. Whatever punishment the law eventually gave you, you would have deserved that. But punishment isn't meant to be forever. You didn't get away with anything by running away. I know you—both of you. I'm sure you've spent years punishing yourselves."

"I'm sorry," Kath had said.

And then Anna had put their father on the phone, and he had blamed himself. "I should have gotten on a plane and met you in LA and made you give me the truth. I should have seen what was going on, but I'd gotten too used to locking myself away in the study. That's on me. I couldn't bear to look around and see the mess I'd made of my own life with your mother, and that cost us all fifteen years when we could have been rebuilding ourselves as a family instead of only growing farther apart."

Waiting for the sunrise, Dai's heartbeat was as sure as a metronome against Kath's cheek. He wouldn't have made the kind of mistakes her family had made. His sense of honor was a moral compass, and he would never be afraid to do the right thing, no matter how hard that was.

"I always knew Dad and Anna had no idea about that night," she told him, "but deep down—" She cut herself off, floundering to find the words.

"You were afraid they knew and blamed you anyway?" he asked.

Kath hadn't even formulated that thought in her head. But he was right. "Dad was furious at himself and my mother. Anna was just sorry for all the time we've wasted."

She thought back to the conversation, to the tears in Anna's voice.

"Before meeting Connal," Anna had said, "I might not have been ready to hear this, but he was worth waiting for. I have him, and Moira and the baby, so I can't help thinking things turned out how they were meant to. But I wish I'd stopped to think there had to be more to the story than we knew."

"I wish I'd been closer to you and Meg back then," Kath said.

"I doubt Mom wanted us close. She wasn't secure enough for that. As long as we didn't trust each other, we needed her more. That's her skewed idea of love, and I'm sorry for that, too."

"Can you imagine what her childhood must have been like?"

"Aunt Elspeth is great. She's normal."

"Is she? She makes up stories about everything in her life because she thinks she isn't enough on her own."

"You know, I've never thought of it like that." Anna

sighed. "At least she and Dad are getting to know each other again, and maybe they'll have their own happy ending." She paused, and then her voice grew less certain. "Would you come and visit here when you finish filming? I'd love that."

"Me, too," Kath said.

Anna's invitation was enormous, a bridge across wasted years and too many miles of misunderstandings. Kath had hung up and sat on the bed with her arms wrapped around her knees, crying with pain and relief and regret until Muppet made his way upstairs to check on her.

Sitting beside Dai now, she closed her eyes and listened to the whisper of the wind through the grass. His breath was warm against her hair.

"I know I have to talk to my mother at some point," she said, "but I think of all the time we've lost. All of us. My mother didn't keep the secret to protect us. She did it to avoid an even bigger scandal. She was afraid of what people would think, of us and her. HT and I were so numb we didn't question anything she told us."

"You were seventeen and in shock, and she was your mother. What you did was an enormous mistake, but she set the events in motion to make it worse." Dai held Kath close, his chin resting on her head.

"I'm going to let Anna and Dad make their peace with her before I call her. She's never going to see that she did anything wrong."

"Can you forgive her?"

"She's my mother. Hating her is like hating myself, and I've done that too long already." Kath was breathless at the truth of that, and she paused to let herself absorb it.

If she ever had a daughter, she was going to break the cycle of this. She would do things better for her children, so they could do better for theirs.

"I suspect she was probably a lot like Lona when she met my father," she continued. "A bit like me. Seeing someone she wanted, and not being mature enough to process that it was wrong. Maybe on some level she knows it. She keeps herself busy with a swirl of activities so she doesn't have time to think, and she numbs herself with alcohol and sleeping pills at night to keep herself from dreaming."

"Guilt grows bigger until you stop and face it." He was quiet for a moment, that deep, still, and conscious quiet Kath was starting to recognize. It made her feel quieter, too.

"What were you guilty about?" she asked.

"I lived and Robbie Hanmer died. We were on the roof together, so that makes no sense. I feel a bit responsible for Lona as well. I should have paid more attention to what Caradoc was doing."

"Her own parents didn't see it. And Glenys didn't see Wenny's fear. We hide the things that make us vulnerable. That's probably human nature. Self-defense instinct."

Dai brushed Kath's hair off the nape of her neck and kissed the small, vulnerable hollow above her spine. Then he stood up, took his phone out of his pocket and searched for something.

"The sun's not fully up yet," Kath said, not ready to go back to the world.

He held his hand out to help her up. "You're ready for today, but I don't want you leaving here thinking about pain or guilt."

He pushed his screen and music spilled out of the iPhone's speaker.

Kath smiled as she heard the opening to Jason Mraz's "I Won't Give Up."

"Will you dance with me, Kath?" He pulled her to him, then stepped back and spun her around before drawing her back toward him like a magnet.

They danced while the sun rose, Dai's eyes on hers the entire time, never flinching away from the ugly places she'd tried so hard to keep buried out of sight. Then she laid her cheek against his shoulder as the song wound down, and his cheek rested against her hair. Wrapped in his warmth, she felt grounded. She felt safe enough to say anything, try anything. To be anyone and be herself.

She didn't want to analyze what she felt for him. Words had too much power to use them carelessly. They became labels that people had to live up to or live down. All Kath wanted was to live the best day she could manage, today and every day. She wanted to feel joy and live out loud.

She raised her head to look at Dai, and their eyes met again. Eyes, then lips, and she wanted more. She wanted—needed—to pull his shirt over his head and let their kisses take their natural course. His eyes darkened as if he read her thoughts.

"We'll have to save that for later," he said hoarsely, and he kissed her again, thoroughly and deeply. They both stepped back at the same time and cleared their throats. He brushed a finger along her cheek. "We need to go back so that you can go be brilliant. And you will be."

Her heart gave a few uncertain beats at that, but she smiled at him. Then she let herself fly down the trail again, too fast and out of control, and pushed herself until her muscles burned on the run back to the village.

Dai didn't stop when they reached her door. Instead, he jogged backward while she turned the lock.

"See you in forty minutes," he said.

She showered and slipped into leggings, ballet flats, and a long, white tunic sweater in record time. The car pulled up a few minutes early, but she was ready. Muppet was in his carrier, and she had her purse and her big tote bag packed with her annotated script, the sides and information for the day's filming, Muppet's food, bowls, treats, and everything else she might need.

Dai opened the car door for her as she came out, and he caught her lips in a fast, firm kiss before she slid inside.

She gave him a wary look. "Should we—"

"Yes," he said, standing there with his arm hooked over the top of the door. "Because life is short. Do you disagree?"

"That life is short?" She watched him as she took her seat. "No, I can't disagree with that."

"And the other thing?"

She shrugged. "The jury's still out, but so is the gossip. So what the hell."

He grinned, closed the door, and went around the back of

the car to slide in beside her. They had the distracted driver again, but for once, he wasn't on his phone. He watched them in the rearview mirror until Dai had settled in. Then he put the car in gear and pulled out onto the road.

Dai scooted closer along the leather seat. "Alan asked me about us again yesterday. With the whole Caradoc mess, it's bound to come out that we're seeing each other. Since I'm seeing you and HT was seeing Nia, there's a chance that someone will say I'm allowing unsafe conditions for women."

"Seriously?" she asked. "Then we shouldn't—"

"We've learned this lesson, haven't we? There's always going to be someone who knows what we should or shouldn't do. Alan agrees it's better if we're honest as long as I do my job and make sure everyone can see how brilliant you are as Margaret."

Kath winced and closed her eyes. "Which means I have to *be* brilliant."

He turned to study her, one shoulder resting against the seat beside her. "I've been thinking that I don't want to start with a full rehearsal. We'll do the setup with the stand-ins, then get you and HT and the others in to do the blocking for the master shot. We're using multiple camera angles, so we'll run the action and dialogue straight through, and I want you and HT to find your way spontaneously. Then we can all look at the master before we go back for a second take and close shots and reaction. But I don't want either of you overthinking."

"What if I freeze up again?"

"Then we'll do what we did before. Let you have all the time you need."

He leaned forward and put his hand on hers. And the touch of his fingers on hers—just that—was enough to make her fill up like a helium balloon. She'd been empty for far too long.

She must have let out some small sound because he gave her a questioning look, and then he touched her face and brushed the back of his hand against her cheekbone.

"You're so bloody beautiful, Kath. Sometimes I look at you, and it's like I'm seeing you for the first time and being surprised all over again. But it's this and this"—he tapped two fingers gently above her heart and then brushed her temple—"that I want to show the world starting today. It's what I want you to see in yourself."

BELIEF

"She'll be a soldier too,
She'll to the wars."

WILLIAM SHAKESPEARE, *HENRY IV, PART ONE*

T HE SCENE DAI HAD CHOSEN for Kath to shoot first was one they had rewritten together. By adding Kath, it catered less to HT's daredevil streak, and there was a bit more theatre to make Alan happy. Still, Dai was confident it would work.

To simulate a chokepoint along the road from Chester into Wales, they set up the master shot on a ridge overlooking a wide dirt track. Glyndwr's Welsh archers and foot soldiers waited on the slopes on both sides of the valley while the English army stood ready for Dai's signal to march forward below.

As luck had it, the weather predictions had been right so far. The morning grew increasingly overcast as they blocked the action and set up the cameras, rain rigs, fans, fog machines, and lighting and practiced the shots with stand-ins a half dozen times to get the positioning and camera angles down before he did an action run-through for the actors and sent them back for costumes. By the time the crew was ready, the wind pelted cold needles of rain against the ridgeline, making a good backdrop for the almost supernatural storm he needed.

He gathered everyone under the rain shelter before the cameras started rolling.

"Any last questions?" Dai asked.

"Yeah, do you have to be so damn authentic? And does it have to rain all the time?" HT asked. "Sorry, rhetorical questions. I'm freezing my balls off."

Dai smiled grimly, then pulled Kath aside. She wore her hair braided into a crown similar to the style she had worn at the first audition and mostly covered by a dark green, fur-lined hood. The bold color around her face made her skin translucent and pulled the shards of green out in her eyes. Her back was as tense as a dagger.

"Stop worrying," he said. "The anticipation is the worst of it. As soon as we start, you'll forget your nerves."

"I want to get it right."

"Right is whatever works for you. We'll do this as many times as you want, but don't second-guess yourself during filming. I'll let you know after the take if there's something we need to change."

He turned to go, and her finger brushed his hand as she nodded and moved away. The contact could have been accidental, but he knew it wasn't, and he felt that certainty like a cloak of warmth settling over them both. He smiled without saying anything else because all that he felt would have been there in his voice.

When he was back in position, he signaled for Kath and the men to mount up. HT and the dozen men with him settled into their hiding places behind boulders, looking down at the valley while their horses waited out of sight nearby. Below them, the English army stood in billowing drifts of manufactured fog, visible and then lost again. The crew wiped down the lenses and checked the sleeves and umbrellas that would keep the cameras dry, snapped the backlights and blacklights and rain rigs on, and scattered leaves and fine dry dirt around the rocks for the powerful fans to send swirling in the air.

Dai called "Action."

Kath and her men kicked their horses into a gallop up the sheep track toward Glyndwr and his captains. The fans and the way she sat forward in the saddle made the heavy wool cloak stream behind her. Her black horse stood in stark contrast against the clouds.

HT heard the horses approach. He and the others jumped to their feet and unsheathed their swords. Then, seeing it was Kath, HT ran toward her, his progress slow in the chain mail while she was a streak of green and black.

Sheathing his sword again, he called to her as she reined the horse to a stop. "What's amiss?"

She swung off the horse, barely breaking stride as she

continued moving toward him a step ahead of Gareth Teale, who played their young son Gruffudd. Rain had soaked Kath to the skin, and mud splattered her cloak and the horse's legs perfectly for the shot.

She took Dai's breath away.

"That is only a third of the army Bolingbroke has sent against you." She gestured toward the men marching down the valley. "The rest advance from Shrewsbury and Hereford in equal numbers."

HT took an instant to absorb it. "The king has sent a hundred thousand men?"

"He sees the danger," Harri Rice said, playing the bard Iolo Goch. "Despite the messengers he's killed, the Irish chiefs and Scots show interest. France is ready to commit. If he loses today, it could turn the tide in our favor and even parts of England could rise against him."

"Aye, Richard was not without friends, and even his enemies balk at king slaying," HT agreed. "Refusing to ransom Mortimer, breaking oaths to the church and Parliament... He does himself no favors."

"That's all very well, but a hundred thousand men? We cannot stand against half that number, much less be in three places at once," Harri said.

HT frowned, deep in thought. "We must, though it would be magic indeed to conjure a victory in Shrewsbury and the south when we are fighting here."

Kath studied the army below, and then the rocky slopes on either side. Dai could almost see the cogs turning behind her eyes.

"The appearance of magic is all you need, so long as you do not stand and fight," she said, gesturing for the others to move closer.

They crouched low behind the boulders, then wiggled on their bellies to the lip of the bare granite overhang, and Kath pointed at the army below where individual men vanished and reappeared through the drifts of fog.

"How many English do you see?" Kath asked. "Can you count them? If you cannot, neither can they know how many men you have. Divide your force three ways, and you can be everywhere at once."

"Whether the English can count us makes little difference if our numbers are too few to stop them."

"You are still thinking like a soldier on a battlefield in France, commanding an army to meet an army. Look at where we are." Kath waved at the steep slopes strewn with boulders. "Our numbers may be smaller, but the very mountains will fight for us. Your victories in France and Scotland have earned respect. Your victories here have already taught the English to fear you. You can use that fear to defeat them. Fear is the hardest weapon to overcome."

Her eyes slid off to the side on the last sentence, and she let every bit of the fear that she had lived with over the years show in her eyes and the set of her jaw, all the fear and self-doubt that she had carried.

Dai's throat caught, and he was glad he was going to have this moment from multiple camera angles. He wasn't sure it would be as powerful on a second take. And he couldn't help wondering whether HT, or anyone, had ever understood how afraid and alone she had been all these years.

Maybe HT did understand. Instead of delivering his next line as written, HT placed his hand on top of Kath's where it rested against the granite. He laced their fingers together and looked down at her with such a fierce mixture of love and respect, guilt and regret that the air almost shimmered with it. She held his eyes and let the tension draw out, and everything they had been through together was there in that look between them. Then they turned to look back down at the valley side by side again.

Dai made a mental note to get a close shot of their hands like that. Then they'd pull out to get that look

"The weather would have to hold," HT said. "But a hundred horsemen would seem like ten times that number if they cloak themselves in fog and rain and arrows from our bowmen."

"The storm will hold for several days," Harri said beside him. "Long enough to make the English fear they are fighting ghosts. Between that and how our women avenged themselves on the dead at Bryn Glas, they may turn and run like rabbits back across the border."

"What say you?" HT asked his men. "Do we dare to split the army?"

None of them wanted to be the first to speak.

Kath waited through the silence a long moment, then she responded softly, "Caution is admirable, but today is not that day. We must dare, or we will lose." Drawing back, she put her hand on HT's arm and silently asked him to trust her. "Keep a third of your men here. Gruffudd and I can each ride with another third and carry your standard to Hereford and Shrewsbury to meet the English there."

HT did a good job of looking torn, looking at Kath as if he was seeing her—all of her—for the first time and simultaneously realizing that he could lose her.

"I would wish you safe at home in Sycharth," he said softly.

She placed a hand against his cheek. "Every man here wishes his family safe, Owain. I would wish you safe, but my own fears do not matter. You are not mine alone. You are the red dragon of Wales, the symbol of what we have lost and what we must not lose again. If the English win now, no corner of Wales will ever be safe."

HT was silent, studying her as if he wanted to memorize every feature in case he lost her. Then he nodded and slid down off the overhang of rock. Crouching low, he gestured for Kath and the men to follow and returned to where the horses and remaining men were waiting to receive their orders.

Men ran in all directions, and Kath went to stand beside the boy who played her son. He was nearly the same height, a boy on the edge of manhood. Kath allowed herself a moment where she placed the back of her fingers across his cheek. He was fighting to be brave and older than his years, and he didn't respond. But as her hand dropped away, she inched closer, and their arms rested against each other from shoulder to wrist, touching without seeming to touch.

Dai needed to make sure they had a good back view of that.

The tension in Kath's shoulders, that almost invisible lean. She said so much without words.

HT finished with his men and went back to his family. He placed a hand on his son's shoulder and held it there without saying anything—without needing to say it. The boy nodded, equally silent. Then HT held out his hand for Kath and led her back toward her horse. She gripped the saddle, waiting for him to cup his hands and give her a leg up. Instead, he bent and kissed her. Her hands moved to tangle in his hair as she kissed him back. They pulled away slowly, their foreheads pressed together. For a moment, then two, they stood like that, saying goodbye to all they had been, releasing each other. Forgiving each other. Then HT straightened and cupped his hands to help her mount.

None of that was in the script, but it was there between them, visible and perfect.

It worked. It all worked.

This was the master shot. Dai and the crew would reset and film it all again at least once more. They would shoot closeups and pieces of the action from different angles. But even if this had been the only shot, no one could doubt Kath's talent after seeing her like this. Dai had wanted to show the crew—the world—what he saw in her, and it was all right here.

The cameras continued rolling while HT went to his own horse. He and the boy mounted their horses simultaneously, and with Kath beside them, they kicked into a gallop. The other men fell in line behind them, banners flapping wet and heavy and steam rising from the horses' bodies.

Dai waited until the last of the group had rounded the hill and disappeared before he shouted, "Cut! Great job, everyone. Take a half hour while we reset."

He walked down the track toward the tents and shelters, pulling his collar tighter around his neck. Kath had ridden down, so she beat him. She stood beside her horse, loosening the girth and tucking the stirrup irons up beneath the saddle skirt while she waited for the horse's handler.

"How was it? Did you get what you needed, Dai?"

The horse stamped his feet and tossed his head, and she took a breath and patted him on the neck. Dai debated how to answer, sorting through all the different emotions he felt and trying to find the words she needed to hear. She looked so fragile, as if the slightest mishandling would break her. She had no idea how strong she was. How much talent she had been holding back. But she needed to rely on her own opinion, not his.

"How did you feel about it?" he asked.

She lifted her head to meet his eyes, and the look she gave him brimmed with joy. Her lips tipped up into that brilliant, beautiful smile that knocked him sideways.

"It worked," she said. "Didn't it? I think it did."

"It did. The rewrite was a brilliant idea." He nodded, wanting to keep making her smile like that.

"And HT was fantastic. I felt the fear and the hope between him and Margaret, and how personal the war was to them—to everyone. Like they were fighting for each other, even if that meant one or both of them would die. It's hard to believe their dream for Wales is going to end the way it does."

The handler took the horse from her and led it away, the hoofbeats a steady cadence like the rain and Dai's heartbeat.

Dai wished he could hold Kath. He stepped back instead.

"I've been thinking about the end," he said. "I'd like to rewrite it to leave a bit more hope. What would you think about closing with Margaret walking into the Tower of London holding hands with her daughters as they carry a grandchild each? Then a last scene with Glyndwr and a few of his men riding away into the mountains and fading into mist."

She tipped her head up to look at him, her beautiful eyes shining. "That's much better. Perfect. And thank you."

"For what?" he asked.

"For taking a chance on me. For helping me learn to believe in myself."

She raised a finger and brushed it along his hand, one of those barely-there touches that sent a live current through him. Then she smiled, and they walked down to the rain shelters together, their footsteps in sync and their hands swinging in rhythm scant centimeters apart as if an invisible string was laced between them.

PREMIERE

"If you get the chance of the mad kind of love,
grab it with both hands. . ."

KEN FOLLETT, *WINTER OF THE WORLD*

THE SANTA ANAS HAD COME early again, driving wildfires across the foothills some twenty miles away. Looking out her windows as she tied her shoelaces, Kath scanned the ridgeline in the pre-dawn darkness, searching for any sign of an orange glow on the horizon. It was hard to believe a year had come and gone since that disastrous breakfast meeting when Joel had fired her, the last time she had been home when the Devil Winds blew.

She had hoped for too much that day and secretly believed she deserved the worst. It had been a long road from there to here. Miles of running before dawn with Dai, innumerable phone calls rebuilding ties with her family, and long days on set to get *The Last Prince* on film. She had also found a better agent.

Typically, Joel had insisted that was a mistake when she'd

stopped to tell him in person a couple of weeks after production wrapped. By then, things had already changed for her enough that he got off the phone immediately and came out to reception to bring her to his office.

Sitting behind his glass desk with photos of his stars on the surrounding walls, he'd tried to convince Kath that she needed him. "You need to be taking advantage of all the momentum right now, not making changes. I'm already hearing potential Oscar buzz for you, and the film isn't even out of post-production. Offers are coming in. You need me working for you."

"I need someone who believes in me. Someone who will do the work when the offers aren't coming in. You didn't do that when I needed you, and instead, you made me doubt myself. That's not my idea of working well together, so I've found someone who's a better fit."

"Who?" Joel asked.

"Fiona O'Connor."

"She's a dialogue coach."

"She's been in the business for forty years and knows it well enough that William Morris jumped at the chance to hire her. She has me, and at least four of her other former clients are also switching over."

"You can't keep making rash decisions, Kath. You need to think things through—"

"What I don't need is you telling me what to think. I'm done being afraid of mistakes. But thank you for the time you spent with me. You gave me a start, and I won't forget it."

She meant that. This past year, she had learned to be grateful for all the people who had come into her life, and those who had come back into it. She had a standing girls' night out with Olivia, Fiona, and a half dozen other friends who often brought others along. Then there was her father, sleeping upstairs in one of the guest rooms with Elspeth beside him. Meg and her husband, Niall, were also still asleep after flying into LAX from Ireland the night before. Anna and Connal hadn't been able to make it for the Los Angeles premiere, but they'd all had a great visit together when Kath had finished on location, and they planned to be in Wales for the UK opening.

Kath's mother was the only holdout, stubbornly clinging to outrage over the fact that Kath had told everyone else the truth. She would come around eventually; at least Kath hoped so.

"Ready, Kath?" Dai walked in from the kitchen after feeding Muppet.

His hair was longer than it had been when Kath first met him. Not too long, but longer, and it had fallen across his forehead. Kath went and brushed it back, loving the way it felt beneath her fingers. Small touches like that had become almost a secret language between them.

He smiled at her. That warm, honest smile she loved. "Alright, *cariad*? Nervous?"

"Mildly terrified and trying to focus on positive things," she said. "What about you?"

"I used to get shot at for a living, remember?" He grinned and shook his head. "Of course I'm anxious, but I know what we've achieved with it. We can both be proud of what we've done. All of us can."

She picked up the blue Dodgers cap off the table in front of her and adjusted it around her ponytail. He caught her hand, and they walked toward the door.

The house was no longer all white inside. Kath had added warm accents of terra-cotta colors to the walls and furnishings, making the interior blend more seamlessly with the outside spaces. Working around the last mad rush before *The Last Prince* released, she and Dai had also started to integrate furniture from his LA house in with her own pieces.

They ran along the canyon and up narrow winding streets squeezed between homes with privacy hedges or painted stucco walls. Kath missed their old route in Wales, the valley with its lush, ancient greenness. But as they reached the Griffith Observatory and LA spread out beneath them clad brightly in ribbons of light, the view was beautiful in a different way.

A mule deer grazed on the hillside below with twin fawns beside her. Kath took Dai's hand, and he pulled her close while they stopped to watch, then they walked east and sat on the wall, waiting for the sun. Dai wrapped his arms around her to ward off the morning chill, and she settled against him comfortably, sinking into all the right places as if he was a well-used pillow. His heartbeat had already returned to normal, steady and strong. Unflappable.

"I wish I could watch the film like this tonight," she admitted. "Your heartbeat always calms me down."

He turned his head toward her. "You've never said that before."

"There are a lot of things I haven't said yet."

His smile was unusually serious. "I've been thinking about that lately. I wanted to be sure you were ready, but I think it's time. Unless you haven't noticed yet that I'm moving in?"

"The sofa was a clue," she said, laughing.

He slipped off the wall and stood behind her, and when she shifted around to look at him, he caught her by the waist and set her down.

"What are we doing?" she asked.

"There's something I need to tell you before the premiere, because after tonight, your life will change. You've been so cautious about putting a label on our feelings, so I haven't told you how much I love you. Not aloud, at any rate." He smiled down at her, a slow, wonderful smile with his eyes darkened by emotion. "I've never been more certain of anything than I am about the two of us together," he said. "Katharine Cameron, I want to sit beside you every morning as the sun comes up, and I want to be with you in the evenings when it sets again. I'll hate the time when we're apart, but I'll support whatever you want to do and never hold you back, and I know you will do the same for me. I love you. And I think—I hope—that you love me."

Kath's heart hammered within her chest.

"Will you marry me and spend the rest of our lives together?" Dai asked.

He'd taken a ring from his pocket and held it out, and the sunrise turned it to liquid fire.

Kath's hands flew to her lips, a hundred thoughts tumbling in her head. But he was waiting for an answer, and she said what she'd known in her heart for almost a year. "I love you, Dai. And yes…" Her voice broke. "Yes, I'd love to spend the rest of my life with you."

He slid the ring on her finger. It fit perfectly, a three-stone emerald-cut diamond on a platinum band. Simple but elegant, and Kath would have married him with a ring from a funfair claw machine or no ring at all.

He kissed her, a kiss full of promise and all the things they had a lifetime to put in words. Things they had already said in a thousand other ways.

"I never knew it was possible to love someone so that your heart could almost burst with it. And the ring is perfect. Your timing is perfect."

"In that case, I hope you don't want a big wedding because I don't want to wait."

"Our families are the only guests I want. Well, and Fiona and Olivia and a few other people."

"They're all here for the premiere, almost all of them. If you're willing?"

So much joy welled up inside her that she couldn't speak. She let her smile say it all, and Dai traced the outer corner of her lips with his finger. "I love this smile," he said. "It was one of the first things I ever noticed about you."

She stood on tiptoe to kiss him fiercely, feeling as though a dam had burst inside her, letting out all the love and happiness she had missed out on over the barren, lonely years.

MARTINA BOONE

Then he drew her back against him and they held each other until the sunrise had faded from the sky.

It was only when they were home again, and Muppet had come to growl at her because the house was in chaos with everyone pitching in to make breakfast and talking about the engagement and weddings and plans, that Kath realized she'd stopped worrying about the premiere. She wouldn't have put it past Dai to have saved the proposal for that morning on purpose.

She stopped on her way out to the terrace with a platter of bacon and a bowl of scrambled eggs in her hands, and Dai was right behind her, carrying a carafe of coffee. She turned and stood on her toes to kiss him.

"What was that for?" he asked. "Not that I'm objecting."

"What if we had the wedding in Scotland after the UK premiere? I want Anna and Connal to be there, and it would be easier for your parents."

"What about your mother?"

"I'd have to talk to Dad and my sisters about that, but I'd like to invite her," Kath said, and she realized she didn't want to get married without her mother there. For all the damage Ailsa had inflicted, she was still blood and bone, and it had been easier to forgive her than it had been for Kath to forgive herself. She didn't want to start a life with Dai nursing ancient wounds, not her mother's and not her own.

They called Anna and put her on speaker during breakfast, everyone throwing out suggestions and making plans. Anna and Connal offered to host the wedding, and their daughter,

Moira, offered to be the flower girl and wanted to have Muppet carry the rings down the aisle. There was laughter and more noise and joy packed into those few moments than the house had known in all the years Kath had lived in it combined.

She had never been good at letting go of things, but she was learning to hold on to what mattered and release the rest, to accept that she didn't need to be perfect or play it safe. She meant to love Dai and her family fiercely and welcome everyone who came into her life. And she hoped to be loved in return.

That thought came back to her later that evening while she and Dai, along with HT and Nia, walked the red carpet for the cameras. She wanted to be loved by the people who really knew her, and she needed to keep reminding herself to put the media—especially the tabloids—into better perspective.

Fiona had recommended a new publicist to replace Jane Kim, and Kath didn't read social media at all. She was learning to ignore the tabloids. But what people thought of her work, of Margaret, did matter, and that still scared her. The thought of letting down Dai and all the crew and cast members who had worked so hard on *The Last Prince* scared her. But maybe that was okay. Bravery only came through fear.

Dai slipped his arm around her waist, and together they turned and smiled as photographers called to them. Each of them gave brief answers in response to reporters' questions, and then they moved on to the theatre. Dai squeezed her hand as he led her down the aisle toward their seats. The theatre was full—of people, of sound, of smiles, of anticipation.

The curtain opened, and the action began, and even though she had told herself that she wouldn't, Kath watched the audience as much as she watched the screen. She had always done that, though. And maybe that was part of being an actor, she realized. Maybe the best part of being an actor. Being part of something bigger than herself that brought everyone, including the audience, into a shared adventure and shared emotions.

As if he'd had a similar thought, Dai leaned closer and pointed down the row of faces all looking up at the screen, their reactions mirroring the action. "Look around," he whispered. "You see? They love you. I love you."

And every cell and fiber in Kath's body filled with joy.

"It's your film," she said. "You made all of this possible, and I love you even more."

AUTHOR'S NOTE

If you look on a map of Wales, you'll find a Ty Newydd village up the valley from the mouth of the Conwy River. That's pure coincidence. "New Village" was the perfect name for my fictional reconstructed village, so I decided to stick with it. The idea of Ty Newydd is based loosely on several abandoned villages in Wales, but the story of reconstruction for holiday rentals is purely fictional, as is the Obaith Estate. You will, however, find Bodnant Gardens near the real life Ty Newydd. The whole of North Wales is gorgeous, including the beautiful Snowdonia area, the valleys, and Conwy and Caernarfon with their magnificent castles.

While the title "Prince of Wales" now refers to the heir to the British throne, the title once referenced the ruler of an independent country. Like Ireland, which once had many princes, Wales comprised different regions with their own rulers. At various points in history, leaders combined or split apart these regions, until Edward I finally conquered the whole in 1282. He completed the ring of enormous castles and handed out Welsh estates to Englishmen, creating a de facto occupation. Finally, for a few years during the early part of the fifteenth century, Owain Glyndwr led an uprising that not only regained Welsh territory but expanded it as part of an alliance with English lords who rebelled against Henry IV.

The Glyndwr Rebellion forms the backdrop for *Heart of Legend*. Not only did Glyndwr fight to regain a nation, he set a full government in motion, including a robust foreign policy, an independent Welsh church, reestablishment of Welsh laws, and plans for two universities on a scale of Oxford and Cambridge. Compared to the rights offered to commoners under Norman English rule, the idea of this government was in many ways like the Camelot of King Arthur. And like Arthur, legend has it that Glyndwr never died, that he merely sleeps until the day when Wales will need him once again.

Using my fictional film version of *The Last Prince* as a backdrop in *Heart of Legend*, I touched on how life was different for women in the Celtic nations. The Welsh laws codified under Hywel Dda before the English conquest gave women more equality than the Norman laws that the English later forced them to adopt. Actions by peasant women on the battlefield provide intriguing hints about the role that women's grievances played in Glyndwr's rebellion, and the cry of "Revenge for Gwenllian" used by the Welsh in battle was a centuries-long tribute to a king's daughter who commanded a Welsh army against the English. All this inspired me to build the character of Margaret Hanmer, Glyndwr's wife. Margaret existed, but apart from her relationship with her father, Owain, her children, and her imprisonment in the Tower of London, relatively little is known about her.

THANK YOU

A heartfelt thank you to my family, friends, and writing circle for their unwavering support and daily words of encouragement. Enormous thanks to Jodi Meadows for her late-night discussions and reassurance when I feared that redeeming Kath would be too hard. Thank you to Kelsey Gay for her eagle-eyed editing; to Jennifer Harris for copyediting; to Linda Au for proofreading; to alpha readers Alisha Vincent, Kate De Silvestre, Scott Knight, Deena Guptil, and Adriana Cuabu; to Kalen O'Donnel for the beautiful cover; to Rachel and Joel Greene for the interior design; and to everyone involved at Mayfair who made this collection possible. Most of all, thank you to my wonderful ARC team and all the readers who enter the worlds within these pages.

ABOUT MARTINA BOONE

Martina Boone is the award-winning author of the romantic southern gothic Heirs of Watson Island series for young adults, including *Compulsion*, *Persuasion*, and *Illusion* from Simon & Schuster, and heartwarming contemporary romances for adult readers beginning with *Lake of Destiny*. She lives in Northern Virginia with her family, Phineas the Shetland Sheepdog, Zoey the lopsided cat, and assorted deer, foxes, birds, and wildflowers that come and go with the seasons. She writes romantic fiction set in the kinds of magical places she loves to visit, and when she isn't writing, she's addicted to travel, horses, skiing, chocolate-flavored tea, and anything with Nutella on it.

More Information:

http://www.martinaboone.com/
Twitter: @MartinaABoone
Facebook: https://www.facebook.com/martina.boone/

Made in the USA
Monee, IL
27 March 2024

55877021R10246